SEA OF SHADOWS

AMY MARONEY

Artelan Press

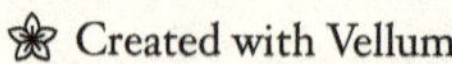 Created with Vellum

Sea and Stone Chronicles, 1400s
To FRANCE
To ARMENIA
VENICE
GENOA
CROATIA
FLORENCE
SIENA
ITALY
ROME
NAPLES
SALERNO
Black Sea
N
W
E
S
BULGARIA
ALBANIA
CONSTANTINOPLE
Aegean Sea
TURKEY
GREECE
ATHENS
SICILY
BODRUM CASTLE
KOS
SYMI
ANTIPAROS
NISYROS
TILOS
*RHODES
KARPATHOS
NICOSIA
*CYPRUS
SYRIA
BEIRUT
DAMASCUS
CRETE
Mediterranean Sea
JERUSALEM
ALEXANDRIA
EGYPT
ST. HILARION CASTLE
KYRENIA FORTRESS
ABBEY OF BELLAPAIS
RHODES TOWN
ARCHANGELOS
NICOSIA
LINDOS
FAMAGUSTA
LIMASSOL
0
200 Kilometers
0
200 Miles

CHAPTER 1

Summer, 1459
Rhodes Town

Anica Foscolo hurried through a crowd gathering in the marketplace under the blazing sun, trailed by her slave, Maria. All around them, traders unloaded their goods from donkey carts. The sugar sellers up the hill had already attracted a swarm of customers.

"Let's stop at the sugar stalls on the way back," she told Maria over her shoulder. "I want to make a lemon tonic for Mamá."

Maria nodded, stone-faced. She had not wanted to come on this errand, and she was never one to put on a false smile.

Two spice merchants leading heavily-laden donkeys ambled into their path, sending whiffs of cinnamon, ginger, and cloves into the air. Slowing her pace, Anica caught sight of a ceramics trader setting out bowls on a nearby table.

"Good day," she greeted him, moving closer.

Placing a hand over his heart, the man smiled in recognition.

"When will your family return to Archangelos, signorina? It's been too long."

"Perhaps this autumn we'll be back." Anica traced the outline of a dolphin on a bowl with her fingertip, unwilling to explain the reason for their absence. "You're using blue paint for your designs now, like the Italians?"

His smile fading, he bent to rummage in a pannier filled with crockery. "Latins don't care for the Greek style. They want what they can get in Genoa or Florence, and they pay well for it."

At the mention of Florence, she tightened her grip on the canvas-wrapped parcel tucked under one arm and turned away.

There was no avoiding the Kastellania, where onlookers congregated at the whipping post as two guards hauled a chained inmate from the building's interior. Anica swallowed hard and sped her step, the prisoner's cries echoing in her ears. For the first time all morning, Maria matched her pace. The girl had always been terrified by the sight of a public flogging.

When they reached the Florentine banker's home, Maria hung back again, scowling.

"A slave is safer in the streets than in that man's house," she said in a voice dripping with venom.

"He's not your master," Anica retorted. "Come inside with me. All will be well."

Maria shook her head and stood her ground, refusing to meet Anica's eyes.

"If you prefer to broil in the sun, so be it." Anica regarded the polished cypress wood doors, wishing for her father's comforting presence. Then she drew in a breath, steeled herself, and lifted the heavy iron door knocker.

Signor Salviati kept her waiting in the high-ceilinged parlor for what seemed like an hour before he emerged from an adjoining chamber.

He approached, his silk tunic rustling. "Signorina," he said in a clipped voice, his expression cool. "I am eager to see your father's work."

Anica unwrapped the painting and presented it to him. It was exactly what he had asked for: a portrait of the Madonna and her child. The Virgin's shimmering blue robe, made of lapis lazuli pigment, had cost a small fortune. The banker held the panel at arm's length, pursing his lips. A long moment of silence passed. Anica's left knee began to tremble.

Finally, he spoke. "Exquisite." When he smiled, his graying teeth showed evidence of too many years' enjoyment of red wine. "Signor Foscolo is indeed a talented man. He shows much discipline, working to this standard even while he mourns his son. Although it has been some time since your brother's death, I suppose—"

"Six months today," Anica said shortly.

Since Benedetto's death, Anica had fought back her own sorrow and finished her father's commissions one by one. She'd sourced the pigments, prepared the panels, and layered on the tempera paints herself. From the backgrounds to the most intricate details of a shining eye or a silken sleeve, she was responsible for it all. But Signor Salviati would never know that.

A young, clean-shaven man also clothed in silk entered the parlor and came to stand at Signor Salviati's side.

"Ah! Troilo, look at the painting." The banker tilted the panel in the newcomer's direction. "Lovely, isn't it?"

The young man gave the painting a cursory inspection. Then his deep-set brown eyes fixed on Anica. "Not as lovely as you, signorina."

Signor Salviati lifted an eyebrow, his smile deepening. "Do you remember Troilo, my eldest son, signorina?"

She eyed the young man, who was a stocky, fleshy-faced version of his father. The Salviati family attended Santa Maria, where she often worshipped with Papa. But if she'd ever interacted with Troilo as a child, she had no recollection of it. "Yes, of course I do," she lied smoothly.

"We've both grown up since I was last in Rhodes," Troilo said. "You speak Italian as beautifully as if you'd been born and raised in Venice instead of Rhodes Town."

"My father did not overlook my education," she replied.

"He's a true citizen of Venice, then?" The banker's son narrowed his eyes. "Or a white Venetian?"

Anica stood taller. "He comes by his citizenship naturally—he did not buy it, I assure you."

"You're fortunate to possess some Latin blood, signorina," he said with a thin smile. "Though some might mistake you for Greek." He flapped a dismissive hand at her long cotton headpiece.

She felt the sting of shame, followed by a wave of anger. With effort, she kept her face impassive.

"Her mother is a Georgillas," Signor Salviati put in. "One of the first families."

When the Knights Hospitaller took ownership of Rhodes generations ago, a handful of Greeks had forged lucrative alliances with them. Mamá's family was descended from one of those men.

"Indeed?" his son said in a slightly more respectful tone.

Anica repressed an impatient sigh, eager to receive her payment and flee. Her gaze fell to the coin purse on Signor Salviati's belt. "My father expects me back straightaway."

He gave a start, one hand going to his waist. "Oh, he did not tell you? We've made other arrangements for payment. I shall not be giving you any coin today."

Anica studied the Florentine's face with suspicion. Her father had said nothing of this, but in his current state Papa could not be counted on to communicate anything of importance. She thought of the ducats she'd spent on pigments and other supplies to create this painting, of the expenses her family had faced for Benedetto's funeral. Words of protest rose up in her throat, but she gritted her teeth and pushed them back down again.

Speak with Papa first, she counseled herself. *Keep this encounter pleasant, for his sake.*

So rather than protest, she gave a quick curtsy. "Thank you, signor."

The younger Salviati put up a hand. "Wait." He plucked the wooden panel from his father's grasp. "I've spent the last five years in Florence, signorina. I saw dozens of portraits hanging in the finest homes there. Portraits of the men who've made their fortunes in wool and wine, done in a new style, with paints of oil."

"Oil?" repeated Signor Salviati.

His son nodded. "It's a style that started in the north. Flanders, I believe." He stepped closer to Anica. "Surely, you've heard of this?"

Anica resisted the urge to edge away. There was a wide space between his two front teeth. His pink tongue protruded slightly through the gap, and his breath smelled of fish and garlic.

"No," she said. "Artists use egg to thin the pigments. That is how it's always been done."

He shook his head. There was a hint of triumph in his expression. "Things are changing," he told her. "Oils are the new fashion. Your father had better learn this new style, or he shall soon find himself out of work."

Signor Salviati turned a sour expression on the panel that he had complimented a few moments before.

"If that is the case, then we shall have portraits made in oil, too. One of me, one of you, and one of your mother." The two men exchanged a satisfied look. Then the banker turned back to Anica. "Tell your father of my wish, Signorina Foscolo. He'll welcome the commission, I have no doubt."

Something in his tone sent a stab of worry into Anica's chest. "I will tell him, signor."

When a manservant let her out the front doors, she found Maria standing still as a statue where she'd left her, face covered with a sheen of sweat.

They pressed against the wall as a donkey cart piled with fruit rolled by. Anica looked back at the banker's home, her eyes aching from the glare of the sun against the white marble façade.

She should have been glad for another commission from the man. But instead, she felt certain no good would come of it.

CHAPTER 2

Summer, 1459
Rhodes Town

WHEN THEY RETURNED HOME, Anica stood in the center of the courtyard a moment. The sun spilled over the roof and drenched her mother's garden with gold, warming the air and filling it with the scents of citrus fruits and herbs. She watched a ruby-red dragonfly soar skyward from a potted rose, its wings glinting in the light.

Crossing to the niche in the wall where a small bronze statue of a boy stood, she swiped at a spiderweb in the crook of his arm, searching for its maker. But the silk clinging to her fingers was the only evidence she could find of the spider's existence.

Straightening, she headed to the studio. She loved stepping into the airy workspace each morning—or had loved it until grief turned every room in the house into a painful reminder of the little boy who lay entombed in a crypt, fading to dust.

Last night, sleepless, Anica had decided to prepare a half-dozen icons of Greek saints. With the help of her Aunt Rhea, it would not be difficult to find buyers in their network of wealthy Greeks, both here in Rhodes and on neighboring islands. She had painted so many of these portraits it had become as easy as breathing, but there was no challenge to it—and, unfortunately, little reward. The small works brought in a pittance compared to larger portraits and frescoes.

She eyed the rectangular pine panels stacked on her battered supply table, whitened with a thick layer of gesso. There were four. Soon she'd have to buy more wood and cajole her father into making more panels, but this was enough to get her started. Setting out pots of ground pigment and a row of ceramic dishes for mixing the paints, she calculated in her mind how much egg she would need for today's work. She had no goldleaf for the backgrounds, but there was a goldbeater in the Jewish quarter near their old neighborhood, a friend of Papa's. He often let them purchase goldleaf on credit.

The door opened and her father shuffled in.

"Papa?" A thread of hope rose in her chest. "I didn't expect to see you here. Will you be working today?"

Her father looked at the easel standing ready by the window. "You don't need me at all anymore, do you?"

His voice was rough with lost sleep, with too many hours spent weeping. Benedetto had been the second boy born to their family, and the second to die. The pain of it was nearly unbearable—once again, Papa's dreams of a son and heir had been shattered.

She came to his side, slipped an arm around his waist, felt the hard edge of a rib.

"The painting I delivered this morning was the last of them," she said quietly. "I'm starting a series of icons, though we have no buyers for them yet."

"We'll take up such matters soon, my dear."

"When? We'll never stop mourning Beno, but you can't ignore the world much longer." Swallowing, she softened her tone. "We may have another commission from the Salviatis. Securing it will be up to you. I wish it weren't so, but there is only so much I can do." She hesitated. "Signor Salviati told me you'd made other arrangements for payment, so he gave me nothing."

Papa's gaze dropped and a muscle worked in his jaw for a moment.

Then he cupped her cheek with a hand, the deep hollows beneath his eyes making her heart twist. "Our work, your betrothal—everything has been pushed aside. We'll take it up again tomorrow, I promise you. But today is your brother's day."

He turned away, vanishing as silently as a wraith.

Anica closed her eyes, steadied her breath. Every month on the date when her small brother Benedetto had died, her parents marked his death in the chamber off the entry hall where a row of icons hung on the wall. Mamá was likely already there, kneeling before Santa Maria. Any moment now, Papa would take his position at her side.

Her throat aching with an insistent urge to sob, Anica got back to work.

The next day, she did several household errands with Maria, then ate a quick meal of flatbread, cheese, and grapes in the kitchen before heading to the studio. She worked in silence, the afternoon punctuated by the tolling of church bells that marked the hours. As she was sanding a panel, the door swung open.

"My dear, I did not ask you yet—was Signor Salviati pleased with the painting?" Papa asked, stepping inside.

He looked better today, she thought as he closed the space between them. More alert.

"Yes. How much had he agreed to pay you?" she asked. "Can you show me the contract? I want to make sure it's enough to cover our expenses."

Papa avoided her gaze. "That's better left to me, my dear."

Anica watched him with narrowed eyes. Papa had never hesitated to share information about their commissions before. What was her father concealing from her?

Let it go. The last thing he needs today is an argument with me.

"His son was there, too," she told him.

"Ah, yes. Young Troilo. I thought they'd shipped him off to Florence for good." Papa cocked his head to one side. "Did you say they wanted another commission?"

She nodded. "Three more portraits. They want them in oil paints."

"Oil paints?" her father repeated dubiously.

"It requires oil to thin the pigments rather than egg," she explained. "Troilo claimed the finest homes in Florence have works in oil hanging on their walls."

"I've heard a few merchants bragging about portraits made in oil they've had sent over the sea from Flanders and Holland," he said. "But there's no one schooled in the technique on this island."

"Perhaps you could be the first," she suggested.

He gave her a rueful smile. "My dear, I'm having enough trouble as it is. The last thing I need is another complication."

"Is it getting worse?" She examined his brown eyes with concern.

"The world is blurry, as if a veil of mist conceals everything I look at," he confessed.

"Do they hurt?"

"No, no. Other than a headache now and then, especially when I work by candlelight, my eyes don't hurt at all. And I'm still quite capable of wielding a brush. You've done more than your share of the work ever since"—his voice faded for an instant—"these past few months. You won't toil alone much longer. This week I shall write to a cousin in Venice and have an apprentice sent on the next ship to Rhodes."

"But you've tried that before." Anica's heart sank. Three Venetian apprentices, all relatives from her father's family, had come and gone in the same number of years. None of them had shown any talent nor any motivation to work.

"My Foscolo relations have proven disappointing on that count. I think they save all the best apprentices for their own studio in Venice, and I suppose I can't blame them. No, this time I'm turning to my mother's family—the Loredans."

"We have artists on that side of the family, too?"

She knew little about her grandmother's family other than the story of her father's arrival on Rhodes. He had come here by way of the island of Antiparos, where his mother's cousin Giovanni Loredan had built a grand home and married a Greek woman. At Cousin Giovanni's invitation, Papa had journeyed from Venice to Antiparos and painted frescoes on the walls of his new house. From there, it was a quick voyage to Rhodes. Once Papa set foot on this island, he'd been in no hurry to return to Venice.

He shook his head. "No. But the Loredans have connections everywhere. I can cast a wide net through them, and who knows how big a fish I'll land?"

Anica smiled a little, glad her father was making an attempt at lightness.

His expression sobered. "Your betrothal hasn't been forgotten either. Mamá and I are ready to begin the search again. Aunt Rhea is eager to help us find a match."

She put her arms around him. "Thank you."

The shroud of gloom was finally lifting from her father's shoulders. And perhaps the weight of responsibility would now lift from hers.

A door slammed. The quick slap of sandals on stone echoed in the corridor.

The servants and slaves walked so silently they often appeared in a room without warning, like puffs of smoke. As for her parents, they both moved through the world with calm, measured steps.

But not her sister.

"Anica!"

Heleni flung open the door, Maria close on her heels. The two of them were about the same age, but Maria looked much older than Heleni. In her sixteen or so years on the earth, she had experienced enough heartbreak for a lifetime—and the furrow of worry between her brows was already deep. Heleni, in contrast, was coming into the bloom of womanhood like a flagrantly scented scarlet rose. Her full lips and enormous brown eyes turned heads whenever she left the house, and to their parents' dismay, she loved the attention.

"A merchant fleet is approaching Rhodes," Heleni reported breathlessly. "Along with Hospitaller ships from France."

Anica turned to the slave with a questioning look.

"It's true." Maria drew two eggs from a pouch and laid them on the table. "I heard the news in the lane from the soap man."

Anica nodded her thanks for the eggs. "And you had to tell my sister because . . . ?"

Maria shrugged. "She asks so many questions. I can't lie to the girl, can I?"

"Everyone's going to the harbor in the morning to watch the crews unload their cargo." Heleni turned to Papa with a pleading look. "Can't we go, too?"

"Your mother—" he began, then trailed off, looking thoughtful.

"It would be good for her to get out of the house," Anica said. "A distraction could raise her spirits."

He nodded slowly. "You're right. Perhaps I can talk her into it."

"Help me sand some panels while Papa speaks with Mamá," Anica said to Heleni.

Heleni stayed where she was. "I hate such work."

Her sullen tone was nothing new, but for some reason it grated on Anica more than usual.

"Do you like this house, Heleni?" Papa asked, his voice flaring with irritation. "Do you like to eat? Do you want fine silks, pearls, and silver plate in your dowry chest?"

She glowered at him in silence.

He gestured at the easel, the pots of pigment, the brushes lined up on a rectangle of canvas. "The gold earned in this studio makes your comfortable life possible. It's your duty to help. In fact, we won't go to the harbor unless you sand the panels Anica prepared."

Without another word, Papa stalked from the room.

Anica went to the table where the pine panels lay. In silence, she handed one to her sister.

Snatching up a square of parchment coated with a fine layer of crushed seashells, Heleni set to work with a heavy hand, making deep slashes in the gesso.

"Gentle!" Anica warned. "You'll go all the way down to the grain."

"Who cares?" Heleni flung a dark glance at her.

"I do. Papa does. Mamá does. Your attention to the smallest details is important."

Heleni rolled her eyes. Anica tried to steady her breath. Later, she would have to go over Heleni's work and correct any mistakes.

Her father's reputation—indeed, their entire family's—depended on it.

CHAPTER 3

Summer, 1459
Aegean Sea

The rising sun warmed Drummond Fordun's back and cast a golden
glow on the familiar curves of Rhodes. Shifting waters spread out
before him, blue-black as a raven's wing. He stared mesmerized at the
waves for a moment, savoring the dance of light and color. Scotland's
sea had never inspired awe in him as the Aegean did. Then again, all
this beauty came with a price.

He glanced over his shoulder at the distant shores of Turkey. No
swift Turkish *fuste* were in pursuit, he saw with relief, but that meant
nothing. Infidels could be gathering in coastal villages or quiet coves
along those shores even now, preparing their sleek vessels to launch an
assault on Rhodes tonight.

Overhead, the sails billowed and snapped in the shifting breeze.
The wind had been their ally on the voyage south to Alexandria. The
return journey was a different story. A sudden gale had scattered their
convoy like errant twigs, cracking one galley's mainsail mast. The craft

trailed the convoy now, a lame sheep struggling to keep up with the flock. Drummond prayed no further harm would come to the damaged ship or its crew.

He strode to the steps leading to the hold. "I see Rhodes!" he bellowed. "Your wives and families await!"

A cheer went up from the rowers on their benches below decks, soon followed by the lilting refrain of a Greek folk song. As usual, his Rhodian oarsmen brightened at the thought of home—and the extra pay Drummond would portion out as soon as they docked. He knew how to keep his men loyal.

Drummond signaled to his Genoese first mate, a mercenary who'd seen years of action on these seas and was as handy with a crossbow as he was with a compass.

"More power from the starboard oarsmen when the harbor walls come into view," he ordered. "This wind has half a mind to blow us to the Black Sea."

"As you command, Captain," the Genoese said in his best approximation of Scots-accented English.

"Och," Drummond said. "You've been practicing. I'm impressed."

The man put a hand to his chest and bowed slightly. "*Grazie.*"

Two gulls appeared over the galley and glided on a current of air near the mainsail mast, studying the men with cold yellow eyes.

"We've got nothing for you," the Genoese informed the birds. "If it's fish you're after, or biscuit, you'd best look elsewhere."

It was true. Their hold was nearly empty. Besides ballast, the last soggy rations, and the ever-present barrels of wine and ale, they'd little to show for the journey. But that was as planned. A small wooden box, a letter for the Order's grand master from the Mamluk Sultanate of Egypt, and several passengers were the only items of value they'd brought back from Africa.

"The lighter the load, the swifter the journey," Drummond said. "Once we dock, see that the galley is tied up and put to rights. I've got to escort the knights to the palace—if we can get through the crowds. With this merchant fleet coming in, the harbor will be jammed."

"What about our special guest?" the Genoese asked, jerking his head at the figure shrouded in a dun-colored silk cloak who sat under a canvas shade at the stern of the galley. "Is he a man or a statue, I wonder? Every time I glance his way, he's sitting like a lump of stone."

Drummond kept his eyes on the island ahead. "He moves. And talks."

"You speak to him?" The Genoese looked astonished.

"He's an interesting fellow."

"Careful what you say to the man. You know these infidels. Can't be trusted, no matter how charming they seem."

Drummond raised an eyebrow. "Who made you the expert on Syrians?"

His crewman shrugged. "Syrians, Turks, Egyptians. They'd slit our throats to a man if given half a chance."

"In this case, you're mistaken. He's saved more lives than you or I can imagine. And Christian ones at that."

"How so?" The Genoese seemed genuinely mystified.

A gust of wind flapped the sails, died down, then rose again.

"This wind's no help, and we're close enough," Drummond said, ignoring the question. "Have the crew trim the yards and sails."

The stone towers standing sentinel over Rhodes harbor came into view as the Genoese turned away, dispensing orders to the crew. A fleet of merchant ships was clustered at the entrance to the commercial harbor, which was already crowded with vessels. Small rowboats ferrying goods from the ships to the quays wove in and out of the bobbing crafts. Two light galleys rowed past the chaos, heading toward the Mandraki, the Order's military harbor.

Drummond drew in a breath and bellowed, "Let's skim around this tangle of ships and follow those galleys to the Mandraki."

The familiar sounds of the harbor descended upon them. Men shouting, the clang of iron on rock from the weapons arsenal under construction nearby, the harsh screams of seabirds circling overhead. Citizens of the city streamed through gates in the massive stone walls, attracted by the arriving fleet.

As they entered the calm waters of the inner harbor, the tension Drummond had carried in his chest ever since they'd left Alexandria began to ease. For a moment, he allowed himself to imagine the night ahead. Dice, cards, a big meal, a visit to the bathhouse, perhaps a few hours in the city's finest brothel—or a visit to the lovely Genoese courtesan who kept a private apartment near the marketplace. Then a long, peaceful night of rest in his rented chambers near the Inn of the English. The possibilities swam in his mind, tantalizing him.

Reluctantly, he pushed them aside. The first orders of business were tying up the galley, paying his rowers, transferring three of his passengers to the palace, and delivering a letter to the grand master. Only after all of that would he have an opportunity to relax.

"Prepare to dock!" he called as the galley slipped through the water toward the quay. "Let's show the Order how a landing should be done!"

The port-side rowers pulled in their oars while the starboard oarsmen put the last bit of their strength into maneuvering the craft alongside the quay. As ropes flew and sailors swarmed over the galley, Drummond touched the amulet hanging from his neck, murmuring a prayer of thanks to Santa Maria for seeing them safely back to Rhodes.

A slight man with a closely trimmed beard and a fur-edged cloak hurried forward from the crowd of knights, servants-at-arms, and bureaucrats who stood assembled along the quay watching the boat tie up. He was followed by two guards leading a mule and cart.

"Did you secure it, Captain?" the man asked in French, stopping short in front of Drummond.

"Yes," he said.

"All of it?" The man widened his eyes meaningfully.

"Yes," he repeated, louder. Did the fellow think he was daft?

At Drummond's signal, two sailors lugged a compact wooden chest forward, staggering with the effort, and deposited it at the Frenchman's feet.

"To think such a small thing weighs so much," the man observed with a satisfied little smirk.

Drummond shrugged, making no response.

"Any plunder of note on the return journey?"

Drummond's hackles rose. He had retrieved the captives and gold he'd set out for; he had safely returned with none dead. And yet the Order still wanted more.

"I chose to hurry back rather than waste time and put more lives at risk by chasing random vessels at sea."

"And the knights you transported?"

"They don't have a scratch on them. The infidels treated their captives well, it seems."

"As they should. We did the same for theirs. What message for the grand master?"

Drummond regarded the man steadily. "Lord de Milly asked me to personally deliver my report along with the captives. I'll be up to the palace as soon as your guards load the chest into that cart. I'm sure the treasurer is expecting you."

The man's expression darkened. Without another word to Drummond, he signaled for the guards to come forward.

Watching the guards load the wooden box into the waiting mule cart, Drummond didn't notice his silk-clad passenger appear at his elbow, a servant at his side.

"My gratitude for a safe journey, Captain Fordun," the man said, inclining his head in thanks.

Drummond turned to face him. "Any time you need transport, sayyid, I'd gladly be of service. I'm often tasked with voyaging to Cyprus, and I've no doubt I'll be called to journey to Alexandria again."

The physician had traveled from Damascus, the city of his birth, to Alexandria, where he'd boarded Drummond's vessel for the return journey to Rhodes. During snatches of conversation under the canvas shelter in calm weather, he'd told Drummond tales about the medical techniques of doctors in Damascus—stories that were almost too incredible to believe. He'd described observing and even participating in surgeries in which patients' skulls were opened or their internal organs were repaired. The thought of a man undergoing such procedures and not only surviving but being cured seemed fantastical.

"I won't forget the offer," he replied. "And if you have an injury that needs attention, come to me."

Drummond looked at him in surprise. "I'm just a privateer, sayyid."

The doctor's bearded face broke into a smile. "You have better manners than most of the high-ranking members of the Order, though. I can't recall the last time a knight called me 'sir' in my own language. Here, I'm known as Signor Syriano or, more often, 'the Syrian.'"

"I understand. Most people call me 'the Scot,'" Drummond returned with a wry smile. "Thank you, but I hope I'll never need to take you up on your offer."

The Syrian's expression grew contemplative. "You take great risks for the knights. You're lucky to be alive, from what I hear."

Drummond's fingers flew to his amulet again. "Santa Maria has been generous."

"May she ever be so." The doctor fumbled in his purse and withdrew a length of black silk embroidered in white with the eight-pointed cross of the Knights Hospitaller. He slipped it around his neck. "You've your amulet to keep you safe; I've my mantle."

"These streets aren't always friendly to your kind," Drummond acknowledged. "For my part, I sometimes wear robes in the Arab style when I'm in Alexandria and Damascus. Why court trouble if you can avoid it?"

"Trouble will find us no matter how well we prepare," the doctor said softly. "Good day."

A familiar figure strode into view as the doctor departed. The English knight's slightly bowed legs made his gait a bit awkward, but his broad shoulders and powerful chest hinted at the warrior within.

Drummond's smile was so wide it hurt. "Glad to see a friendly face, Sir Peter."

"Good to see you alive, Scotsman." His friend clapped him on the arm. "Praise God, you made it back in one piece. You look a sight."

Drummond glanced down at his salt-stained leather armor and boots. He stank, too. Worse than usual.

"There were a few moments I thought we were in real trouble," he admitted. "A gale blew up and separated the fleet."

"Did you lose anyone?" the knight asked, looking beyond Drummond at the galley.

"Not a soul, praise Santa Maria," Drummond replied. "Though we're still awaiting the arrival of a ship that was crippled in the gale."

One of his sailors appeared from the bowels of the galley leading three young Frenchmen with bushy beards, dressed in threadbare cotton tunics. To a man, they wore triumphant grins. Drummond shook his head. If he were in their shoes, he'd be slinking along like an alley cat, hoping no one would recognize him.

"Those knights look as Christian as Arab spice merchants," Sir Peter observed. "How did they fall into the hands of the infidels, anyway?"

"The wee bairns were captured in Cyprus," Drummond said with a dismissive grunt. "Caught up in some brawl started by Catalans near the Famagusta harbor. They say they were defending a Genoese merchant family that was in the wrong place at the wrong time."

"Their story's not so far-fetched, really," Sir Peter mused. "You can't walk three steps in the Famagusta harbor without tripping over a Catalan pirate."

"True. But their swords are meant to defend Christendom, not the honor of merchants."

Sir Peter snorted. "I'd wager they were defending the honor of the merchant's daughters, if I were a betting man."

"If?" Drummond chuckled. "You've never met a pair of dice you didn't like."

One of the young knights pointed at a vessel in the commercial harbor. "See that ship's banner? It's from Narbonne. I want to speak to the captain. If he's heading back to Provence soon, I'll send a message with him to my family, tell them I'm safe."

"I'm in no hurry," said one of the others, stretching his arms over his head. "We could spend the afternoon at the marketplace, and no one at the palace will be the wiser."

"I've got my orders," Drummond said curtly, "and leisure time for the three of you scunners is not on the list. We can make inquiries of that ship captain, but then we're heading straightaway to the palace."

"What's a scunner?" asked one of them, regarding him with interest.

A nuisance, he replied silently. Aloud, he said, "A young person of note."

He glanced at Sir Peter, who was having trouble repressing a laugh. "Want to come along?"

His friend's eyes lit up. "It would be my pleasure, Captain."

CHAPTER 4

Summer, 1459
Rhodes Town

Anica followed her family out the front door, Maria and a manservant close behind. Outside, the sun blazed overhead and life pulsed in the streets as if their family's private tragedy meant nothing. Trumpeters at the grand master's palace up the hill bugled a serenade to mark the fleet's arrival. It was clear, though, that news of the arriving ships had already spread. Merchants and their wives, artisans, traders, notaries—it seemed all of Rhodes Town was streaming downhill toward the harbor.

Hurrying to match Heleni's stride, Anica adjusted her violet headpiece embroidered with silver thread, a recent gift from Aunt Rhea. It was the first time she'd worn any color other than black for six months, and she'd felt a twinge of guilt when she put the garment on. Heleni's headpiece was bright fuchsia, the color of the deadly but beautiful oleander flowers blooming in gardens all over Rhodes Town, and it glittered with gold thread. Glancing at her sister sideways, Anica realized Heleni had rimmed her eyes with black kohl and stained her lips with pink-tinted beeswax.

"Too slow." Heleni pulled at Anica's arm. "We're missing everything!"

Anica shook her off. "The boats aren't going anywhere. It takes ages to unload them." She raised her voice, directing her next words to Papa. "I hope there's a vessel from the Black Sea carrying oak for panels and another from Alexandria full of minerals for pigments."

Heleni let out an exasperated sigh. "You would. I hope there are silks in every color of the rainbow and a Hospitaller ship full of strong, handsome knights."

Papa glanced at them over his shoulder. "Heleni, have you painted your face again?" he asked.

When she didn't answer, he looked at the sky as if to implore God for patience. Next to him, Mamá clutched his arm, her face concealed by a gauzy black veil. Before Beno's death, Mamá would have wiped Heleni's face clean at the door, scolding her all the while. Now she was listless and unseeing, her mind preoccupied with the one person who wasn't there.

Santa Maria, Anica prayed. *Give my mother a reason to smile today.*

As they passed the Salviati home, the banker and his family, along with an entourage of slaves and servants, were filing out the door.

"*Buon giorno*, Signor Salviati," Papa said. He nodded at the banker's wife. "*Buon giorno,* signora."

The woman inclined her head at Papa but studiously ignored Mamá. Anica's heart pounded a little faster at the slight. Her mother had once taken in one of this family's house slaves, a woman who had been beaten half to death by Signora Salviati and flung out on the streets. That was nearly five years ago, and Signora Salviati had shunned Mamá ever since. Luckily, Signor Salviati himself had overlooked the matter.

"Troilo has just arrived from Florence," Signor Salviati said, sweeping a ring-laden hand at his son. "He'll be joining me at the treasury this week. Your gold could not be in better hands."

Anica dropped her chin, studying the cobblestones underfoot.

"What good fortune," Papa said politely, turning to the young man. "How do you find Rhodes after so many years away?"

"Florence has its advantages. But Rhodes suits me. The climate, the sea air, the beauty." The young man's gaze returned to Anica. "Yes, there is much to recommend it."

After another moment of polite conversation, Papa bade the Florentines farewell. He turned down a narrow side lane rather than following the main street past the Kastellania.

"But the other way is faster!" Heleni protested.

Papa ignored her. Anica knew his detour was for her mother's benefit.

When Mamá and the aunts had wailed during the funeral procession for her brother, spectators had warned they could be flogged for defying the knights' rules.

Anica herself had not wailed. She'd distanced herself from her shrieking Greek relatives, clinging to her father's arm during the entire procession, his quiet strength keeping her upright as tears rolled down her cheeks.

She clenched her teeth, forcing the memories away. Here in these bright streets, she could escape the worries marching through her mind. At the very least, she had to try.

They passed through the Sea Gate with the jostling crowd and descended toward the harbor. Azure waters shimmered within the embrace of the honey-colored stone seawalls. The canvas sails of windmills along the eastern wall turned in the wind.

The heavy iron chain that separated the harbor from the sea had been released. Sleek galleys, ponderous merchant ships, and battered fishing vessels entered the harbor one by one. Sailors fanned out over the decks and riggings, their commanders shouting orders. A fisherman's wife screamed a curse at the gulls circling her husband's small craft.

Anica eyed the place where Colossus had once straddled the entrance to the harbor. She wondered for the hundredth time how the great bronze statue had been constructed and assembled—or if it had even existed. Perhaps it was just a figment of some ancient storyteller's imagination.

Once on the quays, they drew near an enormous merchant ship. A short distance away stood a group of knights in black tunics emblazoned with the white eight-pointed cross of the Order. Seabirds soared overhead, their plaintive cries mingling with the voices of the sailors, fishermen, merchants, and others who milled about.

Papa bent down to murmur in Anica's ear. "How many today?"

She looked at him with delight. "You wish to play?"

He nodded, smiling. It was a game they played, honed to perfection over the years. They each got one point for Catalan or French, two for Arabic or Hebrew, three for Armenian, Russian, or any Balkan language, four for English or German, and five for any language completely unintelligible to either of them. They had not played the game since her brother's death.

"One point for French," Papa said, cupping a hand to his ear, pointing in the direction of the knights. "And another for Catalan."

Before Anica could respond, the knights began moving in their direction.

Heleni pushed her headpiece back so her luxuriant black hair gleamed in the sun and her face was naked to the world. At this, Mamá came to life. She took hold of the trailing edges of her daughter's headpiece and tugged it forward.

"Mamá, it's so hot!" Heleni protested, batting away her mother's hands.

"Cover your hair, or we leave at once," Papa warned her, his expression darkening.

Heleni pouted, crossing her arms over her chest as Mamá arranged the folds of cloth around her face.

The knights paused in front of them, watching Heleni's antics with amusement. Anica's face burned with shame. Why did her sister have to draw attention to their family in this way? She moved forward, partially blocking their view of Heleni, and raised her chin.

"I notice many families standing along the quay," one of the knights said in French, his tone silky and polite. "What brings the townsfolk to the harbor?"

Anica stared at him in astonishment, her protective instincts derailed. He had a finely wrought face, with heavy brows over startling blue eyes, and a clean-shaven jaw. And he looked very young—like her, he had likely not yet seen twenty winters.

She felt her sister take a breath to speak and squeezed Heleni's hand in warning.

"The whole town turns out when a merchant fleet arrives," Papa responded, also in French. "There is much to see and hear. And goods on display."

"What kinds of goods are you in search of today?" the knight asked, his eyes sliding from Papa to Anica and back again.

"When the vessels unload their cargo, we'll see what's on offer and make our choices, sir," Papa said coolly.

"My father is an artist, *seigneur*," Anica interjected, giving Papa a pointed look. These knights were all nobles. A mere "sir" would not do. "Sometimes merchants bring materials he needs for his work."

"An artist, you say," the knight mused. "I shall need ornament in my quarters. Perhaps I shall visit your atelier and see your work, then. I've heard there are few here who speak French the way it ought to be spoken, but you and your daughter prove otherwise."

Papa looked taken aback. "I bring examples of my work to patrons, *seigneur*. It's easier that way."

A flicker of disappointment arose in the man's eyes. "I am Émile de Chambonac," he said. "From the *langue* of Auvergne. I shall lodge at the Inn of the French until my home is ready—ask for me there."

The knights were divided up into *langues*—or tongues—depending on their kingdom of origin, each one responsible for different duties within the Order. Anica could never keep straight what each tongue actually did, nor did she care to. The less time spent thinking about the knights, the better. Their presence was a continual reminder of war, of preparations for the siege that everyone believed would come one day soon from the shores of Turkey.

"I will look forward to it," Papa said.

"Good day to you all," the knight replied, his gaze lingering on Heleni. His lips quirked as if he were holding back a smile. "I hope you find what you're looking for."

Anica glanced sideways at her sister. Heleni's mouth was slightly open. She was studying the knight under half-lowered lids, an expression of abject admiration on her face.

Papa gave the knight a curt nod. "Thank you, *seigneur.* Good day."

With obvious reluctance, the knight bowed and moved away.

CHAPTER 5

Summer, 1459
Rhodes Town

With their three wards in tow, Drummond and Sir Peter navigated the busy waterfront. Servants of the Order were everywhere, scurrying from the quays to the warehouses by the dockyard.

Peering at the sea, Drummond caught sight of a vessel heading toward the Mandraki, the top third of its mainsail mast leaning drunkenly to one side. "Praise the Virgin. They made it."

Sir Peter patted him on the back. "You can rest easy now, my friend."

Several knights of the Order approached from the direction of the Provencal merchant ship, followed by servants hauling carts full of luggage. They all fell silent at the approach of Drummond and his small group.

"What's this?" one of them called out to Sir Peter. "Keeping company with Arabs now, are you?"

Sir Peter shook his head. "Long story. These are Christian fellows." Under his breath, he added to their young companions, "If tongues start wagging about your return before he claps eyes on you, the grand master will be displeased. Keep your adventures to yourselves."

A young man whose black velvet doublet bore the eight-pointed cross of the Order stepped forward. "Is this how Christians dress in Rhodes, then?" he asked in French. "I'm woefully unprepared, it seems. Where did you procure those interesting robes?"

One of Drummond's charges waved a hand dismissively. "We're not at liberty to say. We've been muzzled by our guides. And you are . . . ?"

"Émile de Chambonac, knight of Auvergne." The young man bowed, one hand on the tooled leather hilt of his sword. His boots glowed with a sheen of oil. "And cousin to Jacques de Milly."

Drummond barely suppressed an eye-roll. This young fop was the worst type of knight—not only rich and spoiled, but related to the grand master himself. No wonder the Order relied so heavily on mercenaries. These days, they were often the only soldiers guaranteed to have seen action in battle.

"Were you aboard that merchant vessel, sir?" asked one of Drummond's wards, eyeing the wealthy newcomer eagerly.

"I was."

"Is it returning to Narbonne soon or heading farther east?"

"How am I to know? Such details bore me." The man signaled to his valet, who stood near a mule cart loaded with a teetering mountain of wooden crates. "Let's away to the palace so I can give my family's greetings to the grand master."

Another man spoke up. "Cyprus after Rhodes, that's the usual itinerary for merchant vessels. The captain said he's continuing east, at any rate."

Drummond glanced at the crestfallen face of the young knight at his side. "Don't worry," he said quietly. "There'll be a Hospitaller ship heading to Narbonne soon enough. Your message will get home quicker than you think. Come, follow me."

But the way was blocked now. The knight from Auvergne and his entourage had stopped, engaged in conversation with a group of townsfolk just ahead. Drummond sighed in impatience. It seemed all of Rhodes Town had turned out to watch the merchants unload their wares.

His annoyance vanished when he clapped eyes on a woman in the cluster of townspeople. Her hair was hidden by a colorful headpiece of the style favored by Greek women. He studied her large dark eyes and slanting cheekbones, admiring the fullness of her lips. By God, she was lovely. As the thought lodged in his brain, the woman lifted her eyes to his, returning his stare with unabashed curiosity. For a long moment, he forgot to breathe.

"So what else have you got in your hold?" Sir Peter said in Drummond's ear as they edged around the group. "It's rare you enter this harbor without some treasure or a hold full of captives."

"It's not all raids," he replied. They were passing within an arm's length of the woman. "All I wanted was to get my cargo back here safely. Whenever I transport valuable passengers, plunder is the farthest thing from my mind, believe me. In addition to those knights, I had a Syrian doctor on board whose knowledge is worth a dozen chests of gold."

Sir Peter gave him a sidelong glance. "Truly?"

In the next instant, the woman smiled. Drummond filled his lungs and expelled the air with a whoosh, barely registering his friend's question.

Good Lord in heaven.

He wanted more than anything in the world to stop and bask in the light of her smile. It was as if he'd just drunk a cup of strong wine. A burning sensation forged a path down his throat, through his chest, settling just under his belly. When she looked away, it felt like a blow to the gut.

"Aye," Drummond said, forcing his attention back to Sir Peter. As they hastened toward the city walls, he fought a powerful urge to glance over his shoulder, catch one more glimpse of that smile. "The Order gave him safe passage and a home here not long ago, and he's been back and forth to Damascus and Alexandria a few times since then."

"I shall have to keep the fellow in mind next time I come down with a fever," Sir Peter remarked.

Drummond burst out laughing. "The day the grand master lets his prized physician tend to an English knight is the day I sprout wings and fly."

CHAPTER 6

Summer, 1459
Rhodes Town

"Émile de Chambonac," Heleni said, drawing out the words with dreamy pleasure. "A name befitting a knight. Did you see the tooled leather of his boots, the silver tracery on his belt? He must be from one of Auvergne's richest families."

Anica kept silent, her eyes fixed on two men following in the knight's wake: a bow-legged English knight alongside a tall, bareheaded fellow with a face in need of shaving, his skin burned reddish brown from the sun.

She watched the tall man curiously. He wore a rough linen blouse with an iron-studded leather vest over it. A dagger and short sword were sheathed at his waist. His gait was more a lope than a walk, and yet it was graceful. He glanced at the sky as if to chart the sun's position, one hand shading his eyes, then he dropped his chin and responded to some query of the knight's.

She had caught fragments of their conversation when they'd passed by, though the tall man's English was oddly accented. But she was certain the English knight had spoken of captives, and she'd distinctly heard his companion say "Syrian doctor."

Anica's heart had hammered against her ribs when she realized the stranger was looking at her. She'd stared back, fascinated by his gray-green eyes. His mouth curved up a bit at the corners, countering the slightly melancholy look lent him by his downturned brows. When Papa had reprimanded her for staring, she'd given her father a guilty smile.

"Four points for that one," Anica said now, gathering her composure. "I'm certain of it."

"Why's that?" Papa's mouth twitched, as if he were hiding something from her.

"Because he's a Scotsman," she asserted. "Not English."

"Your ears did not deceive you," Papa said. "I've seen him before. He's a privateer in the employ of the knights. Has a sleek galley of his own. I heard he's been rewarded handsomely for his part in raids for the Order in recent years."

"Don't you mean he's a pirate?" Anica asked, recoiling in distaste. "Raiding is what pirates do."

"Pirate or privateer—they play by the same rules at sea, whether they're working for the Order or for themselves . . ." Papa paused, distracted by a vessel entering the harbor. An unfamiliar banner flapped on its mainsail mast. "What have we here?"

"If there is any quality silk on that ship, I want some before it all gets snapped up at the marketplace," Mamá said.

The animation in her mother's voice made Anica draw in a quick breath. An outing had been the perfect distraction indeed—Mamá's sorrow had receded like a swiftly moving tide.

Over Papa's shoulder, she could still see the Scotsman's retreating figure moving quickly through the crowds.

Why would a Scotsman venture all the way to Rhodes? What rewards has he received for his service to the Order? And what exactly did he do to earn them?

Then a woman's shout made her forget all about the Scot.

"Did someone say silk?" a voice rang out, brassy and familiar.

Anica caught sight of her Aunt Rhea's rotund form pushing through the crowd. Two armed manservants and a female slave followed at her heels.

Reaching them, Aunt Rhea embraced Mamá. "Cali, my dearest sister. It warms my heart to see you out and about. I've so much to tell you."

She bent her head to Mamá's. They began talking in low tones, occasionally glancing at Anica and Heleni. Anica hoped her aunt would keep the conversation to pleasant, diverting topics. Anything but the horror of Benedetto's illness and death.

As the vessel anchored and its crew readied it for unloading, Anica caught snatches of the foreign sailors' conversations.

"Papa." She leaned toward her father. "What language is that?"

He smiled, and for a moment the mask of mourning he'd worn these past few months fell away. "I'll claim four points for Basque."

A group of Catalan sailors moved closer when the Basque sailors disembarked. Insults were lobbed in Catalan, then the Basques fired off a volley of obscenities in their own language.

"Saints above," Papa said in alarm. "The company grows rough on these quays."

Two of the men rushed each other. Scuffling and grappling rippled along the harbor like a wave as more sailors joined the fray. Panic took hold of the townsfolk gathered along the water's edge, and the crowd began surging back toward the city walls.

Papa herded the women behind him and ordered the manservants to guard them at the rear.

One sailor took a hard blow and staggered into Mamá's path. Heleni screamed. Before Papa could react, Anica darted in front of her mother and pushed the man away with all her might.

"Get back!" she shouted.

He regarded her in astonishment, then slunk away into the crowd with his hands up in a gesture of surrender.

"To the Sea Gate," Papa cried. "Quickly!"

CHAPTER 7

Summer, 1459
Rhodes Town

THEY JOINED the restless mass of citizens waiting to file through the immense doors of the Sea Gate. Anica watched the Catalan and Basque sailors being rounded up by their officers while several guards of the Order dispersed along the harbor to keep the peace.

Aunt Rhea turned to Anica, her eyes gleaming. "You've always been a brave one."

"Only when I have to be." Anica tried to steady her breath.

Papa gave her a stern look. "Brave? Or foolish? You've no weapon, for one thing—"

"Oh, go easy on the girl," Aunt Rhea broke in. "She was only protecting the ones she loves." She shaded her eyes with a hand, studying the quays. "That was no brawl—just a scuffle, easily mended. See there?" She pointed. "The knights have sent guards to straighten things out, and the sailors are all back to work. I've a mind to return, see what I can get from those merchants now that all my competition has scattered like leaves in the wind."

Aunt Rhea was one of the few women in Rhodes Town who moved through the world like a man. She had taken the helm of her husband's many businesses after his illness struck and grown them into a small empire. Papa called her bossy, a henpecking busybody—but even he admitted she had a good heart.

"Rhea!" Mamá said sharply. "You're not serious."

"Where there's danger, there's opportunity," Aunt Rhea retorted. "Believe me, I've been knocked around plenty in my life. A little flap in the harbor doesn't scare me. Besides, I don't travel with armed manservants for show. They're trained to use their weapons."

"Paolo, go with her," said Mamá after a moment's hesitation. Then she took Anica's hands in hers. "You go, too," she said softly. "Keep your aunt and father company."

A bit bewildered by her mother's words, Anica watched their manservant clear a path toward the Sea Gate, Maria and Heleni following close on Mamá's heels. Then she reached for her father's arm.

"The Basques will take ages to unload all their cargo." A sheen of sweat glimmered on Aunt Rhea's upper lip. "I've a long list of items to buy, starting with wine from that merchant over there." She indicated a hulking ship that was a frequent visitor to the harbor. It trundled back and forth between Cyprus and Rhodes, its hold stocked with the finest Cypriot wines. "He's one of my best suppliers. Let's see what he's got today."

She took firm hold of Papa's other arm, clearly pleased to have an escort for her outing. Anica fought a smile at the resigned look on Papa's face. Aunt Rhea's husband was trapped at home, crippled by a strange illness that years ago had robbed him of his speech and sapped the strength from his legs. It had been years since he'd squired his wife around the harbor, and he likely never would again.

"As you wish, Auntie," Anica said.

"The sun shines upon us, the breeze is pleasant, the harbor is full of merchants carrying fine goods. And I'm with you. Family is my greatest joy, you know."

"And ours as well," Anica said, her heart warming at the tenderness in her aunt's voice.

"How are plans for Valossi's wedding?" Papa asked absently.

Anica's uncle, a notary in Lindos, had lost his wife and three of his five children to the sweating sickness last year, but he was now betrothed to wed again.

"His new wife will be a balm for his soul," Aunt Rhea replied. "She is a sweet little thing, eager to wed, and her dowry is generous. He'll have a fresh start."

"I'm happy for him," Anica said, sure that Aunt Rhea had engineered the match.

"I promised Valossi I'd buy only the finest Cypriot wine for the wedding," Aunt Rhea continued. "If I can get it at the right price today, I will. Why wait? Who knows if this merchant will be back again before spring. All the pirates in these seas, plus the Turks and the Mamluks. You never know if a ship will disappear forever, whether a storm takes it or a raid." She clucked her tongue.

Papa made a vague sound of agreement.

"Speaking of weddings," she went on, glancing at Anica sideways, "we are all eager for a joyous occasion to look forward to in the Foscolo household."

Anica's face grew hot. This was one of her father's main gripes about Aunt Rhea: she barged into personal matters without being invited.

"We've been in mourning, Auntie," she pointed out, trying not to sound rude. "My marriage plans have to wait."

Aunt Rhea made a sympathetic noise in the back of her throat. "Our dear Cali is in no state to make betrothal arrangements, but I am."

"What do you mean?"

"Your mother's asked me to help, and I've given her my promise to assist in any way I can."

The sun was now directly overhead. Sweat coursed down Anica's back, tickling the knobs of her spine. Before she could speak again, a turbaned spice trader displaying samples of his wares on an olive-wood tray bustled up.

"Good day, kyria," he said to Aunt Rhea, then turned to Papa. "Kyrie, surely you are in need of the best spices available on this island."

Papa studied the tray. "Offering a bit more variety would bolster your claim. So many peppercorns. They're as common as figs and grapes here."

The man gave him an odd look. "Peppercorns and *cloves*! See? The finest, rarest cloves."

"Ah! So they are." Papa straightened, shrugging. "My wife buys the spices, not me."

The man returned his gaze to Aunt Rhea, his lips curling in a smile. "Ah, kyria, forgive me. What a lovely gown you wear—"

"Save your breath. I am not his wife. But I do consider myself an expert on spices." Aunt Rhea leveled a hard stare at the trader. "Give me a sample, and I'll decide for myself if your wares are as good as you say."

The man reluctantly scooped out a few cloves and peppercorns and deposited them into Aunt Rhea's outstretched palm.

"Now away with you!" she ordered him. "If I like what I taste, I'll find you again."

Frowning, he scurried off. Anica held back a laugh. Aunt Rhea was like a sirocco that blew in without warning, leaving all in her wake stunned and disoriented.

"The plain fact is you must wed soon," Aunt Rhea went on briskly as if their conversation had never been interrupted, stuffing the peppercorns and cloves into a cloth sack attached to her belt. "You long to be married, don't you, poor girl?"

Anica hesitated, glancing at her father. Yes, it was time for her to marry. But until he had a new, reliable apprentice, how could he even contemplate letting her leave their household? Papa could not execute the fine details of a portrait without her—something she was certain Rhea knew nothing of.

Aunt Rhea swiveled her gaze to Papa. "How much easier it will be for you, Paolo, once Anica's settled into a new life with a husband, under another man's roof. Then you can get Heleni married off, too, and your worries about these precious girls will be over."

"Tell me something I don't know," Papa muttered.

Anica knew what he was thinking. Aunt Rhea had been blessed with sons. She would never have to amass dowries or protect the virtue of daughters.

"I know the funeral was costly," Aunt Rhea added with a confidential air, drawing close to Papa. "You need gold, and quickly. I've a partnership with an Arab merchant from Alexandria whose family has been trading in spice for generations. For the last few years, I've helped him finance his shipping business, and he gives me a cut of his profits from pepper, cinnamon, ginger, and cloves."

"What are you proposing?" Papa asked.

"You can join me in the endeavor," Aunt Rhea said. "Give me whatever you've saved for a dowry. I'll invest it in the spice business and triple your earnings in a few months."

"*If* your trader returns from Alexandria," Papa said. "You just told me how dangerous these seas are."

"There's chance in everything," she countered. "He's returned faithfully since we began this venture. I'd rather put my money into spice than let it molder in the knights' treasury or the Florentines' bank, where it will benefit foreign men instead of me. We have to be inventive these days, spread out the risk."

"Like your trade in illicit statues?" he asked, his voice sharp.

Mamá's family possessed a collection of marble statues from ancient times, mostly depicting pagan gods and goddesses. Such things were officially the property of the Order, of course. They were meant to be turned over to the knights upon discovery. But the Georgillas clan—along with other Greek families—kept such treasures hidden all over the island, some in caves that were accessible only at low tide.

"Can I help it if the Italians are mad for such things?" Aunt Rhea asked. "When the price is right, I'd be a fool not to part with a statue or two. But I can't always find a trustworthy ship captain for such delicate matters. So I'm having my Dimitri apprentice in the shipyard here with a master builder. Soon he'll go to sea under the wing of a merchant friend of mine. One day he'll captain his own ships. Then I'll no longer have to put my trust in strangers."

"You truly want Dimitri to take such risks?" Anica asked, shuddering at the thought of her cousin at the mercy of privateers and pirates.

Aunt Rhea shrugged. "He's seen twenty winters and he's a bright, strong lad. There will always be work for shipbuilders and sea captains from Rhodes, and I want to have a way out if there's a siege. Besides, our sword master says he's the most skilled fighter of all our boys. With God's grace, he'll always be able to defend himself on land or at sea."

They had drawn close to the Cypriot merchant ship now. Sailors unloaded wooden casks of wine onto the quay. Aunt Rhea rapped on the side of an oak barrel.

"Where's the captain?" she demanded of a passing sailor. "Tell him his most loyal and generous customer, Rhea Georgillas, awaits."

The man nodded. "Right away, kyria."

Anica contemplated the perspiring face of her aunt as she inspected the wine barrels arrayed in front of them. She understood now why Mamá had sent her back to the quays with Aunt Rhea and Papa. It was her mother's way of including Anica in a discussion of her future, of matters that until now had been kept from her. Pride unfurled in her chest at the thought.

"Aunt Rhea," she ventured. "Do you have a suitor in mind for me?"

"It is not a matter of finding a suitor, but of fending them off. You and your sister are rare flowers on this island." Aunt Rhea gestured at the heavens and dropped her voice. "We won't speak of beauty because the gods are listening."

Anica's Greek relatives had no problem combining their respect for the old gods with their adherence to the Orthodox Christian tradition, though they knew better than to exhibit this tendency in front of the knights. "But you've got Latin blood *and* Georgillas ancestry—it's an irresistible combination for men seeking a good match. You're a lucky girl."

Anica turned to her father, thinking of all the responsibility she had taken on these past six months. With her changed role within the family, she felt certain Papa would give her some authority over her own future.

A lone gull circled overhead, screeching plaintively.

"Who are these men, Papa?" she asked. "Will I get to choose among them?"

His eyes were unreadable. "When the time is right, we shall select the suitor who is the best match for you and our family."

She looked from her father to her aunt, wrestling with an urge to protest. The pride she'd felt a moment ago vanished, replaced by a rising sense of indignation. Since Beno's death, it had seemed as if she were the head of the household—when in reality she was being discussed behind closed doors like a sack of grain or a basket of grapes to be sold off.

"Surely, this doesn't surprise you," Aunt Rhea said. "I didn't choose my husband, nor did your mother." She leaned closer, raising her voice over the gull's screams. "And neither will you."

CHAPTER 8

Summer, 1459
Rhodes Town

Drummond and Sir Peter led the way through the city gates to the Collachium, where most of the Order's knights and servants lived. Their three companions trailed them, talking loudly amongst themselves in French as they took in the sights. A few passersby—pilgrims from Western Europe, by the looks of them—stopped to stare. Drummond eased his stride as they entered the Street of the Knights and climbed the curving hill to the grand master's palace.

As usual on this street, the cobblestones were clean, swept morning and evening by servants in the employ of the knights. The new hospital lay to their left, still under construction. Just past the hospital on the right was the Inn of France. He craned his neck, admiring the windows fitted with tiny diamond-shaped panes of thick glass, the doorway framed by intricate stonework.

"It's the best of the lot," he remarked to Sir Peter.

"For my part, I prefer the simple comforts of our English inn.

Though I'll never tire of the sight of her." Sir Peter's gaze traveled to the statue of the Virgin Mary in a niche on the wall of the building.

"Aye," Drummond said, one hand going to his amulet. "Bless the sainted lady."

At the entrance to the palace, huffing a bit from the climb, they bypassed the queue of locals who milled about, hoping for an audience with the grand master.

"Poor sods," Sir Peter said as they stepped around the crowd and filed through the palace gates. "Now that you're here, they may not get their time with the big man."

Drummond raised an eyebrow. "Is that what you call Lord de Milly these days?"

They reached the door leading to the formal chambers of the palace, where a young page awaited them.

"It's no insult," Sir Peter protested. "You can't dispute the fact he's nearly as tall as you. With the bones of an ox."

"I'll refrain from telling him you said that."

Sir Peter's eyes twinkled. "Saints praise you."

"See you at the inn this evening," Drummond said. "I hope your chess game has improved in the past month."

"Be prepared to kiss your queen good-bye," Sir Peter replied. "You'll be so deep in your cups by the end of the night that you'll use the chessboard as a pillow, I wager."

Drummond scoffed. "No offense, but I'll not be sleeping at the Inn of the English on this night or any other."

"None taken, my friend." Sir Peter inclined his head and turned on his heel.

Drummond and his charges followed the page through the door and down a shadowy corridor laid with squares of marble, then up a sweeping staircase. Torches burned at intervals on the walls. His companions had fallen silent, either cowed by the majesty of their surroundings or exhausted by their long journey.

After surrendering his weapons to a pair of guards, Drummond and the men were ushered into a small chamber near the cavernous receiving hall. The grand master spent many hours each week in a high-backed chair on a dais in that hall, hearing grievances, approving marriages, giving permission for men to free their slaves.

This study, in contrast, was a quiet, contemplative space. The wood-paneled walls were hung with colorful tapestries; stained-glass windows let in jewel-toned sunlight. Lord de Milly sat behind a desk flanked by two attendants. A falcon sat quietly on a perch nearby, a leather hood covering its eyes.

"Master Fordun, you are safely returned to us," the grand master said to Drummond in French. "As are your companions."

Drummond bowed, thanking God for his French mother and grandmother. "Yes, my lord."

The grand master stood and came around the front of his desk. His gaze settled on the three men behind Drummond. They shuffled their feet nervously, hands clasped behind their backs.

"Well?" he demanded. "What do you have to say for yourselves?"

Only one of them had the courage to speak, the man who had wanted to send word home on the merchant ship from Narbonne.

"We were well-treated, my lord," he ventured. "The infidels fed us, though not much meat. Mostly vegetables and biscuit. They took our tunics and boots and our swords—"

"You are fortunate to be alive." The grand master advanced on the men, his eyes dark with fury. "Your swords are meant to protect Christendom—not the honor of merchants in Famagusta! I do not spend my days negotiating ransom agreements with the Mamluk Sultanate so I can send my best privateer across the sea to rescue the likes of you."

The three young men hung their heads, terrified. No doubt they were imagining themselves tied to the whipping post by the Kastellania or locked up in its dark cells. Knights were sometimes flogged in public, but it was rare, especially for knights from the most powerful noble families of Europe. Drummond had no idea who these three men were, though, nor how valuable their families were to the Order. They were cargo to him, in the end, goods he had safely delivered.

"You will not return to your private residences," said Lord de Milly in a cold, clipped tone. "You will sleep in a dormitory at the Inn of the French, and you will not leave the Collachium until further notice. You will hear mass at St. John's Church each day, and you will assist the physicians in the hospital each afternoon, washing the feet of the ill and poor. You will not attend any social functions until I give permission for you to do so. I will assign pages, monks, and priests to observe your habits and report back to me, so do not think for a moment you can flout these rules. Is that clear?"

The three men stared wide-eyed at the grand master as the details of their punishment sank in. Drummond nearly laughed aloud at their indignant expressions. They must be quite rich, then. Only knights from the wealthiest families enjoyed the luxury of private homes.

"Yes, my lord," said the knight who had spoken before. "Thank you, my lord."

The other two repeated the words with sullen reluctance.

"Go now," the grand master ordered them. "A guard will accompany you to the inn." He glanced at Drummond. "Stay a moment longer, please."

"As you wish, my lord."

When the three dejected knights had disappeared into the corridor, the grand master returned to his seat.

"All went as planned?" he asked.

"Yes, Lord de Milly. I turned over the Arab merchants we'd held captive, and the Mamluks were satisfied the men had been treated well. My men and I stayed in the Genoese quarter in Alexandria, and no trouble visited us there. The gold you'd been promised was delivered without incident. All around, it was as peaceful a transfer as I could have hoped for."

One of the Egyptian merchants he'd exchanged for the knights had arranged a deal with the Order. During his captivity in Rhodes Town, the knights had allowed him to live in an elegant home complete with cook and servants. The chest full of gold Drummond had carried back from Alexandria was payment from the merchant's family for his lavish treatment.

"Do you bring news from the Sultanate?"

Drummond thrust a hand into his leather pouch and fished out the letter. He handed it over with another slight bow.

Lord de Milly turned the letter over in his hands, nodding in satisfaction at the unbroken seal. "Excellent. And I've been informed that Signor Syriano has returned to his home as well."

Drummond nodded. "He was a pleasant companion on the voyage, my lord."

The grand master's mouth tightened. "Even though he carries safe-passage papers, I worry each time he journeys east. He's a valuable asset to the Order. I only let him return to Alexandria and Damascus to get training and supplies that are impossible to obtain here."

"I'd be happy to accompany him east on his next voyage, Lord de Milly."

The grand master pulled a small velvet sack from a drawer and tossed it to Drummond. "I wish I had a dozen privateers of your caliber. There are many missions requiring skills that only you seem to have. You're a seasoned sea captain, your fighting instincts are superb, and you speak—what, a half-dozen languages?" He leaned back in his chair. "I've come to expect the highest standards from you, Master Fordun, and I've yet to be disappointed. It would be a huge blow to the knights if you were to return to Scotland."

He put his elbows on the arms of his chair and tented his fingers together, contemplating Drummond with a probing gaze.

"I've no intention of returning to my homeland," Drummond said brusquely.

"Your family must long for your return."

"My life is here. This is where I belong." Even as he spoke, the lurch of sorrow in his heart pinned Drummond to the floor like a lead weight. The falcon shifted on its perch, opening its wings and beating the air for an instant. It was as if the bird felt his emotions shift and could not help but react.

"You do have a family, do you not?"

Drummond swallowed. "Of course. My father and mother are dead, God rest their souls. But I've brothers and sisters left to me."

Half his pay went home to them, had always done. If he could, he would take the form of a falcon this instant and wing his way back to Scotland. For his family's sake, though, he would not return—not as a man, a bird, or a puff of wind. With each letter from a sibling, his heart railed wildly against his ribs, throbbing with hope. So far, the words he'd prayed for had not appeared. It was more than ten years since he left Scotland, and he'd almost given up hoping his chance to go back would come. Hope sometimes hurt more than missing home.

"Do not imagine I take you for granted." The grand master's voice softened. "I know exactly how valuable you are to the Order. What can I do to show you our gratitude?"

Drummond looked at him in surprise. This was unexpected. The Order had already been extraordinarily generous to him. Asking for more money when he had a bag of gold in his hand seemed greedy. All he could think to do was stall.

"I—I'd like to reflect on it, my lord, if you find that agreeable."

"As you wish. At the very least, you must join me for a feast at my villa on Saturday. You'll be quite entertained, I imagine. And you'll no doubt make some beneficial acquaintances."

Drummond weighed the sack in his palm and inwardly groaned. The last thing he wanted was to share a table with fancy folk all spewing hot air. He longed for the freedom to spend his scant time off as he wished. But the grand master was king in all but name. To refuse his invitation would be disastrous. For starters, velvet sacks full of gold coins would never come Drummond's way again.

"That's generous of you, my lord," he replied in as polite a tone as he could muster. "I'd be honored."

CHAPTER 9

Summer, 1459
Rhodes Town

ON THE DAY of the grand master's feast, Drummond exited his rented rooms in the small stone building near the Inn of the English and paused in the doorway. Across the square from him, the heavy doors of the old hospital creaked open as a pair of monks departed. To his left, merchants stood near the entrance of the Church of Santa Maria, deep in conversation. The waning light of late afternoon illuminated the bell tower, gilding the stone with gold.

Smoothing his black velvet doublet—the only valuable item of clothing he possessed, in excellent shape because he rarely wore it— Drummond headed for the city gates, his freshly polished boots tapping out a rhythm on the cobblestones. Once outside the walls, he moved north past the shipyard, then climbed a small rise overlooking the gardens that extended for miles on the city's western side.

He stood for a moment watching canvas sails on a wooden windmill turn slowly in the breeze, powering a fountain that distributed water through canals to the various villas and their lushly planted plots of land. With slow, measured steps, he moved through the gardens, admiring the graceful branches of fig and pomegranate trees. The air was redolent with citrus and floral scents. He wished he could stay out here, watch the sky darken and the full moon rise.

When he arrived at the grand master's villa, he heard the roar of laughter, the hum of conversation, a melody being plucked out on a lyre. At the door, he relinquished his weapons to a guard.

A cry of welcome rippled through the high-ceilinged space as he entered. Light flickered from oil lamps set on iron pedestals and from candelabras on the tables along the chamber's perimeter. The black tunics of knights contrasted with the bright silks and velvets worn by merchants, notaries, bankers, and other high-ranking men of Rhodes Town. Drummond smiled uncomfortably, hating the attention, and bowed.

Lord de Milly's voice rang out. "Find this man a cup and fill it. Master Fordun is our honored guest this night."

A silver cup was thrust his way, and he drank deeply, eager to dull his nerves with a deluge of fine Cypriot wine. Two Italian knights approached, full of questions about his voyage. In a nearby alcove, the lyre player was flanked by a flautist and tambourine player; all three of them wore doublets of rose-pink crushed velvet and pale green hose.

"These melodies are nothing like the Greek folk songs I hear in taverns," he remarked to the Italians. "And I've never seen such finely dressed musicians."

A voice spoke up from behind him in French. "These musicians are a gift from my father in Auvergne to Lord de Milly. They play the music of the French court, the latest arrangements favored by the king himself."

Drummond turned to confront the searing blue eyes of the young knight Émile de Chambonac.

"They'd be better suited, in my opinion, to a gathering that includes ladies so that the guests might dance together," he replied.

Every guest here was male, a concession to the knights' vow of chastity. It was a hollow vow since plenty of knights openly visited brothels, had mistresses, even had children roaming the streets of

Rhodes Town. And then there were the knights who took pleasure in the arms of other men. Unlike dalliances with women, such transgressions were treated harshly by the Order—so they were kept more closely guarded.

"The players will accompany me to a brothel later this evening," de Chambonac said, lowering his voice. "You're welcome to join us. There are ways to work around the vows, as I'm sure you're aware."

His tone was so pompous that Drummond wanted to slap the back of his head. Eighteen if he was a day, and yet he spoke as if he were a wise old veteran of the Order.

"You were on the harbor the other day," the knight went on, studying Drummond with curiosity. "With those knights dressed as Arabs."

One of the Italians spoke up, his expression tight. "Did you not hear the grand master announce this man's name? He's Master Drummond Fordun, the Order's finest privateer."

"Ah?" A gleam of excitement flared in the young man's eyes. "How many infidels have you killed, Master Drummond Fordun?"

Drummond stared at him in silence for a moment, bristling with irritation. Finally, he said, "As many as necessary to do my job and keep my men safe."

The knight frowned. "I'd kill them all in your place. I'd leave none alive."

"Have you ever killed a man in battle?" Drummond asked him.

"No," de Chambonac admitted. "But I killed an infidel on the journey here."

Drummond regarded him dubiously. "How did you manage that?"

"It was easy. We saw a fishing craft sailed by a man wearing a turban. He shouted insults at us in the infidel language. I wanted to capture him and hang him from the mainsail yard of our vessel, but the captain said it was too dangerous to stop. So I paid the captain to let me use one of his mounted crossbows." He let out a gleeful laugh. "I skewered the fellow to his mast! My aim has always been true. I can't wait to raise a sword in the name of God and strike down every infidel in my path—"

Applause drowned out the man's words as a parade of servants entered bearing platters of steaming meats and vegetables. Drummond stared in disbelief as an entire roasted peacock with its gaudy tail feathers intact was placed at the head table.

"Finally!" De Chambonac's face brightened. "I could eat a camel, I'm so famished. Sit next to me, Master Fordun. I'm sure you have amusing tales to tell, and you speak excellent French for an Englishman."

"I'm not English," Drummond growled. "I'm Scottish."

The knight regarded him blankly. "Ah? But there is no tongue of Scotland in the Order. Just as the knights of Auvergne pledge fealty to the French king, the Scots in the tongue of England must also be loyal to the English king, yes?"

Drummond's spine stiffened. "No. I work for the grand master, not the tongue of England. And Scotland has its own king." He raised his cup to his lips, draining his wine in an attempt to drown the three words hurtling up his throat: *Ye wee idgit*.

A man appeared at Émile de Chambonac's elbow, dressed in a long tunic of burnt-orange silk. Drummond recognized him as the agent who had taken the gold from him at the harbor. The man smiled, revealing small, widely spaced teeth.

"Our supper awaits," he said smoothly. "Lord de Milly has promised me the Scotsman's ear, and I'm eager to take my place at his side."

Drummond studied him. "And you are . . . ?"

"Guillaume Lopic, at your service. Servant of the Order."

Servant? The man was dressed like a noble. Gold rings adorned nearly every finger on his hands. His short brown beard was painstakingly oiled.

"I'm surprised we haven't already met," Drummond said. "I'd never clapped eyes on you before that day at the harbor."

"I've been living in Genoa these past few years, representing the Order and protecting its interests with our allies. Please, Master Fordun, follow me. The grand master desires us both to sit at the high table with him."

The young knight made to follow them, but Monsieur Lopic put up a hand. "Émile, I believe you'll find a place on a bench at that table over there, with the other novice knights."

The man frowned, his lower lip thrust out in a display of petulance that nearly forced a laugh from Drummond, and slunk away.

Drummond took his seat in a heavy oak chair at the head table. A servant poured a long stream of wine into his cup. He began to guzzle it, then stopped himself.

Steady, man. You've got to keep a few wits about you tonight.

Before him lay a knife, a spoon, and a two-pronged silver instrument with a long mother-of-pearl handle he recognized as a fork, an item common on tables in Alexandria and Damascus but something he rarely saw anywhere else. The knights' vow of poverty—it, too, was merely a guideline, Sir Peter always said with a wink.

The musicians strolled into the center of the room, playing their courtly tunes. Shoveling in a spoonful of roasted peacock mixed with saffron-scented rice, Drummond relaxed a little. He might as well enjoy the feast itself.

"So, Master Drummond," Guillaume Lopic said. "The Mamluk peace holds, thanks to you. A fragile peace indeed, all too easily frayed."

"I just do my job and follow orders. I don't know much about the Mamluks or peace accords."

This wasn't entirely true. Drummond did know that the Mamluks were descended from elite Turkish slaves who had been taken from their families and raised to be ruthless warriors. They'd turned their fate around when they overthrew the Egyptian Sultanate, making them the rulers of Egypt to this day. What he had little knowledge of was the patchwork of diplomatic arrangements between the Mamluks and various other powers in this part of the world, including the Order. And quite honestly, he didn't care to learn all the details.

"I find it confusing myself," Lopic said, spearing a morsel of peacock with his fork. "No sooner is a truce arranged than it falls apart again."

He was clearly no stranger to the utensil in his hand. Drummond, for his part, had no intention of handling his own spindly little fork, especially not when he was sitting at the high table during a lavish feast. Why invite embarrassment to an already charged moment?

"As long as we rule the seas, the Mamluks will continue to negotiate with us," his companion went on. "So a man like yourself—well, your service to the knights is equal in value to my own, though our work is quite different."

"What is it you do, then?" Drummond asked, eyeing him sideways.

"I began as a notary, and my skill with languages launched me to the highest ranks of the Order's servants. I help smooth over diplomatic tangles for the knights, usually by wielding a quill and an inkpot, unlike you with your swords and crossbows."

"Ah." Drummond helped himself to a pile of grilled octopus from a platter offered by a servant. He'd been slow to warm up to this popular treat when he first arrived in Rhodes, but now he eagerly consumed it every time he had the chance.

"Of course, as a Frenchman, my loyalties are twofold: to the Order and to my kingdom."

"Naturally." Drummond reached for a piece of flatbread glistening with olive oil, wondering how many slices he could consume without looking like a complete glutton. He had not eaten this well in months.

Lopic put down his cup. "Tonight, I have a delicate matter to address, something that encompasses both loyalties at once."

Drummond swallowed an enormous mouthful of bread and stifled a belch. "Is that so?"

"Yes. I've been instructed to find a suitable protector for a newcomer to the Order, someone whose life is very precious indeed. Someone who needs a bit of extra guidance in the art of war."

A sinking feeling struck Drummond in the gut. "Who do you speak of?"

Lopic took up his cup again and gestured to one of the lower tables. "Émile de Chambonac. His father is Lord de Milly's cousin, and a generous benefactor to the Order."

"Has he seen any action at all?" Drummond asked bluntly.

Lopic smiled. "Only at the hands of his sword masters. Of course, he's got enthusiasm and the courage of youth. But he needs seasoning. Lord de Milly will send him out on a mission or two, to please him and his father, but only under the strictest surveillance of a trusted man. You would be the ideal candidate for such a role. Despite the risks, the great danger of the seas, you and your men return alive from every mission, against all odds. There's no one better suited to take De Chambonac under his wing."

A slow burn of uneasiness crept up Drummond's throat. He watched the young knight regale his seat mates with some story, then sulk peevishly when their attention was diverted elsewhere. He was barely more than a child. A spoiled, daft child. One who'd made sport of killing a lone fisherman at sea. And Drummond was supposed to invite him onto his vessel? Be a mother hen to a strutting little cockerel?

He turned and looked Lopic full in the face. "I'm guessing I don't have the option to refuse," he said. "But know this. When I'm on the seas, it's as an agent of the Order. If a knight joins my crew and puts all of us in danger, he will be breaking the one vow that has any teeth in this organization—the vow of obedience. If that boy—forgive me, *man* —does not follow my commands at sea, I'll have no choice but to return him to Rhodes. Have I made myself clear?"

Lopic nodded, his shrewd brown eyes never leaving Drummond's. "Perfectly."

Drummond raised his cup and drained it dry.

CHAPTER 10

Summer, 1459
Rhodes Town

Anica awoke to the gentle sound of the bedchamber door shutting. She thrust a hand in Heleni's direction—but her sister was not in the bed. Her eyes fluttering open, she glanced at the shutters. The first light of dawn seeped through the cracks.

She slipped out of bed and unlatched the shutters, peering at the enclosed yard where they hung their laundry out to dry. Today was Tuesday. The soap man would soon make his rounds along the alley behind the house, peddling his product. It was high-quality soap made of olive oil, lye from the ashes of a scrubby beach plant, and essence of lavender.

Trumpets blared up the hill at the palace, making her flinch. Here, in the heart of the knights' quarter, the presence of the Order was inescapable. She knew that should make her feel safer. Instead, it gave her a perpetual feeling of dread.

An orange cat stepped daintily along the top of the wall, then leapt into the alleyway and disappeared. Anica stretched her arms over her head and yawned just as the soap man's lilting cry rang out. Through the window, she saw Maria heading toward the gate leading to the alley. Then Heleni appeared and overtook her, unlatched the gate, and went outside. Her sister returned a moment later with the sack of soap, lugged it past Maria, and vanished.

Anica lingered at the window, watching Maria slowly spin around, her face twisted in a scowl. Slipping on a shawl, she hastened downstairs, bare feet silent on the floor.

Outside the kitchen, she nearly collided with her sister.

"Why did you fetch the soap, Heleni?" Anica asked.

"Maria has so much to do on laundry day. And I was up early. I needed the fresh air, anyway."

Heleni sauntered off.

Inside the kitchen, Maria stood at the table, spooning yogurt into a ceramic dish. The sack of soap lay in the shadows near the back door.

"Maria," Anica said quietly. "I know my sister. She never helps with chores unless she's forced to."

Maria set down the spoon. She crossed to the hearth and stabbed at the glowing embers with the iron poker until a flame ignited.

"The wind blows where it wants, when it wants." She kept her back to Anica. "I'm glad for the help, whatever the reason for it."

Anica entered the studio a few moments later to find her father at his easel next to the window. He stood less than a hand's breadth from the panel, squinting earnestly as he daubed a bit of paint on the face of a saint. At her approach, he lowered his brush, looking at her with consternation.

"Papa, you must leave this sort of work to me," she said. "We've already agreed I shall be your eyes."

His shoulders drooped. "I thought with this brighter space my problem would be solved," he admitted. "But instead it grows worse, I'm afraid." He fumbled with the purse at his waist, pulled out a letter with a broken seal, and handed it to her.

She unfolded the square of linen paper and studied it. "Signor Salviati wishes to have a notary draw up a contract for the oil paintings I mentioned."

He stared at her in distress. "I've no idea how to work with oils. It's not easy to learn a technique without a master to guide you."

She put a hand on his arm. "But you are a master, Papa!"

"A master with failing vision," he said miserably.

"We must learn the technique," Anica urged him. "The Salviatis may be the first to ask, but others will follow. We'd be foolish not to accept this commission. Who do you know in this city with an oil painting hanging on his wall?"

He considered that. "Three merchants have bragged to me of such works. A German, a Flemish man recently come from Bruges, and a Genoese."

"Let's pay them each a visit," Anica suggested. "Between us, we can work out how it's done."

During their morning meal in the courtyard, Papa said little, clearly preoccupied by their upcoming errand. Heleni fiddled with her spoon, tapping it against the side of her dish of yogurt.

Mamá's gaze settled on Anica. "After you return, you and I will go to Aunt Rhea's. She has some items for your dowry trunk."

Anica swallowed. "Does this mean—"

Papa scraped the last bit of yogurt from his dish. "Nothing is certain. We've had inquiries from a few interested parties, that's all."

Tightness constricted Anica's ribs. "Who are they?"

Mamá shook her head. "There is no point discussing anyone until we've come to an agreement over his suitability."

Heleni put down her spoon with a thunk. "I don't think it's fair. Why doesn't Anica get to choose her suitor? When it's my turn to wed, I shall have a love match."

"Any marriage can become a love match over time," Mamá retorted. "And any love match can turn sour. The fates will turn our plans upside down—that is all we can count on. A match arranged by family is safer than one sparked by a lovesick young woman." When Heleni opened her mouth to protest, Mamá waved a dismissive hand in the air. "No, Heleni, I won't hear another word. You will come to understand the wisdom of what I've said one day, I promise you."

Anica expelled a long, low breath, thrilled at her mother's display of spirit. After all these months of wandering the house like a hollowed-out shell, Mamá was coming back to herself. Stealing a glance at Papa, Anica saw him staring at her mother with a mixture of tenderness and pride.

"Was your marriage a love match?" she blurted out.

"For me, it was," Papa said without hesitation. "I knew the first moment I clapped eyes on your mother that I would marry her. It took a while to convince her family I was suitable, though."

"Why?" Heleni pushed her cup and dish away and leaned her elbows on the table.

"I was new to Rhodes. I was Venetian. I was an artist. The list goes on." Papa let out a wry chuckle. "I had to work hard to get my foot in the door of the Georgillas household."

Mamá smiled at him, her brown eyes lighting up. "Once you learned Greek and secured your first patrons, things went smoothly enough. Your talent dazzled my family, and your kind heart captivated me. I've never had a moment of regret for the choice my family made for me."

"Didn't your family want you to marry a Greek man, not a Latin?" Anica asked.

"They wanted to make a match that would benefit not just me, but the whole family." Mamá leveled her gaze at Anica. "That is what a good marriage does. It's not just for the husband and wife."

Papa threw his napkin on the table and got up. "Wise words indeed. Now, Anica, let us be on our way."

To their disappointment, the German and Flemish merchants were not at home. Anica's purposeful strides faltered a bit as they set out through the streets one more time and finally drew up before the doors of the Genoese merchant's residence. At Papa's signal, she lifted the iron door knocker and let it fall. It was an interesting ornament, crafted in the shape of a dragon's head. Perhaps it had been inspired by tales of a dragon a knight had supposedly slain in Rhodes long ago.

A servant admitted them and they were ushered into the parlor, a spacious room overlooking the central courtyard. Two impressive oak armchairs sat on either side of a hearth topped with a carved stone mantel.

On the wall opposite the hearth hung a portrait. Before Anica could study it closely, the Genoese merchant swept into the room. He was dressed entirely in black. She had met this merchant and his wife at church a few times and recalled being impressed by their pleasant manners and fine clothing.

"Signor Foscolo, Signorina Foscolo," he said to them. "You are very welcome in my home. May I offer you refreshment?"

Papa shook his head. "We are sorry to infringe on your privacy when you are in mourning, Signor Lomellini," he said uncertainly, gesturing at the man's black velvet doublet and hose. "I was not aware . . ."

"I welcome the distraction," the merchant said politely, though his expression sagged a bit. "My dear wife perished in Genoa six months ago. She was ill for some time, and despite the care of the best doctors in the city, I could not save her in the end. I've only just returned to Rhodes. It took some time for me to find the will to travel."

"You have our condolences," Papa murmured.

The man eyed Papa's clothing with a thoughtful air. "And you are in mourning as well, signor."

Papa nodded. "Our little boy died six months ago, too." His eyes glinted in the sunlight pouring in from the courtyard. Anica prayed he would not begin to weep.

The merchant sucked in a breath. "God rest his soul." He looked at Anica, allowing Papa to gather himself again. "As difficult as it is, life must go on, mustn't it? Let us talk of other things. How can I be of service to you?"

Anica felt a rush of gratitude at his understanding tone. Observing that her father was still regaining his composure, she said, "We came to look at your portrait. Is it made with oils?"

Signor Lomellini nodded. "It's the work of a Flemish artist who is making a fortune off all the merchants of Genoa. A talented man. You're welcome to examine it."

Anica stepped closer to him, inspecting the portrait. Signor Lomellini stood but an arm's length away. She could smell the faint scent of cypress wood on his clothes. It was a scent she had always loved.

Papa came to her side. They both studied the painting in silence. It was a modestly sized portrait of the merchant and his wife, an interior scene. While the composition was not remarkable, the details and lighting were exquisitely rendered.

"What a lovely portrait," Anica said, breaking the quiet. "The artist has captured your wife's image perfectly."

"Yes." Signor Lomellini's voice thickened with emotion. "She was so young, so lively, so happy. I still imagine I hear the tread of her slippers on the stairs or her laughter when I first wake. But of course, it is all in my mind."

"It's the same for us," Anica said. "My brother was so full of life. It scarcely seems possible that he's no longer in this world."

Papa made a humming sound in the back of his throat. "But we descend into sorrow again, and that is not what we came here for," he said. "Signor Lomellini, I'm eager to paint using oils, but I've never been trained in the technique. I thought perhaps by studying such a work, I would gain insight into how it is done."

"Ah! An excellent idea," said the merchant. "I can tell you what I recall from our sittings with the artist. He spoke of making many layers using slightly different hues of paint, of the time it took to let the layers dry. He claimed that by using all those layers, he could create an impression of depth and light that are impossible with the old ways."

"He was right," Anica said, her eyes on the portrait again.

The painted figures were bathed in light from an open window, their faces glowing with lifelike radiance. On the table before the couple stood a silver pitcher, a glass beaker of wine, and an arrangement of flowers. Anica moved closer, scrutinizing a detail.

"Is that a man's image reflected in the beaker?" she asked in disbelief.

Signor Lomellini let out a delighted chuckle. "You've spotted it! Yes, the artist put his reflection into the portrait. It's a trick these northern artists use. One I find quite amusing."

Anica looked at him sideways. His smile was so engaging that it made him look boyish, though there were fine lines around his eyes. She was comfortable in his presence, as if she had known him a long time.

A servant entered with wine.

"Ah! Please join me for a cup of wine," Signor Lomellini said. "I can have another chair brought in, and the three of us can talk about the portrait, the artist, and his ways. Ask me anything . . . anything at all."

Anica glanced at Papa, willing him to say yes, and her heart leaped at his next words.

"With pleasure, signor," he replied. "We won't forget this kindness."

CHAPTER 11

Summer, 1459
Rhodes Town

Anica shifted in her seat, her gaze flicking to the painting above
the altar. It was one of Papa's most prized works: the Virgin and her
child, commissioned by the archbishop of Rhodes Town for the
Church of Santa Maria.

Stained-glass windows above the painting illuminated the church
with a faint ruby-tinted glow. Anica glanced higher, into the nave. Long
ago, someone had painted the sky up there, a wash of dark blue span-
gled with gold stars. But much of it had peeled off in the intervening
years.

Her ears pricked back, alert to the small sounds of people breathing, coughing, adjusting their positions on the hard pews, whispering
amongst themselves. Seagulls shrieked outside. The harbor was a
stone's throw away, just beyond Santa Maria's eastern flank. For a
moment, Anica felt sorry for the priest. He had to compete with restless parishioners and the distracting sounds of the sea. She studied his

face. His lips moved ceaselessly, his words vanishing into the murky upper reaches where the stars glimmered under their shroud of dust and soot.

As the mass concluded, she and Papa filed outside to the small square where worshippers gathered in the sun to exchange gossip. At the far edge of the crowd, she spotted the Salviati family. Anica positioned herself so there would be no danger of making eye contact with any of them. She dreaded another interaction with Signor Salviati or his son, especially since Papa had put off the meeting the banker had requested.

"Paolo!"

The grand master's French falconer approached.

"Monsieur de Montavon," Anica exclaimed, glad to see his warm smile.

"Cédric!" Papa flung his arms wide, and the two men embraced.

"I can't stop looking around for Estelle," Anica admitted, wishing the falconer's daughter would appear at his side.

"You're not alone," the falconer replied. "We all miss her." His wife and children stood with a group of Latin women a short distance away.

"How goes it for her in Cyprus?" Papa asked. "I imagine the prince's death has cast a shadow over everyone there."

Not long after her friend had sailed to Cyprus to join Princess Charlotte's court last year, the princess's husband had died. Rumors quickly spread that he had been murdered. Worried for her friend, Anica had written Estelle several letters—all of which had gone unanswered. Since Beno's death, though, she'd nearly forgotten about Estelle. The whole world had shrunk down to the walls of their household.

The Frenchman's expression sobered. "You've not heard?" He leaned closer, lowered his voice. "Sorrow has visited Cyprus again, I regret to say. Princess Charlotte has been not only widowed but orphaned."

"How cruel fate can be," Anica said, stunned.

"Were the king and queen ill?" her father asked.

"That's what they say, but . . . ." The falconer's voice faltered a moment. "When King Jean died, so did my faith in his court. I'm trying to get Estelle back to Rhodes. Unfortunately, Princess Charlotte does not respond to my entreaties to release Estelle from her service."

"Let me know if we can help," Papa told him, reaching out to grip his arm. "I'd no idea."

"Grief is all-consuming," Monsieur de Montavon said quietly. "You're not to blame for that." He mustered a smile and tilted his head at the church doors. "I must compliment you on your painting in there. It is splendid. You must be proud of it."

Papa threw a sidelong glance at Anica. "Yes, I am."

Anica stayed quiet. No one but she and Papa knew the truth. From the hidden layer of gesso under the paint, to the lapis lazuli pigment that made the Virgin's blue gown so luminous, to the faint specks of white in the lady's eyes that gave them the illusion of life, Anica had been responsible for it all.

Another man approached, giving his greetings. Anica turned, relieved to see Signor Lomellini.

"How goes it with the new painting technique?" Signor Lomellini asked Papa in Italian. To the Frenchman, he added, *"Bonjour, monsieur le fauconnier."*

The falconer put up a hand. "I speak Italian well enough. Truth be told, Genoese slides off my tongue in a way the Venetian dialect never will. Apologies, my friend." He glanced at Papa with a grin.

"There aren't too many on this island who speak in the Venetian way," the merchant said. He looked at Anica again, his eyes twinkling. "I find that style of speech charming, even if most of my fellow Genoese would disagree with me."

The falconer chuckled. "Yes, you Genoese and Venetians are constantly at war on the seas. But on land, things can be different."

"We've no reason for enmity," Papa said. "And luckily, I've no need to venture out to sea these days."

"I wish I could say the same," Signor Lomellini said a little wistfully. "Genoa will never let me go, but Rhodes is my home now, too. I haven't spent enough time here. I'm determined to change that."

His last words made warmth flare in Anica's chest. Something about Signor Lomellini lifted the weight of grief that clung to her day and night. Perhaps it was because he bore the same burden himself—and despite his grief, he still managed to smile.

Across from her, the convivial look in her father's eyes vanished, replaced by a mask of cool politeness. She glanced over her shoulder, following his gaze. The Salviati men pushed through the crowd with purpose, headed their way.

"Good day, good day," Signor Salviati boomed.

His wheat-colored silk tunic was edged with gold thread. A velvet purse dangled from his belt alongside a tooled leather sheath. Judging by its glittering, jewel-bedecked handle, his blade was meant to be admired more than feared, Anica guessed.

The younger Salviati wore a silk tunic of pistachio green and emerald-green hose. Somehow all the green conspired to turn his olive skin a sallow, almost gray tone.

"Signorina," he said to Anica. "It is a pleasure to see you again."

"Thank you, signor," she returned.

"Have you heard?" The elder Salviati surveyed them all with a self-satisfied air, as if he were about to impart a valuable secret. "A traveling theater troupe arrived in Rhodes Town last night from Crete. They will perform in the marketplace next week. It will be quite amusing, I'm told. Acrobats, singers, puppets—something for everyone."

Anica looked at Papa, her fingers tingling with excitement.

"Excellent news," Papa said with enthusiasm. "We need pleasant diversions to keep our minds off our troubles."

Monsieur de Montavon nodded. "My wife and children will not want to miss that. Speaking of them, my wife is waving at me. I'd better not keep her any longer. Good day to you all."

He bowed and strode off. To Anica's disappointment, Signor Lomellini made his excuses, too.

"I'm glad your companions have left," Signor Salviati said. He licked his plum-colored lips. "I've a matter to discuss with you, Signor Foscolo. Perhaps you did not yet open my letter?"

"I did. Forgive me for having kept you waiting," Papa said in a conciliatory tone. "I would be more than happy to discuss the terms of more commissions with you."

"I could not be more pleased to hear that," Signor Salviati said.

"Perhaps you can visit my home tomorrow to talk about the details. My notary can write up the contract . . ."

As the two men bent their heads together in conversation, Anica avoided the younger Salviati's gaze.

"There are few educated, well-born females in this city," he murmured, leaning in. "They are as rare as snow in Rhodes Town."

Anica felt as if a stone had been flung against her stomach. She fought for a breath, wishing the earth would open up and draw her into its cool, dark depths.

"I thought you made your home in Florence, signor." She lifted her chin and stared back at him. His eyes were pools of murky ink. "I am sure there are many eligible young women in that city."

His mouth twitched. "I have opportunities here that are far greater than anything Florence could offer me. Both in work and in . . . life."

"You will not return to Florence, then?" Her heart sank at the prospect.

Before he could respond, the bells of Santa Maria began to strike noon, signaling the end of the social time after mass. People began dispersing as bells rang out all over the city. Anica glimpsed several men crossing the square from the direction of the English tongue's inn. She recognized two of them: the slightly bow-legged English knight and the tall Scotsman they had seen in the harbor not long ago. The Scotsman turned his head, studying the crowd as he walked. When his eyes met hers, he slowed his gait. She imagined she saw a glimmer of something in his expression—was it curiosity? Then she banished the thought. Such fanciful imaginings were best left to her sister.

Papa touched her shoulder. "Forgive us," he shouted to the Salviati men over the din of the bells. "My wife expects us home at noon. We'll be late."

Moving through the crowded square, they fell in behind the knights and the Scotsman, the vigorous chimes pursuing them to the Street of the Knights. As they passed the intersection, Anica peered up the curving cobblestone lane and caught one last glimpse of the Scot.

"I'm still uneasy about this commission, but Signor Salviati seems intent upon brokering an agreement," Papa confided, offering her his arm. "Signing a contract to do work I've never attempted before is foolish. Though I'm afraid I have little choice."

His words floated past Anica in an unintelligible jumble. She chewed her lip, unable to remove from her mind the image of the Scot's tall figure striding up the hill. He was a ruthless agent of the knights, a brutal privateer, a pirate in everything but name. Surely, she should despise him on sight. And yet he intrigued her. Meanwhile, the man who made her shudder with distaste was the educated son of a wealthy Florentine.

Like many things in this world, it made no sense at all.

CHAPTER 12

Summer, 1459
Rhodes Town

WHEN ANICA, Papa, and Heleni arrived at the marketplace, the din was almost overwhelming. A temporary stage dominated the space. Bakers, fruit vendors, and purveyors of sweets in stalls near the stage peddled their wares to the crowd. Small groups of knights in their black tunics strolled among the townsfolk.

Amongst the gathered citizens, Anica recognized several merchants from church, some of whom had their wives and children in tow. She glanced furtively around for the Salviatis but saw no sign of them.

A wagon repurposed as a puppet theatre stood at one edge of the stage. Children screamed in delight at the antics of the colorful puppets being manipulated on its stage by unseen actors.

For a moment, Anica fought a wave of sorrow. Little Beno would have loved this scene. He'd have rushed to the front of the crowd, bubbling with laughter, his brown eyes joyous. Praise the saints, Mamá had decided not to accompany them here today. This would have rubbed her grief raw all over again.

She stole a glance at Papa. He was engrossed in conversation with the falconer and his wife, seemingly unaffected by the laughter of the children. Heleni drifted toward the puppet show, pulling Anica's hand.

"Let's get closer," she urged.

At the same instant, Papa beckoned to them.

With reluctance, Heleni followed Anica to where their father stood with the French couple.

"Monsieur de Montavon has just told me the grand master may be interested in commissioning a portrait," Papa said.

Anica's mouth fell open. "Truly?"

The falconer nodded. "I've been singing your father's praises to Lord de Milly for years now. He's finally listened."

She locked eyes with her father. He was beaming.

"What kind of commission, did he tell you?" she asked the falconer.

"A triptych for his private chapel in the palace."

A three-paneled painting was a rare and lucrative job. It would do much to strengthen her father's position as the finest artist on Rhodes. A surge of gratitude rippled through her. The falconer and her father had been friends since the Frenchman arrived here several years ago, and his loyalty had never wavered.

"We'll go to the palace tomorrow and meet with Lord de Milly," Papa said to her. "The two of us."

The breath leaked from her lungs in a whoosh. "What? You mean me?"

Heleni dropped Anica's hand. "That's not fair! I want to go. I've never been in the palace."

Anica ignored her sister. She looked at Monsieur de Montavon. "Are you sure?"

He nodded. "I told the grand master you assist your father with his work, and he had no quarrel with that."

She felt buoyant, as weightless as a dragonfly.

Madame de Montavon ran her eyes over the long cotton headpiece covering Anica's hair and shoulders. "You shouldn't dress like *that* when you go, though."

Anica bristled. Madame de Montavon had always harbored a superior attitude. In recent years, she had shown respect toward Mamá and other members of the Georgillas family. But her mistrust of Greeks in general was still obvious.

"Why is that, madame?" Anica asked.

"The Order will treat you respectfully if you appear to be Latin because they are Latins, and they prefer to do business with their own kind. In my fabric enterprise, I've seen it play out every day."

The Frenchwoman ran a business exporting fine fabrics from Cyprus and Syria to France, so Anica had to admit she possessed knowledge of such things.

Madame de Montavon threw her another appraising stare. "I had a dress of brocaded silk and sleeves to match made for Estelle, but who knows when she'll return? She would want you to wear them." She reached out and fingered Anica's headpiece. "I've a silk head wrap in the French style that will suit you, too."

Anica swallowed, surprised by the kindness. "You are certain?"

Madame de Montavon gave an emphatic nod. "Yes. Come to our house tomorrow to fetch it all. This meeting with the grand master is important. A detail like clothing mustn't mar his impression of you."

Heleni let out an indignant sigh. "She gets a silk dress and sleeves, too?" Turning to Papa, she pulled the corners of her mouth down in a pout. "What about me? What do I get?"

Papa considered her words. "You get an iced-sugar bun," he said in a measured tone. Fishing a few silver asper coins from his purse, he handed them to Anica. "Both of you, go get a treat."

When they returned with their buns in hand, the de Montavons had moved along, but the Genoese merchant had taken the couple's place alongside Papa.

"A beautiful day for a bit of amusement," Signor Lomellini said, nodding at Anica and Heleni.

Anica greeted him warmly while Heleni dipped her head in a careless nod, her eyes wandering to a group of knights a little distance away.

"How does your new experiment progress?" he asked Anica. At her bewildered look, he added, "The oils? I've been wondering ever since your visit to my home."

"I've bought enough linseed oil to get started," she said, flattered by his interest. "We may have to experiment with brushes a bit. In your painting, I noticed the brushstrokes are quite small. I can't be certain if that's due to the artist's own preference or if small, fine-haired brushes are better for oils. It will be a matter of experimentation, I suppose."

He cocked his head to one side, an eyebrow raised. "You know much about this work. Your father is lucky to have such a diligent assistant."

Heat flooded her neck. Why had she divulged so much? It felt easy sharing information with this man. He had such a warm, attentive manner.

"But surely you will put down your palette and brushes one day soon and marry," he said.

"Yes, one day soon," she agreed, glancing at Papa.

Her father's gaze was fixed on the players dispersing across the stage. The crowd pushed closer, buzzing with anticipation, and a drummer sounded out a low, persistent beat.

"I hope your future husband allows you to continue painting," he said. "It would be a shame to cease an activity which you so clearly enjoy."

Anica smiled. "Thank you, signor. I hope so, too."

"I would like very much to purchase some of your small icons," the man went on, raising his voice over the sound of the drum. "I saw your father's work in a ship captain's home a few days ago. My entry hall needs just such adornment."

Hearing this, Papa turned his head. "As it happens, we have a series of icons in progress. You must come visit our studio, signor," he invited the Genoese. "You would be very welcome in our home."

Another male voice rang out behind Anica. "What is this, signor? You told me patrons were not allowed in your studio the day we met."

She spun around to confront the young French knight who had engaged them in conversation at the harbor not long ago. His expression held a trace of amusement, but his tone had been indignant. Beside her, Heleni drew in a quick breath, her lips parting in a radiant smile. The knight's gaze traveled from Anica to Heleni, then settled on Papa.

She watched her father trying to sort out what to say. The drumbeats came faster now, thickening the air with their sonorous rhythm.

Thankfully, Signor Lomellini spoke up first. "But I am not a patron, monsieur," he said. "I am a friend."

Papa's shoulders relaxed, and he tossed the Genoese a look of gratitude.

The knight frowned. Before he could speak again, a troupe of musicians launched into a raucous tune, signaling the start of the performance.

With a sidelong glance, Anica examined the French knight's profile. He was so young. The thought of him wielding a sword in combat with Turkish soldiers or Mamluk warriors filled her with sympathy. He couldn't possibly have seen combat on a battlefield. How would he survive if a siege came? Perhaps he was fiercer than he appeared.

The acrobats executed a complicated series of flips and somersaults, eliciting whoops and cheers from the audience. Anica clapped her hands in delight when two of them launched a companion into the air, where he curled into a ball, turned over twice, and landed on his feet, grinning.

Next to her, Heleni screamed—but it was a sound of outrage, not pleasure. A street urchin with Heleni's iced bun in his hand careened away from them, darting through the crowd with the agility of a cat.

"He stole my bun!" Heleni shrieked, pointing after him.

The French knight sped after the thief and seized him. He dragged the boy to Heleni's side with a triumphant gleam in his eyes. The boy dropped the bun, his face twisted by fear. He sank to his knees, his filthy tunic pooling on the cobblestones.

"Shall I take him to the Kastellania?" the Frenchman asked. "They'll throw him in the stocks, I imagine. Unless he's already made a name for himself as a thief. Then they might chop off one of his hands."

"Yes," Heleni said with vehemence. "He must be punished."

A Catalan merchant's wife nearby said, "The Greeks can't be trusted. They should be grateful to the knights for protecting them from Turks and Mamluks, but instead they steal and connive in the shadows." She turned to the knight. "Look under his tunic, monsieur! He's probably got a merchant's coin purse hidden there. Who knows what else he's stolen today?"

Anica shot her an icy glare.

"He's bone-thin," she said. "He must be starving. Have pity on him."

The young knight's proud countenance slackened a bit, his bravado wavering, but he kept his grip on the thief.

"Where does your family live?" Anica asked the boy softly in Greek. "Have you nothing to eat at home?"

A ripple of shame passed over his face. He dropped his gaze. "I have no home," he muttered. "No family."

"No family? He's lying," Heleni declared, tossing her head. "Trying to gain our sympathy." She spoke in French for the knight's benefit.

"Off to the Kastellania with him, then." The knight yanked the boy up, emboldened by Heleni's words. "I'd heard the Greek commoners will resort to anything to escape the rule of law, and now I believe it. We must make an example of him, or none of us will be safe."

His last proclamation elicited a murmur of approval from several Latins nearby.

A prickling sensation ran from the base of Anica's spine up to her neck. This man had just arrived in Rhodes. How dare he make such sweeping and offensive statements about his hosts?

"No!" she said, her voice flaring with anger. "He's just a child. An orphan."

"An orphan, perhaps. A thief, most certainly." The knight's blue eyes raked over her, cold and imperious. "The Order does not tolerate thieves."

A deep voice cut in. "I'll take him."

Anica looked up, startled to see the Scottish privateer, his face set in a furious scowl. The sheer towering presence of him made her take a step back.

"Let me handle this, my lord." His words, in perfect French, were directed at the young knight. "You've done your part for justice. I'll take care of the rest."

The knight's expression transformed into one of relief. Anica sensed he'd regretted his impulsive act and was glad to wash his hands of the matter. Without a word of protest, he relinquished the youngster to the Scot.

"See that he receives the harshest penalty possible when you deliver him to the gaoler," he told the man.

"The Kastellania's too good for him," the Scot growled. "I'll give him the fate he deserves."

"As it should be," the young knight replied, a glimmer of uncertainty in his expression.

The Scot gave one quick nod in the Frenchman's direction, then looked Anica full in the face.

Anica's heart pounded as she met his gaze. The poor boy looked twice as terrified now that he was in the hands of this man. What would the Scot do to him? Would he keep him for himself, make the boy his galley slave? Sell him across the sea? The privateer's gray-green eyes revealed nothing, but his clenched jaw, the flat line of his mouth, the furrow of his brow gave him an impression of barely repressed fury.

You made it worse by drawing attention to the boy, she castigated herself. *Now he's in the hands of a coldhearted killer. He'd have been better off at the Kastellania.*

The drummer pounded out a climactic rhythm as the acrobats readied for their final round of stunts, capturing the attention of the onlookers who had been distracted by the incident.

Anica ignored the troupe, balling her trembling hands into fists. She watched the pair move away, the Scotsman hulking over his cowering charge, and could swear she felt the blood boil in her veins.

CHAPTER 13

Summer, 1459
Rhodes Town

THE RISING sun spilled over the city walls, warming Anica's face as she
and Papa threaded their way past fruit vendors leading donkeys loaded
with heavy baskets. She smoothed the edges of her borrowed head
wrap, self-conscious. The embroidered sleeves belonging to Estelle
hung to the cobblestones, and she held her arms up awkwardly to keep
them from dragging. Next to her, Papa wore his finest black silk tunic
and a pair of chestnut-brown hose. His face was freshly shaved, and
Mamá had sewn him a black velvet cap lined with russet-colored silk
for the occasion.

When they turned onto the Street of the Knights, she saw they
were not the only townsfolk climbing the hill to the grand master's
palace. Once a week, Lord de Milly welcomed citizens of Rhodes
Town to hear grievances, settle disputes, and grant permission for
various endeavors. Though the people chafed at the oversight of the
Order, everyone understood the knights were the only defense

between them and an infidel siege. For this reason, there had been no major rebellions against the Latin masters of Rhodes—at least, not yet.

"Now remember," her father murmured in her ear as they passed the Church of St. John, "if the Grand Master asks you anything—"

She glanced at him sideways. "Papa, don't worry. You're the artist. I'm just your assistant."

He looked sheepish. "Forgive me. I'm a bit nervous."

"I won't embarrass you," she promised. "I know when to keep silent and when to speak."

They joined the queue of people massed before the palace's wood-and-iron doors. A pair of bearded Greek priests stood shoulder to shoulder behind them, immersed in a lively argument about tariffs on spices.

Anica bounced on the balls of her feet, trying to expel her nervous energy. Then she heard English voices and caught her breath. Fighting an urge to turn and stare, she concentrated on the fragments of conversation drifting overhead.

"Why do you hesitate?" one Englishman complained. "We're not islanders."

"You go ahead," said another.

Anica recognized the Scot's deep, lilting voice and stiffened.

"I'm waiting for a shipbuilder," he went on. "I'll see you inside."

Anica watched two English knights hurry around the crowd and enter the palace at a signal from the guards.

She turned her head, trying to catch a glimpse of the Scot. To her shock, he stood mere steps away, looking over the heads of the priests directly into her eyes. She wheeled around and stared at the ground, her heart wriggling like a water-starved fish. An image of the small boy he'd hauled away from the marketplace consumed her thoughts. What had he done to the child? Where had he taken him? Oh, why couldn't the Scot just disappear? Anica gritted her teeth, willing herself to stay calm. Today, of all days, she needed a clear mind. Anger would cloud her judgement—or worse, inspire her to spew dangerous words.

Finally, it was their turn. Papa explained to the guards who they were and what their business entailed. After being waved inside a cool, dim entry hall, they followed a young page up a broad staircase and along a marble-floored hallway to a reception hall. At the doorway, a guard told them to wait.

Anica peered inside the vast space, awed by the grandeur on display. Wood-paneled walls soared to meet a crisply plastered ceiling. Fine molding in the plaster bore a recurring pattern of fleurs-de-lis. Her gaze traveled to the center of the room, where a black-clad man sat in a heavy oak chair on a dais. A canopy fitted with lengths of embroidered silk towered over him, and a colorful Moorish rug lay at his feet. Two assistants stood alongside a table stacked with papers, books, and scrolls, awaiting Lord de Milly's command.

At the guard's signal, Anica followed Papa across the polished stone pavers, praying she would not trip on her dangling sleeves. The grand master watched them in silence. His close-cropped silvery beard matched his hair, and his sun-weathered skin stretched taut over high cheekbones.

Papa bowed. "My lord."

Anica lowered herself into a deep curtsy.

"Welcome," Lord de Milly said in French. "So. You are the Venetian artist I've heard so much about from my falconer, and from the knights as well. Your work hangs in several of the chapels along the Street of the Knights. I've seen your portraits, and I am impressed."

"Thank you, Grand Master," Paolo replied.

"How did you happen to come to Rhodes from Venice?" Lord de Milly asked. "Surely, you did not just stumble across this island."

Anica knew Papa had been dreading this question. Venetians weren't always favored by the knights. The Order had a history of aligning itself with the Genoese, taking their side during naval battles between the two Italian city-states. So far, Papa's Venetian citizenship had not imperiled his reputation in Rhodes Town, but his heritage could one day become a liability.

Papa hesitated a moment, clasping his hands at his waist. "It was a fortunate twist of fate, my lord. I had a patron—a cousin, in fact—who invited me to a Greek island to paint frescoes in his villa there. When I finished the job, it was a short journey to Rhodes, and once here I quickly found my place in the world."

"Which island did your cousin live on?"

Papa cleared his throat. "Antiparos."

The grand master's expression grew thoughtful. "You're a Loredan, then? That island is in their possession, if my memory serves me."

"I—well, the Loredans are my mother's family, yes."

"Interesting." Lord de Milly's eyes slid to Anica. "This is your daughter?"

"She assists me in my workshop," Papa replied. "And with frescoes. They are quite time-consuming to execute, on account of their size."

The grand master studied Anica for a moment. "Do you enjoy such work, signorina?"

She hadn't expected him to speak to her. Somehow she found her voice. "Yes, my lord. I do my father's bidding, helping him prepare panels and mix paints."

A look of faint surprise glimmered in his eyes. "You speak superb French." Examining her dress and sleeves with new interest, he added, "You look French, too. Is your mother from France?"

She shook her head, unsure if she should admit her Greek ancestry.

Papa jumped in, rescuing her. "My daughter speaks a half-dozen languages. She picks them up with ease. She learned French from the falconer's daughter, Estelle. We are fortunate in Rhodes Town to live amongst citizens from all over the world. Anica's language skills help us communicate with my patrons to their satisfaction."

Lord de Milly tented his fingers together, gazing at Papa. "The falconer's daughter . . ." He trailed off, his mind working something out. Then he sat up straighter in his chair. "You were one of the girls involved in that unfortunate incident during the plague year."

It had been four years since the terrifying day when Anica, Estelle, and Maria had been caught up in a dark scheme that would have cast them out of Rhodes forever and sentenced them to a horrible fate.

Anica drew in a deep breath and met his gaze. "Yes."

He nodded and sat in silence another moment, contemplating her.

What would he say next? Why did he not speak? A bead of sweat trickled down her spine.

"It pleases me to see you standing here before me, healthy and strong." His expression softened into a smile.

She took in his words with astonishment, glowing at the unexpected kindness.

"Thank you," she murmured.

"As for the commissions, I spoke to Monsieur de Montavon about a triptych for my private chapel. Did he mention it to you?"

"Yes," Papa said. "I would be pleased to undergo the work, my lord."

Anica's fingertips tingled at the idea of creating the three-paneled work alongside her father. It would take ages to complete, but she looked forward to the challenge.

"Excellent. I wonder if you would take on another commission as well," Lord de Milly went on. "I want a portrait of Santa Maria, too. And both works should be done in the Flemish style, with oils."

Papa shifted his weight next to her. Anica's heart pounded so furiously she was sure the grand master could hear it. Oils again! It was one thing to commit to a commission using the technique for Signor Salviati, but another thing entirely to promise such work to the Grand Master of the Order of St. John. She knew her father shared her thoughts, and she fought an impulse to slip her hand in his.

Courage, Papa.

"Yes, of course, my lord," her father said slowly. "It would be my honor."

"Excellent. Now that I know you're experienced with frescoes, I've another idea as well. A knight of Auvergne, my cousin's son, has lately come to Rhodes. He'll be taking over residence of one of the garden villas outside the city walls. It is in need of renovations, especially its frescos. Would you be able to revive them?"

Anica's gut twisted. Could this be the knight who had taken too bold an interest in Heleni at the harbor and then made a scene when the boy stole her iced bun? He had spoken of such a villa when they first met.

"It would be my great pleasure," Papa replied, dropping his chin to hide his discomfiture. "Shall I discuss the matter further with the knight himself?"

"No. It is to be a gift for him from his parents," said Lord de Milly.

"My secretary will give you instructions for carrying out the work, along with funds for the materials needed."

Papa bowed again. "My deepest thanks to you."

Anica sank into a curtsy once more, begging all the saints to let her rise again with grace.

CHAPTER 14

Summer, 1459
Rhodes Town

THE PAGE who led Anica and Papa down the sweeping staircase took a different route to exit the palace. They followed him through a door leading to a vast courtyard. Massive iron grain silos were sunk into the cobbled ground at intervals, and marble statues stood around the perimeter. Anica saw a figure emerge from the shadowy stone arcades opposite them, a bird perched on his wrist.

"Papa! Isn't that Monsieur de Montavon?"

The man approached them, dismissing the page.

"I asked the boy to bring you this way so I might see you. How did it go?" The falconer's eyes betrayed a trace of anxiety.

"Better than I could have imagined," Papa told him, grinning. "And I've you to thank for it."

"I planted the seed, but your work speaks for itself," the falconer returned, his own face breaking into a relieved smile.

"That is a beautiful creature," Anica said, mesmerized by the falcon.

"She's a saker falcon. Born in Crete, raised here. One of our best hunters."

The bejeweled leather hood on the falcon's head sparkled in the sunlight. The bird was large, her sharp talons gripping the falconer's gloved wrist, and she cocked her head in his direction when he spoke as if she understood his words.

"She sits so quietly on your wrist," Anica marveled. "Yet I can see the power in her, too. Under those feathers, she must have muscles as strong as steel."

"Not quite that strong," Monsieur de Montavon said. "But few creatures can match her for strength or courage, I'll say that." Something caught his eye behind her, and he stuck his free hand in the air. "By the saints, here comes the man who delivered her to me."

Anica and Papa turned as one, and her stomach lurched at the sight of the Scotsman approaching. For a moment, she stared in fascination at his loping walk, admiring his graceful and confident way of moving through the world. Then she remembered his menacing presence in the marketplace and looked away.

"Captain!" The falconer clearly had no such qualms about the man. "Join us."

When the Scotsman drew up before them, there was no sign of the fury he had displayed in the marketplace. His gray-green eyes regarded them steadily, and his wide mouth curved in a friendly smile.

"Monsieur," he said to the falconer. "Is that one of my charges riding on your wrist?"

Monsieur de Montavon inclined his head. "Indeed, it is." He glanced at Papa. "The Captain manages to deliver a dozen saker falcons a year to me without fail. I'm not sure how he does it, to be honest. With all the other demands the Order puts on you, where do you find the time to voyage to Crete each year?"

The Scotsman shrugged. "I get restless when I'm not at sea. And Crete is not much more than a stone's throw away from here."

His deep voice resonated in Anica's ears. Why was his French so good? She kept her eyes averted. The only place she could think to rest them on was the falcon. So she stared at the pattern of pale spots on the bird's gray-brown feathers as if they were objects of intense fascination.

"But you possess lands on Rhodes, I thought," the falconer said. "Surely, you have things to attend to there."

"I do," said the Scot. "A villa on the coast, south of here. But I'm rarely at liberty to visit it. When I'm on this island, Rhodes Town occupies most of my attention."

"If you don't mind my curiosity, Captain, why buy a villa you cannot use?" Papa asked him.

The Scot let out a short laugh. "I did not buy it. It was a gift from the Order. If it were up to me, I'd sleep there every night. But my duties lie elsewhere."

A movement to Anica's left distracted her. She watched a man padding quietly across the great expanse of the courtyard, dressed in the rippling silk robes and turban of an Arab. What on earth was an Arab doing in the grand master's palace, the heart of all Christendom in this part of the world?

"Good day, sayyid," the Scot called out to him.

The falconer's eyes lit up in recognition, too. "Signor Syriano," he cried, gesturing to the man to join them.

The fellow reversed course, his smile revealing even white teeth above his generous beard.

"I've heard of your skills, Signor Syriano," Papa said to the doctor. "They say doctors who are trained in Damascus have no equals."

"You are too kind," the man said in heavily accented French. He nodded at Anica. "Signorina."

Anica murmured a greeting in Arabic.

The doctor's eyes widened. "What's this?" he asked, astonished. "A Latin woman who speaks lovely Arabic? That is rare indeed."

Anica's flush deepened. She eyed the other men, self-conscious all over again in her unfamiliar clothing. Reverting to French, she said, "My father indulged my interest in languages when I was young."

"Anica has a talent for languages," Papa said, a note of pride creeping into his voice. "A gift."

Heat flooded Anica's cheeks. Now the Scot knew her name. The urge to steal a glance at him was irresistible. When she did, she stifled a gasp. He was staring soberly at her. His eyes were speckled with gold, she noticed. They seemed to emit sparks of light. Flustered, she trained her gaze on the doctor again.

The doctor looked from Papa back to Anica, and wistfulness washed over his face. "I have a daughter who is similarly talented," he said.

"Is she here in Rhodes? I'd like to meet her," Anica said.

He shook his head, his shoulders drooping. "She lives in Damascus. But my family may visit Rhodes soon, so perhaps you will meet her one day."

Anica wondered why the doctor lived here, so far from his family. With his next words, though, she had her answer.

Glancing up at the interior windows of the palace, he stood a little straighter. "But I must not linger. I'm off to the apothecary to fetch some medicines for my lord."

Of course. He worked for the Order, for the grand master himself, and there was every possibility that he had been forced into the position. Her heart ached for him, for his family, for the daughter who lived across the sea.

They all said their farewells to him. Before Anica and her father took their leave as well, Papa's gaze lingered on the privateer.

"Whatever happened to that boy who took my daughter's sweet in the marketplace? He seemed destined for a dark fate."

The Scot's mouth flattened into a hard line. "He won't get into any more trouble in Rhodes Town, signor, I assure you."

Anger flared in Anica's chest. A scathing retort pushed against her throat, ready to launch itself at him like an iron-tipped arrow.

Don't look at him. Look at the falcon, only at the falcon.

But for some reason, the falcon seemed as unsettled as she. The bird extended her wings and flapped them several times, rising off the falconer's wrist with each thrust. The leash attaching her to his arm kept the falcon from making any progress, though. She emitted a frustrated shriek.

Monsieur de Montavon spoke to her in soothing tones, backing away. "Too many unfamiliar voices, perhaps. I must bid you farewell."

"As I must," the Scot replied. He dipped his head at them and turned on his heel. "Good day."

CHAPTER 15

Summer, 1459
Rhodes Town

ANICA and her father entered their home, bursting with the good news. They found Mamá in the parlor with Aunt Rhea, heads bent together, sitting in the two armchairs before the hearth. Something dreadful must have happened, for both women's expressions were etched with worry.

"Look at you," Aunt Rhea said to Anica, trying to inject her voice with merriment. "Dressed like a proper Latin woman. Those sleeves!"

Mamá did not smile. Her eyes were fixed on Papa.

"What is it?" Papa's voice was sober, the energy waning from his expression.

Aunt Rhea rose from her chair and offered it to him. "I had a visitor today."

Maria came to the door, and Anica sent her to fetch wine.

"Who?" he asked warily as he sank into the chair, both hands gripping its arms as if he were bracing himself for the reply.

"Signor Salviati."

Papa exchanged a long look with Mamá. "So it's as we feared," he murmured.

She bit her lip. "Yes."

Anica brought two stools from the opposite side of the room for herself and Aunt Rhea. When Maria returned with the wine, Anica whispered, "Where's Heleni?"

"She's upstairs, embroidering. Shall I fetch her?"

Anica shook her head.

Heleni's presence never made things easier, though she could be counted on to divert everyone's attention—which, since Beno's death, Anica had a new appreciation for.

Maria withdrew, shutting the door gently behind her.

Anica poured wine for the others, then sat on the remaining stool, clutching her cup.

"Signor Salviati approached me about Anica and Troilo making a match," Aunt Rhea said. "Apparently, he is not going back to Florence and will make his home here."

Anica realized her hands were shaking. She set her cup down on a nearby table and laced her fingers together. "No." The word came out like the crack of a whip. "Please don't make me marry that man."

Aunt Rhea's expression darkened. "The Salviatis are confident the match will be made."

"Why?" Mamá asked. "Their arrogance is astounding."

"Because we are in their debt," Papa said, passing a hand over his face.

"So are many citizens in Rhodes," Mamá pointed out. "Signor Salviati may consider himself superior to the average moneylender, but he cannot dictate our affairs."

"The knights promised to reimburse us when we moved, but the purse they gave me was light," Papa admitted. "I had to find a loan to cover our expenses."

Anica stared at him in astonishment. After an attack by the Ottoman Turks several years ago, many houses near the city walls had been demolished to make way for massive reinforcement projects.

Theirs had been one of them. But she'd had no idea how much the move had cost her father.

"Oh no!" Aunt Rhea said in horror. "Why did you not come to me, Paolo? I could have helped you make other arrangements. How much do you need to pay back the Florentines? I'll loan you the sum today."

Papa shook his head. "More than you can afford."

Mamá put down her cup, frowning. "You never told me."

"I did not wish to concern you with it," he said. "I've been paying off the loan little by little."

"Saints above. The Florentines always attach such outrageous terms to their loans," Aunt Rhea spluttered. "Is the interest rate twenty percent? Thirty?"

Papa just stared at the floor.

Anica tried to organize the jumble of thoughts careening through her mind. "We just got commissions from the grand master himself," she said. "Surely, the payment will go far to cancel this debt."

Her father lifted his head. His face now held an expression of alarm. "Dear God, the commissions." He turned to Aunt Rhea. "We promised Lord de Milly to deliver him works made in oils. Neither of us have ever painted using that style. It will take our combined talents to get it done to his standards. Plus, there are frescos for a villa—a massive job, one I cannot undertake alone. Until my new apprentice arrives, I need Anica more than ever."

Aunt Rhea's eyes widened in surprise. They had never divulged the exact nature of Anica's help in the studio to her. Before she could probe for more details, Mamá stood and paced restlessly around the room.

"Why in the world is the Florentine's son putting down roots in Rhodes Town? That family bragged of his future in Florence ever since they arrived here, then put him on a ship to Italy what, five years ago? It makes no sense that he's come back."

Aunt Rhea watched her sister stalk back and forth. "My guess is that something went awry in Florence. Perhaps a business deal soured, perhaps he wronged a man—"

"Or a woman," Mamá said darkly. "I've never trusted that family.

You can tell a lot about a family by the way they treat their servants. When we took in the Salviatis' slave woman all those years ago . . . the things she told me!" Mamá's lips compressed. Her eyes were black with anger. "No, I couldn't bear letting Anica become that family's property."

Aunt Rhea took a long swallow of her wine, ruminating over the problem. "Refusing will be treacherous, for Signor Salviati holds much influence within the Order. He could make life difficult for you."

"There might be a way," Papa said. "The Genoese merchant, Signor Lomellini, is also interested in a match with Anica; I met him yesterday to discuss it."

Everyone stared at Papa in astonishment.

"He has not reached out to me yet," Aunt Rhea said a bit reproachfully.

"He likely doesn't know your reputation as a matchmaker," Mamá told her sister in a soothing voice. "He hasn't spent much time in Rhodes Town, has he?"

Anica shifted in her seat. "I do not know the man very well, but I like him," she said. "If we could spend a bit more time together, I would feel more confident about the idea, but I'm not opposed. He's kind to me, and I enjoy his company."

"He's wealthy enough," Aunt Rhea put in. "And an upstanding citizen. I've never heard a complaint about the man."

"Neither have I," said Papa. "Not from merchants, not from agents of the Order. And I've been inquiring."

Anica raised an eyebrow. "Since when?"

"Since the day we entered his home to see his portrait," Papa confessed. "I saw how the two of you looked at each other. It was clear you found him pleasant company."

She smiled a little. Papa had been so distracted since Beno's death that she assumed he paid scant attention to such details. She'd been wrong, evidently.

Mamá frowned. "Well, I've never met him. Let us arrange for a meeting so I can see for myself what kind of man he is."

"It must be soon," Aunt Rhea warned. "The Salviatis won't wait long for an answer."

"I need Anica's help with these commissions," Papa said. "She cannot be wed until all of this is finished."

"We won't consider a wedding until the one-year anniversary of Beno's death has passed and our official period of mourning is over," Mamá declared. "No one can argue with that. That will be enough time, won't it?"

Anica looked at her father. "I think so," she said. "Although, with these oil paints, I can't be sure . . ."

"It's enough," he said. "It will have to be. And with God's grace, our new apprentice will have arrived by then." He stood. "Tomorrow I'll call upon Signor Lomellini with your mother. If he meets with her approval, I'll go to the grand master for his blessing. Then we'll have our notary draw up the marriage contract."

It was customary for citizens to ask the grand master's permission before planning a betrothal. Anica had never heard of such a request being denied by the Order; the custom was a mere formality.

Mamá turned to her sister. "Rhea, can you put off the Salviatis?"

Aunt Rhea nodded. "Leave it to me. If all goes well with your Signor Lomellini, I'll tell them Anica is betrothed to another. If they protest, I'll inform them this arrangement has been under discussion for some time and they made their proposal too late. A contract is a contract, after all. That is something even Signor Salviati must respect."

As her parents and aunt continued to discuss the details, Anica's mind darted to the conversation she'd had with the Genoese merchant after church. He'd said he hoped her future husband would allow her to continue painting. Had he been imagining himself as that man? She hoped so. Unbidden, her mind recalled the searching gaze of the Scot, the golden flecks in his gray-green eyes.

Consider yourself lucky you're not betrothed to the likes of him.

If he was so repellant, why did he linger in her thoughts? That was a question she did not want to dwell upon, for the longer she mulled over it, the more uneasy she became. Trying to ignore the fierce pounding of her heart, she willed all thoughts of the Scot away.

With any luck, she would never cross paths with the man again.

CHAPTER 16

Autumn, 1459
Rhodes Town

ANICA POURED a measure of linseed oil into the small dish of red-ochre pigment. She mixed the concoction into a congealed mass with a palette knife.

"It doesn't look right." She glanced up at her father. "Too thick?"

He shrugged, looking doubtful. "Pour in a bit more oil. Just a drizzle. Then stir again."

Anica followed his instructions. Now the liquid looked more like paint. Though not at all the same texture as egg tempera.

Two panels, already sanded and primed with gesso, stood on easels by the windows.

Heleni pushed open the door. Her gleaming black hair was wrapped around her head in complicated braids. "I've got what you wanted."

She carried the faint scent of rose with her into the chamber. Crossing to the battered pine table that served as a work surface,

Heleni laid down the day's purchases: half a dozen small corked ceramic jugs and several ceramic bowls.

Papa straightened and gave Heleni a long stare. "I trust you kept your hair covered while you were out."

"Of course. Maria fussed over me like a mother hen." Heleni peered at the dish in front of Anica. "It's quite odd looking, this paint. And it smells." She wrinkled her nose.

"It may look odd, but I've seen what this strange mixture can do on the panel," Anica said. "It is a marvel." She turned to her father. "Should we practice by painting Heleni?"

"Excellent idea. One of the commissions is to be of Santa Maria, so why not model it after you?"

Heleni's expression brightened. "Where should I stand?" she asked eagerly.

"By the window," Papa said.

Heleni did as he instructed.

"Turn a bit toward the light," Anica said, moving her easel to a better angle. "That's it."

With a slender piece of charcoal, she set about drawing the basic structure of her sister's face on the prepared panel.

Papa filled several more bowls with pigment and oil, readying a full palette of colors for Anica.

Mamá entered the studio wearing a flowing gown of delicate deep-blue cotton, prompting a gasp from Papa. Startled, Anica dropped her stick of charcoal. Heleni raced across the room, flinging her arms around Mamá.

Their mother had worn black each day since Beno's death. It had become as much a part of her as the finely arched dark brows over her eyes. Anica had assumed she would never put on colorful garb again.

Mamá smiled a bit self-consciously and kissed Heleni's cheek. "I can't hide away from the world forever. I have much to do and much to look forward to."

"Uncle Valossi's wedding," Heleni exclaimed. "We need dresses. I want mine to be pink."

Mamá laughed indulgently. "And pink it shall be." She glanced over

Heleni's head at Anica. "We shall need things for your dowry chest," she said. "Including gowns sewn in the Latin style."

Heleni pulled out of Mamá's embrace and resumed her position by the window, where slanting rays of sunlight bathed her with gold. "Is that because she's marrying a Latin man?"

"Yes," Papa said. "Signor Lomellini, a Genoese merchant."

"I've never met him." Heleni crossed her arms over her chest, frowning.

"I have, and he is a fine man. A good match for our Anica," Mamá said firmly.

Anica reached for her mother's hand. She pressed it to her cheek, her heart full to bursting. When her parents had returned from their visit to Signor Lomellini's residence last week, they'd both borne broad smiles. A few days later, Papa had secured a notarized letter of permission from Lord de Milly. Anica had felt a strange mixture of excitement, relief, and disappointment at the realization that she was now betrothed. A small part of her had hoped Mamá would dislike Signor Lomellini, Troilo Salviati would go back to Florence, and her marriage plans would be postponed.

All childish hopes, she knew. It was time for her to wed. Signor Lomellini was a man she could imagine sharing a life with—how many betrothed women could say that? After all, she barely knew him and she already felt affection for him. That affection could easily grow into love.

Anica's spirit soared at the sight of her mother's joyous expression. Lately, she'd forgotten what joy felt like—but now it gripped her with a buoyant, fizzing sensation. She grinned foolishly, seeking Papa's eyes. His expression was full of tenderness.

"The wedding is in six months; there's plenty of time to pack the dowry chest with any kind of clothing you wish." He exchanged a glance with Mamá, and his face broke into a smile. "Signor Lomellini has invited us to return and study his portrait again, Anica. Today, as it happens."

Her hands went to her paint-splattered apron, then to the linen head wrap concealing her hair. "Today? I . . ."

"Don't worry," Mamá told her. "You are as luminous as the moon."

Heleni surveyed Anica with a disdainful expression, then slowly twirled in the sunlight. "That may be, but the moon's beauty pales next to the sun's."

"We don't discuss beauty in this household," Mamá said. "It's bad luck. Go pray to the saints for forgiveness, Heleni. And relight any of the candles that have gone out in the prayer room while you're there."

Pouting, Heleni dragged her feet across the floor and exited the studio.

"Then return straightaway so your sister can finish the portrait," Papa called after her.

"When are we going to his house?" Anica asked her father. Her heart was thumping wildly. She had not seen Signor Lomellini since their betrothal had been settled. It would feel odd encountering him with the knowledge that one day soon they would share a marriage bed.

"When the bells toll three this afternoon," Papa replied.

Anica's trembling hands kept returning to the violet-hued headpiece that swirled around her shoulders. Over and over, she adjusted the circlet holding it in place. The Genoese merchant's residence was not far from their home, but the walk seemed longer than usual. What if her initial impressions of Signor Lomellini had been completely wrong? What if he was cold to her, or rude, or dismissive, or . . .

"Anica?" Papa's voice penetrated her thoughts. "Are you unwell?"

She shook her head. "No. Just a little nervous."

He offered her his arm. "Understandable considering the circumstances. All shall be well."

Inside Signor Lomellini's parlor, a servant offered wine and ushered them into dark wood chairs outfitted with silk-damask seat cushions. When they had visited here before, Anica's attention had been fixed on the painting. But today, she could not help observing minute details of furnishings and ornament. One day soon she would live in this home and care for all of these belongings. To her relief, Signor Lomellini had taste she admired. The hand-hooked Moorish rugs on the tile floor bore pleasing patterns in red and green. The silverplate on the oak chests glinted softly in the light from the courtyard window.

Footsteps rang out in the entry hall and Signor Lomellini entered the chamber.

"Signor Foscolo, Signorina Anica," he said, approaching them with a smile.

Papa stood and bowed. Anica made to rise, but he waved her into her seat again. He took her hand and raised it to his lips. The warm pressure of his mouth made her heart leap with anticipation. How would it feel to have those lips on her own?

"That is a lovely color on you," he said, studying the headpiece.

Her cheeks blazed with heat. "Thank you," she murmured.

He sat in an armchair across from them, directly underneath the portrait. It was slightly disconcerting to see his dead wife's face peering over his shoulder. Did she harbor an expression of slight disapproval? Anica shook off the thought. The woman simply looked contemplative.

Signor Lomellini turned to glance at the painting. "Surely, we can have a short visit before your attention turns to matters of work." His jovial tone conveyed that he meant no ill will by the comment.

She flushed anew. "Forgive me. The craftsmanship is admirable, that's all."

Signor Lomellini nodded. "You will be able to admire it at your leisure very soon." He gestured around the chamber. "All of this shall be yours. If you prefer to move the furnishings, or replace them, you may do so."

She sat up a little straighter in her chair, clutching her silver cup with both hands. "Thank you, signor."

He laughed. "Let's dispense with formalities, Anica. I'm called Marino."

Papa put down his cup. "When we drew up the marriage contract, I was surprised," he admitted. "Marino is one of the most popular names in Venice. I'd no idea the Genoese favored it as well."

The merchant nodded. "The first Marino among us made his fortune off the seas, through the spice trade. Our family has honored his legacy ever since by naming our firstborn sons after him. And as our fortunes keep rising, with God's grace, we'll not drop the habit anytime soon."

His gaze settled on Anica with those last words. Would their future sons *all* be named for his family members?

"And if you—we—were to have a girl?" she asked.

He smiled. "Marina, naturally."

They all laughed.

"Once we've ticked off that box, we're free to name any other offspring as you please," he added, his tone more serious.

A wave of relief washed over her. He was the same man she had met on their first encounter. He had a warm manner and a streak of humor that she found appealing. She kept her eyes on him for a moment, realizing that her heart has ceased fluttering. She turned her gaze to Papa, and he met it with an understanding smile.

Her father had been right. All would be well.

"Though I long to spend the next six months at your side, I must return to Genoa soon," the merchant told her, sipping from his cup. "The spice traders will be back from the East in October, and it's never wise for me to be absent during the autumn. There's much to oversee. I'll hope to be back before winter ends."

Anica stared at him in dismay. She'd already begun imagining afternoons spent with him in the marketplace, visits to the harbor when merchant ships arrived, the social hour after church spent in his company.

"I am sorry to hear that," she said. "But of course, I understand. Your business affairs come first."

Papa shifted in his seat. "Will you return to Genoa each autumn going forward, then?"

"Until I can find someone trustworthy to stand in for me there. I hope that in three years or so my younger brother will be ready to take the helm of our business in Genoa and I'll be able to spend most of my time here in Rhodes Town." He looked at Anica and smiled. "With you."

Warmth spread through her as if the wine they drank was hot and spiced rather than cool and sweet. It made sense that her marriage would be full of separations—her future husband was a merchant from

Genoa, not a Greek. Rhodes was not his home, not really. Her parents had told her they found this appealing. He owned several ships and a residence across the sea. In case of a siege, he would have a means of escape and a safe, comfortable place to resettle. And so would Anica.

"I'll take you with me to Genoa one day," he promised. "My family will be eager to meet you."

His words sparked a new pulse of anxiety within her. Would a Genoese family truly approve of a Venetian-Greek wife for their son? It was hard to imagine.

He seemed to know her thoughts. "You will make them proud," he assured her. "They will find much about you to admire."

She raised her cup to her lips, still unnerved.

"Now you must have your fill of time with the portrait." He stood. "I have another engagement, I'm afraid, and I must leave you both. But you can stay as long as you wish."

He bowed as they stood and murmured their good-byes.

When he left the parlor, Anica's eyes swiveled to the painting. To her consternation, the woman's expression held a hint of reproach, even a flicker of suspicion. Anica blinked several times, then looked again. It had been another trick of the light or her imagination. For the dead woman's face was serene, and her eyes bore nothing but peace.

CHAPTER 17

Autumn, 1459
Rhodes Town

NOT LONG AFTER Marino Lomellini set sail for Genoa, Anica joined her family for the morning meal in a fog of exhaustion. A strong wind had rattled the shutters all night, jerking her out of slumber each time she drifted off.

In contrast, Heleni had slept next to her oblivious of the noise, and her mood today was light. She chatted with Mamá about the parakeets Aunt Rhea had recently purchased from the marketplace, about the garnet earrings she had seen at a goldsmith's shop. Then she informed them all that a French countess had arrived in Rhodes Town on her way from Cyprus to Paris and would be attending mass at Santa Maria on Sunday.

"She'll be wearing the latest French fashions," Heleni reported.

"Where did you hear about this countess?" Papa asked Heleni, helping himself to a large portion of sliced figs and yogurt from the bowl at the center of the table.

She picked at an errant thread on her sleeve. "At the apothecary. When Maria and I were there to buy lapis lazuli powder the other day. There were servants of the countess waiting behind us. I overheard them." Turning her attention to Anica, she added, "You must study every detail of her garments at church on Sunday. Then you can have your wedding dress made in the same fashion."

"Perhaps I won't want a dress in the Latin style," Anica said, bristling. Her sister could be as bossy as Aunt Rhea. "Perhaps I'll have it made in the Greek way."

"But you're marrying a Latin man. You'll have to adopt his ways."

Anica could not shake her prickly mood. "Why don't you come with us to Santa Maria and see the countess's dress for yourself?"

Heleni recoiled. "I don't attend Latin mass."

"I go to Greek and Latin services. You can do both, too."

Mamá looked uncomfortable. "We can't force Heleni to worship at Santa Maria."

Mamá and Heleni only went to the Greek Orthodox Church favored by the Georgillas family. Anica sometimes accompanied them, especially for Easter services, but she was more often at her father's elbow at Santa Maria. It had been that way ever since she could remember.

"This is a tiresome discussion." Papa drizzled a stream of honey over his food and spooned up a few bites. "I've some good news to share. We shall have help in the studio before too long."

Anica glanced at her father in surprise. "An apprentice?"

Papa nodded. "He's already received training in a studio. He can draw well. I was sent a sample of his work. It's far superior to anything my previous apprentices could turn out. He's under contract with another artist until the spring, though. Then he's free to travel here."

"I'd like to inspect his work, too," Anica said. She felt jealous at the idea of a young man taking her place at Papa's side, even though she ought to be relieved and happy at the news.

Church bells across the city began chiming to mark the hour.

Papa stood, tossing his napkin on the table. "Saints above, this morning is already half-over. The marketplace is in full swing at this point. The oil purveyor will be there today, Anica," he added as he walked away. "Perhaps he'll have the linseed oil we need."

Heleni sprang from her seat and bolted for the door. "I'm getting ready," she hurled over her shoulder. "I can't go out looking like this."

Anica's shoulders shook with laughter as her sister's footsteps pounded up the staircase. She rose when Maria entered and began clearing the dishes.

"You'll come with us, Maria. I need you at my side to help carry things."

Maria nodded in silence, continuing her task.

Anica glanced at Mamá. "Will you come?"

Her mother stood. "Yes. Rhea will be there with a friend, a newcomer to Rhodes she's taken under her wing. She wants me to meet the woman."

Anica followed her mother through the doorway. "So like Auntie. She has such a warm heart."

The wind had vanished with the rising of the sun. Their little group wove through the streets to the marketplace, engaged in animated conversation. This was almost like the days before Beno died, Anica thought. It felt as if she could turn around and see him hand in hand with Mamá, his little face beaming up at her, full of excitement at the prospect of visiting the marketplace. She forced herself not to glance back. He was not there. He'd left them, and this was their life now. It could be full again, she knew. It could spill over with moments of joy— even without his presence.

As they passed the Sea Gate, the sound of wailing made her pause. Near the guards' station by the iron-studded doors leading to the harbor, a woman dressed in rags squatted on her heels, begging passersby for aid.

Heleni tugged at Anica's hand. "Why do you stop?"

Their mother drew in a sharp breath. "Look at her face! They've cut off her ear."

Anica sucked in a breath at the sight of a bandage wrapped around the woman's head, dark with blood where her ear had once been.

"She must have stolen something from her master," Heleni said. "Jewelry, perhaps."

Anica kept silent. When slaves or servants stole or lied, they could lose a tongue, an ear, even a hand in punishment.

"That's what betrayal brings," Heleni went on. "Serves her right."

Out of the corner of her eye, Anica saw Maria flinch.

Mamá approached the wounded woman.

"Cali," Papa called, a note of warning in his voice.

But Mamá ignored him. She slipped a coin in the woman's hand and talked to her for a moment.

When she returned, her mouth was set in a grim line. "I told her to go to St. Catherine's convent. The nuns will see to that injury. If she's still here when we return, we must take her there ourselves."

"Why?" Heleni demanded. "She's nothing to us. And she's clearly done something horrible, to be punished so."

Anica turned on her sister. "We know nothing of the woman's troubles. Who knows if she was justly punished? Her master may simply be cruel."

Their little group proceeded again through the streets, but the energy that had propelled them forward a moment before was dulled now by Heleni's resentful silence.

Just before they reached the marketplace, Mamá waved at Aunt Rhea, who stood with several servants and a woman wearing a simple linen veil over her hair in the Latin style.

"This is Signorina Giovanna," Aunt Rhea told them when they reached the group. "She's a physician. Trained in Italy at a medical school."

"I didn't know women were permitted to become doctors," Anica said in surprise.

The woman smiled, falling into step alongside them as they turned up the market street.

"It never fails to astonish people, but it's true. The school in Salerno has trained women alongside men for hundreds of years," she said.

Her delicate features, smooth skin, and large brown eyes made her appear young, but she must have been older than she looked.

"Signorina Giovanna is a fine physician," Aunt Rhea said. "Better than most of the Latin ones in Rhodes, I can assure you. She'll be helping me aid your uncle with all of his maladies."

Now Anica understood. Her uncle had been an invalid for many years. Rhea had hired seemingly every doctor in Rhodes, whether Greek, Arab, or Jewish—and yet his suffering only increased. It was just like Aunt Rhea to cast her net all the way to Italy in search of relief for him, despite all the pain he'd inflicted on her.

"When did you arrive in Rhodes Town?" Anica asked the doctor.

"Just a few days ago," the woman said. "I've been living in Genoa for the past several years, but I was ready for a change. I visited Rhodes some time ago and found the climate to my liking. When the opportunity came to move here, I could not resist returning."

"And was it a good decision?" Papa asked.

She smiled. "I've not yet had any reason to regret it."

There was even more activity than usual in the marketplace. A merchant fleet from Alexandria had sailed into the harbor last night. Spices, pigments, silks, all manner of goods from the East were flowing into Rhodes Town today. Maria's basket already contained several items they'd use for the oil paintings, including marten and rabbit fur for brushes. Standing in a queue at a purveyor of oils, Anica hoped Papa was making headway with the merchant of precious minerals who was rumored to possess cinnabar.

"Good day to you," a male voice said behind her. Startled, she turned to confront Troilo Salviati. His skin was oddly pale for one who lived under the Greek sun, but then he spent most of his time indoors at the knights' treasury, counting ducats and florins.

She stepped back a bit. "Good day, sir."

"What are you seeking in the market today, signorina?" he asked, adjusting the billowing sleeves of his linen blouse. He wore full Latin regalia with a green silk tunic over brown hose.

"Supplies for my father," she said shortly.

"Ah, the artist is ever in need of paints for his palette," he observed.

Wishing he would melt away into the crowd, Anica nodded politely and directed her gaze back to the vendor's stall. The matron ahead of her yammered on about the differences between olive oils from Crete and Cyprus, the merchant absorbing her words with utmost seriousness.

"You look fetching today," the Florentine said, leaning closer.

Anica flinched, her shoulders tightening. "Thank you, sir."

She studied the fine stitching on the hem of the matron's cloak. Why wouldn't the woman make her selection and move along?

"You weren't at Santa Maria on Sunday," Troilo observed. "Why do you not attend mass regularly?"

His tone rankled her. What business was it of his?

Anica gave him a sharp look. "My mother is Greek, as you no doubt recall. I sometimes attend the Greek Orthodox Church. I'm sure you're aware the practice is permitted by the Order."

He pursed his lips. "Of course, of course. I simply meant to say I miss your presence when you're not at church."

Anica stifled an exasperated sigh. Her coolness was not having its intended effect.

"Some say your sister is the beautiful one," he went on, lowering his voice to a silky purr. "But I don't know. There is something about you I cannot resist." He put a hand out, touched the thin gauzy cotton of her flowing headpiece. "It cannot be true that you will marry a Genoese merchant. Contracts can be broken, you know."

She pulled away, seized by a combination of revulsion and anger. But he did not relinquish his grasp on the fabric.

"You go too far," she snapped.

Over his shoulder, she saw a man striding toward them. It was the Scot, and his eyes were on her. Shame and panic flooded her at the same time.

"Signorina," the Scotsman called out. "Is all well?"

The Florentine lowered his arm. The matron in front of Anica completed her purchase and bustled off.

"Yes, sir," Anica said, cursing the heat flooding her neck. "Thank you."

The Florentine stalked off, giving a wide berth to the Scot.

Distracted by the merchant's greeting, Anica lost sight of the Scot. When she finished her transaction, the man had vanished. She handed the cask of linseed oil to Maria, then headed out into the sunshine again, half hoping to catch a glimpse of the Scotsman, half dreading another interaction with the Florentine.

"Come," she said. "Let's find Papa."

They hurried through the busy marketplace. A vivid memory of the Scotsman's powerful stride entered her consciousness for the tenth time since she'd clapped eyes on him.

Banish him from your mind, she ordered herself.

Then she spotted Papa in conversation with Signor Salviati near the spice stalls.

"God save me," she said under her breath. "They're everywhere, those Florentines."

Maria glanced at her sideways. "Should we go to the goldbeater's stall, then? Your mother asked for gold thread so I can embroider your headpieces for your uncle's wedding."

"Ah! I nearly forgot."

Catching sight of them, Papa concluded his conversation and hastened in their direction.

"Did you get the items on your list?" she asked him.

He nodded. "And you did, too." He took the cask of linseed oil from her.

"We just need the gold thread for Mamá," she said.

He matched his pace to hers. "You rescued me from a tedious conversation."

"You with the father, me with the son," she replied.

"What do you mean?"

"Troilo is not satisfied with your answer to his father, it appears. He brought up the subject of marriage, of contracts."

Papa looked at her soberly. "I'll see that the matter goes no further. Don't worry, my dear."

But her father's soothing words did not comfort her. Ever since she'd learned her family was in debt to the Salviatis, a pit of dread lodged in her belly each time she thought of them. Until Papa paid off the loan, they would be at that family's mercy, she was sure of it.

CHAPTER 18

Autumn, 1459
Rhodes Town

THE NIGHT before his departure for the south, Drummond stayed up late playing chess with Sir Peter at the Inn of the English by the warm hearth, listening to the innkeeper interrogate a group of pilgrims about matters of the English court. The pilgrims, wealthy wool merchants from York, professed ignorance regarding English royalty and preferred to discuss border wars with the Scots. One of them bragged about the role his family had played in keeping Roxburgh Castle in the hands of the English. Drummond found it difficult to concentrate on the game while the man spouted his nonsense.

Roxburgh Castle will be ours again one day, he vowed.

If only he could sail home and help King James wrest it back from those English dogs. Of course, there was no chance of that happening, for his return would imperil the lives of everyone he held dear. A border conflict had gotten him into this predicament, he reflected bitterly—a fight the Scots had won. Drummond had survived the battle only to learn he'd killed the wrong man. He was still paying for it.

Caught up in his thoughts, he lost a bishop and a knight to Sir Peter in quick succession.

"Why not stay in Rhodes Town for a while longer?" his friend asked, assessing him with a shrewd gaze. "You'll be lonely in your cliff-top hideaway. No one to play cards with, no one to beat you in chess."

"You know I'm not one for city life," Drummond told him, draining his cup of wine. *Go easy*, he told himself. *You can't captain your vessel tomorrow with a head dulled by drink.* "I can't wait to get back to Archangelos, but work awaits me there, not leisure. I'll be training new guards for the fort at the Bay of Malona. Then I'm due back here to prepare for another sea voyage."

"Have you been tapped to lead the inspection of fortresses on Kos and Symi? I heard two galleys will be dispatched for that."

Drummond raised an eyebrow. "Word leaked out fast."

"I've been ordered along," Sir Peter confessed. "I'll be on the vessel accompanying yours."

Relief flooded Drummond's veins. Thank God. There were few knights with Sir Peter's battle experience or his reliable instincts at sea —and most of all, his unflappable calm.

"Some good news at last," he replied, clapping a hand on Sir Peter's shoulder. "I'm obliged to bring along that young knight from Auvergne, the bairn who's barely cut his milk teeth. It seems he's never wielded a blade in battle, though he brags of his crossbow skills."

Sir Peter nodded in sympathy as he captured one of Drummond's pawns. "He'll be in the way, I've no doubt. Let's hope he's a fast learner."

"As long as he obeys orders, I'll keep him aboard. But if he defies me . . ."

Drummond pondered his next move. His remaining bishop looked woefully exposed without the pawn that had been flanking it.

"What will you do? Toss him to the sharks?"

"Maybe." Drummond moved the bishop to safety. "I won't have a willful pup putting my crew and vessel in danger, and he strikes me as the kind who won't listen to his superiors."

"That's because he doesn't believe he has any," Sir Peter rejoined with a wry smile.

The next morning, Drummond was up before dawn. He collected his satchel of navigation instruments and the large sack stuffed with clothing and personal effects that accompanied him everywhere. After locking the door to his chambers, he descended the stairs and stepped out into the chilly morning air.

It was a short walk to the dockyards and warehouses abutting the Mandraki harbor. Just before he arrived at the city gate, he caught sight of the well-dressed Italian man he'd put off from harassing the lovely young woman at the marketplace the other day. The fellow was deep in conversation with two companions, but he quieted when he saw who was striding past. Squaring his shoulders, Drummond ignored the man's pointed stare and made for the gate.

Sir Peter had filled him in on the scant details he knew of the woman and her family. Her father was a talented painter of Venetian origin, her mother from a prosperous Greek family that owned many of the best taverns on the island. And by a stroke of luck, he now knew her name.

Anica.

He turned the word over in his mind, wondering if he would ever get the chance to speak it aloud. Then he dismissed the thought. That day at the theater performance, when she'd defended the street urchin, he'd sealed his fate with her. She'd given him a look of pure hatred when he'd hauled the wee lad off. He'd felt her eyes burning into his back like flame-tipped arrows. In the palace courtyard not long afterward, she'd saved her kind words for the Syrian doctor and had done her best to ignore Drummond. Aye, he'd seen a measure of relief in her eyes when he'd scared off the Italian by the oil merchant's stall the other day, but that meant nothing. She no doubt thought he was little better than a beast, a hired killer. Which he could not fault her for. In his darkest moments, he believed it to be true.

He reached the Mandraki at the same time that the massive iron chain stretching across the gaping mouth of Rhodes harbor was released. Shouts went up from bystanders on the stone quays as the iron links vanished deep under the water. The atmosphere, already charged with anticipation, exploded with excitement.

Vessels jostled for passage through the crowded waterway to the open sea. A half-dozen languages filled the air as captains shouted instructions to their crews. Sleek, oar-powered galleys maneuvered around ponderous merchant ships, their captains eager to be first out of the harbor. Gulls shrieked overhead, darting between tall masts.

Drummond clambered aboard his galley, barking orders to his crew. He supervised the untying of ropes and the launching of his vessel, eager to escape the chaos. His rowers' oars dipped and pulled, leaving swirls of white foam in their wake.

When his vessel passed into the sea, he glanced up at the tower guarding the mouth of the harbor. Two guards stood on the parapet scanning the waves for enemy ships. One of them raised his hand. Drummond returned the gesture.

As was his habit, he went through a list in his mind, reassuring himself that the weapons were stowed and ready for use, that the hemp ropes used to hoist the canvas sails were in good shape, that the sails themselves had been inspected for signs of wear.

He'd had to swap out a few of the oarsmen in Rhodes. The longer they were at sea, the more they griped about the costs of their absences to their families. It was better to keep fresh faces entering the mix, with clear minds and hands not yet swollen with blisters.

"Sails up, oars in!" he shouted, one hand touching the amulet around his neck.

The crew unfurled the sails, catching the strong northwesterly wind. The rowers pulled in their oars. He heard a shouted order from below decks, envisioning the scene as the oarsmen got out their dice and cards. Drummond had no quarrel with gaming during lulls in the work. It kept the men busy. As his mother often reminded him in his youth, idle hands did the devil's work.

Drummond sucked in a great gulp of air and let himself relax a bit when Rhodes Town faded from view. He was always on his guard in the bustling harbor city. It was full of scheming, power-hungry men bent on building wealth, whether through property, goods, or the slave trade.

Human bondage was the worst thing about the knights' world, the thing that made him wake with nightmares, covered in sweat. He hated taking part in it. But the knights demanded that he take captives at every opportunity. There were never enough slaves to satisfy them. Where he was going, thank God, he'd be far from the sight of slaves shuffling through the streets of Rhodes Town strung together by chains.

His family had known poverty, but they were fiercely independent. The idea of owning other folk was both outlandish and sinful where he came from. His grandfather had been squire to a powerful and generous earl, well-rewarded for his loyalty and courage. But his family's modest fortune had vanished long before Drummond was born. By the time his eldest brother inherited the estate, the family home was falling into disrepair. Their only income was rent from the few tenants who worked the land—just enough to feed and clothe the Forduns. That was why Drummond sent home most of his earnings.

The knowledge that he had a home and a loving family had gotten him through the past ten years. The hope of returning to Scotland fed his dreams, buoyed him during his bleakest nights.

But the likelihood of ever returning to Scotland was slim. The man he'd killed in a border skirmish more than a decade ago had been the favorite bastard son of an English lord. The lord had promised retaliation, and his men had hunted Drummond relentlessly for the next several months. Though Drummond evaded his hunters by taking refuge in the Highlands, the English lord had set his sights on Drummond's family and the earl his father was loyal to. To avoid more bloodshed, his family had invented a mad plan to get Drummond to safety and placate the English lord.

With God's grace, the ruse had worked—but Drummond had lived in exile ever since. Only when the English lord died would it be safe for him to return. His most recent letter from home relayed news that the nobleman was ill. Perhaps the next letter would hold the words he'd dreamed of for ten years now: *It's safe to come home.*

The uneasiness that always accompanied brooding thoughts began burrowing into his chest. He turned his back on the horizon and moved to the canvas-covered area in the stern where the Syrian doctor had spent most of the voyage from Alexandria this summer.

"Put that cloak on. It's cold out here on the water," he said in Greek to the small figure huddled there.

The child peered at him under dark lashes. "Is it really mine?"

Drummond sighed. "Yes, boy. It's yours. You won't be punished for wearing it."

The lad snatched up the cloak from its resting place on the small wooden box next to him and shrugged it over his shoulders. It was clear he was holding back tears.

Drummond squatted next to him. "You'll see when we get there. It's better in Archangelos than Rhodes Town. You'll be a big help in the fort. The cook needs someone to haul water and chop wood for him. And the horses need brushing twice a day. You'll have plenty to eat, and no one will harm you."

The boy bit his lip, his enormous brown eyes searching Drummond's face with apprehension. Then he gave a slow nod.

"Tell me your name."

No response.

"We can't call you 'boy' forever," Drummond pointed out. "What'll we call you when you're no longer a boy? It's not a fitting name for a man."

"My name is Angelos." The child's voice was faint, barely more than a whisper.

"Dame Fortune must have seen to this! What better place for Angelos to live than Archangelos?" Drummond said. When the boy did not respond, he added, "I'm Master Fordun, Angelos. Pleased to meet you."

He attempted a reassuring smile, but the boy's sober, wide-eyed gaze did not soften.

Giving up, Drummond returned to the bow deck and studied the horizon. A strong breeze careened over the hull and ruffled his hair. He looked overhead, wondering if a storm would follow the wind. But the northern sky was clear. Nothing marred his view, not even a wisp of fog.

CHAPTER 19

Winter, 1460
Rhodes Town

Anica paid the honey seller and deposited the change—two silver twenty-asper coins—into her purse. She settled the jars of honey in her basket with stiff fingers, grateful that her woolen cloak extended nearly to the ground. Winter's chill had settled over Rhodes Town, and when the sea breeze rippled through the streets, it sometimes set her teeth chattering.

She had one more errand before returning home. With quick strides, she navigated the familiar lanes and alleyways to St. Catherine's convent. Rapping on the door, she bounced on her toes, wishing she had worn two pairs of hose today.

The door creaked open, and a middle-aged nun admitted her.

"What is your business here, child?"

"I'm looking for a boy of about ten winters. He has no family, and I know you sometimes take in orphans here."

Anica hugged herself under her cloak. It was not much warmer in the cavernous entryway of the convent than it was outside.

"Wait here." The nun shut the door with a resounding thud. "I'll inquire with the mother abbess."

She disappeared through a doorway, brushing past a young woman walking in the opposite direction. The woman set a bucket down next to a tall candelabra where beeswax candles burned. She withdrew an iron tool from the bucket and began to scrape splatters of wax from the stone pavers.

Anica studied her for a moment. The woman looked familiar. But why? Then she remembered. It was the poor wretch they'd encountered in the streets one day whose ear had been cut off as punishment.

"*Kalimera*," Anica said to her.

The woman glanced up, startled. Her head and shoulders were covered with a short veil. "*Kalimera*," she muttered.

"I remember you. My mother gave you a coin and sent you here. I'm glad to see you've recovered."

"That was a kindness I'll never forget." The woman rocked back on her heels.

"Is your injury healed?"

"Yes. It's ugly, but I can't help that. And God doesn't care how I look."

"Who did that to you?" Anica asked.

A fearful expression seized the woman's face. "I can't speak his name. He vowed to kill me if I told anyone what he'd done to me."

"Was he a merchant? A banker? An agent of the Order?"

The woman fell silent.

"Was he Greek?"

"Of course not." The woman took up her tool and started scraping again. "He was of Latin blood. No countryman of mine would slice off my ear."

The nun returned. "We had a boy about that age living here, but he ran away so many times the mother abbess gave up trying to help him. A foreigner found him in the streets and tried to return him to us, but the mother abbess wouldn't hear of it. The child was too much trouble."

Anica stiffened. "Was the foreigner a Scot?"

"Who knows?" The nun shrugged.

"Did he take the boy to the Kastellania?"

"Mother abbess said he didn't intend to deliver the child to the knights. Now I must get back to my work." She went to the front door and held it open. "God bless you and keep you well."

"God bless you too, Sister."

The whole walk home, Anica mulled over the boy's fate. What had that Scotsman done with him? Why had she drawn attention to the child with her impulsive words, anyway?

By the time she got home and delivered the honey to the kitchen, Anica had made up her mind to continue her search for the boy. Perhaps the Scot had dumped him near the warehouses by the harbor. Children sometimes earned a few coins here and there from merchants and ship captains, running messages or helping load wares into carts and wheelbarrows. Such wharf rats did not have bright futures.

Not long after the church bells tolled three that afternoon, Papa entered the house whistling. From the studio, Anica heard the front door shut and set her palette and brush on the table. She tore off her paint-splattered apron and met him in the corridor.

"Well?" she demanded.

Without a word, he untied a small leather sack from his belt and shook it. The dull clank of coins rang out.

Nervous anticipation swirled in her chest. "So Lord de Milly liked them?"

"No." He contemplated the bag in his hand with a serious expression.

She sucked in a breath, her belly twisting with worry. They had completed the portraits for the Salviatis and, as before, were paid nothing for the work—Papa was still indebted to the Florentine banker, after all. So, they'd poured all their energies into the commissions for the grand master. If he disliked the results, it could be devastating for Papa's reputation and their finances.

Papa raised his chin, his face breaking into a smile. "He loved them, my girl. He paid me twice what he'd agreed for the triptych. Said he'd never seen its equal."

She hurtled into his embrace, tears pricking at her eyes.

He added in a whisper, "And it was all because of you."

Anica listened to the thump of her father's heart, warmed by a flood of pride and love. "Thank you, Papa."

That evening at supper, her whole family was in high spirits.

"My image hangs on the wall of the grand master's private chapel," Heleni crowed. "I'm sure there's no other girl in Rhodes Town who can say the same."

Anica gave her a considered gaze. "You were not the only inspiration for Santa Maria's face, Heleni. Mamá sat as a model, too. Even Maria had her turn."

"But the Virgin looks more like me than them, in the end." Heleni took up her knife, stabbed at a chunk of grilled octopus on the platter in the center of the table, and popped it into her mouth.

"The grand master is a generous patron," Mamá remarked, her eyes shining in the candlelight. "Paolo, your talent has only grown over the years. The saints have blessed you."

"Our daughter was a big help. I could not have done it without her."

"Of course," Mamá said. "To think just a few months ago you'd never made a painting with oil paints before. I suppose Signor Lomellini gave you good advice, didn't he?"

"And he let us study his portrait as often as we wished," Anica put in.

Heleni looked up from her task of tearing flatbread into tiny bits and dropping them into her bowl of fish stew. "When is he returning from Genoa?"

"When winter turns to spring, he said in his last letter." Anica drank a sip of wine. He'd written her twice since he left for Genoa. Each time someone rapped on the front door, she held her breath, wondering if it was the Genoese notary delivering another letter from him. "And if Santa Maria is willing."

Papa put his spoon down. "I've an idea. We've finished all of our commissions, and I need a few days' rest before we begin the frescoes for the villa. Let's go to Archangelos. It's been too long since our last journey there. We can visit with your cousins, Cali." He leaned forward, clearly warming to his idea. "And we can pay our respects to the Virgin herself in the shrine. She's long overdue for a bit of care and attention."

Anica smiled, watching her father's enthusiasm rise. When Papa had sailed to Rhodes all those years ago, a gale during the crossing from Antiparos blew in and nearly swamped the vessel that carried him. Two sailors had been flung to their deaths and some of the cargo had been spoiled by seawater rising in the hull. But the ship had made it safely to Rhodes in the end. And Papa had vowed to paint portraits of Santa Maria, the saint of all sailors, and install them in every shrine to her on the island. The portrait of Santa Maria he'd placed in a cave at Archangelos overlooking the sea had been his first effort.

"It's been too long, I agree," Mamá said. "An outing to the seashore is what we all need."

"I'd like nothing more," Anica said. "There's a potter from Archangelos who sells his wares in the marketplace here. I want to visit his studio."

Though she did not want to spoil the pleasant mood by mentioning it, she also longed to escape the walls of Rhodes Town and the overbearing presence of the knights, even for a few days.

Heleni heaved a loud sigh. "Well, *I* don't need an outing to the seashore. And I don't care for pottery, and I don't like staying at the inn there. It's so shabby."

"My cousin Spiros owns that inn, and he'd be insulted to hear you call it shabby," Mamá said. "It's comfortable and clean. Besides, you loved Archangelos when you were younger."

"What does a child know?" Heleni said, letting her spoon drop into her bowl with a clatter. "Things are different now."

"I disagree," Papa said tersely. "You may not be a child any longer, but you are still our daughter. The whole family is going to Archangelos in two days' time, and there will be no more discussion about the matter."

CHAPTER 20

Winter, 1460
Archangelos

A SERVANT from Aunt Rhea's household came to their door with a message the morning of their departure for Archangelos. Anica accepted the note and skimmed the words quickly. Then she found her mother in the kitchen, overseeing Maria and the cook as they sorted through the household's supply of linens.

Anica thrust out the note. "Aunt Rhea is ill."

Mamá read the lines. "Pains in her stomach." She shook her head. "This has happened before. It comes on without warning, and she's bedridden for days."

"Perhaps Signorina Giovanna would be helpful?" Anica asked. "Aunt Rhea told me she's skilled with women's ailments."

"I'll call on her at once," Mamá said.

"But we're leaving for Archangelos this morning."

Her mother tossed the note in the fire. "Not me," she said. "I'll not leave my sister in that state. Her husband can do nothing for her, her sons are busy all day with work, and besides, she needs a woman's touch in times like these."

Heleni popped her head around the doorway. "I'll stay with you and help keep Aunt Rhea entertained," she said. "I'll sing to her and tell her stories."

"You just don't want to go to Archangelos," Anica said flatly.

Heleni smirked. "Not true. I want to help."

"Then come with me now, Heleni," Mamá said, bustling out of the kitchen. "Fetch a shawl."

A mule cart and driver stood in the lane. With a manservant in tow, Anica and Papa climbed into the cart and took their seats on the hard bench.

She glanced at her father, who bore a worried expression. "Mamá will be fine, Papa. She's content when she's tending to others, and she wouldn't have enjoyed the time away knowing Aunt Rhea was ill."

He let out a sigh, slinging an arm around her shoulder. "You speak the truth. It will feel good to get away for a few days."

Listening to the creak of the cart wheels on the rough road, Anica let her mind drift to the letters Marino Lomellini had written her. They were in a wooden box in her chamber, bound with a silk ribbon. He wrote with a heavy hand, the ink strokes bold and black on the creamy linen paper. He told her droll stories about colorful people he'd met in the marketplaces of Genoa, about the hounds his brother insisted on collecting even though he detested hunting. About the gifts of silk brocade and pearls he had purchased for her.

She closed her eyes, imagining herself in the marriage bed with him. What would their wedding night be like? She had only ever shared a bed with Heleni. The thought of such intimacy with a man who was essentially a stranger made her nervous. He was a gentle man, and kind, she reminded herself. It would be awkward, but there was nothing to fear.

When they arrived in Archangelos late that afternoon, the only sign of life was at the Georgillas tavern, owned by Mamá's family.

Papa turned to Anica. "I could eat a goat," he proclaimed with a smile.

The mule cart came to a stop. Male voices and the clatter of crockery drifted from the tavern. Papa's smile disappeared.

"There could be soldiers inside." He clambered down from the wagon and instructed the driver to wait. Grimacing, he put a hand to his lower back. "My body doesn't take well to traveling in a wagon over rough roads, that much is certain."

A moment later, Papa returned with the innkeeper, Mamá's cousin Spiros.

"Welcome!" Spiros boomed, arms outstretched. "But where's the rest of the family?"

"Cali is tending to Rhea," Papa said. "She's unwell. Heleni's with them."

"Ah, poor Rhea. She'll be in my prayers. You must be famished." Spiros clapped his hands together. "Come around the back. We'll set the table under the grape arbor. There's a snug canvas cover, and I'll light a fire in the brazier, have the cook grill some fish and octopus for you. There's no wind today; you'll be plenty warm under there."

"Do you host a regiment of *turcopoles* today, Spiros?" Anica asked as she climbed down from the cart, her gaze straying to the door of the tavern again.

To her shock, a tall man with a fierce, wind-burned face and a tumble of sandy hair stepped outside. He hurried toward them, his body outlined by the afternoon sun. When he recognized Anica, his stride faltered.

"My apologies," the Scot said in Greek to Spiros. "We've taken all the tables. I'll hurry my men so you can eat in peace."

His eyes flicked to Anica. He nodded at her, then at Papa. "Signor, signorina."

Papa greeted him politely. Anica said nothing. Heat ignited at the base of her throat and traveled quickly to her cheeks.

"Never mind, Master Fordun," said Spiros, waving the Scot away. "We have it all arranged. Please sit down again, sir. Your meal is getting cold."

The Scotsman dipped his chin. "As you wish."

He wheeled and retreated inside.

Papa told the driver to proceed to the stables. He put a hand on Anica's shoulder, studying her with concern. "Are you feeling poorly? Your face is flushed."

"No, Papa. Not at all." She stared at the ground, trying to steady her breath.

Behind the tavern, Spiros dispensed instructions to two servants, who hurried off to do his bidding.

"Why are all these men here?" Paolo asked him.

"That foreign captain, Master Fordun, he inspects all the troops along the coast each winter," Spiros explained. "His men are lodged at the fort down the road. Lately, he's taken many meals at my tavern."

"Why's that?" Papa asked.

"He owns the villa on the cliffs overlooking the harbor. The knights gave it to him, or so the story goes."

"What kind of man is he?" Anica asked, her curiosity getting the better of her.

Papa gave her a sharp look, which she ignored.

Spiros shrugged. "Generous. Polite. Keeps his distance. Who really knows? He's a privateer; he must have stories to tell. But he doesn't strike me as a talker. He takes his meals, drinks a few cups of wine, and off he goes."

A servant approached with a cloth and spread it on the table that stood under the covered grape arbor. Another woman emerged from the door, lugging a large iron brazier.

"Wash your hands in the basin by the door, then settle yourselves at the table," Spiros instructed them. "I'll fetch my best wine. Ah, it does my heart good to see you here again."

Anica barely heard him.

Master Fordun.

The words tumbled in her mind, over and over. The idea of him sitting just a few strides away made her appetite disappear. She shivered at the idea of catching sight of him again, and the thought made her flush anew. The warmth should have been fueled by revulsion, for he was nothing more than a bloodthirsty hired killer. But instead, the sensation flooding her body was sparked by something else: desire. She held her breath, trying to will the feeling away.

She sat down next to Papa as Spiros appeared with a pitcher and poured each of them a generous cup. But her head was canted toward the tavern, her ears attuned for the sound of the Scotsman's voice.

Papa's eyes were on her. In his expression, she saw something usually reserved for Heleni—a gleam of suspicion.

"Cousin Spiros," she said, forcing brightness into her voice, "I've brought along a gift from Mamá. Some honey and spices for your larder. She regrets she couldn't be here herself to give it to you."

"Your mother's doing the right thing, tending to poor Rhea," he said. "Family is everything."

Papa nodded, holding Anica's gaze. Perhaps she'd only imagined the suspicion in his eyes. The heavy canvas covering the trellis over-head blocked the winter sunlight, putting his face in shadow. When shadows fell, nothing was certain.

"Yes," he said softly. "Family is everything."

CHAPTER 21

Winter, 1460
Archangelos

DRUMMOND STOOD at his bedchamber window staring at the sea, mesmerized by the shifting waters. In wintertime, the English *langue* paid him to inspect and train the island's troops, giving him cherished opportunities to spend time in his villa. He took in a long breath of salt-tinged air, held it a beat, then let it out with a contented whoosh.

The home lay atop a cliff up a hill from the village, overlooking a crescent-shaped bay. It had been a gift from the Order in recognition of his service following a brutal series of battles at sea just over a year ago.

The last of them had been a raiding mission along the Turkish coast. Loaded down with goods and captives, their vessels had been surrounded at dawn one morning by a squadron of small, nimble *fuste*, faster and more maneuverable than the war galleys favored by the knights and manned by soldier-sailors outfitted with bows, lances, and swords.

Drummond had barely had time to sound the alarm to the rest of the fleet, let alone point the bow deck with its bronze swivel gun at the enemy. His ship had been quickly boarded by Turkish warriors screaming their lungs out, but his crew, trained for just such attacks, was ready for them.

With daggers, crossbows, lances, and swords they'd picked the Turks off one by one as they emerged over the gunwale. Meanwhile, his crossbowmen had launched arrow after arrow at the other Ottoman vessels. Overpowered, the Turks had retreated, churning east through the waves until their sleek *fuste* were like specks of glass on the distant horizon.

Drummond's gaze flicked around the spacious bedchamber, taking in the white-washed walls, the lofty ceiling, the hand-hooked Moorish rugs on the floor. He whispered a prayer of thanks to Santa Maria for keeping him safe that day. This house was his reward for such efforts, and he was determined to squeeze every bit of pleasure from it he could. There were so few moments of peace in his life—each one was a gift.

His eyes lingered on the bed with its sturdy wooden frame, its soft white linens, and the pillows where he would lay his head tonight.

Unbidden, the image of the Venetian artist's daughter surfaced in his thoughts. Anica had looked straight back at him outside the tavern without shyness or fear, her golden brown eyes regarding him calmly, mesmerizing him once again. He'd had his share of women, some he'd even felt passion for, but not one of them had occupied so much space in his mind.

A fool's hope, man. Forget her.

Tearing his gaze from the bed, Drummond moved quietly through his home, flinging open each shuttered window as he went.

Archangelos itself was a modest little village with a tavern, a church, and a small shipyard where fishing boats lay propped on wooden blocks in various states of repair. Potters turned out glazed plates and bowls from studios in the village. And of course, the stone fort sat a short distance away, its stable filled with horses, its barracks inhabited by *turcopoles*—mounted troops paid to protect the island from attack.

Visible from his south-facing windows, the stone fort loomed on a hillside overlooking the little bay. It had been refurbished after an attack some years ago. If enemy vessels appeared, soldiers would light the fort's beacon and sound the alarm while messengers would race to alert the knights in Rhodes Town.

When Sultan Mehmed's forces attacked Constantinople a few years ago, they had numbered well above one hundred thousand. Should such a navy appear off these scrubby cliffs, the sight of a few dozen soldiers would do nothing to deter them. In fact, he mused, it would likely encourage them. Everyone in this town would soon be dead or enslaved.

A horn blast reverberated from the fort, shattering the quiet. He stiffened at the sound, his chest tightening. It meant a vessel had been sighted, a ship that bore neither the distinctive cross of the Hospitallers nor the recognizable banner of an ally.

Drummond hurried downstairs. He ordered his servants to lock away the valuables and assemble in the courtyard. A manservant helped him strap on his armor and weaponry while he instructed another to lead everyone else to the fort. He mounted his horse and raced to the village. People were rushing about in varying states of panic, readying themselves for the short trek to the fort.

"Leave everything you can't carry!" he shouted in Greek. "Better to save your own lives than a few possessions."

He saw Spiros and his family emerging from the doorway of the tavern.

"Are all your guests accounted for, Spiros?" he called. "Where are the artist and his daughter?"

"They went to the shrine." Spiros flapped an arm toward the cliffs. "But they haven't returned."

Drummond vaulted into his saddle again.

"Go to the fort with your family and guests," he ordered. "I'll find them."

Spiros began to direct people to the donkey carts that stood in front of the tavern. A stream of people and carts already headed up the long hill to the fort.

Good. The villagers knew what to do. Drummond didn't need to hand-hold them through the routine.

He spurred his horse into a gallop, following the trail to the shrine.

CHAPTER 22

Winter, 1460
Archangelos

Anica and her father had slipped out early with their manservant to walk to the shrine. They'd followed a steep, rocky trail overlooking a half-moon-shaped beach. The shrine was tucked away inside a cave in the cliffs, a natural room used for worship longer than anyone could remember.

Stubby candles burned on low tables near the modest altar. Atop a burnished mantel of olive wood stood a miniature carved wooden galley, complete with oars and a sail. Above the altar, affixed to the cave wall, hung Papa's painting of the Virgin.

"She's still in fine condition," Papa said, approaching the portrait with reverence.

The brilliance of Santa Maria's blue dress, the sheen of her tawny skin, the curve of her rose-colored lips were flawless.

"I've aged two decades since I placed the painting here, but she looks as good as new," he mused aloud, grinning. "I was so full of energy in those days. To think I planned to install a painting of the Virgin in each seaside shrine on the entire island."

"How many did you install, in the end?" Anica asked, coming to stand at his elbow.

"Three, I think. Perhaps four. Then I got married to your mother, you and your sister came along, and my expenses started growing. I needed money, so I sold the next series of Santa Marias to knights and merchants for their private chapels."

He knelt before the altar, and Anica sank down on her knees beside him. The scent of beeswax mingled with the soft, salty sea air and the faint dampness of the cave. The distant rhythm of waves crashing on the beach was soothing. Anica lost herself in prayer, lulled by the music of the sea. It was so peaceful here on this little bay, so different from Rhodes Town.

Then a long, mournful horn blast shattered the calm.

She scrambled to her feet at the same time as Papa, and they hastened outside. The manservant stood facing the sea, both hands shading his brow.

"Does a ship approach?" Anica asked.

"I see nothing but waves," he replied.

"There's likely no cause for alarm," Papa said. "Perhaps the soldiers at the fort are conducting a drill. Still, we should go back to the tavern now."

He led them up the steep trail. Anica picked her way along the rocky path, fighting the urge to glance over her shoulder at the water.

"I see something now!" cried the manservant from behind them.

She whirled and stared at the sea. Sure enough, a dark shape marred the horizon. A galley with its sails up, bolstered by a favorable wind.

"Let's not tarry," Papa said in a tight voice. "Make haste for the inn, and mind your footing."

Anica gathered her skirts in her hands and hurried after the men. A knot of fear pushed against her throat, stripping the moisture from her mouth.

In the next instant, Papa slipped on a stone and fell, striking his head on the ground. He cried out in pain.

"Papa!" She raced to his side.

"My ankle," he groaned. "I twisted it."

A trickle of blood ran down his forehead.

"Your face is bleeding," she said in alarm as the servant helped pull him upright.

He grimaced. "Let's keep walking, fast as we can."

But their progress was slow now, with three of them abreast on the narrow trail and Papa lurching unsteadily in the middle.

The horn sounded again. Panic rippled up Anica's spine. It took all her concentration to keep Papa upright. She jumped in shock when the manservant let out a hoarse shout.

"Get behind me," he yelled. "Someone approaches."

Anica pulled her father into her arms. The pounding of hooves on hard-packed earth thundered in her ears. Then she realized who was astride the horse in their path.

Master Fordun drew his mount to a halt and surveyed them.

"What happened to your father?" he asked Anica in Italian.

"He fell," she answered. "He hurt his ankle."

The Scotsman dismounted, eyeing the servant. "You've a blade. Do you know how to use it?"

The servant nodded.

"Let's get Signor Foscolo onto my horse," Master Fordun said. "Then you ride with him. Take the road out of the village and follow the donkey carts to the fort."

"What about my daughter?" Papa asked.

"I'll see her to the fort. We'll be right behind you."

"I'm not leaving my father's side," she said levelly.

"He needs the strength of your manservant to hold him safely on my horse—and an armed escort," the Scot growled. "We'll follow on foot."

"Do as he says." Papa mopped blood from his forehead with a sleeve. "We've no other choice, and we must hurry."

The Scot helped her father and the manservant mount his horse. Soon they disappeared over the top of the cliffs, heading toward the village and the fort beyond. She glanced sideways at the Scotsman, who was studying the approaching ship.

"God's teeth, but those scoundrels are moving fast," he muttered in English.

Signaling to her to follow, he stalked in the horse's tracks.

"Hurry, signorina," he tossed over his shoulder in Italian. "We've a lot of ground to cover."

"I am hurrying, sir," she responded in English. "Perhaps not as quickly as those scoundrels, but I'm doing my best."

He stared at her in astonishment. "Where did you learn to speak English so well?"

"It's easy to pick up languages in Rhodes Town if you have the interest. Which I do."

They were nearing the village now. It was empty of life. A few open doors swung in the breeze. The sight made her stomach drop. Beyond the village, a path snaked to his cliffside villa. She saw his gaze stray in that direction.

"Is your house well-protected?" she asked.

"I pray so." Dust rose from under the heels of his boots, trailing in his wake.

"Why do you live here, so far from Scotland?"

The question shot out before she could stop it.

"I go where the work is," he said coolly. "The knights pay me well."

"To raid and loot and capture innocents?" Her tone was sharper than she'd intended.

His pace slowed a fraction, but he kept his gaze straight ahead. In profile, his unsmiling face looked formidable.

"To do what the knights order, not what I please. That's the lot of the privateer. I work for them."

Anica felt a stab of remorse for her rude question. But then the memory of the small boy he'd hauled away from the marketplace surged into her mind. She put some distance between them, clenching her fists.

The tracks of donkey carts led up the hill. Anica concentrated on avoiding rocks and furrows in the ground, her breath labored now.

"Why did your father bring you to the grand master's palace that day?" Master Fordun asked abruptly, glancing at her sideways.

She should not answer, should volunteer nothing about her life to this strange, fierce man. But something made her want to tell him.

"He has no sons. Sometimes he calls upon me to act as one."

"You must be brave, then."

"No one has ever called me a coward," she allowed.

"Are you not afraid now? With this ship approaching the harbor and the whole village fleeing to the fort?"

"The thing I should fear at this moment is you," she pointed out. "You are the most immediate danger."

He looked at her soberly. Close up, she saw each fleck of green and gold in his gray eyes. His sharply protruding cheekbones and square jawline contributed to the sternness of his appearance, and his wide-set eyes were framed by dark lashes. She longed for a stick of charcoal and a scrap of paper so she could draw his features.

Yours is a beautiful face.

Her breath hitched in her throat. Had she spoken the words aloud, or only thought them? She dropped her gaze, feeling vaguely guilty. It was disloyal to Marino Lomellini, having such thoughts.

"You have nothing to fear from me, Miss Anica. I vow it."

His voice was earnest, soft.

"How do you know my name?" she asked in suspicion.

"That day in the palace courtyard, when you met the doctor . . ."

"Oh yes." She felt foolish.

They climbed the rest of the hill in silence. The Scot's leather armor creaked with each stride, his sword clattering against the iron studs on his high boots. A guard shouted at the sight of them, and the tall armored doors of the fort swung open. Another horn blast reverberated through the air, deep and insistent.

Anica's knees buckled at the sound. She staggered and nearly fell. Master Fordun extended his hand. Without hesitation, she gave him her own. Easing his pace, he guided her through the gaping doorway. Then he gently relinquished her.

"You're safe now, Miss Anica." His voice was low and calm in her ear.

She nodded, unable to manage a word in response.

CHAPTER 23

Winter, 1460
Archangelos

As soon as they were within the fort's walls, Master Fordun left
Anica's side. She searched for her father. He and the manservant sat in
a shady alcove with Spiros and his family. Other villagers were clustered in small groups nearby, some standing, some huddled in the
shade of the fort's wall. Panicked conversations flew overhead. She
tried to ignore the chatter, not let their fear seep into her own skin.

Examining her father's wound, she saw dirt mixed with the blood
on his forehead and cheek. With her sleeve, she dabbed at it until her
father swatted her away in irritation.

"Who is in charge here?" She stood up and approached Spiros. "My
father needs help."

"We'll get no help from anyone until this attack is dealt with," he
said grimly.

Anica glanced around the bustling courtyard, her eyes settling on
Master Fordun. A crossbow was strapped to his horse's flank, and a

shield hung from his saddle. He jammed on a helmet and mounted his horse.

Several more armed men followed suit. Then the lot of them cantered away, sending a cloud of dust into the air. The fort gates were shut and barred. On the parapets, guards stood with their bows at the ready. Some of them were readying cannons set into the crenellated walls.

"Where are they going?" she asked Spiros.

"They'll head to the bluff overlooking the harbor. If it's an enemy ship, they'll shower the marauders with arrows."

Spiros's words were rendered less convincing by his worried tone.

For the first time, she was grateful for the knights. They had reinforced this island's defenses for generations. And now, facing impending attack, she understood how critical they were to everyone's survival.

"Has this happened before?" she asked Spiros.

"It happens every few years." He glanced at his weeping wife, who clutched their daughter in her arms. "It's terrifying each time."

All her life, Anica had heard whispered conversations between adults about the horrors of war. About attacks on coastal villages where none were left alive. Or all were enslaved. Or the women and girls were raped in front of their husbands and fathers, then taken as concubines.

"That man, the Scot." Anica lowered her voice. "Are we safe with him in charge?"

"We're lucky he's here," Spiros replied. "But even the strongest among us face bad fortune. Today might be his last."

She flinched. Master Fordun, dead? No, that could not happen today. Their paths might cross again . . . *must* cross again.

The horn sounded three short blasts.

"The vessel's entering the harbor," Spiros interpreted, his eyes wide with fear. "That's the signal to attack. The archers will start shooting soon."

His wife's weeping was inflated by a chorus of other cries and wails from the villagers.

Anica returned to her father's side and sank down next to him. His blood-smeared face filled her with dread.

The day passed with excruciating slowness. When dusk fell, the men were still gone, and there were no sounds of battle, only the whisper of wind through chinks in the fort's stone walls. Many of the villagers complained of hunger. Their panic had receded with the encroachment of silence. Anica crouched over her father, studying his face in the fading light.

"That wound needs cleaning." She stood, smoothing her skirts. "And we all need food. I'm going to the kitchens."

He looked at her in alarm. "Take Spiros with you, by the saints. You're in a fort full of soldiers, Anica."

"Most of the men are gone, fighting to defend us." She gestured around them to prove her point.

A few soldiers patrolled the parapet, and two men moved through the interior, lighting torches affixed to the walls. But the vast majority of people left inside were villagers.

"Still, heed my words," Papa said sternly.

With Spiros at her side, Anica found the kitchens. A cook and a young boy were the only staff in sight. The cook stood over a massive iron pot affixed to a chain in the hearth, a spoon in his hand. The boy had his back to them. He stood atop a block of wood so he could reach the counter, and he was chopping a mound of onions.

At the sound of their approach, he whirled, the knife still clenched in one hand.

The cook turned. "What is it?" he asked, frowning. "The men will be back any moment, with God's grace, and we've a stew to prepare."

"You've got a hundred villagers in the courtyard who need to eat as well." Anica's words were directed at the cook, but she could not tear her gaze away from the boy. He stared back at her, a defiant gleam in his eyes. She drew in a sharp breath of recognition. "I've seen you before," she said in disbelief. "In Rhodes Town, at the marketplace."

He dropped the knife, and it clattered on the stone floor. He regarded her with fear.

"Now why've you done that, boy?" asked the cook in exasperation. "Next thing you know, you'll cut off your own toe."

Anica bent down and retrieved the knife. Gently, she placed it on the table. "Are you treated well here?" she asked him in a low voice. "I've been worried about you since that day."

His face relaxed. He nodded in silence.

"That urchin doesn't hold with talking." The cook hefted a canvas bag of grain from a ceramic urn and deposited it on the table next to a bowl filled with cleaned and gutted fish. "He gets nervous when folks speak to him. Only person he trusts is the Scot."

Anica took that in, her eyes on the boy. "Is that true?" she whispered.

Again, he nodded.

Straightening, she exchanged a glance with Spiros. "What can we do about the hungry villagers? My cousin feeds the Scot and his men often at his inn. Surely, the Order can spare a meal for his family and the villagers who caught the fish you'll be eating tonight."

The cook let out a long sigh. "I don't have the help. This boy's all I have today, and he can't feed an extra hundred mouths."

"With me at his side, he can." Spiros rolled up his sleeves. "Where's a knife? I'll try to match this little fellow's blade skills, but I'm not altogether sure I can do it."

The boy lifted his chin and pushed back his shoulders with a hint of pride. His cheeks were rounder than they'd been that day in the marketplace, and his flax shirt and leggings were fairly clean. He looked taken care of, Anica decided. As if someone was looking out for him.

"What's your name, little one?" Spiros asked kindly. "I'll need to know it if we're partners here today."

The boy glanced at Anica, then back at Spiros. "Angelos."

He hopped off the wooden block, trotted to a cabinet, and retrieved a knife, which he thrust handle-out at Spiros.

"You know your way around a kitchen," Spiros said with admiration.

Angelos glowed at the compliment.

Watching him, Anica's mind churned. So this is what the Scot had done with the boy. He'd not enslaved him; he'd not sold him off or left him in the streets. He had brought him here and put him to work under the care of this cook. She eyed the man once more. He was grumpy, but he did not seem cruel.

"I need some hot water and clean cloths," she told him. "My father is wounded."

"We're not handing out free supplies here," he retorted. "We've only got so much."

She thrust a hand into her purse and pulled out thirty silver aspers. "I can pay."

The man relented. He accepted the coins and waved a hand at the storeroom.

"You'll find clean linens in there. There's a ladle by the hearth and bowls on those shelves." He jerked his head toward the wall, where wooden cabinets held an array of kitchen goods.

Hurrying back to her father, she set about cleaning the wound on his forehead, then tore a length of linen into strips and bound his ankle with it. He winced at her touch, especially when she handled his foot. She wished for a doctor as she covered him with her shawl and positioned a leather satchel under his head for a pillow.

"We'll be all right, Papa," she whispered in his ear. "The Scot will keep us all safe."

His face was sober in the torchlight. "You put much faith in a man you just met. He's a stranger to us, Anica."

She shook her head. "Not a stranger any longer. His name is Master Fordun, and I trust him."

"You've always been my steady girl, a voice of reason and intelligence. So different from Heleni." Her father sighed. "But this time, I wonder . . ."

Anica rocked back on her heels, chewing her lip. Perhaps he was right. Perhaps her interest in the Scotsman was clouding her ability to judge him as he ought to be judged.

But today, she took comfort in believing Master Fordun would keep them all safe.

She prayed she would live to thank him for it.

CHAPTER 24

Winter, 1460
Archangelos

For the three nights they'd been in the fort, sleep eluded Anica. Every time she drifted off, the clank of armor or a guard's shout spurred her back to consciousness. Lying awake, her body tense with dread, she finally understood the threat that gathered in the East. How could a tiny island withstand an attack by the army that had sacked Constantinople?

That first night, Master Fordun and his men had frightened off the ship, letting loose a torrent of arrows from both sides of the harbor, keeping up their vigil until the vessel disappeared into the vast blue sea.

When he returned, the Scot had told the villagers they would stay in the fort until more soldiers came from Rhodes Town. He said war galleys would patrol the sea to ensure no further threats lurked offshore.

He'd made a point of checking on Anica and her father, and did so again tonight.

Papa was asleep, but Anica was wide awake, thrumming with nervous energy. She still expected another attack from the sea. At Master Fordun's approach, she sat up.

He crouched next to her in the flickering torchlight, producing a small jar from a sack. "This is healing ointment." He placed it in her palm. His fingertips brushing her wrist filled her with a fierce, strange longing. She fought an impulse to catch his hand with hers, to feel the warmth of his flesh one more time.

It took a moment to regain her composure. "Thank you."

He reached into the sack again and pulled out a woolen blanket. "This'll help keep you warm. I've a few more; you can share them with those who need them most."

She nodded in gratitude.

"Have you wrapped his ankle?" He jerked his head at Papa's feet.

"Yes. He's in a lot of pain," she admitted.

In the guttering light, his eyes registered concern. "He may have broken a bone. He should see a doctor when you return to Rhodes Town. A good one."

"He will," she promised.

"Signor Syriano would be happy to take a look at him, I warrant. He's the best of them."

She regarded him in surprise. "But he's the grand master's personal physician. He can't be bothered with townsfolk."

"Did you see how he looked at you when you spoke beautiful Arabic to him? He'd make an exception for you, Signorina Anica. And if you tell him I sent you, he'll be doubly glad to help."

His kind words felt like a caress. The thought made her heart leap.

"He's better trained than any doctor in Rhodes Town," the Scot went on. "Damascus is the place for cures of the rarest ailments. Signor Syriano says he's even witnessed surgeries that restore men's sight."

"That can't be true," she said in astonishment. "There is no cure for blindness."

"I don't know about blindness," the Scot conceded, "but the doctor told me about a fellow from Cyprus who sailed to Damascus to cure his failing vision, and he returned with his sight restored."

A pulse of hope throbbed in Anica's belly. Could this be possible? A cure for Papa's ailing eyes?

"It sounds fantastical," he said, perhaps interpreting her silence as skepticism. "My family would never believe what I just told you."

"Do you miss them?" she blurted, amazed at her own boldness.

"I do," he confessed. "And I miss Scotland."

"What is it like there?"

"Green. Much colder than here."

"Why did you leave?"

"A knight hired me to be his guard on the voyage to Rhodes when I was not yet twenty. Things went wrong on the way, though."

"What things?"

He considered her question in silence.

"It's far too long a tale to tell," he said after a moment.

Anica found herself wishing for the chance to hear his story, spun out slowly in front of a winter hearth. He was so close, only an arm's length away. The shifting torchlight illuminated the planes of his high cheekbones, set his eyes aglow. Again, that longing to capture his face on paper struck her.

You are golden light and bronze shadows, bold lines and fierce angles.

Her heart thumped so powerfully against her ribs she was sure he could hear it.

"Will you go back to Scotland one day?" she asked, trying to keep her voice smooth and reserved.

He hesitated again. "Even if I could, I've no way to earn money there. And my family needs money."

Anica realized he must send home a portion of his wages to help them.

"What about you?" he countered. "Your father is Venetian. Do you have family there?"

"Yes, but I've never met them."

"You've not journeyed to Venice?"

She shook her head. Before he could ask her anything that might lead to talk of Genoa or Marino Lomellini, she turned the conversation back to him again.

"Do you have sisters?" she asked.

"Two."

"How old are they?"

"Both younger than me by several years. One wants to marry. Thanks to my work with the Order, she has a dowry. The other says she'll never wed." He chuckled.

"Why?"

"She earns the family a good income with her work," he said. "Making embroidery on silks that I send home with gold thread I buy in Cyprus. Then she sells the cloth to rich folk in London, Bruges, other places."

"She's an artist, then."

A faint smile curved his lips. "Like you."

She stiffened. No one could learn the extent to which she helped her father. Especially now with the oil paintings. Papa was still struggling with the technique, and she was doing the bulk of the work.

Master Fordun stood, responding to some shouted request by a soldier.

"I'm going to check on the signal fires along the cliffs in the north," he said to her.

"In the dark?" she asked, alarmed.

"I know these trails well. As does my horse."

He nodded a farewell and walked into the gloom.

CHAPTER 25

Winter, 1460
Archangelos

WHEN THEY WERE RELEASED from the fort the next morning, Master Fordun again gave her father his horse to ride back to the tavern, then insisted on dispatching two mounted soldiers to accompany them home. After their manservant hitched the mules to the cart and took the reins, the Scotsman helped Paolo up into his seat. He turned to Anica, one hand outstretched, and smiled.

Papa would expect her to wave him off. But the chance to touch Master Fordun again made her reckless. When she placed her hand in his, her stomach lurched. His hold on her was gentle. Even her lungs seemed affected by his presence, able only to draw in the tiniest sips of air. His large hand was warm, and the touch of it made her fingers tingle. The back of his palm bore a scar that traced a thin white line along his sun-browned skin.

She settled into her seat on the hard bench.

"Thank you for all you have done for us," she said in English as he released her hand, smiling back at him.

His own smile deepened, revealing a dimple in one cheek. "It was my pleasure."

She knew she should look away, but the desire to hold his gaze won out.

Adjusting his position on the bench, her father looked at the Scotsman and cleared his throat. "You've been very kind, sir. We will not forget it."

Master Fordun nodded at Papa. He stepped away, one arm raised in farewell. The cart rolled down the dusty track toward Rhodes Town.

Anica longed to turn back and watch him recede into the distance, but she forced herself to stare at the road. The soldiers rode ahead of the cart, their horses' hooves sending up torrents of dust.

Her father leaned close. "You held that Scotsman's hand far too long. And spoke to him with as much boldness as a man. What's gotten into you, Anica? You're behaving like your sister, I'm sorry to say."

Anica avoided his gaze. "He saved you. Me. All of us."

As explanations went, it was weak. But her mind had been emptied of logical thought a few days ago.

"That may be, but he's a soldier above all else," he reminded her in a sharp voice. "A privateer in the service of the knights. Not someone you should be talking to, let alone touching. You're a betrothed woman, after all."

"You have nothing to worry about, Papa." Anica straightened her spine, staring straight ahead. "I've not forgotten about my marriage."

He snorted. "Your marriage isn't what concerns me. There are other fates for women, much worse fates. What starts out innocently enough can soon tangle into a web of disaster."

She glanced at him sideways. "In all likelihood, we'll never see him again. Stop worrying, Papa."

He frowned. "I'll worry about you and your sister until the day I die. That's the lot of fathers, whether we like it or not."

"What we should be more concerned about is Mamá's reaction

when she sees your face and your ankle. I'm sure she's beside herself with worry anyway. We won't hear the end of it for weeks."

Papa said nothing. But the set of his jaw told her he agreed.

As the cart rolled toward Rhodes Town, Anica thought only of the warmth of Master Fordun's hand on hers, the easy joy of his smile, the light in his eyes. Each time he invaded her mind, she was struck by a strange combination of pleasure and guilt.

Why has fortune put Master Fordun in my path?

If it weren't for him, she would be eagerly anticipating her future as the wife of Marino Lomellini. Instead, she was fluttering with nerves, mesmerized by a man she could never have. This would have to stop. Such fantasies were in Heleni's realm, not hers.

As they approached Rhodes Town later than afternoon, a falcon winged overhead.

Anica watched its silent progress across the sky until it disappeared behind the walls of the city. The sight of the massive stone fortifications and towers thronged with armed guards filled her with relief. When they passed through the city gates, she thanked God for the knights and soldiers trooping through the streets.

It would be rude not to thank Master Fordun. I'll write him a note expressing our appreciation. After all he's done for us, it's the least I can do.

The idea made her brighten a little. Perhaps she could even bring the note to him herself. As soon as she had the thought, she dismissed it. No, Maria would deliver the note. Seeing the Scotsman again would make the tumult in her heart even more distressing. It was better to avoid him entirely.

The mules clattered through the narrow lanes for what seemed like an eternity, finally coming to a halt in front of their residence. Anica regarded her home with a strange mixture of relief and disappointment. The ordeal in Archangelos had shifted something in her. She was not looking forward to navigating daily life with its repetitive tasks and duties, to the sameness of her days. Even the studio, which she always thought of as the beating heart of their home, did not hold its usual allure. The longer she and Papa concealed the truth about her role in that place, the less joy she experienced within its walls.

As they disembarked from the cart, two well-dressed men ambled by, immersed in conversation. They spoke Catalan. Their talk was of ships and commerce, of journeys made and voyages to come. She and the manservant helped Papa down from his perch on the cart bench, and she regarded the passing men with something close to envy.

The domestic sphere was something men took for granted, a place they could enter and exit at will, a quiet respite from the excitement and terrors of the outside world. How would it feel to live like them, free to come and go as she pleased?

Her ruminations were interrupted by her mother and sister, who burst weeping from the front door and rushed to embrace them amid a deluge of questions. Anica caught Papa's eye, knowing his resigned look matched her own.

Tears flowed down her own cheeks as she gathered Mamá in her arms. It felt good to come home to love and affection, she had to admit. She was lucky to have a comfortable place to live, to know that her family was safe within these walls.

She linked arms with Heleni and walked into the tile-floored entry-way. Mamá's icons, glowing from the light of a half-dozen oil lamps, beckoned to her through the open doorway of the prayer room. The mingled scents of citrus and roses drifted in from the courtyard. Anica took in a long breath. Had she ever truly realized her good fortune before now?

Papa was right. Idle fantasies about a foreign privateer were a waste of time at best.

She would write Master Fordun a letter of thanks and have Maria deliver it to the Inn of the English. And then, somehow, she would force him from her mind. She would erase him like charcoal dust from a scrap of linen paper.

She saw Maria standing quietly in the shadows, watching the family enter the house.

"Maria," she said. "We're back safe and sound."

Maria stayed where she was, a wan smile on her face.

"Welcome home," she said softly, then turned and made for the kitchen.

"Is she ill?" Anica asked her mother.

Mamá took Anica's hand again and pulled her toward the staircase.

"She's been quiet these past few days. Everyone's been worried about you. Let's have a quick meal, then go to the bathhouse so you can wash off the dust of your journey."

"While we're there, you can tell us everything about the attack," Heleni called after them. "And you'd better not leave out a single detail."

CHAPTER 26

Winter, 1460
Rhodes Town

ANICA BALANCED the palette in one hand and carefully ascended the ladder, shivering in the chilly breeze. She spied rain wetting the shrubs and citrus trees through the open windows. She hoped the clouds would vanish by afternoon and allow sunlight to flood this chamber.

"That peacock's tail needs filling in," Papa called from his perch on a stool nearby. "It will be slow getting all the colors done." He let out a frustrated groan. "I wish I could help. If only that apprentice would arrive."

Without turning her head, Anica said, "He will. We must be patient."

"A pair of young eyes will ease my worries a thousandfold. My hands can hold a brush just as steadily as ever, but my eyes—well, if it weren't for you, I'd be sunk." He hauled himself up and, with the aid of his cypress-wood cane, hobbled to the small table holding their supplies. "I'll mix you some green paint."

"I can do it," she replied. "Your ankle needs rest."

He grunted. "I'm envious, to be honest. I've always enjoyed painting frescoes. The mixing of egg and pigment, the daubing of paint on the whitewashed wall—it's satisfying. Soothing to the soul."

With her father calling directions from his stool, she had completed the general outlines first with charcoal and then with a thin wash of paint tinted with yellow-ochre pigment. And now, day by day, Anica climbed the ladder and brought the fresco to life.

The design was a landscape populated by animals with an elegant château in the background. At one point, she'd had to scour the library of an old friend of her father's, a Jewish goldsmith, to find an illustrated bestiary. Hounds, horses, and hawks were easy to draw, and she had little trouble with deer, but the correct proportions for a bear were impossible for her to construct out of nowhere. Now, with the outlines finished, she was doing the tedious work of filling in the colors.

Praise all the saints, they'd yet to clap eyes on the new resident. Apparently, Émile de Chambonac was away. A servant had said something about a voyage—some mission at sea for the knights.

So it was just herself and Papa, the master gardener and his crew of slaves, and a few house servants moving about the spacious villa and its grounds today. Wetting her brush with deep blue paint, she set to work on a peacock. Perhaps the château in the fresco was a place special to the knight, she mused. Possibly his own home in Auvergne.

A sudden crash made her jump. "Papa!"

She clambered down from the ladder. Her father lay prone on the polished tile floor, surrounded by spatters of green paint.

"I dropped a rag and leaned down for it, then lost my balance." He gritted his teeth, working the muscles in his jaw. "I'm afraid I've injured my bad ankle again."

Anica helped him up to a sitting position and fetched a rag to clean the paint from his hands. "Let's go home. I'll put our supplies away. The storm clouds make it nearly impossible to see, even for me."

She bustled around, cleaning the palette and brushes, tucking all the jars of pigment into a small wooden cask, and removing her apron. Then she stuck her head out the doorway, looking for someone to help her assist Papa back to their mule cart. A manservant was hurrying down the corridor, but when she called out to him, he turned a corner and disappeared. She let out a sigh of exasperation, then moved to the windows. Two turbaned men were weeding a path just outside, where jasmine climbed iron trellises.

"Excuse me," she said in Arabic. "I need help."

They looked up from their work with reluctance.

"We aren't allowed to speak with you," one of them replied in a worried voice.

Anica turned away and went to her father's side. "Come, Papa. Lean on my arm."

Papa's cane tapped the tiles as they walked slowly through the villa. In the entryway, they found two servants to help him back to the mule cart and located their driver, who had been napping in a garden shed. Soon they were on the road, the gardens falling away from them on either side, the foreboding stone fortifications of Rhodes Town rising in the distance. Thunder rumbled somewhere over the sea, and a heavy rain began to fall.

Once they were through the city gates, the shower abated and Anica pulled her shawl off her head. She glanced at the Inn of the English to her left as the cart rolled over the cobblestones. If Drummond had received her note of thanks, she'd never heard a response. Perhaps he, too, was at sea. His work for the knights seemed to entail a series of dangerous voyages. They rattled past the Church of Santa Maria. She closed her eyes a moment.

Santa Maria, please keep him safe.

When she opened her eyes, she observed a man just ahead wearing the flowing silk robes and turban of an Arab, a mantle embroidered with the eight-pointed cross of the knights over his shoulders.

"Good day, sayyid," she cried, an arm raised in greeting.

Recognition lit the doctor's eyes when he saw her. "Signorina."

The cart drew abreast of him. Papa told the driver to stop.

"Good day, Signor Syriano," he said, the tightness in his voice betraying his pain.

The doctor studied him for a moment. "What ails you, signor?" His gaze ran up and down the length of Papa's body, then came to rest on his feet. The linen bandage around Papa's ankle bulged over the top of his low leather boots. "Ah. A fall?"

Papa nodded. "At Archangelos, during the pirate attack. But I fell again today, and I fear I've done more damage."

Anica felt a stab of remorse. She'd not followed Master Fordun's advice to seek aid from the doctor. Now she wished she had.

"Come to my home," Signor Syriano invited them. "I'll take a look."

"Oh no," Papa protested. "You haven't the time . . ."

The doctor gave a quick shake of his head. "I'm free to do as I wish this evening. Follow me, please."

Papa glanced ahead at the Street of the Knights, his mind clearly working through possible adverse outcomes to being seen entering the home of the physician to the grand master. Finally, he nodded. "As you wish."

The Syrian strode through the streets, and their driver urged the mule after them. Anica noticed some of the Latin folk moved out of his path at the sight of him, bending their heads to whisper together, casting furtive glances in his direction. Were they impressed by his status as physician to Lord de Milly or fearful of him because he was an infidel? Perhaps a bit of both.

Once inside his small but elegant home, they proceeded to a parlor overlooking the interior courtyard. The doctor waved Papa into a wooden chair topped with a velvet-covered seat cushion, its armrests and legs inlaid with tiny mother-of-pearl tiles. He sat on a squat stool and took Papa's foot in his hands, carefully removing the bandage.

"Ah." He put gentle pressure here and there on Papa's ankle and foot, watching Papa's face for his responses. "It's quite swollen. But I do not believe it is broken. You haven't given it a chance to fully heal." He frowned at Papa. "Too much walking. Too much painting."

"I've not been doing enough of either," Papa protested.

"I'll have to enlist your daughter to keep you from putting too much strain on that ankle, or you'll make the injury worse."

Anica half-listened, still mesmerized by the ornate pattern of the mother-of-pearl tiles in the chair. Feeling the weight of the doctor's gaze, she raised her head.

"I'm sorry, but I've never seen the equal of this chair," she admitted. "It's beautiful, isn't it, Papa?"

Her father peered at the armrests, squinting at the intricate pattern of tiles. "Yes, I suppose it is."

Signor Syriano watched Papa with renewed interest. "How are your eyes these days, Signor?"

Papa shifted in his seat. "Not bad, not bad. Well, not as good as they once were, but one can't stop the progression of time."

The doctor got up, fetched a glass oil lamp from a table, and brought it close to Papa's face. "Tilt your head back and look at me," he said.

Papa did as he was told. The doctor inspected his eyes in silence, then replaced the lamp on the table.

"You have a common condition," he said. "Cataracts. Does it seem as if a veil of mist lies before you and all you see?"

"Yes, a mist that grows thicker every day," Papa admitted.

"Do you have trouble seeing things that are close to you, especially in low light?"

Papa nodded. "It's getting worse, too."

"There are different types of cataracts," the doctor explained. "Some develop more rapidly than others. If you don't have the condition treated, you may lose your vision entirely."

"Papa could go blind?" Anica cast a worried glance at her father. "How can this condition be treated?"

The doctor slipped the embroidered mantle off his shoulders, folded it, and placed it on the table. "With surgery."

"Surgery on the eyes?" Papa asked in astonishment. "That sounds terribly dangerous."

"It can be. In the wrong hands, a person can be blinded by such surgery. But done correctly, it can restore one's vision."

Papa looked at Anica with an expression of hope that made her heart twist.

"Can you do such a surgery?" he asked, turning to the doctor again.

"No. I've seen it performed many times in Damascus, though."

"Is there a doctor in Rhodes Town with such training?" Anica asked.

He shook his head. "There is one here who will perform a surgery called 'couching' to correct cataracts, but I would not recommend it. In Damascus, surgeons use a hollow needle and suction to remove the cataract. It's far safer, and far more effective."

Anica knelt at Papa's side and took his hands in hers. His strong, capable hands had always comforted her, had always given her strength. But today, for the first time, her father seemed vulnerable, his hands fragile in her grip. "Perhaps you can journey to Damascus for the surgery, Papa."

His hopeful look faded. "It must be costly. So is a sea voyage. Besides, we have too many other expenses."

She knew he was thinking of her wedding. "We can postpone things," she said quietly.

He did not answer.

Breaking the silence, the doctor observed, "You've been helping your father, I see."

She looked at him, startled. "How do you know?"

"Your hands."

She glanced down at them. Her fingers were stained by the paint she'd been using for the peacock feathers. "Oh. Yes." She lifted her chin. "I assist him here and there. An apprentice will come soon. Then Papa won't have to worry so much . . ."

She trailed off. Why was she divulging this? They were strangers to the man, after all.

The doctor regarded her with a gleam of understanding in his brown eyes. He went to a small cabinet, where he retrieved a vial of pale liquid and a sealed pot. He handed the pot to Anica. "Milk of the poppy and ointment for the swelling. I'll show you how to wrap his bandage properly, too."

Kneeling before Papa again, he spooled the bandage around the injured ankle with practiced movements. "You must stay off that foot for at least a week, preferably two."

"I won't find it easy," Papa admitted.

"If you continue to ignore the injury, you may end up limping for the rest of your life." The doctor's tone was grave.

A wave of despair welled in her chest. Learning there was a cure for her father's vision problem had felt exhilarating for a moment—but Papa would never journey across the sea to a foreign land, chasing a treatment that might not even work.

She helped him up and thanked Dr. Syriano.

"My father will stay off his foot," she promised grimly. "I'll see to that."

CHAPTER 27

Winter, 1460
Rhodes Town

ANICA AND MARIA followed the Greek manservant into the spacious main chamber of the villa. The servant told Anica he would be back later to make sure she had everything she needed. She thanked him. They stood in the quiet, listening to his footsteps fade in the corridor.

Through the windows, she saw gardeners snipping branches from shrubs and weeding the paths. Maria, who had never seen these sumptuous villas and gardens, wore an expression of dazzled astonishment.

Anica surveyed the half-finished frescoes and sighed. There was so much left to do. Most of the forested background remained unfinished, but it was the easiest part and would go quickly. She began unpacking her supplies and laying them out on the small table near the windows. Then she rooted around for eggs in the willow basket she'd brought.

A high-pitched, eerie shriek rang out from the gardens. Next to her, Maria flinched, though the sound was not new to her. Citizens in

Rhodes Town kept peacocks in their gardens, and some roamed the city without apparent oversight, taking refuge beneath oleander shrubs and overgrown jasmine vines as it suited them.

"Such a hideous sound from such a beautiful creature," Anica muttered under her breath, cracking an egg against the edge of a ceramic bowl. "I've never understood the appeal of a bird that screams."

After measuring pigment into the bowl and mixing a quantity of paint, she climbed the ladder and set to work on a banner fluttering from one of the château's towers.

The peacock shrieked again, making her jump. Her wet brush bumped against the wall.

I hope this doesn't go on all day. I'll end up spending more time fixing my mistakes than getting anything done.

"Fetch me a rag to wipe away the smear, please," she said to Maria.

Maria handed her a rag.

"Will you dampen it? A dry rag doesn't work as well as a wet one."

"There's no more water," Maria reported from the table a moment later.

"Will you go to the kitchens and fetch a bowl, then?"

Maria vanished into the corridor. A blessed silence settled over the villa. Anica worked diligently, grateful that the peacock had stopped its plaintive cries.

When she heard footsteps, she thanked Maria without turning her head. "Just dip the rag into the water," she instructed, "and hand it to—"

"I'm not Maria, I'm afraid," said a man in French.

She stopped what she was doing and climbed down the ladder in surprise. Before her stood the young knight Émile de Chambonac. He wore a pale blue doublet and white hose, and his long brown hair tumbled around his shoulders. His clean-shaven face was just as handsome as she recalled, with high cheekbones and a square jaw.

"My lord, forgive me." She set the palette and brush on the table and bobbed a shallow curtsy. "My father injured his ankle in Archangelos during the attack there and needs to stay off his foot."

The man approached. His eyes, the exact shade of the midday sky over Rhodes, inspected her with interest.

"Were you at Archangelos, too?"

She nodded. "We took shelter in the fort with the villagers."

"The Scotsman led the charge against the pirates, I heard."

"Yes, he kept us all safe."

The knight turned to the fresco. "I was not aware a woman could do such work."

Anica's body went rigid. "I help my father when he needs me. Once he does the skilled work of the outlines and details, I fill in the colors."

The knight strolled along the wall, studying the composition. She went to the table, pretending to be busy with her paints. He turned and wandered back. She was glad for her shapeless leather apron, for the brown linen wrap that covered her hair.

"I don't meet many respectable women on this island," he remarked. "But I miss the company of cultured ladies. Women I can talk to. Even the courtesans here speak loathsome French. Yours, on the other hand, is beautiful."

She struggled to breathe, refused to meet his eyes. Where was Maria? Picking up a paintbrush, she began wiping it clean with a rag.

He stopped in front of her. Lowering his voice, he said, "This villa would benefit from a woman's presence. I could make someone very happy here, see that her every wish was granted. I also have the perfect small nest in Rhodes Town. It lies empty, waiting for a woman's touch."

Anica steeled herself to look at him. She wanted to slap his face. But he was a powerful knight, and this work had to be completed to the grand master's satisfaction. Insulting him could be catastrophic.

Still wiping the brush, she took a breath. "My lord, I am sure you'll find that woman. I imagine there are many who would give their eyeteeth for the opportunity."

He looked at her with amusement, reached out to touch the back of her hand. "Perhaps you are one of them."

She dropped the brush and tugged her hand away, hoping anger did not show in her expression. "No, forgive me, my lord. I'm betrothed."

He picked up the paintbrush and twirled it in his fingers. His hands were slim and pale as milk, with carefully filed fingernails. They were the opposite of the Scotsman's large, brown, weather-worn hands.

"You've a sister." He tapped the end of the paintbrush against the table. "Quite lovely, too. I see her from time to time. She always returns my greetings with enthusiasm. Perhaps she'll make the perfect companion for my little nest."

Anica's breath caught in her throat. If only she could seize the paintbrush and poke him in the eye. Instead, she said evenly, "We are a respectable family. My sister is not a candidate for your scheme."

He scoffed. "Respectable? I'm not so sure."

"What do you mean?" Her chest tightened with anger.

He turned away from her, strolling the length of the wall again. "So finely wrought. You said your father does the detailed work and you just fill in the colors. That's not true, though, is it?"

Slowly, he pivoted and fixed his gaze on her.

"It *is* true!" she protested.

He raked her up and down with a long, cold look. "My servants are my eyes and ears when I'm not here. And they've heard you and your father, seen you working. It's you who does everything, isn't it? He's not just injured. His eyesight is failing. He can't see." With a sweeping gesture, the knight indicated the fine details of the château on the wall. "This is your talent at work, not his."

He approached her, his soft leather shoes quiet on the tile floor.

Anica's throat was dry as dust. "I help him," she said, horrified to hear a quiver in her voice. "But he is the artist, not me."

"Lord de Milly just received some work of your father's for his private chapel. He told me your father is an artist of magnificent talent, trained in the ateliers of Venice. How disappointed he would be to discover that a common-born girl with a Greek mother painted those portraits. How embarrassing for him to learn he'd been lied to by the Venetian." The knight circled the table, his eyes never leaving hers. "Do you know what I think? I think such a revelation would be quite a blow to your father's reputation. I imagine his commissions would dry up entirely. Perhaps he would even find himself banished from Rhodes altogether—sent back to Venice in disgrace."

The words struck Anica like physical blows.

At that moment, Maria entered the chamber. When she saw the knight, she faltered, and water slopped over the rim of the bowl in her hands. He ignored her and stepped closer to Anica.

"I leave soon on a mission across the sea. When I get back, I will make arrangements for you to get a key to my little home within the city walls. And when I call for you there, I'll expect you to obey my wishes. Or your father's secret will be a secret no longer."

CHAPTER 28

Winter, 1460
Rhodes Town

THEY ROLLED through the city gates heralded by the discordant chimes of bells marking the hour. The familiar sound seemed ominous today, amplifying the dread in Anica's gut. With a trembling voice, she ordered their driver to stop near the Inn of the English, then told Maria to wait in the cart. Pulling her shawl over her head, she approached the steps with trepidation. When she walked in, the lively chatter in the parlor faded away. Every eye in the place was on her.

Then, thankfully, a man bustled over to her. His brown wool doublet and green hose bloomed with dark stains. He gestured at his soaked clothing with an apologetic smile.

"A bit of a spill. Wasted ale is always a sad sight, but there's more where that came from. I'm the innkeeper. How can I help?"

The lodgers in the parlor began speaking amongst themselves again. Anica spied flames leaping in a small hearth on the opposite side of the parlor. Two men near the fire were engaged in a game of chess; another group sat around a small table covered with playing cards.

She took a shaky breath. "Is the Scot, Master Fordun, in residence?"

The man looked surprised. "Drummond Fordun never lodges here. Takes refreshment here from time to time, but he lives across the square."

Anica faltered.

Drummond.

She stood very still a moment, savoring the knowledge of his first name. One of the chess players got up from his stool and approached. He was silver-haired, with a carefully trimmed beard and a ruddy face.

"You're the artist's daughter."

She recognized him. He had been on the harbor that day when she'd first clapped eyes on Drummond Fordun.

"Yes. You are a friend of the Scot?"

He nodded. "Do you need to get a message to him?"

"I hoped to speak with him," she said in a low voice. "To thank him for helping my father in Archangelos."

"Ah." Understanding dawned in the man's eyes. "You're in luck. He's here in Rhodes Town, just across the square at his lodgings. I'll take you there myself."

She tensed.

"Don't worry, signorina," he said kindly. "I'll fetch him down, and you can talk to him in the square."

Anica nodded, relieved. "Thank you, sir . . . ?"

"Sir Peter's his name, miss," said the innkeeper. "Although I like to call him Nosy Nellie."

Sir Peter waved a hand at the innkeeper's damp clothing. "Just as I like to call *you* Mr. Butterfingers."

Chuckling, the innkeeper returned to the parlor.

Outside, Maria waited on the cart bench, her features arranged in the expressionless mask she wore like armor in these streets.

"I'll be right over there," Anica told her, pointing after Sir Peter. "I won't go out of your sight."

Maria inclined her head, her lips compressing into a flat line.

Sir Peter disappeared into a two-level stone building and returned with the Scot in tow. Then he retreated across the square with a wave.

Master Fordun stared wide-eyed at Anica as if she were a ghostly apparition. "Signorina Anica."

The rich, deep rumble of his voice ignited a flame of longing just below her breastbone.

"Master Fordun," she said, trying to ignore her leaping pulse.

"My thanks to you for the letter and the thread. My sister will be pleased."

She'd written her letter of thanks to him after Archangelos, and Maria had delivered it to the Inn of the English. Within the folds of the single page, she had placed a precious packet of gold thread from Cyprus, which her aunt had gifted her a few years ago. She'd told Drummond it was for his sister the embroiderer.

"I—we—were grateful to you for all you did for us. And for Angelos."

A look of faint surprise appeared on his face at the mention of the boy.

"I thought you'd taken him to a cruel end, and instead you found him a better life," she added, feeling a tingle of shame at the hateful feelings she'd harbored toward the Scot.

A group of French pilgrims wandered by, chatting about the Colossus of Rhodes and whether it had actually existed. She waited until they passed, then spoke again.

"But that's not why I'm here. I've come to ask for your help."

He softened his stance, bent his head toward her. "I'd be honored."

"Signor Syriano said there is a cure for what ails my father in Damascus. I must get him safely there and back again. I thought of you and—"

Anica tightened her shawl around her neck. Could she really trust this man? Take him into her confidence? Then the thought of Émile de Chambonac's smug arrogance hardened her resolve.

Steadying her breath, she said, "I wondered if you might help him make the journey."

"I'm leaving soon for Alexandria, with a merchant fleet. He might be able to secure a place on a merchant vessel."

"Truly?" She felt a tiny loosening of the tension in her chest. "But Damascus is yet another journey."

"If he accompanies my fleet to Alexandria, I can find safe passage for him to Damascus." He paused. "How long will this cure take?"

"I have no idea," Anica admitted. "Signor Syriano did not tell us."

"Then let's go to his house and ask him now," suggested the Scot. "I'd be in a better position to help if I knew the details. And I don't have much time to make arrangements before the fleet sails."

"Very well." She glanced over her shoulder at Maria, whose glowering face trumpeted her disapproval of the situation. "Can we meet you there?"

"Do you know where Signor Syriano lives?" Master Fordun asked.

"Yes, Papa and I visited him not long ago. We'll take the Street of the Knights and then cut through the side lanes to his house."

"Suit yourself. I'll be taking a different route."

"Why? Is there a faster way?"

He chuckled. "No. My route is slower. But it avoids the Street of the Knights. I'll be less likely to run into sergeants of the Order wanting to whine in my ear like mosquitoes. Or the wee knight I've been tasked with keeping track of."

"I'm sorry?" Anica asked, bewildered by his last statement.

He shook his head. "A young knight from Auvergne. He's been put under my care. Every time he catches sight of me, he's got a hundred questions. And he's coming to Alexandria with me."

She backed away. A wave of panic left her knees weak.

"Émile de Chambonac?" she asked.

"Yes. Are you acquainted with him?" Master Fordun's forehead furrowed in a frown.

"Yes—no, not really. My father was commissioned to paint something for his villa." The words came out in choppy bursts.

"Is something wrong, Signorina Anica?" His voice held genuine concern.

She forced herself to meet his gaze. "Would my father be making the journey in your galley?"

"To Damascus? No. He'd be on a merchant galley in the fleet. My vessel will carry only knights and servants of the Order."

Anica swallowed, trying to force down the lump that had formed in her throat. When she found her voice, it was tight and cool. "Let's go, then. My family is expecting me at home. I don't want to worry them."

He waited until she was seated in the cart and the wheels were turning, then hastened into the streets ahead.

Anica and Master Fordun emerged from Dr. Syriano's home together, Maria a few steps behind them. The mule cart stood waiting, the driver singing a Greek folk tune, apparently for the mules' benefit. Their long ears twitched back and forth in response to his melody. As Maria climbed into the cart, Anica turned back to the Scot.

"It's an opportunity that won't happen again," she said. "To think that Papa can stay in Dr. Syriano's home in Damascus during his recovery! That will make the idea of a month or two there easier for him to accept. He'll be worried about traveling in winter, though. And how will we arrange his return?"

"I can see to it. I'll find a voyage back to Rhodes for him with trusted allies," Drummond said. "If your father has questions about the journey, he can call for me at the Inn of the English or find me at the Mandraki."

Two men dressed in Latin garb approached, engrossed in conversation. They fell silent as they passed, staring at Anica and Drummond with cool interest. One of them bent to the other, murmuring in his ear, his gaze fixed on Anica.

The Scot eyed the retreating men. "Do you know them?"

She shook her head, distracted by an alarming thought. "A voyage like this will be costly. Do you know how much my father will have to pay?"

"I'm afraid not. I know little about merchants and their passengers," he apologized. "The merchant vessels in the fleet to Alexandria are Genoese. If he wants to meet the captains and inquire about payment, he'll find them at the Inn of the Italians."

Anica gave him a pleading look. "You and Dr. Syriano are the only people who know why Papa must go to Damascus. Please don't tell anyone else."

"I don't have a wagging tongue," he assured her.

Her pounding heart must have been audible, but he showed no sign of hearing it. In a voice that was barely more than a whisper, she said, "Thank you, Drummond."

His eyes shone when she spoke his name aloud. "What for, Anica?"

On impulse, she reached out a hand. "For helping my father get his sight back, and for guiding him safely across the sea."

He took her hand between his own, and for a moment they stood joined in touch. Everything else in the world fell away from her—everything except the warm pressure of his hands cradling her fingers with astonishing tenderness.

Maria dissolved in a coughing fit so violent that the mule cart driver started pounding her on the back. Anica slid her hand out of Drummond's grasp and stepped into the cart.

"May Santa Maria keep you from harm on the journey," she murmured, not wanting to break their gaze.

He looked almost shy, studying her beneath long, dark lashes, his tall form defined against the warm glow of the sunset.

"May all the saints keep you well every day of your life," he said softly.

The cart lurched forward. Anica savored the tingling warmth that lingered on her fingertips from his touch. It took every ounce of her self-control not to turn around and watch Drummond vanish into the gathering dusk.

CHAPTER 29

Winter, 1460
Rhodes Town

THEIR LITTLE GROUP waited on the stone quay in the weak winter sunlight, watching the sailors ready the fleet to sail. Anica and Papa stood on either side of Mamá, their arms linked with hers. Heleni had stayed home, complaining of a stomach ache. Anica was grateful for her sister's absence; a quiet farewell would be best.

"When you stop in Famagusta, will you inquire about Estelle?" she asked Papa, leaning forward to catch his eye. "If you have time."

Mamá clutched Papa's arm tighter. "Don't step foot on the soil of Cyprus, Paolo, not even to ask after the falconer's daughter. Promise me! The harbor's overrun with pirates, and the Genoese there can't be trusted."

"What do you mean? My betrothed is Genoese." Anica gave her mother an exasperated glance. "These merchant ships are Genoese."

"That's different. Signor Lomellini is a true Genoese, born and raised in Genoa. And these ship captains are true Genoans as well.

Famagusta is different—it's crawling with white Genoese. They're ruthless. They'll do anything for money. My family knows this to be true. Ask any Georgillas."

Papa kissed Mamá's cheek. "My dear, I'll do nothing that puts me in harm's way. Besides, I'll have our nephew at my side." He gestured at Anica's cousin Dimitri, who stood nearby making his own farewells to his mother and brothers. "Nothing to worry about."

Mamá's eyes welled with tears. "There's everything to worry about! Your health, your very life, not to mention these winter seas . . ."

"Mamá, he'll be in good hands with Dr. Syriano's family." Anica slid an arm around her mother's waist. "And he has a letter of introduction from Dr. Syriano himself to the physician who will perform the surgery."

"There are too many dangers." Mamá began to weep in earnest.

Aunt Rhea shooed Anica off and took Mamá in her arms. Anica excused herself and went to Dimitri's side. She embraced him and thanked him for making the journey.

It had been fairly easy to convince their family that Papa was ill and the only cure for him lay in Damascus, for medical care in the Syrian city was far superior to that in Rhodes Town. But no one besides Anica, her parents, Drummond, and Dr. Syriano knew the real reason for the voyage.

Even her own parents did not know the full truth. In the end, Anica had told them nothing of her encounter with Émile de Chambonac. She had only said rumors were spreading that she, not Papa, was responsible for the portraits made in their studio.

This revelation, combined with Papa's own admission to her mother that his eyesight was deteriorating, had not quite turned the tide. It was Aunt Rhea who had offered a solution acceptable to Mamá in the end, by pledging Dimitri to Papa as his companion for the voyage.

Anica was reassured, talking with her cousin now. A strong, bright young man, capable with a sword and destined to be a ship captain, he would make an ideal protector on the journey.

"What is that Scotsman's name, the one accompanying the merchant vessels?" Aunt Rhea called to her.

"Drummond Fordun. He'll take special care of Papa. He gave me—us—his word." Heat rose on her neck as she spoke.

"How is it you find a foreign privateer trustworthy, Paolo?" Aunt Rhea looked at Papa with a raised eyebrow. "You often say there's little difference between a privateer and a pirate."

Papa lifted his chin. "I believe this fellow is worthy of our trust. Archangelos gave me a chance to see the measure of the man. We'll be safe with him on the voyage, if Santa Maria is willing."

With Émile de Chambonac absent, Anica could complete the frescoes at his villa without further difficulties. She alternated that project with several new commissions from merchants.

One cool morning a few weeks after the fleet departed, when the air was thick with moisture and a gusting wind rattled the shutters, Anica entered the studio. She was eager to get started on a portrait of Santa Caterina that would require both precious lapis lazuli and gold leaf. She glanced at the easels lining the walls. Because the oil paint took so long to dry compared to tempera, she had taken to starting multiple projects at the same time and adding thin layers of paint as needed.

Anica searched for the linseed oil on Papa's supply table. Uncorking the little jug, she poured the last few drops into a small dish. Had they really used it all?

She would have to send out for some oil. Their apothecary did stock the substance, though it would be more expensive than buying a large quantity in the marketplace.

She padded through the quiet house to the kitchen. Maria was at the hearth, bent over a steaming kettle of water filled with linens, and the kitchen maid was preparing vegetables for tonight's supper at the table.

"I forgot today is laundry day," Anica said as she entered the chamber. Maria wiped the back of a hand across her perspiring brow, greeting her with a nod. "Did you fetch the soap this morning?"

"I did." Heleni stood in the doorway, her eyes heavy-lidded, as if she weren't quite awake yet. "I bought Mamá orange-blossom water from the soap man, too. She asked me for some."

Anica studied her sister in silence.

"You say you have work to do in the studio," Heleni said, twirling one of her long braids with a finger. "Instead, you wander about interrogating the rest of us."

"I need more linseed oil," Anica said.

Maria stopped stirring the laundry but didn't turn around.

Anica nodded in the direction of the kitchen maid, who wiped her hands on her apron, brightening at the idea of getting outside. "Take her and go to the apothecary for me."

Maria glanced over her shoulder, looking anxious. When she realized Heleni would be accompanied by the maid, not her, the slave's expression relaxed.

"Are you unwell, Maria?" Anica asked.

Maria resumed her work, shaking her head.

Anica fixed Heleni with a stern gaze. "I know how long it takes to get to the apothecary. If you're not back when the churches ring ten bells, I'll send Maria out after you."

Heleni shrugged. "There's a queue most days. If I'm trapped behind some old woman with a thousand ailments, it won't be my fault."

"Shall I come with you, then?"

"No. I'll manage." Heleni strode away, the kitchen maid following.

"And cover your head!" Anica called after her sister.

She went to Maria's side. "If you're feeling ill, you can tell me."

Maria bit her lip. "Your father told me I would get my freedom once seven years in his service had passed, perhaps sooner. But with him gone, I wonder what will happen to me if . . ."

"We must all wait and be patient and pray every day for Papa's safe return. What will you do when you are freed?" Anica asked in a soft voice.

"He says I can keep working here if I choose," the slave said. "And if I wish to marry, he will pay the dowry."

Though Anica rarely asked Maria about her past, curiosity got the better of her. "Do you want to return to your homeland?"

Maria's eyes narrowed. "There is nothing but death for me in that place." She bent over the kettle again.

Walking to the studio, Anica mulled over the slave's behavior. Maria had been a shy, fearful girl when she first came to them, covered with sores and bruises. She'd never told them a word about her origins, despite Heleni's pestering. After Mama's careful attention restored the girl's health and she'd adjusted to her new home, Maria's true character emerged. She had a dry sense of humor and could even get saucy at times. But lately her spirits were low.

The prospect of freedom must weigh on Maria's mind. No one was immune from worries about their fate, least of all a slave.

That afternoon, Anica sat in the courtyard on a cushioned bench, wrapped in a shawl against the chill. Overhead, dark clouds knitted together, veiling the sky. A storm was coming, she was sure of it. Despite the poor weather, she needed fresh air. The quality of her work had been laughable today.

By rights she should have been thinking about her future husband, but her thoughts were on Drummond Fordun as she mixed paints and applied layers of color to the panels. She had even sketched an image of his face in charcoal on a gesso-covered panel, then scrubbed it off with a damp cloth.

If only he were sitting before her now. If only she could study his features one by one, taking all the time she wished, and compose a portrait of him that truly captured his essence.

She recalled the sharp angles of his cheekbones, the fullness of his wide mouth, the light in his gold-flecked eyes. The exquisite moment when she had offered him her hand, had seen how quickly his fierce demeanor could melt into tenderness.

A movement caught her eye. She sat up, her dreamy torpor interrupted.

It was Heleni, moving toward her. Anica slid over to make room on the cushioned bench, surprised that her sister would seek her out. Heleni was so combative these days.

"You look tired, Heleni. Sit with me." She patted the bench beside her.

"I thought I heard thunder. I'm frightened," Heleni admitted, sinking down next to Anica.

The air grew heavy and thick. A growl of thunder sounded in the distance, then lightning bleached the sky.

"Help me move this bench back a bit," Anica said. "Rain will follow any moment."

Together they slid the bench against the wall near the bronze boy in his niche, beneath the overhang of the roof. They settled down again, Heleni leaning against Anica. For a moment, a wave of nostalgia struck her. Moments of sweetness between them were rare these days.

"I'm envious," Heleni confided, her head heavy against Anica's shoulder. "You'll soon be wed and mistress of your own household. And I'll be stuck here alone."

"As soon as I'm wed, Aunt Rhea and Papa will line up a bevy of suitors for you." Anica rested her cheek on Heleni's head and slipped an arm around her shoulders.

Her sister was silent. Another rumble of thunder rolled across the sky. Moments later, a steady rain began to fall.

"I don't want suitors. I have a husband in mind," Heleni said. "I'm promised to him."

Lightning turned the sky bone-white.

"Who?" A current of dread snaked through Anica's stomach.

"He's a nobleman. A Latin, and best of all, a knight."

Anica sat like a stone, dumbfounded.

"He knows everything about me," Heleni continued. "We write notes back and forth. It's a lovely game. And he has our future all arranged. We're to marry and live in a beautiful house not too far from here. It's our little nest."

"That's why you've been fetching the soap," Anica said dully.

"Yes. The soap man carries our notes for us. Émile pays him well for the task. Though there was nothing from him this week." A trace of dejection entered her voice. "He's always answered my letters with a note of his own."

"You speak of Émile de Chambonac." A roaring filled Anica's ears.

Heleni pulled away and gave Anica a defiant look. "He loves me," she asserted. "And I love him. Nothing will keep us apart."

Anica fought to keep her voice calm. "Heleni, the knights are not permitted to marry. He does not wish to wed you; quite the contrary."

"You're wrong," Heleni retorted. "He found a monk who will marry us."

Anica chose her next words with care. "I'm afraid he lied to you, Heleni. He's not what you think he is."

Heleni let out a scornful laugh. "You know nothing of him."

"I know he sailed across the sea in the fleet with Papa."

"That's a lie!"

"You weren't there," Anica pointed out. "I saw him sail away on the Scot's galley."

Heleni took that in, chewing her lip. "But I got a note from him last week. He did not mention such a journey."

"He concealed the truth from you."

Reluctantly, Anica told her sister what had happened at the villa, how the knight had propositioned her. This would surely make her see the folly of her plan.

But Heleni slid away from her as the words spilled out, crackling with rage.

"I should have known not to confide in you," she hissed. "You always find a way to stick a needle in my joy. You're jealous, aren't you? You're betrothed to a man who cares more for his life in Genoa than he'll ever care for you."

"Heleni—"

"Don't speak to me." Heleni sprang up and slapped Anica on the face. "Stop telling me lies. Your envy is sickening."

She whirled and stalked inside.

Anica stared after her in horror, a hand pressed to her cheek. She tried to steady her breath, tried to ignore the sting of the blow. What kind of web had that knight woven? And how could she extricate her sister from his plan before their parents—or worse, Rhodes Town's many gossips, with their loose tongues—found out?

CHAPTER 30

Winter, 1460
Aegean Sea

AFTER DRUMMOND'S leave had been cut short by the pirate attack at Archangelos, he'd raced through his inspections of the *turcopoles* at the island's various military forts and made it back to Rhodes Town just in time to ready the galley for another voyage—the one he'd been dreading.

The only bright spot in his time at the port city was the unexpected encounter with Anica Foscolo and his opportunity to help her father. He was still scratching his head over their conversation near the Inn of the English, though. It had been going well until he mentioned Émile de Chambonac. Then she'd shut down like a tortoise withdrawing into its shell.

The morning of the expedition to Alexandria, four galleys set out from Rhodes harbor a little after dawn—Drummond's own vessel, another war galley owned by the Order, and two Genoese merchant ships. Aboard one of the Genoese ships was Signor Foscolo and his young companion, a strapping Greek fellow who was apparently a relative of his.

As they glided away from Rhodes, Drummond called Émile de Chambonac to the bow deck. Instead of coming straight to his side, the young man strode to the bronze swivel gun mounted on the bow quarter.

Drummond intercepted him with two quick steps, putting his body between de Chambonac and the gun. "Only those trained to use this weapon can touch it. You'll get that training in due time. But your job today is to shadow my officer."

He pointed at the Genoese first mate, who'd come up beside them with the stealth of a cat.

"Why must I learn the lowly tasks of a sailor?" the knight demanded. "Your crew is responsible for such things. I must save my strength for battle."

Drummond suppressed an urge to slap the insolent whelp on the back of his head. "You're on my vessel now, and you'll do as I order. Is that understood?"

The young knight glowered at him. The first mate glanced at the sky, perhaps imploring God for patience.

"At sea, you're at risk if you don't know how to handle yourself on a ship," Drummond said, forcing himself to speak in a measured manner. "You must know where every weapon is stowed, how the wind affects our speed and direction, how to furl and lash a sail, how to drop an anchor. These things can be the difference between life and death on the waves. You may not be a sailor, but I promise you won't survive out here if you don't bother to learn their ways."

"But I—" de Chambonac began.

"The Order is a naval organization at heart," Drummond interrupted. "You may or may not see battle on land. But there's no doubt you'll see it at sea. Do you want to be ready?" He took a menacing step forward. "Well? Yes or no?"

"Yes," the young man managed to choke out.

"Excellent. Then do as you're told. First, you'll learn port from starboard, bow from stern, and a few basic facts about the wind and waves." He nodded at the Genoese, who led the knight along the gunwale to the stern.

Their sister galley drew abreast of them, its long wooden oars slicing through the water with precision. On its deck stood Sir Peter, one hand shading his eyes. Drummond could swear he saw a smile on his friend's face at the sight of him disciplining the spoiled little knight. He ground his teeth, dreading the days ahead.

That evening, they anchored in a sheltered bay on a small island south of Rhodes. The merchant vessels were positioned between the two war galleys, the better to protect them in case of attack.

If they had not been in the company of the merchants, Drummond would have gone ashore and explored the ruins of an ancient structure whose foundation stones were still intact in the ground. Such places littered these islands; some of them were astonishing, with immense pillars reaching toward the sky, triangular pediments leaning drunkenly on their sides, eroding in the blazing Mediterranean sun. Sometimes, he discovered shards of rust-red pottery in the soil when he explored such ruins. Once he'd unearthed a marble hand, its fingers rendered with marvelous detail. It was stored in a chest at Archangelos, along with other odds and ends he had found during his travels.

When the others were asleep, Drummond went to the bow quarter and stood watching the night descend. Silver moonlight unfurled before him, a gleaming path leading to the beach. Tiny waves lapped on the sand. He longed to strip naked and plunge into the water, wash the day's frustrations away. But tonight, he would satisfy himself by watching the moonlight dance on the waves.

His mother used to say, "Snatch moments of peace when you can, my boy, and savor them." When he was small, he did not understand her words. He was always in motion, always running, jumping, climbing, swimming, pursuing some quarry in the meadows near their home. It never crossed his mind to seek out peace in those days.

But now—oh yes, he understood his mother's sentiment exactly. He needed these quiet moments to still his mind and steady him for the terrors to come. He had to stay calm and strong for his men. How could he do that if he was a seething tangle of anger and nerves?

He stood there a while longer, listening to the waves, breathing the salt air, then retreated to his bedroll under the canvas shelter in the stern to catch a few hours' sleep before dawn. His last thought before slipping into unconsciousness was of Anica. The letter of thanks she'd written him was in the pouch he carried at his waist. Carrying such a memento at sea was risky, for it could get soaked with seawater and ruined. But that didn't matter. After all, he had read the lines so often that every word was etched in his heart.

When they struck out for Alexandria at first light, Drummond's sole focus was navigating the wintery sea. Gusty winds made for choppy, restless waters; a swirl of lead-gray clouds stalked them. Soon after they launched, a steady drizzle set in. Visibility was poor, and Drummond had to rely on his compass to keep their bearings. From time to time, they lost sight of their companion vessels, but the four ships stayed fairly close together despite the poor conditions.

While he was at the stern consulting with the seaman in charge of the rudder, making adjustments to the course with the aid of the compass, a shout rose from the bow.

"Ship! Ship!" came the excited voice of Émile de Chambonac. "I spy an enemy ship, men! Prepare for battle! We shall vanquish the infidels in the name of St. John, we shall—"

Drummond scrambled to the bow and grabbed the young knight by the arm before any more idiocy could spew from his lips.

"It's not your place to sight ships nor decide if they're enemies," he growled. "Go below decks and sit on an oarsman's bench until further notice."

"I'm ready to do battle—" the man protested.

"Move. Now." Drummond ordered, pushing him toward the hold. He signaled to a crewman. "Take him down there and keep your eyes on him."

As de Chambonac skulked away, the first mate came to Drummond's side.

"It's a *fusta*, Master Fordun. The sails are furled, no sign of oars. No crew on deck either."

"What?" Drummond followed his gaze. It was true. The graceful little galley bobbed in the waves, seemingly unoccupied. No banner fluttered from its mainmast.

Their companion vessels appeared off the port side. The captain of the other war galley looked to Drummond, arms raised in a questioning manner.

In a low voice, Drummond said to the Genoese, "It's a Turkish vessel, to be sure. But what's afoot? Were they boarded by pirates and plundered?"

"Or are they hiding, waiting for us to board them so they can slit our throats?" the Genoese asked. "Odds are fifty-fifty, I'd say."

Drummond nodded. The galley lurched crazily in the unsettled sea. He bent his knees so as not to be thrown off balance. It would be difficult to board the *fusta* in these conditions, and if an ambush awaited them, even harder to get away.

The Order expected him to plunder every Turkish or Mamluk vessel he encountered, to take their crew captive. But in this instance, he hesitated. His reluctance was born of three things. First, the knowledge that Signor Foscolo sailed with the fleet. Taking any unnecessary risks that might put Anica Foscolo's father in danger was not an option. Second, that damn de Chambonac. Unseasoned men desperate to prove themselves as warriors were dangerous companions on an outing such as this.

The third, perhaps most worrisome reason of all, was stowed belowdecks in an iron-studded oak chest. Hundreds of golden florins, a tribute payment to the Mamluk Sultanate of Egypt. Lord de Milly had tasked Drummond with delivering the gold personally to the Mamluks upon arrival in Alexandria. Just knowing the value of that precious cargo made Drummond's breath grow shallow. He could not wait to hand it over to the Sultanate.

He watched the Turkish craft bob in the waves for another moment. Then he shot a glance at the other war galley. Its hold did not contain a pearl as precious as Émile de Chambonac, nor did it carry a gift of gold for their enemies. If a battle did commence, by God, de Chambonac could launch a few arrows from the crossbows rigged to Drummond's gunwales. That counted as seeing action.

Drummond signaled to the captain of the other vessel to approach the *fusta*. Their oarsmen quickly closed the distance between the two crafts. He signaled to the merchant galleys to keep well back.

A dozen armed men disappeared into the belly of the *fusta,* their actions muted by the sound of wind and rain. Drummond's stomach tightened as he waited for the men to re-emerge. What had they found?

Within a few moments, the signal came that the vessel was unmanned and empty of cargo.

"We found dead crewmen in the hold," a sailor called out to Drummond. "They've got nothing valuable on them. And there's water rising down there. The hull's damaged in several places."

"It will sink before nightfall," Drummond said, shaking his head.

Some pirate ship had encountered this craft not long ago.

The men crossed back from the Turkish vessel to Drummond's galley, and the fleet set off again. Though the wind was favorable, a driving rain made for a day of cold misery. And the usual banter of Drummond's crew was silenced—quashed by the unspoken fear of being hunted by pirates.

The band of anxiety around Drummond's chest squeezed tighter. He searched the horizon, his eyes aching from his efforts to see through the sheets of rain, his muscles tense from a constant state of alert wariness. His responsibility for Émile de Chambonac was oppressive, but he was more worried about Signor Foscolo. Nothing could befall that man on the journey, by God and all the saints. If he returned to Rhodes with the news that the Venetian painter was dead, Anica would be devastated.

And that was something he could not abide.

CHAPTER 31

Winter, 1460
Rhodes Town

EVERY TIME ANICA attempted to speak with Heleni about Émile de Chambonac, she refused to talk. Furious at her sister's mulish behavior, Anica lost herself in work. Weeks rolled by as she completed Émile de Chambonac's frescos, finished the oil portraits, and churned out a dozen icons of saints.

Finally, Anica entered their bedchamber one evening to find Heleni lying on the bed with her back to the door, her hair loose around her. The shutters were closed against the driving wind.

Anica went to the bedside and looked down at Heleni. She drew in a long breath, composing herself. "Let's end this silence between us. You can't ignore me forever."

Heleni rolled over and assessed Anica with disdain. "You want to destroy my happiness. I'll not tell you another word beyond the fact that I love Émile and he loves me."

Anica's jaw tensed. "Will you ever understand that he can't marry you? He simply wants to make you his concubine."

Heleni sat up, eyes blazing. "Get out. Now."

"You will destroy all our lives if you do not end things with him. If you continue with this foolishness, think of how our mother will suffer," Anica said. "Surely, you can understand what this will do to her."

"Mamá will be honored that a nobleman wants to marry me." Even as she said it, there was a slight hesitation in Heleni's voice.

"How many times must I say it?" Anica cried in exasperation. "He will never marry you."

Heleni flung herself down on the bed face-first. "I hate you," she said through muffled sobs. "I'll always hate you."

Anica made for the door.

"That may be, Heleni." She reached for the latch. "But we are sisters. We are family. I won't see you—or us—ruined by that man. I have no choice but to tell Mamá tonight, since you refuse to."

Striding away from their bedchamber, all she could think of was the knight's false promises. How long could they keep this matter private? Who had he told?

The swirling thoughts were suffocating. Desperate for fresh air, anything to cool the emotions raging within her, she headed for the courtyard. Somehow she must summon the will to break this news to Mamá. Her mother had only recently begun emerging from her suffocating mantle of grief. This would send her into despair all over again.

Clouds obscured the stars. A gust of wind set the leaves of the lemon trees trembling. She moved to the very center of the courtyard, her face turned up to the sky, and began praying to God. The winter air soothed her hot skin but did nothing to quell the emotions churning in her heart.

This is my fault. I refused Émile de Chambonac's offer, so he drew my sister into his web.

She fought off a sob, struggling to calm herself.

Be strong. Don't succumb to tears.

Heleni burst into the courtyard, bare feet silent on the stone, her flimsy shift rippling in the wind.

"Don't tell Mamá," Heleni shrieked. "It's not your right—"

She slipped and tumbled down on the stone floor with a sickening thud.

Anica rushed to her side. Heleni curled up in a ball, her arms cradled protectively around her belly. In that moment, Anica knew the worst had happened.

She crouched and whispered in her sister's ear, "When was the last time you bled?"

"I—I don't remember." Heleni turned her head away.

Mamá entered the courtyard, Maria following with an oil lamp in her hands.

"What's happened?" Mamá cried.

Anica seized the oil lamp from Maria and ordered her back inside.

"What is wrong, my girl?" Mamá pulled at Heleni's arm. "Stand up."

"Let's help her to the bench," Anica said.

They settled Heleni on the bench near the bronze boy's niche. Anica held up the lamp so her sister's face was lit by its glow.

"Heleni is with child," Anica whispered. "By a French knight, Émile de Chambonac."

Mamá recoiled. "Impossible!"

Anica ignored her mother. "Heleni. Look at me. When did he . . . How did you . . . ?"

"We have a quiet nest." Heleni stared at her with defiance. "We go to the little house I told you about. It will be our home once we marry."

Anica gasped for air, sinking down on her knees.

"You have never left this house alone," Mamá said in disbelief. "How did he lure you into such a trap?"

"He did not lure me. I went willingly. The kitchen maid didn't care if I made her wait in the streets. I gave her asper coins to keep her quiet. But Maria—she made it difficult. She tried to keep us apart." Heleni fell silent, a vague expression of guilt on her face.

"Heleni!" Mamá took her daughter by the shoulders and shook her. "You are making no sense at all. Stop these falsehoods!"

"I will bring our family such honor," Heleni said, earnest now. "Imagine, one of us marrying into a noble family."

"This is no honor. The shame on our family, on you—" Mamá broke off, rendered speechless by rage.

"There will be no shame, Mamá. I will marry him. It's all arranged."

Mamá reeled back, eyes wide with horror. "You stupid, stupid girl. That knight will not marry you. He lied to get you into his bed."

Heleni looked away. "You don't know him. He's an honorable man. He loves me."

"Your father won't stand for this." Mamá dragged her gaze to Anica. "What will we do? That blue-eyed devil—he ravished her! He's destroyed her future. And our family!"

The wind tugged at loose tiles on the roof, the brittle rhythm driving into Anica's skull.

She took her sister's hand. "Let's get her to bed. Nothing can be solved right now. In the morning, we'll find a solution."

Hooking her arm around her sister's waist, she led Heleni out of the courtyard, Mamá following close behind.

All night, Anica lay awake next to her weeping sister, dreading the dawn of a new day.

CHAPTER 32

Winter, 1460
Aegean Sea

On the voyage back from Alexandria, Drummond slept under the oiled canvas sailcloth rigged over the stern deck of the galley. He hated being cooped up in the hold. Down there, men slept and rowed in shifts, sleeping on benches or in the spaces between them. The stench and darkness below decks felt like a smothering cloak at night.

No, better to be out of doors, breathing the sea air, watching the velvety sky shimmer with stars. It had been an uneventful return journey so far. Two of his three concerns were now assuaged: Signor Foscolo had been safely escorted to Damascus, and Drummond had personally delivered the gold tribute payment to the Mamluks.

His remaining task, getting Émile de Chambonac back to Rhodes Town unscathed, seemed in reach. But Drummond knew better than to assume the final leg of their voyage would go without mishap.

On the final evening of the journey, a tablecloth was spread over several wooden crates beneath the canvas shelter. Though the oarsmen ate nothing but hard biscuits and cheese for their evening meal, things were different above decks. Drummond, his officers, and the knights shared roasted goat, salted fish, and stale flatbread drizzled with olive oil, which Émile de Chambonac observed with a disdainful stare before consuming. The Genoese passed around a jug of wine he'd just uncorked and pronounced divine.

"It's been months since I had butter," de Chambonac complained, studying his flatbread with hostility. "I'll have my father send a few milking cows from Auvergne. And Burgundian wine. This Cypriot stuff tastes like piss."

"Then don't drink it," Drummond replied, stuffing in another bite of flatbread.

The last amber light of sunset glowed in the west. A soft breeze filled their sails, nudging the vessel through the glassy water. It was unusual for a winter voyage to be so calm, but he'd take it. Restitution for all the near-death moments he'd experienced in winter seas.

"How did you end up here?" de Chambonac asked him. "There are not many Scots in Rhodes."

Drummond regarded him with surprise. The young Frenchman rarely expressed interest in anyone but himself.

"When I was about your age, a Scottish knight hired me to be his guard when he voyaged from our homeland to Rhodes. Never been at sea before then."

"And now you're captain of this galley." A note of respect crept into the knight's voice.

"Aye. It's my ship."

"From a guard with no sea experience to captain of a war galley for the Order. This must be quite a tale."

"I'm in no mood for storytelling," Drummond said. "A captain loses himself in spinning yarns, he'll soon find himself without a ship."

"But when we return to Rhodes Town, surely you'll have time for a bit of leisure," de Chambonac cajoled him. "Cards, dice, chess? Perhaps a fine tavern for a meal."

Another young knight spoke up. "Those brothels of quality are good gathering spots. Not the ones by the harbor, mind you. The fine homes within the city walls, where red lamps glow in the windows after dark."

The Genoese cocked his head at the young man. "What about your vows to the Order? Chastity, for example?"

De Chambonac picked up another slice of flatbread and lobbed it at him. "Mind your insolence, sir. We must have some comforts on this lonely island. There's no harm in it."

Drummond barely listened to their banter. He was caught in memories about those early days, the first voyage from Scotland to Flanders and then on to Genoa. He'd left Scotland in a hurry, with no knowledge of what lay ahead. All he'd known was if he wanted to live, if he wanted his family safe, fleeing was the only option.

The knight who'd employed him was pious and humorless, devoted to the idea of protecting all Christendom against the rising tide of infidels who threatened to engulf the West. Drummond had found himself caught up in the man's tales of warring knights on distant seas. Despite the searing homesickness he felt, he could not wait to get to Rhodes and see some action himself.

But when they arrived in Genoa three months later, the Scottish knight took ill and died in a matter of days.

Out of a job and far from home, Drummond notified the Order of their brethren's death, took what paltry earnings he had received, and found lodging in a tavern near the shipyards and harbor. He spent his evenings playing dice and cards with all manner of seafaring men: sailors, merchants, pirates, and privateers—who, as far as he could make out, were also pirates, though hired ones. With a mother and grandmother from France, he spoke French fluently, and many in Genoa also spoke it. Italian came easily to him, too, and he was soon offered work as a day laborer in the emporium at the harbor, where warehouses, administrative offices, brothels, and inns all crowded together.

After a life spent in the wild beauty of Scotland, he had no appetite for the crowds and stink of the city. So, one night in a tavern when a Genoese spice merchant offered him a job on his galley, Drummond had only hesitated a moment.

"I'm willing," he'd said, draining his cup of wine.

The spice merchant had looked hard at him. "Can you fight?" he'd asked.

"I came here as a knight's guard," Drummond had replied. "I was hired because I can fight and do it well."

"I need a guard myself where I'm going." The spice merchant had studied him with a long look. "You're big. And you look fierce. If we're attacked, we'll need you out front to frighten the infidels."

A week later, they'd set off along with several other merchant vessels for Alexandria, on the Egyptian coast. That first voyage had gone well. Drummond had proved his worth, gained the captain's trust, and earned himself a place on the next voyage to Alexandria. He'd also earned a generous ration of pepper, which he sold at great profit upon returning to Genoa. Repeating the pattern again and again, he'd eventually amassed the capital to purchase his own galley, hire a crew, and call himself captain.

It would be a few years before he made his way to Rhodes, and in that time he'd experienced only one true catastrophe at sea—an experience that would haunt him until the end of his days. Whenever thoughts of his greatest failure got the best of him, he drowned his despair in drink and women. There had been no shortage of lovely courtesans in every port he visited, and he'd grown attached to a few of them.

Since he'd met Anica Foscolo, though, he'd less and less interest in the company of courtesans. Her presence was what he desired. Her eyes on him. Her smile, lighting up the world but meant for him alone.

Émile de Chambonac's voice intruded on his thoughts.

"Brothels are full of disease, and the women in them disgust me. No, when you want a woman, the thing is to find a mistress. A lady of quality you can have all to yourself. I've got my eye on one. She's a dazzling beauty, and she's got a sister I'd be willing to share with you."

Another knight chuckled. "I'll not refuse such an offer."

Drummond glared at them. "Enough chatter. To bed with all of you. Dawn will be here sooner than you think."

"I've no need for sleep. I'm not tired." De Chambonac's face twisted in a scowl.

"Put the lamps out except for the one on the mainsail mast,"

Drummond instructed the Genoese, ignoring the young knight's protest. "I expect silence from all aboard until dawn."

As he watched his first mate extinguish each lamp in turn, a sudden realization made Drummond suppress a laugh. The biggest threat to Émile de Chambonac at this point in the journey was not pirates, Turks, or Mamluks. It was Drummond's own growing desire to fling the whingeing pup overboard.

When they sailed into Rhodes Town at dawn, Drummond was startled to see two Venetian merchant vessels anchored in the commercial harbor. Venetian traders were subject to stiff tariffs that Genoese merchants were exempt from, so it was rare to see them in these waters.

God's teeth, but that's a strange sight. There's a story behind this, and I'm betting it can't be good.

He put the vessels out of his mind and focused on the chaos of tying up and unloading cargo. While he was paying his oarsmen, he found himself under the scrutiny of an unwelcome figure: Guillaume Lopic, the man who, at the grand master's feast, had extricated Drummond's promise to watch over Émile de Chambonac.

"Master Fordun." Lopic advanced, two guards at his heels. His gaze shifted to Émile de Chambonac, who was swaggering along the quay with a few other young knights. "I see you've brought back your charge unharmed."

"I've done my duty, as promised." Drummond jerked his head toward the commercial harbor. "What brings Venetian merchants to Rhodes Town?"

Lopic smirked. "I'm afraid the captains did not come willingly. They sought refuge in the harbor, fleeing a storm. There were infidels aboard and plenty of valuable Egyptian goods. It's all been confiscated, of course, and the infidels taken captive. The captains have instructions to sail back to Venice at dawn."

"What?" Drummond was incredulous. "When the Venetians hear

of this, we'll have a battle on our hands. Why bring war to our doorstep?"

Lopic's smiled faded. "You forget yourself. Who are you to question the knights?"

Drummond clenched his teeth, not quite trusting himself to remain silent.

"Now." Lopic's expression smoothed into a mask of civility. "Have you done what you set out to do?"

Drummond inclined his head. "The gold's been delivered. I've a letter for the grand master from the Mamluk Sultanate."

Lopic produced a hand from under his cloak. "Give it to me."

"No." Drummond stared at him levelly. "My instructions are to carry it to Lord de Milly myself. I'll not question the orders of the grand master. Will you?"

The man withdrew his hand, working the muscles in his jaw. Then he spun on his heel and hurried away.

CHAPTER 33

Winter, 1460
Rhodes Town

DRUMMOND WAS eager to visit the men's bathhouse and wash off the grime and salt that had accumulated on his skin and hair over the long weeks at sea, then relax in his favorite tavern. Tomorrow, he would visit Anica Foscolo's home and report the good news of her father's safe arrival in Damascus.

But the palace was his first destination. In the receiving hall, high-ranking officials of the Order hovered around the dais, eyeing the grand master speculatively. He caught snippets of whispered conversations about the Venetian ships. Drummond guessed a heated discussion regarding the matter among the tongues of the Order would soon unfold.

When Lord de Milly signaled to him to approach, Drummond bowed and greeted his employer with as much grace as he could muster.

"How did the exchange go?" asked the grand master.

"Perfectly well. Here's your message from the Sultunate." Drummond extracted a letter from the purse at his waist. He waited while Lord de Milly broke the seal and skimmed over the lines.

"Well done." Lord de Milly raised his chin. "The treaty still holds."

His eyes looked sunken in his skull, with dark shadows beneath them. The silver in his hair picked up the light of the beeswax tapers flickering in a nearby iron candelabra. He looked as if he'd aged a year since Drummond saw him before leaving on this journey. Not for the first time, Drummond thanked God he was not burdened with the heavy responsibility borne by Lord de Milly.

One of the grand master's assistants approached, carrying a silver tray. "My lord, a letter for Master Fordun."

Lord de Milly nodded. The assistant thrust the tray at Drummond and he plucked the letter off it. His heart leaped when he recognized his brother's script. But he kept his expression impassive.

"Thank you. My lord, you have others waiting for your attention. I'll take my leave now if it suits you."

The grand master looked past him at the gathered men. Their hushed conversations droned all around them, echoing through the vast chamber. Then he sought Drummond's gaze again. "Wait. How did young de Chambonac fare on the voyage?"

Drummond swallowed. Subtlety did not come naturally to him. But if there had ever been a time to practice the art, it was now.

"He's got quite a lot of enthusiasm, but he's unseasoned. As all young men are. He'll learn."

The grand master frowned. "Yes, he has enthusiasm. Unfortunately, it is sometimes directed at the wrong pursuits."

Drummond considered his next words with care. "As one would expect from a novice knight. But he did not disappoint the Order. In time, he'll prove to be a formidable warrior."

That last statement was close to a lie, but Drummond had no interest in antagonizing Lord de Milly, especially not now.

"Excellent." His employer nodded in approval. "Once again, you've proven your worth." He gestured at the assistant, who fished a velvet bag from a satchel and handed it to Drummond. "Your reward."

Drummond bowed his head, closing his fist around the bag. Its weight told him he'd just received a tidy sum of Rhodian florins.

"Thank you, my lord."

"And what is it you desire?"

Drummond jerked his head up, unsure of the man's meaning. "My lord?"

"Last time I gave you a reward for your efforts, I told you to ask for a favor. You put me off. You've had time to reflect upon the matter."

"I shall think on it a while longer, if I may. And I thank you for the kindness."

"Very well." The grand master's eyes were already raking over the other men in the chamber, taking in the atmosphere of charged tension. He let out a nearly imperceptible sigh and waved Drummond off.

The letter burned like a flame in Drummond's hands as he descended the broad marble staircase to the central courtyard. He retreated into an alcove near the mews and broke the seal. Reading the words, he felt his knees go weak. He leaned against the stone wall behind him, his breath shallow, and tried to absorb his brother's news. Disbelief flooded his veins. He read the letter again, then closed his eyes.

This can't be. It's impossible. After all these years—

"Master Fordun?" The falconer, Monsieur de Montavon, approached. "Are you unwell?"

"No, no, monsieur," Drummond said, a little breathless. "I've just received news from home. Good news." He righted himself, sucking in a great gulp of air, and waved the letter aloft. "I've been waiting for this, hoping for this since—well, it's been ten years now."

He couldn't bring himself to say more for fear he'd be overcome with emotion.

The first line of his brother's letter rang over and over in his head:

It's finally happened, praise God and all the saints—you're free to come home, brother!

The words tumbled through his mind like a beloved song, igniting a current of fire in his blood. He stared at the falconer, tongue-tied, and finally gave a helpless shake of his head.

Monsieur de Montavon regarded him soberly. "I must congratulate you, then. That's a long time to wait. Even good news can be a shock, though. You must take some time to digest it."

They walked back into the courtyard together. The sky was ablaze with amber light as the sun made its descent into the western sky. Drummond folded the letter and pushed it into his purse next to the velvet bag, grateful that the falconer did not press him to reveal its contents.

"Join me tonight at the Georgillas tavern for some wine to celebrate?" he asked the Frenchman.

"I'd like nothing more, but I'm hoping to meet with Lord de Milly tonight. There was a problem with my salary last month, and it still hasn't been addressed." He shook his head. "The banker who dispenses funds to all those who work in the mews and the stables has brought on his son to assist him. Since the young man began working for the treasury, several of us have been shorted funds. We were given receipts with the correct numbers on them, but the purses we received were light. Either he's no good with numbers or he's keeping back florins for himself."

"Who is this banker?" Drummond asked.

"The father, Signor Salviati, has always been a reliable man. But the son—I've no idea what he's called—has lately returned from Florence, where he worked for the Medici family as a banker at their treasury."

"Why would he return? The Medici must be generous employers. They're one of the richest families in the world, by all accounts."

Monsieur de Montavon lowered his voice, though no one was near. "I heard the son ravished the daughter of a Florentine merchant. The merchant wanted to take him to court over the matter, and he fled rather than face prosecution."

Drummond raised an eyebrow. "An ugly mess indeed."

"His private business is the least of my concerns," the falconer said. "I just want to be paid what I'm owed, and so does everyone else. Lord de Milly has been so busy of late I've had no luck arranging a meeting."

"This business with the Venetian ships weighs heavily on his mind," Drummond told him. "I'd not hold out too much hope for a meeting tonight."

CHAPTER 34

Winter, 1460
Rhodes Town

THAT NIGHT, Drummond got extraordinarily drunk, fueled by the knowledge that his future was about to change forever. Slinging back cup after cup of wine at Sir Peter's side, he kept his good news to himself. Instead, he exchanged tales of adventure with a tableful of equally tipsy companions. Too far from the harbor and too costly to attract common sailors, the Georgillas tavern was frequented by shipbuilders, privateers like himself, and well-paid agents of the Order.

Doubled over with laughter at some tale of Sir Peter's, he did not notice the door swing open.

"Look at that," one of the men said, pointing. "Lord Muck himself has entered the premises."

A small entourage of men threaded their way through the tables. At their center was none other than Émile de Chambonac.

When he stopped before Drummond, the chatter faded away around them.

"Gentlemen, good evening," the young knight said. "I'm eager to hear your stories, Master Fordun, and I've got refreshment at my home that far exceeds whatever you'll find here. Bring your friends along." He leaned closer, lowering his voice with a conspiratorial air. "There will be women to entertain us, the finest in Rhodes."

Drummond stared at the young man blearily, trying to summon his self-restraint. How in God's name had the lad found him here?

"I thought you preferred a mistress to prostitutes," he said bluntly.

"I do, but my woman is not at liberty to come and go as she pleases. Not yet."

Drummond squinted at him. "Married woman, is she? That's a dangerous game you're playing."

De Chambonac shrugged. "She's not married. She's as innocent as a rose—or nearly." He smirked. "But until she's installed in my house, there are other flowers just as sweet."

Irritation flooded Drummond, choking off his last reserves of patience. Somehow he managed to keep his expression blank. Why hadn't he eaten anything this evening? The wine pounded at his temples, making him light-headed.

"Forgive me, but I cannot join you," he said. "I've promised Sir Peter here to visit the chapel at the Inn of the English. It's a tradition of ours. When we return safely from sea, we spend a few hours on our knees, giving thanks to the Virgin and to God. Often we pray past midnight."

Sir Peter pointed skyward. "If God does not hear our thanks, the consequences could be grave indeed."

Drummond tapped a finger on his cheek, then widened his eyes as if he'd just been struck by an idea. "Would you and your companions like to join us? Surely, you have your own prayers of thanks to say for your safe return today."

De Chambonac scowled. "I've said my prayers. I have no interest in joining you. My friends await me, and they're expecting your company as well, Master Fordun. I promised them you'd be along to entertain them."

Spoiled bairn, Drummond thought. *Prepare to be disappointed.*

"Lucky you have those women for entertainment, then," Drummond said. "They'll get you through the night, I'm sure of it."

De Chambonac's expression tightened. Without a word of goodbye, he turned and made for the door, his companions at his heels.

The murmur of voices rose around them as knots of revelers resumed their conversations. Drummond struggled to maintain his thoughts. Though wine warmed his innards, it also burned all sense from his brain. Sir Peter leaned toward him.

"You're sure you want to make an enemy of that young pup?" he asked quietly.

"He'll get over it." Drummond raised his cup to his lips again. "I have no choice but to bring him aboard my vessel and guard him with my life at sea, but no one can force me to spend my evenings with the likes of him."

"What is it about the lad that gets under your skin? It's not like you, Drummond."

His exhaustion, his hunger, and above all, his drunken state made him reluctant to answer. And to be honest, even he did not know why he'd taken such a strong dislike to the boy. De Chambonac was not yet twenty, after all. He was spoiled and rich, but he was not a scoundrel, not a rogue. A few more years of seasoning would knock some sense into that thick skull of his.

"Maybe I've worked for the Order too long," he finally admitted. "I'm a hired killer, a pirate, an enslaver of men. Keeping my men safe is the one thing I respect about myself. Fools like him make my job nigh on impossible."

Sir Peter put down his cup. "You're fighting to keep infidels from invading all of Christendom. The Turks and Mamluks capture Christians at every opportunity, after all. Would you prefer we stand by and let them enslave innocents at their whim?"

Drummond snorted. "Turks and Mamluks are one thing, but now I'll be called upon to fight Venetians, too."

"How so?"

"Those vessels in the harbor leave for Venice tomorrow without their passengers or goods. The Council of Ten won't hesitate to unleash the full might of their navy upon us. For what? So the Order can crow about sacking a couple of merchant ships, enslaving their passengers, stealing their goods?"

Sir Peter took that in. "It leaves me with a bitter taste in my mouth," he admitted. "The Catalans were behind the decision, I'll warrant. They and the Genoese are always looking for a reason to humiliate the Venetians."

"When I met with the grand master today, he'd come from a meeting with the commanders of all the Order's tongues," Drummond confided, leaning closer to his friend and dropping his voice. "Half of them want to return the seized goods and passengers back to Venice. The other half won't hear of it."

"The decisions of the knights are not always easy to sit with, but whether we like it or not, we must accept them." Sir Peter's gaze grew hard. "And let's not forget the rewards you've been given. Few men enjoy such privileges. The Order is quick to take such things away from a man whose loyalties are called into question."

Drummond shifted in his seat, taken aback by the intensity of his friend's tone. He'd spent too many years as an agent of the Order to lose favor with the knights now. One hand went to the purse at his waist, where the letter and the bag of coins nestled together.

His brother had written the words he'd dreamed of since leaving Scotland: the English nobleman who'd hunted him for ten years was dead. The revelations in his brother's letter would change everything, but he'd understood years ago that simply returning to Scotland and taking up the threads of his old life would be impossible.

"You're right," he admitted, sucking in a long breath. "I've had a bit of a shock today, and it's addling my mind."

Sir Peter looked dubious.

"I'm leaving the Order sooner than I thought."

"Why?" his friend asked, his face alight with surprise.

Though Drummond longed to live out his days in the land of his birth, he had no source of income there. His family needed the money he sent home. That need would never stop. He'd realized long ago that his ship and his connections in the Mediterranean port cities he visited could be his livelihood long after he left the Order—if he did not burn his bridges in Rhodes Town.

"I've been saving for years with an eye to buying a home in Amsterdam."

"What on earth for?"

"I can conduct a business there importing goods from the East, using all the contacts I've developed in port cities over the years. And I'll visit Scotland as often I can."

He'd never confessed to Sir Peter the true reason for his long absence from Scotland. Though he trusted the Englishman with his life, there was no denying that, back home, they had divided loyalties.

Sir Peter studied him thoughtfully. "You don't look happy about it," he observed. "Is this something you're bound to do for your family?"

Drummond gave a helpless shake of his head. Ever since the attack at Archangelos, when he imagined this life, Anica Foscolo's lovely face entered his mind. It was unsettling. He'd never before harbored fantasies of a future with any of the women who'd shared his bed. And now he couldn't get the idea out of his brain. His throat swelled with emotion at the thought of Anica framed in the doorway of a snug little home in Amsterdam, her arms flung wide to embrace him.

"No. I've just—I've met a woman who figures into my plans now."

"Will she go with you, then?"

Drummond passed a hand over his face. "She has no idea how I feel about her."

"Ah." Sir Peter's eyes crinkled in a smile. "Why don't you put yourself out of your misery and tell her?"

"It's—" Drummond shrugged, feeling foolish. "It's complicated."

"Is she married?"

"No."

"So how complicated can it be, then?"

"She's a local woman. This is her home. I can't see her wanting to—"

"Just talk to her, man!" Sir Peter sighed in exasperation. "What can it hurt?"

Drummond nodded slowly. Laughter erupted at a nearby table,

making him wince. Oh, how his head pounded. He glanced around the tavern, immersed once more in the world of men.

"You spoke the truth. I acted rashly just now," he admitted in a hoarse voice. "The next time Émile de Chambonac extends an invitation, I won't refuse him."

Sir Peter reached for his cup again. "Unless you make things right with him, there won't be a next time."

CHAPTER 35

Winter, 1460
Rhodes Town

A FEW DAYS after their heart-wrenching discovery, Anica awoke to the sound of trumpets from the palace, signaling the arrival of ships into the military harbor. As was her habit every time she heard the trumpets blare, she murmured a prayer to Santa Maria for Papa's safety.

After dressing and braiding her hair, she watched her sleeping sister for a moment, fighting tears. Heleni, so lively, so dramatic, so quick to laugh—and quick to anger. In their early days, they'd been inseparable. Heleni had been a mischievous child, full of energy, unpredictable—but also spilling over with laughter and affection. When she began to develop into a young woman, everything had changed. Her wild moods grew darker, her pride swelled. Fantasies about romantic attachments with knights obsessed her, but they had all assumed the phase would pass soon enough. How wrong they'd been.

Anica reached out a hand and smoothed a lock of hair from her sister's brow.

Why have you done this to yourself, to us?

The bitter thought echoed in Anica's mind as she left the room. She and Mamá slipped out, the morning sun bathing the city with a mantle of gold. She had almost forgotten there was still beauty in the world.

Signorina Giovanna lived above an apothecary near the Tower of Italy in the southeast quarter of the city. Her servant told Anica and Mamá that the doctor was visiting a patient but would return soon. They waited in a small parlor, hands entwined.

For two days and nights, they'd had dozens of whispered conversations. No matter how their discussions began, they all ended the same way: Heleni could not bring Émile de Chambonac's child into the world. The dishonor to their family, to the entire Georgillas clan, would be irreparable. Anica's betrothal would likely be revoked, and Heleni would molder in a convent for the rest of her life. Papa's commissions would dry up, never to return.

And the shame. The shame.

Mamá sat still, her eyes closed and her mouth moving in prayer. Anica tried to follow suit, but her prayers were so vengeful that she instead tried to empty her mind of all thoughts. This, too, failed.

Finally, the doctor entered the chamber with a welcoming smile. Her expression grew sober as Mamá quickly explained what they were after, being intentionally vague about who the treatment was for.

"How far along is this young woman?" the doctor asked.

"Too soon to show," Anica said.

"I can give you something, but it does not always work," Signorina Giovanna cautioned them. "There is no guarantee."

"Can you give me two doses, then?" Mamá asked. "If it doesn't work the first time, we can try again."

The woman frowned. "I am under oath not to harm anyone. I cannot break that oath by letting you administer the remedy as you see fit. You may have one dose. Bring her to me if the treatment doesn't work. She'll no doubt need medical attention."

Mamá's mouth tightened. "Why should I pay you for something that might not succeed—and could even hurt her?"

"Mamá," Anica murmured. "Please."

When Mamá gave a curt nod signaling her acquiescence, Signorina Giovanna disappeared through a doorway and came back a few moments later with a tiny ceramic bottle in her hand. After she named her price, Mamá thrust out a few coins and took the bottle from the doctor, studying it with a worried expression.

"Thank you," Anica said when it became clear her mother was too preoccupied to speak.

"I wish the young woman good health," the doctor replied, sympathy in her warm brown eyes. "And remember—return to me if the remedy does not work."

Neither Anica nor Mamá had the heart to face Heleni with their purchase for most of the day. She had refused to eat the midday meal and returned to bed shortly after noon. Anica understood now why Heleni had been so fatigued lately, why she had so often complained of feeling unwell. The life growing within her had sapped her of energy.

"I'm going to wake your sister. I'll give her the remedy without telling her what it's for," Mamá said that afternoon, approaching Anica in the studio with a determined expression. "We've got to put this behind us before your father returns."

"Let me talk to her first," Anica said, rising.

"Don't upset her," Mamá warned.

When Anica entered their bedchamber, she expected to see her sister fast asleep. Instead, Heleni sat propped against the pillows, the shutters flung open to the light. Her devastated expression and red, swollen eyes made Anica falter.

"What is it?" She sat on the edge of the bed and took her sister's hand.

"The soap man came while you were out this morning." Heleni's voice was dull and flat.

With all the chaos, Anica had forgotten what day it was. She nodded. "Soap day was just Tuesday to you all of your life. Until it suddenly became important. I should have paid more attention."

Heleni's lips trembled. "I was wicked to Maria," she whispered. "I said cruel, cruel things. I even beat her. And it was for nothing, in the end." With a shaking hand, she pulled a tiny scroll of linen paper from her bodice. "In my last note, I told him I'm carrying his child. But he doesn't care. He doesn't even love me anymore."

"Let me see that." Anica held out her hand.

Heleni clutched the scrap of paper tighter. "No," she whispered. "It's too shameful."

Anica pulled her sister into her arms. "Another man must have read your note and inked those words, Heleni. Émile de Chambonac is not in Rhodes Town, I told you. He's across the sea on a voyage."

"This note is written in his hand. I'm sure of it!" Heleni protested.

Anica grappled with her own exhaustion, struggling for patience.

"He cannot escape his fate. He broke his vow to the Order by taking advantage of you."

Heleni absorbed the words in silence, her gaze falling to the paper in her hand.

"That man cannot and will not marry you, Heleni." Anica's voice grew rough. "He'll be punished for what he's done, I promise you."

Her sister looked doubtful. "How?"

"He'll be flogged. Or banished. I've heard of knights receiving harsh punishments for ravishing local girls."

"Émile didn't ravish me!" Heleni protested. "I felt only pleasure in his arms."

"You were tricked by a powerful man into giving up your honor. He must answer for that."

As she spoke, a current of foreboding flickered through her veins. Her uncertainty must have been apparent because Heleni's face crumpled.

"But if he's banished, I'm ruined."

Anica shook her head. "There are potions that can end a life in the womb. We've got the remedy. I can fetch it for you now."

A gleam of hope entered her sister's eyes. Then her gaze fell to the note again, her expression uncertain. "Not now. I'll drink the stuff tomorrow."

She crumpled the scrap of paper and threw it in the remnants of a cup of watered wine standing on her bedside table. Curling into a ball, she screwed her eyes shut and turned away. Anica snatched up the cup, fishing the note from it as she exited the bedchamber. Stains obscured most of the words beyond recognition.

Longing for an escape from her sister's predicament, she retreated to the studio and spent several hours painting and repainting the same details of Santa Caterina's gown. Eventually, she gave up and cleaned her brushes. During a quick supper with Mamá, they both ate in glum silence. Later that evening, by the light of a single candle, Anica undressed and crawled into bed with her sister.

Just before dawn, she was awakened by Heleni, who climbed out of bed to use the chamber pot. When she slid back under the bedcovers, Anica fell asleep within minutes, only to be awakened again by moans.

"What is it?" Anica asked her sister, sitting up.

"My stomach hurts," Heleni gasped. "It feels as if my belly is being stabbed with shards of glass."

In the weak dawn light, Anica went to her parents' bedchamber and quietly roused her mother, then hurried to the kitchen to fetch watered wine and an oil lamp. When she returned to her chamber, she found her mother at Heleni's side.

"The sheets under her are soaked with sweat," Mamá said.

Anica set the lamp down on the small table next to the bed. Turning down the bedcovers, Mamá gasped. All the air escaped Anica's lungs when she saw the linens were stained with blood, not sweat.

"Saints preserve us." Mamá turned to Anica, a look of accusation in her eyes. "You gave her that potion?"

"No. She was to take it today."

"My stomach pains me so," Heleni said. "I'm so tired. He said it would not hurt. Another lie, I suppose."

"Who said that?" Mamá asked sharply.

"There was an elixir with the note." She threw an apologetic glance at Anica, then recoiled in shock and let out a cry. "You've come to ease my passage from this world, haven't you?"

Anica exchanged a worried glance with Mamá.

"You're not my sister, but an angel sent by God," Heleni said, staring at Anica in wonderment.

"I'm no angel," Anica said with vehemence. "I'm made of flesh, blood, and bone, just as you are. What elixir do you speak of? You took some poison sent to you along with that note?"

"He said it would make my troubles go away." Heleni's voice weakened.

"But who sent it, Heleni?" Anica demanded.

"My love sent it to me."

"It could not have been Émile de Chambonac. I told you!"

"He said it was the most expensive, the safest elixir one could procure to end a life," Heleni said faintly.

"To end whose life?" Anica asked, her body seizing with panic. "The baby's or yours?"

"It's better this way," Heleni murmured. "The truth would have come out. Now our family's honor is safe. I'll tell all the other angels that, too."

Anica lowered her head to Heleni's chest, expecting to hear it fluttering like a butterfly's wing. But her sister's heartbeat was steady, even slow.

"You will not die this day," she vowed. "I won't allow it."

Springing up, she went to the chest where Heleni kept her most treasured things and flung open the lid. A quick inspection proved fruitless.

"Where do you keep his notes?" she asked over her shoulder.

Heleni said nothing, but her eyes betrayed her. Anica followed her sister's gaze to her own chest of belongings. A small gap between the bottom of the chest and the wooden floor led her to a velvet sack containing a pile of handwritten notes and a bottle made of Venetian glass. Anica stuffed the notes into the leather pouch she carried at her waist, then raised the bottle high.

"This is the bottle he sent?" she asked her sister.

"Yes." Heleni's skin was ashy, drained of color. She was fading away moment by moment.

Mamá crumpled to her knees. "My precious girl. God, spare my child." She gathered Heleni in her arms, tears coursing down her cheeks.

Anica wheeled and made for the door.

"Wait!" Mamá said in a terrible voice. "What do you think you're doing?"

Anica did not turn around. "I'm fetching Dr. Giovanna before it's too late."

CHAPTER 36

Winter, 1460
Rhodes Town

Anica roused Maria and fetched a torch from the kitchen. In silence, they exited the house and raced through the streets to Signorina Giovanna's residence. Anica pounded on the door with her fist until a bleary-eyed servant answered. Instructing Maria to wait downstairs, she climbed the stairs to the doctor's apartments, gasping for breath.

When Signorina Giovanna opened the door, Anica spoke quickly. "My sister bleeds and complains of stomach pain and weakness. I think she's close to death."

The doctor snatched up her cloak. "Did she take the potion?"

"Not yours. Someone else gave her a potion. I'm not sure when she drank it. But I believe it was meant to kill her." Anica held up the glass bottle. A trace of liquid was still visible within it.

Doctor Giovanna hesitated, her eyes gleaming in the torchlight. She took the bottle from Anica, uncorked it, and held it beneath her nose.

"Is your sister able to speak?"

"Yes, but she's not making sense. She told me I was an angel sent from God."

The doctor went to a cabinet and removed a leather satchel. "We don't have much time." She hastened to the door.

Back at the Foscolo home, they burst into the bedchamber, where Mamá was kneeling in prayer at Heleni's side. Doctor Giovanna went to Heleni and pressed her ear against Heleni's chest. Then she examined the sheets beneath her. "She's bleeding, but not heavily. The life in her womb has ended." Taking Heleni's hand, she asked, "Your stomach pains you?"

Heleni did not open her eyes. "Yes," she whispered.

"And you feel tired, weak?"

"Yes."

Heleni's eyes fluttered open. When she caught sight of the doctor, she gasped in alarm. "Another angel. But this time, the angel of death . . ."

"It's what I thought," the doctor said. "Oleander poison. It slows the heart and blurs the vision. She sees auras around us, like the halos of angels." She removed a pouch from her satchel. After pouring watered wine into a ceramic cup on the bedside table, she added a measure of black powder and stirred it with a silver spoon.

"What is that?" Mamá asked suspiciously, pointing at the cup in the doctor's hands.

"A special kind of charcoal, the only remedy for what ails your daughter. Do you have any idea when she took the poison?"

Anica thought back through the night's events. "When you got up to use the chamber pot, did you drink this potion?" she asked Heleni.

Her sister nodded.

"Just before dawn," Anica told the doctor.

"We may be able to save her, then. Help me prop her up." The doctor held the cup of black liquid to Heleni's lips. "Drink this, and you may live."

Heleni turned her head away.

Anica put a supporting hand behind her sister's back. "Drink it now," she said fiercely. "If not for your own sake, then for our parents."

Reluctantly, Heleni opened her mouth and began to swallow.

By early afternoon, Heleni's moans had become less frequent and she fell into a deep sleep. The doctor gathered her things.

"I must attend a birth. The mother was poorly yesterday, and her pains had just begun."

"But Heleni needs you!" Mamá protested, rising to her feet.

"She will continue to bleed for some time, but that is not what threatens her life. I believe the charcoal stopped the poison from killing your daughter, though I cannot promise anything. Within a few days, she should begin to regain her strength and her appetite. If she does not, come to me again."

Mamá resumed her position kneeling at Heleni's side. Anica accompanied the doctor from the room. In the entry hall, she dug into her purse for gold ducats. "How much do we owe you?"

The doctor shook her head. "Nothing. Your Aunt Rhea has been extraordinarily generous to me. She's told me often how close you are. This is a small way I can repay her kindness." She leaned closer. "You should know that the only apothecary who uses Venetian glass for his concoctions is employed by the Order."

Anica regarded her without speaking for a moment. "Someone from the Order sent the poison," she finally said. "There's little chance he will be punished for it, but I will try to seek justice anyway."

"Be careful," the doctor replied. "A woman's words are not worth much and are all too easily turned against us."

Anica lifted her chin. "I cannot stay silent. My conscience won't allow it."

"God protect you, then."

The doctor had no sooner left than Anica put on her own cloak. As she prepared to go out, she felt the prick of someone's gaze. Maria stepped out from the shadows. Her expression was one of despair and trepidation.

"Can I come with you?" she asked.

"No. This is something I must do alone."

Maria's lips trembled. "It's my fault. She beat me and told me I'd be cast out, that I'd lose my chance at freedom if I gave away her secret . . ."

Anica gripped Maria by the shoulder. "We'll speak about this later. Stay here and watch over my family, as you've done faithfully since you came to us."

Maria nodded, the torment in her eyes diminishing a little. "But where are you going?"

"To the palace." Anica squared her shoulders and turned for the door. "I will put this matter at the feet of the grand master himself."

CHAPTER 37

Winter, 1460
Rhodes Town

ANICA'S MOUTH was dry as she climbed the Street of the Knights. She saw no beauty in the graceful stone structures, paid no heed to the chatter of passing knights, monks, and merchants. She covered the ground in rapid strides, fists clenched, consumed by the darkness in her heart.

In his notes, Émile de Chambonac had indeed promised Heleni marriage, jewels, a fine home, noble status. His words were nothing more than a collection of astonishing lies.

Would those scraps of linen paper in her purse do any good? The knight was family to Lord de Milly and an accomplished liar. He would likely tell the grand master Heleni had written the notes herself, was pregnant by another man, anything to extricate himself from the situation.

She stood before the palace gates, shifting her weight from one foot to the other, her mind roiling with terrible thoughts.

A group of Italian knights emerged from the palace gates with several men in Latin dress. She averted her gaze, tugged her headpiece lower on her forehead. It was not seemly to be standing here without a servant or a slave. But she dared not move. She would wait all day if need be.

Please, she prayed, *let the grand master be merciful and just.*

She concentrated on steadying her breath. When the guard approached, she told him she carried a private message from her father to the grand master and was ushered through the heavy doors.

For a moment, she was sure she would faint, standing at the threshold of the receiving hall. Then she closed her eyes and conjured up her sister's listless form under the coverlet, the scarlet blood staining the sheets. For Heleni's sake, she had to find courage.

Finally, she was allowed forward. Sitting in his heavy oak chair on the dais, the grand master studied her with an expression of faint surprise.

Anica was sure her red-rimmed, swollen eyes did not lend her an air of credibility, but that could not be helped.

"Yes, signorina?" Lord de Milly asked in Italian. "What is your father's message?"

She replied in French. "*Seigneur*, I beg you, may we speak in private?"

He signaled to his assistant, who retreated.

"Proceed," he told her.

"Grand Master," she began, fighting the tremor in her voice, "one of your knights has done a great evil to my sister."

"Go on," he said in a low voice.

"Émile de Chambonac got her with child. When she told him this, he or one of his men sent poison to my sister, claiming it would end the life in her womb." Anica's mouth had never been so dry. "It did as he promised—and worse. She is near death. It was meant to kill her."

"Your claim is quite damning," he said. "We don't involve ourselves in the citizens' private dramas, as a rule."

"This is no private drama," she retorted. "It involves one of your knights—your kinsman."

"I heard your accusation." His voice was cold, his dark eyes unreadable.

"What will you do to punish him for his crime?" Anica asked, her voice rising in anguish.

The grand master's expression tightened. "This is no matter for a woman to broach. Your father should be here in your place. In fact, you claimed to carry a message from him. But I see it was just a ruse to get inside the palace."

"My father is across the sea. He knows nothing of this. But in his stead, I act for our family. And my sister needs justice *now*." She clenched her trembling hands. "If she does not get it, the entire island will know Émile de Chambonac is not a man of honor, my lord."

The grand master's expression turned stony. "Why should I believe you?"

She put a hand on the leather purse at her waist. "I have evidence. Notes he wrote her, full of lies about the noble life she would lead as his wife."

Lord de Milly recoiled. He thrust out a hand. "Show me."

With trembling fingers, she retrieved the note Heleni had cast into her cup of wine. "This one came with the poison." She unfurled it and held it aloft. "It is written in the same hand as the others."

The grand master took the stained note from her, examining it with narrowed eyes. "When did it arrive?"

"Tuesday."

"Émile de Chambonac was at sea that day. This note could not have been penned by him. Besides, it's barely legible."

"Whether a servant of his was responsible, or perhaps another knight, is not the point," she said with rising desperation. "Someone within the Order wanted my sister dead, and they wanted her to believe Émile de Chambonac wrote this note and sent the potion himself."

The grand master's scowl deepened.

"There are more notes." Anica fumbled in the purse, drew out three slips of paper, and handed them to him.

In his large hand, the bits of linen paper looked pathetically small.

"Are these all of them, then?" he asked.

"Some are hidden away." Anica struggled to fill her lungs with air. "If the Order does nothing regarding this matter, I will share the others with my Greek family."

"What do you mean by that?" he demanded.

She drew herself up, taut as a bowstring. "My mother is a Georgillas. We have long been allies and loyal servants to the knights. My Georgillas relatives will not take this lightly. It will test their allegiance to the Order, I promise you."

His expression hardened. "You are threatening the Knights Hospitaller? Is that what I hear?"

Her knees nearly gave way. "You've always been just in your dealings with the people, my lord. My sister deserves your justice, too."

"I could have you flogged for this," he growled. "Or worse. Take your leave, signorina."

She stood her ground, staring into his eyes.

"Your time here has ended." His hand tightened around the notes into a fist. "Good day."

Anica did not know how she got from the receiving room to the palace doors. The mad tangle of emotions clouding her mind drove all rational thought away. She stumbled down the palace steps and out the gates, straight into the path of Drummond Fordun.

"Signorina Anica!" His face lit up with a surprised smile. "You're a welcome sight . . ." He broke off, studying her face with alarm.

She stared at him with shock. "You've returned. How is my father? Did he get safely to Damascus?"

"I got him as far as Alexandria and made sure he boarded a trusted merchant's ship bound for Damascus. I've been occupied with work since we returned, but I was on my way to your home now to tell you."

"And Émile de Chambonac?" she demanded. "Did he return as well?"

Drummond looked startled at her vehement tone. "Yes."

"When did you arrive?"

"Tuesday, at dawn."

Anica stiffened at his words, her mind sifting through the sequence of events these past few days.

So Émile de Chambonac must have written that note and sent that poison, after all.

He stepped closer. His towering presence was like a bulwark against the Order. She covered her face with her hands, warding off tears.

"What's happened?" he asked with concern.

"Drummond." She looked up, met his gaze.

His expression softened and his eyes glowed when she said his name aloud.

But before he could speak, she said, "My sister is near death."

The awful words drifted from her mouth like ghostly birds, congregating in the space between them.

"Has she been struck by an illness?"

"Yes, an illness that came on in the night."

"What can I do?" he asked. "Surely, there's something."

She glanced back at the palace doors. "The grand master is the only person who can help us now."

He burned with questions, she could see, but he kept silent, acknowledging her words with a slight tilt of his head.

"I must get home," she said. "It was unwise of me to come here on my own."

The city noises fell away as she held his gaze. Her throat ached with the urge to weep.

"Let me at least accompany you," he said. "You should not walk these streets alone."

They walked in silence to her family's home. The stares they received should have filled her with uneasiness, but today she did not care. At the door, he reached for her hand. She let him take it.

"I'll help you, help your family," he said. "Lord de Milly favors me. Perhaps there's something I can do."

"I may have made an enemy of him today," she said bleakly. "You would be wise to avoid us."

Drummond shook his head. "No. I'll not do that. You have my word."

"Why make such a promise?" she challenged him. "You owe us no kindness."

He stared back at her without answering for a moment.

"Because I've met no woman like you before," he admitted. "The truth is, Anica, since Archangelos, you've occupied my mind day and night. Your smile lights up the world—some days it's all I think about."

Anica looked at him in astonishment. The longing in his eyes tore at her. She wanted to hurtle into his arms, propriety be damned. To shut out the pain, to smother her terrors in the warmth and safety of his embrace.

"I can't bear to see you weighed down by sorrow," he went on. "I would do anything to ease your worries."

She edged closer to him, memorizing the pattern of light and dark in his gray-green eyes, longing to fit her lips to his. His warm hand cradling her own ignited a flame of desire that made her feel reckless.

How she ached to spill out her own truth: that he inhabited her thoughts without end, that his face, not her betrothed's, featured in her daydreams. If she had any power over her own fate, she would choose a life with Drummond Fordun at her side.

She took in a shaky breath, battling a powerful desire to tell him everything in her heart. The words crowded against her lips, desperate to be free. Anica opened her mouth a fraction, then closed it again.

No.

Honesty would just cause more pain. Her fate was set. She would wed Signor Lomellini. Desire for another man meant nothing in the end. It would only bring shame to her family, and she would never inflict more hurt on Mamá and Papa, especially now.

Her place was inside, with Mamá, facing the horror of Heleni's predicament. Not out here with this foreigner, this agent of the knights.

Her whole body trembling, she tried to keep her voice steady. "Drummond, I wish—I want—"

She broke off, choking back a sob.

What she wished for, what she wanted . . . Those things would never come to pass.

Stepping back, she tore her hand from his. "I'm betrothed," she said in despair. "I shall marry in the spring."

He took in her statement with a look of slowly dawning disappointment. The hope fading from his face made her heart twist.

"To what man?" he asked.

Tears burned her eyes. "A Genoese merchant."

I had no choice. I hardly know the man.

"I see. Forgive me." A note of formality crept into his voice. "I spoke hastily, and I regret it. I'm in Rhodes Town for another week. If I can be of service to you—" he paused, "—to your family, ask for me again at the Inn of England."

Without another word, he turned on his heel and strode away.

Anica climbed the steps to her home on unsteady legs. When the door thudded shut behind her, it echoed like a hammer blow in her ears.

She crumpled to the floor and buried her face in her skirts, trying to muffle the sound of her sobs. Sorrow tore her throat, clamped a vise around her chest, blinded her with bitter tears. The darkness in her mind stripped her of the will to move. She had no idea how long she'd been curled on the cool tile floor when Maria's light touch on her arm roused her.

"Come." Maria gently helped her up. "I'll help you wash your face and change. You'll feel a bit better then."

Supported by Maria's arm around her waist, Anica took a hesitant step forward.

CHAPTER 38

Winter, 1460
Rhodes Town

Two days later, Anica was summoned to the palace. She followed a page up the Street of the Knights, feeling as if her shoes were full of lead. Every whisper, every voice lowered in quiet conversation when she passed others in the street made her flinch. She clenched her jaw, kept her gaze forward. Over and over, she reassured herself with the truth: No one in these streets knew what had transpired in her home. No one knew the real reason Heleni had nearly died.

Her sister was wan and spent, but she still breathed. This morning, Mamá had coaxed a small amount of rice and yogurt sweetened with honey down her throat. Heleni's tongue was black from the charcoal powder she had ingested, but Signorina Giovanna assured them it was nothing to worry about. When Anica left, her mother was asleep next to Heleni, one arm draped protectively around her daughter.

Anica waited in the grand master's antechamber, her muscles taut with anticipation. Voices in the corridor droned in her ears. The sunlight reflecting off the marble floor from the windows in the reception room made her eyes ache. When a pair of guards came to fetch her, instead of going into the formal reception hall, they led her down a side corridor.

A movement ahead startled her. At the end of the corridor, she saw the cloaked figures of two women, their elaborate head wraps marking them as Latins. What were women—who were not nuns, judging by their garb—doing in this palace full of men? Did the grand master bring courtesans into his apartments? Were they artisans of some kind, here to work on tapestries, perhaps? But the figures vanished around a corner, and she forgot them as she was led through a door set into a wood-paneled wall.

Anica's eyes adjusted to the light of dozens of beeswax candles burning in the chamber she'd entered, all thoughts of the women forgotten. A fire crackled in the stone hearth. The grand master sat in a chair by a window, a gleaming oak table at his side. Just beyond him, a falcon balanced on a carved wooden perch, its head covered with a bejeweled hood. Lord de Milly waved her into a matching chair. A servant delivered a small carafe of wine and two silver cups, poured them each a measure, then left.

She took a cautious look around. The entourage that usually surrounded the grand master had vanished. Warily, she glanced at her host.

"Please, drink." Lord de Milly's tone was cool but polite.

Anica picked up the cup nearest her and held it to her lips. Like everything had since Heleni's predicament unfolded, it tasted of nothing at all.

She placed the cup back on the table. Surely, this offering of wine meant he was going to treat her with mercy.

The grand master took a sip from his own cup and stared into her eyes. "Your boldness is intolerable."

An icy terror flooded her. "My family's honor—"

He silenced her with a quick slashing gesture. "You accused one of my knights of poisoning your sister. I looked into the matter and uncovered a different story. My agents found that you and your mother had purchased a potion laced with poison from the Italian woman doctor not long before this incident."

Anica's mouth fell open, but nothing emerged.

"Is this true?" the grand master asked.

"We purchased a potion meant to end life in the womb, but we did not give it to Heleni. I swear it. It's still in my mother's possession. I can show you, if you wish. Heleni took a different potion sent to her by the knight. That's what nearly killed her. It came in a Venetian glass bottle, which only the apothecary to the knights is known to use. It contained a poison made from the oleander plant."

She rummaged in the purse at her waist for the bottle and drew it out. Lord de Milly gave it a cursory glance, his face contorted in a deep frown.

"Do you take me for a fool?" he demanded. "Do you truly expect me to believe the stories of a half-Latin girl?"

"What does your knight say?" Anica replied. "Does he deny he sent her those notes? Or the poison?"

"He would never admit to such an act. Nor would I accuse him of it. Not a man in his position."

"What do you mean?"

"His father is one of the Order's most generous donors—and my cousin."

Anica felt as if she were suffocating. "So you will not punish him, you mean to say."

Now the grand master was silent. His features hardened into something close to a snarl. "You threatened to spread accusations about a knight across the island, inciting the Greeks to rise up against the Order. I cannot abide such a possibility. Not now, when the citizens must be aligned, ready to react together to an attack by the infidels or any of our other enemies." He put down his cup. "By rights, I should have you flogged within view of the entire population."

To her shame, Anica's eyes filled with tears. An image rose in her mind of the whipping post by the Kastellania. Would she be lashed to it, her flesh laid bare for all to see, and set upon with the gaoler's whip?

"But as you pointed out, the Georgillas family is quite influential on Rhodes," he went on in a more measured tone. "I can't risk inciting malice toward the knights among the Greeks. We are at a crucial juncture, Signorina Foscolo. Unity has never been more important on this island. A Greek uprising at this moment would be catastrophic."

Anica's pounding heart eased a fraction. She held her breath, praying he would be merciful.

"Therefore you will be punished by banishment from Rhodes Town. You must leave before the week is out."

She stared at him in mute horror. "But where will I go?" she managed to croak. "What will my family do without me?"

"It is a just punishment," the grand master said crisply. "But remember this: if you or your family spread rumors staining the reputation of our knights, you will not like the consequences. You risk your father's honor, his livelihood, his very future, signorina."

Anica numbly took in his words. As much as she wanted to defy him, her desire to protect Papa won out. She pressed her lips together, forcing back her protests.

"Good girl. As long as you keep quiet, the reason for your banishment—and your sister's shame—will be our secret."

Anica summoned every shred of courage remaining to her. "Please —my father needs me in his studio. His business will fail without me here. I beg you, let me stay until he returns to Rhodes Town."

"You shall have to find another helper. If your father failed to make arrangements for another artist to do his work during his absence, that is not my concern." Lord de Milly pointed at the door. "Now go."

She stood and turned slowly on her heel, praying for the strength to walk without staggering.

The grand master's deep voice followed her to the door. "If you don't obey me, I'll know," he warned. "My agents will watch your movements until you leave this city."

Anica stumbled, flinging an arm out to steady herself in the doorway.

You will not fall, she ordered herself. *You will not show your fear.*

Her heart flailing wildly against her ribs, she found the strength to walk out of his sight with dignity.

CHAPTER 39

Winter, 1460
Rhodes Town

On Sunday, Drummond awoke with a throbbing head. He washed and dressed with barely enough time to make it to mass at the Church of St. John. After securing a seat in the last row of pews, he screwed his eyes shut and clenched his jaw to ward off the bitterness rising in his throat. All the fantasies he'd been weaving about a shared life with Anica Foscolo had shattered like glass the moment she'd told him of her betrothal. Ever since she'd uttered the words, he'd tried—and failed—to obliterate his dark feelings with wine.

And now, before a priest, before all the saints, before God, he would sit here among the Knights Hospitaller with a horrendously pounding head and suffer the consequences.

It wasn't as if you ever had a possibility of a future with the woman.

He stifled a groan, thinking of Anica's liquid brown eyes. Her smile, so full of light and promise, haunted him. She felt something for him, he was certain of it. But he knew how these marriages worked. Her family had likely arranged the betrothal without her knowledge. She'd be lucky if she felt any affection at all for the Genoese merchant. A shudder of jealousy rippled down his spine. Did the fellow have any idea how fortunate he was? Who exactly was the merchant, anyway?

Drummond shook off the thoughts. Learning more about Anica's future with another man would only bring him more pain. His eyes dropped to the stone floor. When knights died, they were entombed beneath these floors. He shifted on the hard wooden pew, imagining the bones of those men crumbling into dust below his feet.

Pray for their souls, he told himself. Then Anica's smile flickered back into his mind. He squeezed his eyes shut, forcing her image away.

He would do well to visit his favorite courtesan tonight and put all thoughts of Anica Foscolo to rest. It would be best to lose himself in another woman's arms for at least a few hours. He'd made a habit of it all these years, and the pleasure he'd gotten from those interludes had kept him from going mad at times. He'd had his favorites over the years, some here in Rhodes Town, others in Alexandria and other ports. Since Archangelos, though, only one woman occupied his thoughts. If he sought pleasure elsewhere, he knew he'd be thinking of Anica and no one else. It was a fool's game he played. She was not his woman—and never would be.

Better to fixate on the good news in his brother's letter. He'd soon be setting his plan into motion, sailing back to the West. He'd rent chambers in Amsterdam and hunt for the right property. Once installed in that city, he'd have a quick sail to Scotland whenever he pleased and a steady income from his importing business to share with his family. It was the plan he'd been dreaming of for years. Now it was finally within reach. If only he could summon feelings of joy.

To his surprise, he realized the mass had ended. He'd not heard a word of it. Blearily, he watched the grand master and various high-ranking members of the Order move down the aisle toward the doors.

Once all the knights exited the church, Drummond rose and followed them. Outside, men milled about in the crisp air discussing the week's events, news from across the sea, plans for supper.

He saw Émile de Chambonac deep in conversation with a small

knot of companions. Flagging him down with a wave, Drummond plastered a smile on his face.

"The Scotsman approaches," de Chambonac said coolly.

"Good day, messieurs." Drummond put a hand to his chest and bowed.

One of the other men smiled. "Master Fordun, we don't often have the pleasure of your company at St. John's."

Drummond inclined his head. "We're lucky to have many fine churches in Rhodes Town."

The truth was he leap-frogged from one Latin church to the next each time he was in the city. He had no interest in the gossip that went on after mass, and this way no group of worshippers ever expected his presence during their after-service social hours. Although ever since he'd learned Anica Foscolo frequented the Church of Santa Maria, he wished he could break his own rule and become a fixture there.

He turned back to Émile de Chambonac.

"I'm afraid I was in my cups the other night," he said, striking a conciliatory tone. "I don't quite recall all that was said, but I believe I refused an invitation. I regret having done so. It was a generous offer you made, and I imagine your home is a fine place for entertainment."

De Chambonac's face softened. "Wine can lead us down some dark roads indeed," he replied. "The invitation still holds. Next time I have a gathering, you'll be the first to know."

There was a tap at Drummond's shoulder. He turned, squinting against the bright sunlight, to see Guillaume Lopic's unsmiling face.

"Please follow me," the man said. "Lord de Milly wants a word with you."

"Of course." Drummond squared his shoulders. The grand master stood near the church doors with several knights and the priest who had led the mass. He broke off when Drummond and Lopic approached and stepped away from the group.

"Master Drummond," he said.

"Lord de Milly."

Signaling to someone, Lopic made his excuses and sidled away.

The grand master tilted his head to one side, gave Drummond a long, assessing stare. "What brings you to St. John's?"

"I've neglected the opportunity to attend mass here too long, my lord. I'd like to make up for that before I leave on my next voyage."

Drummond thought of the letter folded in his purse. He straightened his spine.

Just get it over with, man.

"Lord de Milly, I've a personal matter to discuss with you. Now might not be the best time. But I thought it was wise to broach the topic as soon as possible."

"What is it?"

"I've received word from Scotland that my family needs me." The slight evasion of truth felt safer than explaining the long story behind his absence from home. "With your permission, I wish to leave service for the Order when my contract comes up for renewal in the spring."

Astonishment gripped the grand master's face. It was quickly followed by a look of cool displeasure. "This comes at a very bad time indeed."

Drummond dipped his head. "It was a surprise to me as well, my lord."

"We need you here at least until summer is over." Lord de Milly drew his shoulders back. "In a month, I will be mounting a longer mission to the East, a diplomatic effort."

"Does this involve the Mamluks, too?" Drummond asked.

"No, the Ottomans. Their sultan demanded a tribute payment of us several years ago. At the pope's order, I refused to pay it. The only reason the sultan hasn't mounted a siege against us since then is because of his attack against Belgrade. But now that diversion is over, and his eye will soon be fixed upon us again. We may have a chance to resolve the tribute issue through different channels, though. My man Lopic and some of our trusted Greek agents will be in the contingent. But none of the ships can be owned by the Order. They'll all be captained by privateers such as yourself. I intend you to lead the fleet to our fort at Bodrum in Turkey, and I want Émile to be on your galley."

"Consider it done," Drummond promised him. "I'll look after the young knight as if he were my own kinsman. When we return from the mission, I'll make my arrangements to leave for the West."

The grand master gave him a clipped nod. "You will be sorely missed."

Before his employer could turn away, Drummond cleared his throat. "Lord de Milly, about those Venetian ships—"

"They've sailed." The grand master's eyebrows drew together in a frown.

"With all respect, Lord de Milly, as soon as the Venetian Council hears of this, we'll have trouble on our hands."

"The Order was within its rights to seize the goods and passengers. We respected the freedom of their flag and allowed the crew to withdraw unharmed and return to Venice. Now if you'll excuse me, Master Fordun, I've more business to attend to."

Drummond's head throbbed anew. He wove through the men, dread churning in his gut.

His mind spooled out a month, imagining the day when he would prepare his galley and shepherd important men across the sea into enemy territory, then try to bring them back alive—all while keeping that blue-eyed knight from harm's way. If the Venetians attacked Rhodes, would it be before then or after he was halfway across the sea? The knights could take care of themselves, but what of the townsfolk? What of Anica Foscolo?

He touched a hand to the amulet under his shirt. Even if he could not always be by Anica's side, his patron saint could.

Santa Maria, he prayed, *protect her.*

CHAPTER 40

Winter, 1460
Rhodes Town

CHURCHES all over Rhodes Town chimed nine bells as Anica thanked
the messenger and closed the door, then went to the window and
broke the seal. This was the third letter she'd received from Marino
Lomellini since his departure for Genoa. Holding it up to get a better
view of his neat black script, she felt a tide of anger rush through her
veins. The final lines pounded in her head over and over again.

Heed my words, Marino had written. *Never speak to that privateer in
public again, nor to any other agent of the knights. They are dangerous men
with shifting loyalties and disreputable pasts. As my future wife, your duty is to
protect your reputation and, above all, my honor. If you do not obey me in this, I
will hear of it.*

The Genoese notary who worked for Signor Lomellini had seen her
in company with Drummond Fordun. She remembered the Latin men
staring at them when they spoke outside the door of the Syrian

doctor's home. One of them had looked familiar, and now she knew why.

The scrape of hooves against stone made her flinch. The mule cart was here to take her to Lindos, though earlier than arranged. It had been decided that she would stay with Uncle Valossi for the time being. Eventually, the grand master might relent and allow her to return to Rhodes Town. Lindos was close enough that she could still bring in some income by painting icons of saints and selling them to patrons in Rhodes Town using Aunt Rhea's network of connections.

When a rap came at the front door, she opened it, expecting the mule driver. But it was Signorina Giovanna, the Italian doctor.

"Good morning," Anica said in surprise. "I did not expect to see you today. Did my mother call for you?"

"No," the doctor admitted. "How is your sister?"

"Better, praise the saints. But still quite weak."

Heleni had so little energy she rarely ventured far from their bed, but she was eating small meals and spent more hours awake than asleep now. It would be unbearable to leave if Heleni was still at death's door, but with the support of Aunt Rhea and other relatives, Anica felt her absence would be tolerable.

"I'm glad she's made some progress." The doctor's face was in shadow, her eyes hidden under the folds of a black woolen shawl. "The truth is, I came to speak with you, Signorina," she said softly, glancing around as if to be sure no one was nearby.

"Come in." Anica ushered her inside. "Let's go to the studio."

The doctor followed her down the corridor, her skirts whispering over the tile floor. Once inside the studio, she watched Anica shut the door behind them, then spoke.

"The Order sent agents to question me about the remedy I gave you for your sister."

"Forgive me. It was my fault," Anica admitted. "I went to the grand master to get justice for my sister, and I created more problems than I solved. It was an action born of anger, and I regret it dearly."

The doctor's gaze fell to the letter in Anica's hands. She narrowed her eyes, examining the broken seal that hung from a ribbon attached to the linen paper.

"I would have done the same in your shoes. But that's not why I've come. I learned from your mother that you are betrothed to wed Marino Lomellini."

Anica raised an eyebrow, caught off guard by the statement. "Yes. In the spring, we'll wed. When he returns from Genoa. Do you know him?"

"A little. I knew his wife better."

Anica regarded her in silence for a moment, taken aback. But it was not so great a surprise, considering that Signorina Giovanna had lived in Genoa for several years before coming to Rhodes.

The woman drew her shawl off her head. The pale winter sunlight illuminated her delicate features, exposing fine lines around her eyes.

"I attended her in childbirth twice when I lived in Genoa. I served as physician for many of the wealthy merchant women there."

"Twice? I—I thought they had no children."

"They did not. Both times, the child did not survive. And the second time, the mother did not either."

"I see." Anica mulled over the doctor's words. "Why are you telling me this?"

The doctor hesitated, her expression growing troubled. "On several occasions, I witnessed the merchant's wife covered in bruises, Signorina Anica. She confided to me that her husband beat her often."

Anica recoiled in disbelief. "But he is a kind man, with an easy temperament," she protested.

"There are two sides to every man. His public face and his private one."

Anica's mind went to Aunt Rhea. Her husband had beaten her often, too. His abuse of her had only ceased when he fell ill. Aunt Rhea always laughed off the bruises, saying her hot temper had gotten her into trouble.

"Perhaps she had some grievance against him and incited him to use his fists against her." Even as she spoke, Anica felt hollow with dread.

"If I had only seen it once, I might agree," the doctor said. "But the evidence was on her body more than once. She had been beaten while she was carrying his child. It likely brought about the end of both pregnancies—and perhaps even her own death." She drew in a long breath. "I'm breaking my own vow by telling you this. What I encounter during my visits with patients is meant to be private."

"And yet you told agents of the Order what my mother and I had purchased from you," Anica pointed out, her tone growing cool. She folded the merchant's letter and pushed it into her purse.

"I told them because I was threatened with a blade."

Anica's muscles tensed. "I should have known the knights would resort to violence. Who questioned you?"

"I don't know the men. Two were guards and one was French, a small man clothed in silks and furs. It was he who brandished his dagger at me, even pressed it against my throat when I first refused to speak." The doctor gave a rueful half-smile. "The one who appeared to be a fine gentleman proved to be the opposite."

Anica sank down on a stool and buried her face in her hands. "I'm bound to marry Signor Lomellini whether he beats me or not." Her throat was so dry she feared she might choke on her own words. "We've a contract. I cannot break it without my father's aid. Papa's across the sea in Damascus, and I've no idea when he'll return to us. And even if we were to break it, there's another suitor waiting—a man I loathe. My father is indebted to his family."

"I have no counsel for you," the doctor said, kneeling at her side and taking her hands. "All I could do was tell you what I witnessed, prepare you for what might be in your future."

Anica raised her head. "Thank you," she whispered.

Voices called out from the corridor, searching for her.

"I must go." With the doctor's help, she stood, her knees trembling. "I leave for Lindos today."

"Why?"

"That is my punishment for trying to seek justice from the grand master. Heleni's predicament is the fault of the knights—one knight in particular. I had thought he would face consequences for his foul deeds. Instead, I'm banished from Rhodes Town on Lord de Milly's orders."

Signorina Giovanna's expression darkened. "The man who took

your sister's honor—and very nearly her life—won't be punished? How can this be?"

Anica let out a bitter laugh. "He is the son of Lord de Milly's cousin, from one of the richest families in Auvergne."

"Perhaps God will avenge your sister in time." The doctor regarded Anica with sympathy. "Your sister is in good hands. Your mother and aunt will look after her while you are away. I've done everything in my power to heal her. But there is another on the island who may help her make a faster recovery. Signor Syriano, the grand master's physician. The well of knowledge he possesses is far greater than mine. The only problem is he does not treat the townsfolks' ailments. He is bound to the knights."

"I know him." Movement outside the window caught Anica's eye. A blood-red dragonfly clung to the glossy leaf of a potted lemon tree in the courtyard, its wings pulsing. "But I dare not incite the wrath of the grand master again by asking Dr. Syriano for aid. The Order's spies are everywhere. No, I could not risk it."

Doctor Giovanna put a hand on Anica's arm. "Then I shall make it my habit to pass by here each day and look in on your sister until your return—or your father's."

CHAPTER 41

Winter, 1460
Lindos

DRUMMOND AWOKE to a pounding at his door. Groggily, he stumbled out of bed, pausing only to snatch up his dagger.

"Who's there?" His voice was rough with sleep and drink. Last night, he'd drained two more pitchers of wine. Now his tongue was like sandpaper in his mouth and his eyes burned. Not to mention his throbbing head. All of which was, of course, his own blasted fault.

"The grand master requires your presence at once."

Drummond opened the door a crack, confronting torchlight and the familiar faces of two guards who spent most of their time in the palace.

"What's afoot?" he asked warily. No alarm horns had blared, no trumpets signaling the approach of a Mamluk fleet or the Turkish navy.

"The Venetians," one of them said in response. "There's no time to waste. Hurry!"

Drummond groaned. "God's teeth. Give me a moment." He shut the door and fumbled through the dark chamber to the chest containing his clothes, then tripped and fell over his own boots. "Damn!"

"Do you need aid?" one of the guards asked through the door.

"By all that's holy, give me a moment, I said." Drummond's eyes ached as they adjusted to the weak dawn light filtering through the shutters. His gaze fell to his lap and the brown wool of his breeches. With a start, he recalled that he'd not bothered to undress last night. The wine had made him lazy.

He shoved his feet into his boots, strapped on his sword, and slipped his dagger into its sheath. Grabbing a short cloak from a peg on the wall, he flung the door open.

"Let's be off."

When he arrived in Lord de Milly's study a short time later, the chill dawn air had animated his brain a bit. A small group of knights and agents of the Order clustered around their leader, arguing in strident voices. Drummond hoped he'd not be called upon to offer an opinion.

He could barely string a sentence together after one pitcher of wine. And two—what an idiot he was. He'd been in his cups every night since Anica had told him she was betrothed to another man. This lovesickness was entirely foreign to him, and he hated it. Somehow he had to get that woman out of his head.

"Master Fordun." The grand master's deep voice rang out over the clamor. Everyone else fell silent, and all eyes swiveled to Drummond.

He stepped forward. "My lord."

"Our spies tell us the Venetians have dispatched their top admiral to Rhodes."

Drummond's heart sank. A series of inappropriate responses rose, then faded on his tongue. Saying *I told you so* would not endear him to anyone in the chamber, nor would it solve the problem at hand.

"I see," he muttered thickly.

"If he brings a fleet of warships, we must be ready. Some of my brethren wish to mount a counterattack at sea. Others counsel patience. Perhaps negotiations will suffice."

"What is your opinion, my lord?" Drummond asked.

"We do not have lives to spare. I would rather find a way to placate the Venetians without bloodshed."

Several of the men near him shifted on their feet and glowered at his words. He raised a hand, ran a stern gaze over the group.

"The Venetian fleet's leader is Admiral Loredan."

Drummond nodded, cursing his pounding head. The Loredans were a powerful clan of nobles who seemed to have a finger in every pie related to Venice. He'd heard of the admiral, though he'd not yet encountered the man at sea.

"You are acquainted with the Venetian painter Paolo Foscolo, yes?"

"I am." Drummond blinked, bewildered by the question.

"He once told me that his mother is a Loredan. He could be a valuable asset in the negotiations, but he's not in Rhodes. One of my agents has learned you're friendly with the man. Do you know where he is or when he will return?"

"He's in—" Drummond paused, not sure how much to share. "Alexandria. He had business there. He was on the fleet I led east earlier this winter."

The grand master's determined look faltered. "That is bad news indeed."

Guillaume Lopic stepped forward. "My lord, his daughter Anica might be useful in the negotiations."

Drummond shot him a look of fury. How dare Lopic draw Anica into a potentially violent conflict?

Lord de Milly's gaze hardened, too. "I'm loath to involve a person such as she."

"Such as she?" Drummond asked, his hackles rising. "She's got courage and a quick mind and speaks more languages than I do. Plus, she's got Loredan blood. Who else among us can say that?"

Lopic smirked. "Now we have no choice but to involve her, it seems."

Drummond forged ahead, cursing his impulsive outburst. "I can fetch her for you if you like, Lord de Milly. And offer her my protection in the absence of her father."

His voice was gaining strength now, the dullness in his brain clearing like sun burning through sea mist.

"She is not in Rhodes Town," the grand master said. "You'll need to journey to . . ." He leaned close to Lopic and asked a question, then nodded at the answer. "To Lindos. She is staying there with her uncle, a notary of the Georgillas family."

Drummond absorbed the news with a growing sense of uneasiness. Why would Lopic know of Anica's whereabouts? And why had the grand master spoken of her with a tone of such contempt?

"Shall I bring her back to Rhodes Town, then?" he asked his employer.

Lord de Milly hesitated. The rising tension in the air felt palpable to Drummond. A vise of worry tightened around his chest.

Finally, the grand master nodded. "You'd best leave now. The Venetians could appear anytime, and we want to be ready for them."

When Drummond sighted Lindos after a long day in the saddle, his head had ceased its throbbing. But his mouth still tasted bitter, and his stomach still roiled. Drink had been his solace ever since he left Scotland, to his detriment. Drink was also the reason for his occasion of deepest shame and regret—a betrayal at sea that he could blame on none but himself—and yet he still hadn't learned his lesson. In difficult times, he always reached for a pitcher of wine.

He brushed off the self-flagellating thoughts as his horse pounded along the muddy road. It had rained on and off for several days. The dark sky over the sea was ominous. He hoped a thunderstorm wouldn't delay their return to Rhodes Town. But perhaps a gale would cause difficulties for the Venetian fleet—at the very least slow them down.

The covered mule cart rattled along behind him. He had ordered the grand master's guards to stock the covered area in the rear with wool blankets and cushions to keep Anica comfortable on the return trip. He looked forward to their meeting, mostly so he could drink in the sight of her lovely face, hear the musical lilt of her warm voice, pray for a sighting of that magnificent smile. But he also burned with curiosity. Why had she gone to Lindos, especially with her father absent?

Slowing his horse to a trot, then a walk, Drummond approached the town with one eye on the sky. A hard rain began to fall. He was grateful. His headache dissipated further with each cold splatter of raindrops on his face. The town of Lindos was perched on a hillside, with a fortified castle overlooking the sea at its highest point. A sparkling little bay hugged the curve of the coastline below the town. On a sunny day, the sight was breathtaking. Today, the dark, swirling waters looked treacherous.

The horse's hooves clopped over stone as he made his way through the winding streets. That smug little rodent Guillaume Lopic had given him explicit directions to Valossi Georgillas's home, reeling off the exact location without referring to any man or document.

Most of the whitewashed homes in Lindos were shuttered against the driving rain. Still, he felt the burn of scrutiny as he ventured through the streets. He knew he was feared by the Greeks. A hulking foreigner, an agent of the knights, he could not move about the island without attracting attention. He didn't mind being held at arm's length by the people. It kept things simpler.

Listening for the creak of the mule cart's wheels behind him, Drummond dismounted at the door of the notary's home. Holding his horse's reins with one hand, he lifted the bronze knocker with the other. It was designed in the shape of a leaping dolphin, worn smooth by touch over the years. He stood unmoving for a moment, gathering his composure. Then he let the knocker fall.

The servant woman who opened the door regarded him with a look of sheer terror. Drummond tried to calm her by requesting an audience with Valossi Georgillas in his most polite Greek. She shook her head and called out to someone over her shoulder, her panicked words all but unintelligible to him.

Rapid footfalls preceded another figure, who took the servant's place at the door. Drummond opened his mouth to speak, then closed it again when he recognized the woman before him.

"Drummond?" Anica said in amazement. "How did you find me here?"

He swallowed. Had he detected a note of eagerness in her voice? Was she happy to see him? She was not smiling. But the light in her eyes was undeniable.

"Anica." His voice was gritty, more curt than he'd intended. "My apologies." He jerked his head at the approaching cart. "The grand master sent me to fetch you."

"That can't be. I've been . . ." She trailed off, biting her lip. "My uncle is not here. You'll have to wait until he returns. Whatever the grand master needs, Uncle Valossi can arrange it."

The rain hardened, buoyed by a gusting wind that drove water from the roof directly into Drummond's face. He swabbed at his eyes with the back of his hand. Anica glanced at the sky.

"This is turning into a gale," she said. "Take your horse and the cart through the courtyard gates. The animals can shelter in my uncle's stable. You may come inside and get warm."

He hesitated. His orders had been to bring her back immediately. But there was no way he would force her into that mule cart. She would not leave without giving some assurance to her uncle, as was her right. And the prospect of warming up by a hearth at Anica Foscolo's side was too tempting to refuse.

When he signaled to the cart driver and guard to follow him into the courtyard, the guard put up a protesting hand.

"We were ordered to fetch the girl and return straightaway."

Drummond kept moving, pulling the mare along with a gentle tug on the reins. "Last I checked, I answered to Lord de Milly, not you."

"But Monsieur Lopic said—"

Drummond ignored the guard's retort. "We're not riding all night through a gale—that's sheer idiocy. Stand out there in the rain if you like," he tossed over his shoulder as he strode into the courtyard. "It may be a while. They've offered us refreshment. A chance to dry off and warm up."

When the cart creaked into motion behind him, he repressed a smile. That had gone more smoothly than he'd expected.

Handing off his horse to a stable boy, he turned and saw Anica outlined in an interior doorway. She was smiling at him. All at once, the trepidation vanished from his body. And in its place, a heady sensation rippled through his veins. Something powerful, something he associated with memories of home, of family, of times long gone by.

It was the unmistakable feeling of joy.

CHAPTER 42

Winter, 1460
Rhodes Town

THE MULE CART and its escorts clattered into the immense stone courtyard of the grand master's palace. Anica pulled aside the canvas curtain that shielded her from the world, watching Drummond dismount and hand his horse's reins to a stable boy. She let the curtain fall back in place and drew the hood of her black cloak low over her forehead. Her palms were clammy, though her bones ached from the winter chill.

Hear me, God, Santa Maria, all the blessed saints, I beg you—please give me strength.

Drummond opened the curtain and offered his hand to her. She took it gratefully, savoring the warmth of his flesh on hers. Descending, she clung to him as if he were a lifeline tossed to her at sea. His presence was the only thing keeping her from shaking. Gently, he released her hand, bent his head to hers.

"Courage, lass," he whispered in her ear.

She raised her chin and followed him across the courtyard. The thunderstorm had ended during the night, making their journey less miserable than it might have been—though the road was muddy and deeply rutted in places. Crows had heckled them from the branches of cypress trees along the way, an ominous accompaniment to the journey.

Anica ascended the broad interior stairway of the palace, the dread in her stomach thickening with each footfall. She concentrated on Drummond's comforting bulk next to her, trying to gain strength from his presence.

They entered the great hall side by side. Knights and agents of the Order stood talking in small groups throughout the chamber. Anica spied several clean-shaven Venetians dressed in elaborate silk tunics trimmed with gold thread.

Three long tables formed a semicircle at the perimeter of the chamber. Dozens of beeswax candles glowed in candelabras, illuminating the silver cups and platters positioned on the tables. The thought of dining amongst this group of powerful men sent panic through Anica. She fought an urge to turn and run.

She drew in a breath and let it out. Slowly, her composure returned. Drummond had explained everything to her. Now all she had to do was play her role. But first, she would execute a negotiation of her own. It might be her only chance.

A hush fell over the chamber as the men glimpsed her. The grand master was in conversation with a small group of knights. At their approach, he strode forward and inclined his head to her, then flicked his gaze at Drummond.

Drummond gave a bow. "Signorina Anica requests that I remain at her side during the negotiations."

The grand master frowned, the muscles under his short beard tensing.

"As my father cannot be here, I need a protector whom I trust with my life," she said, somehow finding her voice. "Master Fordun is that man."

Behind Lord de Milly, the Venetians studied her, murmuring amongst themselves.

She kept her composure, took another gulp of air. "I will do everything I can to help you keep the peace with the Venetians," she promised the grand master. "But in return, I have two conditions."

His expression darkened. At a gesture from him, Drummond stepped a few paces away.

"What might those be?" Lord de Milly asked, his voice tight.

"That my sister is treated by Dr. Syriano for the illness she has suffered. Her recovery is slow. She may yet lose her life."

"My personal physician?" he said, eyes narrowing. "You forget yourself, signorina."

"I do not forget I have Loredan blood and a Venetian-born father," she responded pointedly. "Dr. Syriano is the finest physician in Rhodes Town. Heleni needs his aid to find her strength again."

He was silent a moment. "What else do you ask of me?"

"That I may return to Rhodes Town—and live here with my family."

He scowled. "You brought banishment upon yourself with your threats. And it is safer for you to be far from this place."

"Far from Émile de Chambonac, you mean to say." Anger sharpened her tone. She struggled to calm herself again. "My sister will be vulnerable to him as soon as she steps foot outside my father's home. I cannot protect her if I'm in Lindos. And as the Order won't see fit to punish the man, it is up to me to keep her safe from him."

The grand master made a sound that was halfway between a growl and a groan. "I am reminded of the fact that women are rarely allowed in this chamber, and for good reason."

Anica pushed back her shoulders. "But a woman's voice—mine, in particular—is critical to these negotiations. Surely, you see I have no choice but to act boldly if I'm to preserve my family's honor—my sister's very life? Especially with my father across the sea in a foreign land."

His expression relented a bit. A modicum of gruff respect crept into his voice. "You are no fool, that's certain, signorina." He raked his gaze over the Venetians. "But know this. If the negotiations fail, you will not get either of your demands met."

"I understand. Please lead me to the admiral. I'm eager to make his acquaintance."

Lord de Milly shook his head. "He's not here."

She regarded him in confusion. "So I won't be meeting my Loredan cousin, after all?" Anica wasn't sure how exactly she was related to the admiral, but the term "cousin" could apply to just about any distant relation.

"Admiral Loredan is with his fleet in a bay on the western side of Rhodes." Lord de Milly inclined his head at the Venetians. "These men are his emissaries. If all goes well this evening, you'll accompany them and my representatives to the negotiations tomorrow, aboard the admiral's vessel."

The idea of venturing onto a Venetian admiral's galley made Anica's stomach drop. "Will you be at the negotiations?"

"No. Representatives from several of the tongues will join you. As will Monsieur Lopic."

He indicated a slight man with a pinched face and dark eyes that darted here and there, sliding over each face in the room. Anica's skin pricked with unease at the sight of him. Glancing at Drummond, she opened her mouth to remind Lord de Milly of her first condition.

"Yes." He raised a hand to ward off her words. "Master Fordun is also among the contingent. You leave at first light tomorrow. You will lodge in the palace tonight, under my protection."

She swallowed hard. "Master Fordun must guard my door. I won't agree otherwise."

Lord de Milly scrutinized her once more, his dark eyes sober. "You're not the first woman to spend a night within these walls. We often host noblewomen, patrons of the Order and others of high rank. I assure you the accommodations are comfortable and safe."

He offered an arm. Praying her wobbly knees would not buckle, Anica advanced with the grand master into the heart of the great hall, her pulse pounding like a drumbeat in her ears.

❦

With Drummond at her side, Anica followed a pair of guards through the torchlit corridors to the chamber assigned to her by the grand master. The past few hours had been exhausting. She'd done her best to charm the Venetians with tales of her family's history in their city. It was so cold in the vast hall that she'd kept her cloak on, eliminating the worry that the men would judge her Greek-style clothing. She'd brought none of her Latin garb to Uncle Valossi's home in Lindos.

When they reached the bedchamber, she saw the door was open. Through the doorway, she spied a fire crackling in the hearth and candles flickering on a table near a four-posted bed outfitted with vivid pink silk curtains. Moorish rugs lay over the stone floors, and a wooden screen lined with silk that matched the bed curtains stood near the opposite wall. On the table stood a pitcher of wine, a silver goblet, and a covered basket that she hoped contained food. During the elaborate meal served in the great hall, she'd had no appetite.

The two guards took up positions on either side of the door. Anica glanced at Drummond.

"Step inside with me, please."

She left the door ajar. Drummond followed her into the shadows on the far side of the chamber.

"Will you send a messenger for me?" she asked him. The firelight illuminated each plane and angle of his face. Her heart leapt at the beauty she saw there.

Drummond nodded. "What is your plan?"

"I sent some icons to my Aunt Rhea a few days ago. One of them is of Santa Maria. I want to give it to the admiral as a gift. I cannot step foot on his galley without one."

The Scotsman smiled, his eyes dancing in the golden light. "Wise woman." Then his smile faded. "But she'll worry about you. Word might spread about your role in this. Lord de Milly would not abide that."

"Tell her a wildly rich patron has promised me forty ducats for an image of the Virgin before he leaves Rhodes."

He chuckled. "You're wanting me to spin falsehoods for you now, is that it?"

"We do what we must. She'll understand, believe me."

"I'd best be the messenger in this case," he said wryly. "I don't trust anyone else to lie for me."

Anica's spine went rigid. "Please don't leave my side." The words came out as a whisper.

He reached for her hand. "I must. When I go, bar the door behind me and don't open it until I call for you at dawn."

She gripped his hand with all her might. "We may die tomorrow."

He did not argue. "The Venetians could be laying a trap, it's true. But if they are, it's an elaborate waste of time. In my view, they're just drawing this out to make a point." He lowered his voice. "It was foolish of the Order to seize the contents of those merchant ships when the Venetians were seeking refuge from a storm. Now the consequences must play out."

Instead of answering, she guided him behind the wooden screen.

His eyes widened. "What are you doing?"

Anica held his gaze. "I am betrothed to a man I barely know. I will wed him for my family's sake. But he is not the man who lingers in my mind, who has captured my heart. And if I should die tomorrow, that man must know the truth."

"Who is this lucky man, then?" Drummond murmured.

She tipped her face up to his. "You."

He framed her face with his hands and kissed her eyelids, her forehead, her cheeks. With one finger, he traced a path along her jawline and down her throat, igniting a trail of exquisite pleasure. When their lips met, she felt a streak of fire run from her mouth to the very core of her being. She pressed herself against him hungrily. He tightened his grip on her, fitting her body to him with assurance. When his kiss grew deeper, more insistent, she met it with passion, running her hands along the hard muscles of his upper arms. A knot of pitch in a burning log burst with a loud crack. Anica ignored it. She did not care if a cannon shot rang out. She never wanted to relinquish her hold on this magnificent man. His warm mouth sought the pulse point at the base of her neck, and she gasped.

A guard in the hall coughed, and there was a murmur of voices from down the corridor. Drummond flinched. With great care, he disentangled himself from her. He glanced at the screen that shielded them.

"It's not quite high enough," he said with regret. "We can't risk being seen."

They moved to the door. Anica's lips burned with heat. She looked at him in the wavering light, soaking up every detail of his long, lean limbs, his broad shoulders, his powerful hands, the ache of desire in his gray-green eyes.

"Go," she said, her voice low and rough.

CHAPTER 43

Winter, 1460
Aegean Sea

THE SKY BRIGHTENED little by little, washed with amber and gold by the rising sun. Water sloshed in the hull of the *grippo,* a snug one-masted boat whose sail was lashed. The oarsmen sang a folk melody in unison as they powered their wooden blades through the water with practiced grace.

"Why do they sing on such a somber occasion?" Anica asked Drummond, her stomach lurching with the movement of the swells.

Before Drummond could answer, Monsieur Lopic spoke. "To ward off sea monsters, signorina."

She had spoken in Italian, but he'd answered in French, his tone dripping with condescension.

Drummond looked at her. "It keeps their spirits up," he said in Italian.

Lopic fixed his gaze on Drummond. "You'd better keep silent aboard the Venetian ship, Master Fordun."

"Why's that?" The Scotsman's tone was polite, but the hard set of his jaw revealed his dislike of the Frenchman.

"You speak Italian like a lowborn Genoese," Monsieur Lopic declared. "The last thing we want is to insult Admiral Loredan by reminding him of his sworn enemies."

Anica bristled. But Drummond ignored the insult, choosing to remain silent.

Follow his lead. Save your words for the Venetians, she counseled herself.

The galley loomed before them, shifting in the water. A long rope led from its deck to the depths of the shallow bay. Two more galleys were anchored nearby. Archers wearing chain-mail shirts lined the railings of each vessel, their wooden bows at the ready. Anica's heart leaped in panic at the sight of the weapons.

Quickly, she returned her gaze to the great ship before them. Banners flew from each of the three masts, bearing the seal of Venice and the colors of the Loredan family. An elaborate wooden structure covered with embroidered red fabric dominated the stern of the vessel. A goat bleated, and a sound like the lowing of a cow drifted across the waves.

Monsieur Lopic let out a mirthless chuckle. "The galley feeds its men well. I hope the animals they've butchered for our meal were in good health."

"We will eat aboard this ship?" Anica turned to the Frenchman in surprise.

"Negotiations with Venetians always involve food."

Anica glanced beyond Lopic at the knights who'd accompanied them. They were about her father's age, high-ranking members of the Order hailing from various kingdoms, most of them bearded. To a man, they avoided her gaze. The slight Frenchman was the only member of the contingent besides Drummond who acknowledged her presence. Too bad he was not better company.

They drew close to the galley. It was much larger than she'd imagined, with crossbows and swivel guns mounted to the railing along the deck. Three men in red tunics appeared above them near the mainsail mast and raised golden trumpets to their lips. An elaborate interlude of piercing music ensued. Then the shriek of a whistle rang out. A wooden gangway was lowered to their craft.

Anica eyed the gangway with apprehension. The waves were not large, but the choppy waters made both vessels unsteady. Drummond helped her stand, then took the satchel containing the icon from her.

"Gather your skirts and take it slow," he advised her. "Should you stumble, I'll catch you."

She cast a grateful look at him and followed his instructions. When she reached the top, a Venetian envoy she recognized from last night's event was waiting with an outstretched arm.

"Signorina," he said. "Such a pleasure to see you again."

She took his hand and stepped down from the gangway, somehow sparing herself embarrassment by landing on two feet. An orange cat streaked by her and disappeared behind a wooden barrel. The indignant squawking of a hen assailed her ears, only to be drowned out by another blare of the whistle.

"Welcome to Admiral Loredan's galley," the envoy went on, beaming at her.

From the corner of her eye, Anica saw Drummond spring from the gangway to the wooden planks beside her. The knights appeared one after the other, and finally Monsieur Lopic scrambled aboard.

She gave the envoy a polite smile, hoping she looked more confident than she felt.

"*Grazie,* signor," she said. "I am honored."

Monsieur Lopic threaded his way through the group until he was face-to-face with the envoy.

"Signor," he began, inclining his head in a stiff nod. "It is an honor to—"

But the Venetian ignored him. "Hand your weapons to my guards, then follow me to the castle," he boomed, spinning on his heel.

Anica caught an expression of tight rage on Monsieur Lopic's face at the apparent snub. Drummond thrust out the satchel to her, then he and the other men removed their weapons and relinquished them to waiting guards. He met her eyes, gave a nod of encouragement. She followed in the envoy's footsteps, Drummond on her heels, the rest of the group in their wake.

Once inside the ornately carved wooden structure protruding skyward from the stern, where the galley's officers navigated, slept, and ate, they were ushered to a chamber outfitted with a table set for a meal. Oil lanterns hung from pegs in the walls, illuminating the cramped space with a faint glow. The air was dank and oppressive, the smell of unwashed bodies and mildew filling Anica's lungs. Nausea roiled in her stomach.

You cannot waver now.

She recognized a few more Venetians from the palace. But an unfamiliar face stood out. It belonged to a clean-shaven man dressed in black velvet with a brilliantly polished shirt of mail over his doublet. A black cap embroidered with gold thread covered his head. Guessing he was Admiral Loredan, she bowed her head and sank down in a curtsy. When she straightened, Monsieur Lopic had moved in front of her, blocking her view.

"Admiral Loredan," he said with reverence. "It is a great honor to be in your presence, Your Excellency. May I present a gift from the grand master—"

"Where is Lord de Milly?" The admiral craned his neck, peering at each visitor. "I distinctly asked for him to be part of the contingent."

"Our leader is poorly," the Frenchman replied. "He suffers from a fever. He very much regrets—"

"Spare me your lies," the admiral snapped. "You bore me with such explanations. Where is the gift you speak of?"

Lopic gestured to a knight. The man came forward and produced a box made of gleaming black wood. He presented it to the admiral with a bow.

"Two hundred freshly minted Rhodian florins, Admiral," Lopic said.

The Venetian leader did not look impressed. "Venetian ducats are the only currency accepted in all ports of call. As a man who spends my life at sea, what am I expected to do with Rhodian florins?"

He sighed in irritation, his eyes flicking over the group. "Move aside, Frenchman. I see there is a woman amongst you. What brings you aboard, signorina?"

With reluctance, Monsieur Lopic sidestepped two paces. Anica curtsied again.

"Your Excellency," she said. "I am Anica Foscolo. My grandmother was Donata Loredan."

He looked at her in surprise. "She was my aunt. Who are your parents, then?"

"My father, Paolo, is an artist trained in Venice who now makes his home in Rhodes Town. My mother is from one of the most respected Greek families on the island."

"You speak like a Venetian," he acknowledged. "I recall when my brother built his castle on Antiparos, he brought a young relation along to paint the frescoes."

She nodded. "That was my father."

"I've seen those frescoes. They're lovely." He studied her thoughtfully. "Why hasn't your father come himself?"

Her breath hitched in her throat. "He is away, Admiral. He will be disappointed to learn he missed an opportunity to meet you."

The admiral took that in. His eyes fell to the satchel in her hands. "What have you brought me?"

She'd forgotten all about the icon. Fumbling with the straps, she managed to open the satchel and remove it. "My father painted this icon of Santa Maria. I thought she might provide comfort to you on these rough winter seas."

He reached out and took the small painting from her. At a gesture from him, an officer plucked a lantern off the table and held it near the icon.

"A finely wrought image," the admiral said in a tone of genuine appreciation. "Equal to the work of the Venetian masters I commission at home." He eyed her again. "Your father is a man of great talent."

Her cheeks grew hot. Papa had nothing to do with this painting. But withholding the truth was the only way forward.

"He is, Your Excellency." She remembered something. "My father is expecting an apprentice from Venice this year. He arranged it with our Loredan relatives, though I'm not sure which ones."

"There are a lot of us," the admiral admitted. "Our line grows stronger with every passing generation. If the apprentice does not appear as promised, write to me. I'll make sure my brethren keep their word."

A smile of gratitude broke over her face, and he returned it. "Now I know without a shred of doubt that you are my kinswoman."

"Why is that, Your Excellency?"

"You have my grandmother's smile. It was a sight to behold, that smile. It made everything right in the world." He signaled to a crewman. "Hang this icon in my cabin over my berth. I shall treasure it."

Anica felt a rush of relief. Beside her, Guillaume Lopic glowered. She watched the crewman carry away her portrait, caught a last glimpse of the Virgin's calm, luminous gaze.

Santa Maria, she prayed, *give me the courage to survive whatever comes next.*

CHAPTER 44

Winter, 1460
Aegean Sea

As the negotiations began, Drummond sat with his muscles tensed, one ear cocked for trouble. Not that there was much he could do if the Venetians were planning to betray them. He felt uncomfortably vulnerable without his weapons. The plain truth was they were at the mercy of their hosts.

He flicked his gaze to Anica. She'd been frightened on the boat ride across the small bay, but now she looked different: her skin flushed, her eyes glittering in the lamplight. There was not a trace of fear on her face. Either she was skilled in the art of deception or she felt a self-assurance that he did not.

The animals in the stable lowed and squealed, their hooves striking the deck in a discordant rhythm. The ship's timbers creaked with each heave of the massive vessel. The gale that had blown through Rhodes over the past several days was over. But the sea hadn't forgotten what it had wrought. It was still unsettled, just like him.

"We were within our rights to seize the goods and passengers," Lopic repeated for the third time in as many minutes. "The Venetian vessels entered our harbor without permission of the Order."

"During a gale. They did nothing to provoke the knights. They did not intend to disembark nor circumvent your tariffs. They were merely waiting for a break in the storm so they might return to sea and journey back to Venice."

The admiral's voice was even and reasonable. His face could have been carved in stone. He appeared to be an even-tempered man, but perhaps a different side of him would emerge before this day was over. Without waiting for Lopic to reply, he continued.

"We deserve much more than a box of florins and a portrait of Santa Maria in compensation." He glanced at Anica. "No offense to your father, signorina. The Order has long favored the Genoese, a partnership that not only rewards our enemies with its generous tariff schemes but also encourages violence against our naval fleets. It is time the knights extended an olive branch to my people and offered Venetians the same privileges."

Lopic's lips pressed into a hard line. "We are prepared to return the goods and passengers seized from your galleys. The Order owes you nothing more."

The admiral picked up his silver goblet. Sipping his wine, he studied the Frenchman over the rim. He did not look addled in the slightest by the man's remarks.

Lord in Heaven, how long will this go on? Drummond stifled an impatient sigh.

Two crewmen carried in platters piled with salted fish, lentil-and-rice salad, grilled meats, and oranges sliced and arranged in layers. Drummond had no appetite, but he would eat it all. Who knew if this was the last meal he'd ever consume?

"The passengers you've detained have all lost income due to this outrageous treatment. They must be compensated." The admiral speared a thin slice of grilled beef with a two-tined golden fork. "I'm sure you agree."

One of the knights spoke, his Italian flavored with Catalan. "What about the Order's ships that have been sacked by Venice, the knights who've lost their lives to Venetian blades and arrows, the innocent villagers killed by Venetian raiders? We've never been compensated for those losses, Admiral."

Admiral Loredan chewed his food with care, then washed it down with another draught of wine.

"For every incident you can recall of Venetian aggression, I can recall several more engineered by the knights and the Genoese."

The Catalan took up his cup. He clutched it so tightly that the skin on his knuckles turned white.

Drummond tensed. Would the man's anger get the best of him? The tension in the chamber made the stale air even more oppressive.

To his astonishment, Anica spoke before the Catalan could respond.

"Your excellency, though the Venetians and Genoese make war with each other at sea, we live in harmony within the walls of Rhodes Town."

Every eye swiveled to the only woman in the cabin. Drummond said a silent prayer to Santa Maria, begging her to come to Anica's aid.

"The signorina is betrothed to a Genoese, your Excellency," Lopic put in.

The admiral's eyebrows knitted together in a frown.

You cunning little weasel. Drummond longed to muzzle the Frenchman with his own silk cloak. Glancing at Anica, he saw a flicker of panic in her eyes.

Calm yourself, love. Breathe.

"It seems to me we have two common enemies that pose more of a threat to us than we do to each other," she went on, each word clear and strong.

The admiral leaned back in his seat. "Is that so, signorina? And who might they be?"

"The Mamluks of Egypt and the Ottoman Turks. Ever since I was a child, I've been told that a siege is coming to Rhodes. That the Mamluks and the Turks will one day send their armies to destroy Christendom and make us all their slaves." She glanced around the table. "Should we not unite and bring the power of the knights, the Venetians, *and* the Genoese to bear on our enemies?"

Lopic scowled at her. Several of the knights followed suit. Drummond's chest swelled with pride at Anica's bold words. But he feared she had gone too far.

"Well said," the admiral remarked. "Your Loredan blood gives you courage. And what you say makes perfect sense. If only the world made perfect sense, too. Genoa and Venice will never be allies, signorina. As long as the Order extends privileges to Genoa that it withholds from Venice, we will not find peace."

"This is not the fault of the Order," Lopic sputtered. "The partnership with Genoa goes back to the time of the first knights on Rhodes, more than a century ago. We did not forge that agreement, nor can we break it."

"Oh, I believe you can," the admiral said softly, spooning up a bite of lentils. "It's well within the power of the grand master to do so, if he's properly motivated."

"There will be mutiny before that happens," the Catalan knight growled.

Drummond flinched. He'd heard rumors of a schism in the Order as a result of this conflict. It didn't seem worth dividing the entire organization over. But what did he know? He was just a privateer, operating on the outskirts of the Order.

"Name your price for compensation of the passengers you speak of, Your Excellency." Lopic's tone dropped, and he smoothed his expression into a mask of cordiality. "If it is reasonable, I may be able to arrange it. But your other demand is out of the question."

"Forty thousand Venetian ducats." The admiral bit into a slice of orange, spraying juice across the table.

"That is outrageous," Lopic gasped. "The passengers have only been in our custody for a few weeks. And they're well-treated, I might add. We've been sparing no expense for their care."

"Not weeks. It's been more than a month," the admiral corrected, mopping his face with a napkin.

"I might be able to secure five thousand," Lopic allowed.

The Venetian winced. "Laughable. I won't accept a ducat less than thirty thousand."

Lopic had a whispered consultation with the man to his right. "Ten is the absolute limit I can offer," he said.

"I'm insulted." The admiral slammed his fist on the table. "Guaranteed safe passage to any Venetian ship, to its crews and passengers, should they have to seek shelter in Rhodes Harbor or any other possession of the Order—from this moment forward. And twenty thousand ducats."

"Fifteen. But only if you can also guarantee safe passage to the Order's vessels in Venetian territories under such circumstances." Lopic's voice had regained its calm.

The admiral considered the counteroffer in smoldering silence. Drummond felt a trickle of sweat make its way down his spine. He snuck a glance at Anica. Her face was tense with anticipation, her eyes fixed on the admiral. For her sake, he wanted this to be finished; he wanted them back on the small craft gliding across the bay to safety.

Please, Santa Maria, please. Let him agree.

"I shall have to take the matter of safe passage to the Council of Ten in Venice," the admiral finally said. "When a decision is made, you shall be the first to know. In the meantime, I'll remain anchored in this cove until I receive the promised payment."

The Frenchman frowned. "You'll get half now and half when the rest of our agreement is honored. You would demand the same in my position, Admiral."

The Venetian pondered Lopic's words. "Perhaps I would."

One of his crewmen came to his side and whispered in his ear. The admiral nodded, then sent the man away.

"I'm reminded that we have some prisoners you might wish to ransom today. Genoese sailors, most of them. But one is a merchant, a fairly valuable one at that. I've sent for him."

The Catalan spoke up. "Where did you acquire them?"

"A Genoese fleet was caught in a gale between Rhodes and Karpathos. It separated the fleet. One galley was struck by lightning, and the entire ship went up in flames. A few survivors managed to escape, floating on the wreckage. We took them prisoner."

Drummond's heart ached for the men. It was every ship captain's worst fear, a total catastrophe at sea. His ship burning or filling with water, sinking like a stone. His crew flailing in the waves, drowning one after the next. He'd woken shaking from this nightmare more times than he could remember. It was a nightmare born of reality in his case, though. For once, long ago, he'd been a survivor clinging to bits of wreckage, tossed by wind and waves.

A few moments later, a disheveled man wearing a green velvet doublet and matching hose stained by seawater entered the chamber. He had no cap or shoes. Despite his forlorn appearance, Drummond sensed he was a man of standing.

"Speak your name," the admiral said.

"I am Antonio Spinola, merchant of Genoa. Lightning struck our vessel. It caught fire and sank. I lost all my goods, and my servants perished." He looked at the knights in desperation. "Please, good sirs, ransom me. I've a wealthy family in Genoa. They'll reimburse you for your trouble, with interest. I vow it."

Drummond couldn't help himself. "My deepest sympathies to you, signor, on the loss of your ship."

The man shot him a rueful look. "It wasn't my vessel. I was a passenger. It belonged to another merchant of Genoa. I regret to say he perished."

"What was his name, signor?" Anica asked.

The man's shoulders slumped. "Marino Lomellini. May God rest his soul."

Anica put down her goblet so carelessly that it tipped on its side. A crimson stain seeped over the linen table cloth. Yet she seemed to take no notice. Her face was ashen, the confident expression she'd worn during the negotiations erased.

Drummond looked at Monsieur Lopic. A knowing smile played around the man's mouth. He ran his eyes over Anica with a cold, assessing gaze that made Drummond want to backhand him.

And then it struck him like a hammer blow. Marino Lomellini must be Anica's betrothed. The man who stood between them was dead. A kernel of excitement exploded in his chest, spreading warmth throughout his veins. It took all of his self-control to keep from leaping from his seat and letting out a joyous whoop.

Monsieur Lopic began negotiating with the admiral for the

Genoese merchant's ransom payment. And through it all, Drummond watched Anica, hoping for a sign from her that signaled she felt the same overwhelming sense of possibility, of joy, as he did.

But she'd dropped her eyes. She was staring at the untouched food in front of her, blind to the overturned goblet, her mind somewhere far away.

His exultant mood faltered.

Perhaps she had harbored affection for Marino Lomellini. Perhaps she'd even loved him. There was so little he knew about Anica, in truth. And with that realization, the giddiness heating Drummond's blood receded like a waning tide.

CHAPTER 45

Winter, 1460
Rhodes Town

As she climbed the steps from the palace courtyard to the great hall, Anica could not recall feeling more exhausted in her life. Both her brain and her body ached from the day's events. All in all, it had gone better than she'd imagined—until the news of Marino Lomellini's death had sent her reeling with shock.

Even so, she had mustered enough composure to stand, to follow the men back outside to the deck. When they'd disembarked from the ship, Admiral Loredan had bowed to her. And within earshot of all the knights, he'd invited her to return anytime she wished to his galley or any property of the Loredan family.

She savored the memory of his words as the group assembled before the doors of the great hall. Whatever happened now, she had done her part to move the negotiations forward. She glanced over her shoulder to assure herself that Drummond was still there.

He locked eyes with her, gave her an encouraging nod.

Anica straightened her shoulders and walked through the doorway.

The grand master was not in his ornate oak chair on the dais. He stood a short distance away, surrounded by advisors. At the approach of the negotiating party, he broke away from the group, regal in his black velvet tunic.

The group paused before him and bowed in unison. Anica swept into a deep curtsy.

"Well?" Lord de Milly asked, a trace of impatience in his voice.

Guillaume Lopic launched into a description of the negotiations. Other members of the contingent contributed their observations whenever he paused to take a breath. Then Lopic would jump in again, describing his heroic efforts to protect the best interests of the Order. The grand master's face looked etched in stone as he listened.

All around them, more men gathered. Apparently, news of their arrival had spread all over Rhodes Town. Anica recognized a Greek notary who worked for the Order. To her consternation, she realized he was standing alongside Signor Salviati, the Florentine banker.

Lopic fell silent a moment, signaling to someone across the chamber. Before he could speak again, another voice rang out.

"You forgot something important, Monsieur Lopic. Things got off on a better footing than we'd imagined thanks to the signorina." Drummond's words were clear and strong. "She gave Admiral Loredan a painting that her father made."

All the men turned her way. Lopic's eyes narrowed. He gave a slight shake of the head as if to warn her not to speak.

Lord de Milly's countenance was thoughtful. "Your gift made a favorable impression upon him?"

Anica swallowed. "He seemed to like it, my lord."

"Well done," The praise was genuine, the grand master's gaze direct and kind.

She bowed her head. "Thank you, my lord."

Someone let out a hard laugh. "Would he have liked the painting as well if he knew the truth about it?"

Anica's gut twisted. She looked around wildly for the source of the voice. Émile de Chambonac swaggered toward them, a taunting grin on his face.

"What do you speak of?" Lord de Milly asked him in surprise.

"This girl painted the portraits that her father sells to you, my lord. And to all the other wealthy men on this island." He raised his voice to ensure that everyone in the chamber could hear. "Your hard-earned coin—wasted on a woman's work."

A rush of shame swept through Anica's body. Her knees wobbled.

"This is nonsense," Lord de Milly growled. But his eyes betrayed his uncertainty.

"It's true," de Chambonac went on. "Her father is half-blind! He can't see to do the work, so she does it for him. They've deceived you all, I'm afraid. A family without honor."

Anica's shame turned to fury as she watched the man who had ruined her sister's life slander her father in front of Rhodes Town's most respected men. She took courage from Drummond's presence, drawing in a deep breath.

"These are lies. My father is not half-blind, my lord. When he returns from his journey, you will see I am speaking the truth." Anica flicked a withering glance at the young knight. "You, Émile de Chambonac!" His shocked expression gave her new strength. "You're a devil." Several men muttered darkly when she said that, but their disapproval did nothing to cool the fire in her heart. "There is not a shred of honor in your soul. You're more schooled in the art of deception than any man on this island. You have no right to slander my father—a respectable citizen of Rhodes Town, a son of the Loredans, a friend to so many in this chamber!"

The young knight's expression soured. He opened his mouth to defend himself, but Lord de Milly placed a restraining hand on de Chambonac's shoulder.

"Enough," he warned. "Go to my study. I shall meet you there shortly."

De Chambonac sullenly followed the grand master's order.

Relief flooded Anica. She looked at the grand master with gratitude. "Thank you, my lord."

But his expression did not soften. "As for you, signorina, your banishment continues. Master Fordun, escort her back to Lindos at once."

"My lord, you said—" Anica began.

"I never promised you a thing." His tone was like ice.

"But what about Dr. Syriano?" she pleaded. "Please, we need his help."

"You cannot seriously believe that the Grand Master of the Order of St. John would acquiesce to the demands of a mere girl?" he demanded.

Anica almost collapsed. All the air escaped her lungs.

Drummond put his hand on her elbow, somehow keeping her upright. With every eye in the chamber upon them, they made for the doorway.

Halfway across the chamber, Signor Salviati obstructed their path.

"Courage, signorina," he said to Anica in a low, soothing tone. "If you're patient, I think you'll find your family still has loyal—and powerful—friends in Rhodes Town."

His flat black eyes were unreadable, and his words penetrated her ears slowly, as if through a thick haze.

"Thank you, signor," she murmured, unwilling to hold his gaze.

Drummond steered her through the doorway. "Let's get you out of here."

Night fell as they left the walls of Rhodes Town. Anica huddled in the covered mule cart, clenching her teeth to keep them from chattering. The steady gait of Drummond's horse alongside her on the road to Lindos was the only thing that kept her from dissolving in tears.

As the cart wheels rattled along the rocky ground, she replayed the day's events in her mind. Each time Émile de Chambonac's grinning face entered her consciousness, she flared with anger. Then she wished she had held her tongue, or had at least tempered her response to his slanderous words. Perhaps the grand master would have given her what she'd asked for if only she had not been so bold.

There was a sharp crack. The cart lurched to one side, coming to an abrupt stop. Anica nearly tumbled off the bench.

Drummond pulled aside the canvas shield over the window opening.

"Are you all right?" he asked.

"Yes," she said.

"One of the cart's wheels broke. I'll ride you ahead to Lindos."

Anica picked up her satchel and took Drummond's outstretched hand. After a brief consultation with the driver and guard, he helped her into his saddle, then climbed up behind her.

"What about the other men?" she asked.

"They'll wait until daybreak to assess the damage, then bring the animals to Lindos," he replied.

The three-quarter moon glowed down at them, casting a pearly sheen on the undulating hills ahead. Anica leaned back, allowing herself to rest against Drummond's chest. His arms encircled her, his right hand holding the reins, his left resting on the saddle's pommel.

Despite her fatigue, her fury, her sorrow, she began to relax. Drummond's warmth spilled over into her own body. For the first time all day, she was no longer cold.

"Thank you," she said.

"For what?"

"For keeping me safe, for treating me with respect, for . . . everything. Your presence gives me courage. I could not have said those things on the admiral's galley or in the palace without you at my side."

"I doubt that, Anica." He chuckled. "Your boldness is in your blood. It rises up when you need it, that's all." He was silent a moment. "Your betrothed is dead."

"Yes."

"Did you love him?" Drummond's voice was gruff.

"No. I liked him, what little I knew of him. But it turned out he was not who he seemed to be."

"When you learned of his death, you were upset."

"I was," she admitted.

"Why?"

Anica sighed. "Signor Salviati, the Florentine who stopped us when we were leaving the great hall—he wants me for his son."

"Is his son the man who harassed you at the oil stall in the market-place?" Drummond asked.

"Yes. He was meant to stay in Florence, but something went wrong and he's returned to Rhodes for good."

"He was caught up in a scandal there," Drummond told her. "And if the rumor I've heard is true, he'll soon be mired in one here, too. The falconer told me he's either no good with accounting, which seems unlikely for the son of a banker, or he's pilfering funds from salaries and the knights' treasury. He's a scoundrel, Anica. Surely, you can convince your father to refuse an alliance with the man."

"My father is deeply in debt to the Salviatis," she said. "My betrothal to Signor Lomellini was a way to protect me from a marriage with Troilo."

Drummond did not reply for a moment, but she felt him take in a long breath.

"You've no choice in the matter, then," he said.

"I must do what's best for my family. What I want has nothing to do with it." She took his hand from the saddle's pommel and placed it on her heart. "I want this—you. But I can't have you."

He tightened his hold on her. She leaned into him, savoring his touch.

"At least I'll be able to see you in the streets from time to time," she said. "That's something."

He hesitated. "Anica, there's nothing I want more than a life with you at my side. But if I can't have that, there's no reason for me to stay in Rhodes."

"What do you mean?" she asked, bewildered. "You work for the knights."

"I'll be returning to the West this summer."

Anica struggled to find her voice. "To Scotland?"

"I'll visit home as often as I can, but I'll live in Amsterdam, near Flanders. I'll keep my galley there and import goods from the East."

She felt as if a hole had opened up in her heart. "I can't imagine Rhodes without you," she protested. "I can't imagine never seeing you again."

"Nor I you." His voice grew hoarse. "But I can't imagine the pain of living here, watching you embark on married life with a man you despise. I won't do it, Anica."

The hot sting of tears burned her eyes. As much as she wanted to beg him to stay, she knew it would be an act of selfishness. Somehow she would have to accept a future without Drummond in it.

"No," she said, weeping. "And I would never ask you to."

CHAPTER 46

Spring, 1460
Lindos

Anica peeked into Uncle Valossi's study. He sat at his desk, poring over a document by the light of an oil lamp. A distinguished notary, he was a practiced scribe.

"You're up early, Uncle." She tossed a shawl over her cloak in anticipation of the wind. The breeze had been frigid these first few mornings of spring.

He looked up, his round face breaking into a smile. Though he was Papa's age at least, no silver showed in his curly black hair. Uncle Valossi looked much like Aunt Rhea, but his temperament was mellower. He somehow radiated delight despite the hardships he'd suffered in his life.

"Work before pleasure, I'm afraid. I promised my betrothed I would walk her down to the bay this afternoon. The closer we get to the wedding, the more details she wants to discuss."

"I'm happy for you," Anica said. His betrothed was a lively young woman with a kind smile and a contagious laugh. "We've been looking forward to your marriage."

He put down his quill. "Where are you off to?"

"Up the hill. I want to watch the sun light up the sea. I'll be back before nine bells to give the children their lessons."

She'd become a tutor to her niece and nephew and enjoyed it immensely. They were the only offspring of Uncle Valossi and his first wife to have survived the fever that took their mother and siblings a few years ago.

"You're not going all the way to the fortress?" His face registered concern.

Anica shook her head. "I wouldn't be so foolish as to put myself in the path of the knights and their guards. No, I'll go as far as the overlook. Where the broken column from Athena's temple lies—at the cliff's edge."

He looked relieved. "Give my respects to the old gods." Taking up his quill and dipping it in the inkpot, he added, "And be careful."

Anica strode up the winding lanes past shuttered windows and blank whitewashed facades. Dawn had broken, but only just. She cherished the shadowy moments between night and morning. They offered a rare chance to be alone with her thoughts while the sky shed its velvety cloak of darkness and the new day unfolded, ripe with possibility.

Near the top of the lane, she heard a cock crow, then another. Shutters thumped against plastered walls as the citizens of Lindos opened their windows and greeted the morning. Male voices drifted up the lane behind her, probably fishermen heading down to the glittering bay.

A stooped old woman in a worn black shawl opened her door as Anica passed.

"*Kalimera*," Anica said.

"*Kalimera*," the woman said in a wavering voice, stepping out into the light with a servant at her heels.

Anica continued onward. Just ahead loomed the Order's castle and fortifications, built on the vestiges of a stone foundation that had once been a temple to the goddess Athena. The figures of guards patrolling the parapet gave her pause for a moment. She stood transfixed, catching her breath.

The Order was impossible to escape. She, like all her forebears, had to coexist with these foreign men, had to bow to their rule. But after all that had happened in the past few months, bitterness now rose in her throat every time she thought of the knights.

She trudged forward again, sidestepping a jagged chunk of marble emerging from the trail. Bits and pieces of the ancient acropolis decorated the rocky soil all over this hillside. She climbed to her favorite lookout spot, in the shadow of a fallen column that at one time had supported the roof of Athena's temple.

Dwarfed by the massive piece of carved stone, Anica felt the power of the ancients rush through her. She shaded her eyes with a hand, watching the ever-changing palette of colors bloom and fade on the waves.

Soon the water would turn deep blue, reflecting the cloudless sky. For the moment, though, it was slate-colored, awaiting the kiss of the sun to explode in brilliant azure. She stretched out her arms and emptied her mind of all thoughts. The sun inched higher, warming her back.

Despite everything, she thought, *there is still beauty in the world.*

Anica had no idea how long she'd been standing there when a shout startled her from her reverie.

She turned. A man approached from the trail to Lindos, outlined by the sun. His cloak flowed out behind him and a cap covered his head. As he approached, she saw he was clean-shaven, and his quick gait was familiar.

"Papa?" She moved forward hesitantly, then broke into a run. "It's you!"

She raced into his arms. He enveloped her in a long embrace, then held her at arm's length and examined her with care.

"You're well. You're safe. Thank God and all the saints." Tears glistened in his brown eyes.

She studied them with trepidation. "Did you get the surgery? I see no scars."

He took her hands in his. "All was well. I was treated with great respect and given the utmost care. My vision is still a bit blurry, but the surgeon said that is to be expected for a few more months. I feel as if I'm seeing the world for the first time, through the eyes of a child."

She began to weep. "Papa, we've missed you so—and needed you so . . ."

The weight of all she had carried during his absence slammed into her. She leaned against him, taking comfort from his presence as she had so many times since she was a small girl.

"I know," he murmured in her ear. "I worried for you and your mother and Heleni every day."

She pulled away. "How is Heleni?"

"She is better, my dear. Not walking much yet, but her spirits are returning."

Anica used the hem of her headpiece to dry her tears. "Have you heard Marino Lomellini is dead?"

"I have," he said gravely. "It is most regretful. He was a good man."

So say some.

But she would not tell her father what she'd learned about the Genoese merchant. What was the point? Burdening him with more dark revelations would only make things worse.

"There are consequences we must face now," he went on. "That's why I'm here."

She stiffened. "The Salviatis?"

"The Order's payment to Admiral Loredan was financed by a loan from the Salviatis. When they made the transaction, they asked Lord de Milly's permission for a betrothal between you and Troilo. He's now in their debt, so naturally he gave it. Signor Salviati awaits my blessing to give you to Troilo in marriage. He claims that once you are betrothed, you'll be granted the freedom to return to Rhodes Town. And he's crowing about our connection to the Loredans." Her father let out a bitter laugh. "The man has a trick of turning everything to his advantage."

Though she knew it was probably futile, she mustered a protest.

"But I cannot wed without your permission. You can stop this by refusing to agree to their demands, Papa. An alliance with the Salviatis is out of the question—we decided that long ago."

"We are not in the grand master's favor," he said. "Lord de Milly used you when it was convenient, but he will never forgive you for your brashness and your threats, nor your attack on Émile de Chambonac in full view of every high-ranking member of the Order."

Anica's eyes stung. "That man slandered you, Papa. He stole Heleni's honor. He is a scoundrel and a liar. I could not keep silent. Lord de Milly had to learn the truth."

He looked away, his gaze running across the horizon. "The truth is more complicated than you imagine."

"What?" Anica cried. "Did Mamá tell you what happened to Heleni? About our visit to Signorina Giovanna? The notes—the bottle of poison delivered to Heleni by the soap seller?"

"Yes." His voice was tinged with despair. "But Heleni encouraged the knight's advances. She fancied herself in love—"

"Because of his lies! He promised her they would wed. His poison almost killed her. Doesn't he deserve punishment for it?"

Her father's tone hardened. "There are other ways to avenge those who are wronged. You have always been courageous, and I love you for it. But you've made targets of us by reacting in anger, and now we must placate the Order."

"Placate them? We're at their mercy. Émile de Chambonac may still ruin us all."

"Enough, Anica." A note of exasperation crept into his voice.

"I haven't told you everything," she insisted. "Please hear me out."

Her father fell silent, a muscle working in his jaw.

"I never told you of my encounter with him at the villa," she said. "He invited me to be his concubine and threatened to tell the world of our secret if I did not comply."

"What secret?" Papa asked, bewildered.

"That I, not you, am responsible for the art that keeps our family housed and fed! He walked in while I was painting the frescoes and he guessed the truth."

"How?"

"His servants had been spying on us, watching how we worked, listening to us talk. I insisted you get the surgery because of his threats, not because of some rumor I'd heard in the streets. Your honor—and our future—was at stake." She took in a gulp of air. "When he propositioned me, I put him off by telling him I was betrothed. Then he turned his attention to Heleni."

Her father's face drained of color. "Saints protect us. Why didn't you come to me?"

She dropped her chin. "It was just after Archangelos; you were injured and your vision was failing. You did not need another burden, I thought. But now I'm not sure. If I'd shared with you what he'd said, perhaps Heleni would still have her innocence. She walked into his web of lies and nearly lost her life."

Papa considered her words, then reached out and lifted her chin with his fingertips. "You were trying to protect me—protect all of us. You could not know what he would do next." He slipped an arm around her shoulders, and they walked to the edge of the cliff, where an unobstructed view of the restless sea stretched to the western horizon. "The truth is, Anica, Lord de Milly will never punish him—he's too valuable; too much gold flows from his family to the knights."

"But what can we do? If Heleni ever ventures from our home again, Émile de Chambonac will pounce on her as soon as he has an opportunity."

"Perhaps not," Papa said. "I learned from the falconer that the young knight is leaving in a few days' time for a dangerous mission across the sea. He may never return. We can pray that he'll meet his end on the seas, like so many of the knights."

She stared at her father in consternation. "But if he's leaving, that means Drummond Fordun is, too."

"So?"

A sob tore at her throat, rendering her breathless. Anica sank to the ground, drew her knees up, and buried her face in her hands. When she could breathe again, she tilted her head and met her father's eyes.

"Master Fordun is favored by Lord de Milly, too. There's a chance he can change my fate. I must return with you to Rhodes Town."

Her father shook his head. "You can't come and go as you please, Anica. That's what banishment means. Don't be foolish."

She stood. "Do you want me to marry Troilo Salviati?"

"Of course not. It's the last thing I'd choose for you. I don't want that family dictating our affairs."

"Then take me to Rhodes Town," she said fiercely. "I believe there is a way out of this arrangement. But only with the help of Drummond Fordun." She seized his hands in her own. "If I stay here, I promise you, Papa—all will be lost."

CHAPTER 47

Spring, 1460
Rhodes Town

Uncle Valossi did not question Anica and her father when they told him of their plan. He, like so many others, was tolerant of the Order because he had no choice—and because the knights protected them from the infidels. But when Latins took advantage of Greeks, that tolerance gave way to fury. She saw it in his eyes as he handed her a black skirt, blouse, and a matching veil that had belonged to his late wife.

"You'll look like a Greek woman in full mourning. No one will give you a second glance," he said. "May the saints protect you."

The next morning at dawn, she embraced him and told the children she'd be back soon. Then she tied her heavy black shawl around her head and climbed into the mule cart next to Papa in the covered area behind the driver. During the long ride to Rhodes Town, she tried to ignore the anxiety radiating from her father.

This is the right thing to do. The only thing to do.

They clattered through the city gates just after dusk, the guards waving them through after a cursory glance.

Anica squeezed her father's arm. "See? That was easy."

"A stroke of luck," he replied acidly.

She instructed the driver to halt outside Drummond's residence as a light rain began to fall.

"Papa, please go inside and ask for Drummond. I'll be at Santa Maria." She gestured across the square to the church. Though the doors were shut, they were always unlocked. Usually, after the early evening service of Vespers, worshippers hurried home for supper rather than linger at church. "Find me there."

She slipped out of the cart and darted through the raindrops to the church while her father headed in the opposite direction. Pushing open one of the heavy doors, she saw to her relief that the church was indeed empty. The priest was nowhere to be seen, but he was somewhere in the shadows, no doubt counting the moments until he could have his supper.

Anica approached a niche in the wall where several stubby candles guttered under a fresco depicting a saint. Normally, she would study such a work, wondering about its origins and the painter who had put so many hours into its creation. But today, she stared at it unseeing, twisting her hands together, her pulse pounding in her ears.

The door opened and shut with a soft thud. Two sets of footsteps sounded behind her. She turned. The men she loved most in the world approached side by side.

"Drummond!" Her excitement at seeing him was impossible to disguise.

He nodded at her, his face somber in the dim light.

"I'll be over there," Papa said, pointing at the pew nearest the door.

Anica stepped closer to Drummond and raised her veil. "Now that I'm with you, I don't know what to say," she confessed nervously. "Or where to begin."

"Just start talking," he suggested. "If nothing else, it's a chance for me to hear your voice."

She smiled a little at this, taking heart from his calm voice. "The Salviatis arranged a loan to cover the payment to Admiral Loredan.

When the financial arrangements were made, Signor Salviati asked the grand master to approve a betrothal between me and his son, Troilo. Lord de Milly did as he requested."

"You'd no choice in the matter. I understand, Anica, as much as I hate it." He leaned in, the intensity in his gaze startling her. "Why are you salting this wound? We have no future together."

"In the palace, when I said you'd captured my heart, I told the truth. I never knew what it felt like to love a man until I met you. The only man I want to share my life with is you." She fought to keep her voice even. "It is your face that lingers in my thoughts at night, your name that I repeat to myself like a precious talisman, your lips that I want to kiss . . ."

He framed her face with gentle hands. "Anica. My love."

She drew in a breath, luxuriating in his touch. "Papa is trapped. He can't defy the grand master's orders. But you're in Lord de Milly's favor. You can influence his decisions. Perhaps there's a chance for us, after all, Drummond. A future."

"Are you asking me to marry you, lass?" His voice caressed her, throaty and deep. "Because if that's the case, the answer is yes."

She smiled, blinking back tears. "I think, with all things considered, my family would choose you over Troilo Salviati."

"I'll not be working for the Order much longer," he reminded her. "I don't have a future in Rhodes."

"Take me to Amsterdam with you, Drummond."

He looked astonished. "You would leave your family—your work?"

"Yes." Anica stood taller. "Papa's vision is restored. Heleni is recovering. Everyone in Rhodes Town talks of the coming siege, and we all long for a way to escape when that day arrives. If I move to another land, my family will have a place to go."

The logic of her words was sound, yet sorrow gripped her all the same. The thought of sailing away from Rhodes was terrifying.

"Your family would always be welcome in our home." His lips sought hers.

Gratitude and love welled in Anica's chest. She returned his kiss eagerly, intoxicated by the passion thrumming between them. Then a thud echoed from the far end of the nave.

"The priest," she said in consternation, stepping back.

Papa stood and walked down the center aisle. His words of greeting to the priest were intentionally loud. His footsteps faded as he walked toward the altar, engaging the man in conversation. He was giving them a little more time. She had to use it wisely.

"What do we do next?" she asked Drummond.

"This." He pulled her close again and kissed her. Sliding her hands around his neck, Anica lost herself in pleasure for a moment. Then she heard the priest's voice rise and reluctantly disentangled herself.

"Would you—would you ask my father for my hand in marriage?" she whispered.

"It would be my honor."

"And then ask the grand master to give his permission?"

The smile vanished from the Scotsman's face. "If he's already given it to the Florentines, I don't know how he'll take my request. But I vow to you I'll find some way for us to wed. There's nothing I want more."

Her father's voice rang out in response to a muffled comment from the priest.

"I leave soon on a mission for the Order," Drummond told her. "It'll be a dangerous one, Anica. More risky than most."

"Will Émile de Chambonac be on the voyage?"

"Yes." He frowned. "Why?"

Anica dreaded her next words, but she managed to force them out. "My sister did not fall ill, as I told you. She was poisoned by that knight."

"What?" He sounded doubtful. "Poisoned?"

Anica swallowed. "He stole her honor, Drummond. He tried to steal mine. He wanted us for concubines, and—" She hesitated, then made up her mind. "He got Heleni with child, promised to marry her, promised to make her a noblewoman. And when she revealed her condition to him, he sent her poison, told her it would end the life in her womb. It was meant to kill her, too."

Drummond's face was troubled. "He's an arrogant little cockerel, but I'd no idea he was capable of such a cruel scheme."

"Even the most amiable gentleman is capable of monstrous acts," she said, thinking of the words of Signorina Giovanna. "Be careful of him, Drummond."

His grave expression hardened. "Émile de Chambonac is the least of my worries, believe me."

Anica kissed him once more, then spun on her heel and hastened away.

CHAPTER 48

Spring, 1460
Rhodes Town

DRUMMOND GAVE up his weapons to a guard and entered the great hall. The grand master sat like a king in his high-backed oak chair. It was Wednesday, when Lord de Milly met with citizens of the city and denied or permitted their requests. The last of the townsfolk filed out the tall doors as Drummond made his way in.

"Come forward, Master Drummond." The grand master waved off his assistants.

Drummond approached the dais and bowed. "Thank you, my lord. You once told me that much was owed to me and asked if I wanted for anything."

"I did."

"I ask you now to give your blessing to my marriage. I seek to wed the daughter of a citizen of Rhodes Town. Will you permit us to marry? I wish to have the matter resolved within the week."

"A man such as you does not often wed," the grand master said, his eyebrows lifting. "Your future is . . . uncertain. More uncertain than most."

"That may be," Drummond agreed. "But I've a chance at happiness, and I would like to take it."

"This must be quite a bride you've found yourself."

"She is, my lord. A local girl. As you said, I'm engaged in dangerous work. My haste to wed is born of that knowledge."

His employer nodded soberly. "Well, my felicitations to you. I'll have my notary write up a letter of permission. May your marriage be long and bring you many sons. What is the girl's name?"

Drummond squared his shoulders. "Anica Foscolo."

The grand master's expression froze for an instant, then turned hard. "Do you jest?"

Drummond feigned innocence. "Not at all, my lord. Why do you ask?"

"Because I've given permission to another man who intends to marry Signorina Foscolo."

"Forgive me, but there must be some mistake." Drummond frowned. "Anica's father has given his blessing to our betrothal. As I understand it, he has refused all other offers."

"That was unwise."

"My lord, surely we can come to some agreement."

"This matter cannot be revisited, Master Fordun. You'll have to find another bride."

Drummond sucked in a breath and slowly let it out.

Steady, man. Stay calm.

"There is no other woman for me."

The grand master looked skeptical. "You don't strike me as the lovesick type, Master Fordun."

"I'm not." Drummond shifted on his feet, feeling naked without his weapons. There were at least six guards in the chamber. To a man, their eyes were fixed on him.

Lord de Milly studied him for a long moment. "If you had a future here, I might consider your request. But you're leaving the Order in a few months' time. Such arrogance is not like you, Master Drummond."

His eyes glittered. "If you agree to stay on under my command for the rest of my tenure with the Order, I will permit you to wed Anica Foscolo."

Drummond stared at him, stunned. All he'd dreamed of for ten long years was the chance to return home. His plans for Amsterdam, his importing business—all of it would crumble into dust if he said yes. An image of the lush meadow where he'd played with his siblings as a lad rose up in his mind. He'd clung to it all these years, the memory of that place. Would he never see Scotland again?

He tried to steady his breath, tried to untangle his thoughts. The most important thing to him now was a life with Anica—a life that had been out of reach until yesterday. As long as he could be with her, he'd be home.

Squaring his shoulders, he leveled his gaze at Lord de Milly. "Consider it done."

His employer leaned back in his chair, both hands on the armrests, one eyebrow cocked in surprise. "But your family has sent for you. Would you ignore their summons just for the sake of a local girl?"

"Signorina Anica is not just a local girl." The defensive edge in his voice made the grand master stiffen. Drummond cursed himself, summoning the grace to soften his tone. "She's the woman I want to grow old with. I can't imagine life without her, my lord."

Lord de Milly's brow furrowed in a frown. "Are you aware that I hold this position for life? You may never leave Rhodes if you make this vow."

Drummond's mouth was dry as sand. "I understand."

A silence fell. The blood pounding in Drummond's ears roared like waves crashing over the bow of his galley. He swayed a little. The floor seemed terribly far away.

"I want this promise in writing at once, witnessed by my notary," the grand master said. "Then I will give the union my blessing."

Breathe, man. Breathe.

Relief flowed through Drummond's veins. He widened his stance, determined not to sway on his feet. With great effort, he managed to stay upright.

"My deepest thanks to you, Lord de Milly. And as for the matter of her banishment . . . ?"

"I will rescind it, but I advise you to keep her away from Rhodes Town anyway."

"My lord?"

"She's a bold, outspoken woman. The Salviatis will be angered by this decision, and there are other powerful men who make no secret of their dislike for her."

"You mean Émile de Chambonac," Drummond said flatly.

"He is not the only one." The grand master leaned forward and fixed Drummond with a sharp look. "Is it really best for the woman to live within the walls of this city, mingling with such folk, when you are off fighting for the Order?"

When Drummond appeared at Anica's home a short time later, his palms were clammy. He stood in the lane gathering his thoughts. Before he got mired in doubts, he seized the brass door knocker and rapped it several times. Best to just muddle through.

A moment later, he was ushered in and led to a bright chamber facing the interior courtyard.

Signor Foscolo waited for him there, standing by the window. He looked ashen and exhausted.

Drummond got straight to the point. "Lord de Milly gave me permission to marry Anica."

The Venetian stood motionless, squinting at Drummond as if he hadn't understood a word of the Scot's Italian.

Just as Drummond decided to repeat himself, Signor Foscolo opened his mouth. "Praise the saints. How did you manage that?"

The door opened. Anica and her mother entered. Anica's eyes sought Drummond's, and the spark that flew between them made his spirits soar. A surge of determination flooded him. He would have this woman. She was meant to be his.

"Is it done?" Her voice was clear and strong. "What did he say?"

"Lord de Milly is breaking the arrangement with the Salviatis. He gives us his blessing. And ends your banishment, though he thinks it best if you don't live in Rhodes Town—at least, for now."

Anica stepped toward him. He took her hand in his. It was much smaller than his own. But she gripped his fingers with enough power to make his heart leap.

"I love your daughter," he said, turning to face her parents. "I will make her a good husband. I'll cherish every moment with her, I promise you."

Signor Foscolo's expression was tight. "Words mean little. This man is a privateer, Anica. Yes, he's favored by the knights—for now. But he could be taken captive or killed any day. Your future is not secure with him."

Anica's mother gave her husband an assessing stare. "Would you rather have her wed to a dishonorable Florentine whose family would revel in having us at their mercy? Who comes from a home known for mistreatment of servants and slaves? Our daughter will be a piece of property to them, to use and abuse at their will. How is that a secure future for Anica?"

Signor Foscolo's expression sagged. He studied their clasped hands with resignation. "So be it."

"I may have spoken in your defense just now, but I have doubts." Signora Foscolo turned to Drummond, a finger raised in admonishment. "You're a foreigner, and you live a dangerous life. How do you intend to keep our daughter safe?"

"Before you begin questioning him, may Drummond and I have a moment alone?" Anica asked her parents.

Signor Foscolo exchanged a glance with his wife, then relented. "We'll be just outside the door," he said sternly.

Finally alone, they stood facing one another.

"Why didn't you tell my parents about Amsterdam?" she asked.

"To secure his permission for our betrothal, I had to promise Lord de Milly that I'd stay on as long as he's grand master," he admitted.

"You gave up your chance to return home?" An expression of remorse struck her face. "For me?"

"Home is where you are, Anica."

Her expression brightened again. "I love you, Drummond Fordun. I will follow you West, if the opportunity comes again. But I'm grateful not to leave my family—it would have torn a hole in my heart."

"I know how that feels." He glanced away, gathering his composure. His gaze came to rest on the easel near the window.

"You won't stop me from painting, will you?" she asked. "He still needs me."

"I'd sooner stop a wave from breaking on the shore. You're a woman with a talent, like my sister. If you can serve your family with your skills, I won't stop you." He reached a hand out, followed the line of her cheek with a fingertip. "Anica, I'll do my best to care for you and keep you safe. But your mother is right. I may sail away one day and never return."

"We all live on a knife's edge on this island," she said soberly. "If there's a chance for happiness before that day comes, I'm willing to take it."

He took her in his arms as her parents entered the chamber again.

"There will be time for that after the wedding," Signor Foscolo grumbled.

A few moments of awkward conversation ensued, during which Anica's mother asked Drummond no less than a dozen questions about his past and his family. He answered as politely as he could.

"Cali." Signor Foscolo put a hand on his wife's arm. "We have practical matters to decide." He turned to Drummond. "The wedding should take place quickly, before you leave on your next mission."

Drummond nodded. "I agree. I'd like to take Anica to Archangelos, to my villa there, after the wedding." He glanced at her. "If you're willing. The voyage has been delayed for a fortnight while two of the war galleys undergo repairs. We will have a bit more time together than I'd thought."

A smile broke over her face. "I'd like nothing more, Drummond. Archangelos is close to my heart."

"I think it's best if you stay in Archangelos for some time," he added. "So does Lord de Milly. The Salviatis, Émile de Chambonac—

perhaps others—will not make good neighbors for you here in Rhodes Town, and I'm away more than I'd like."

Anica drew in a breath to protest, but her father spoke first.

"You brought attention to yourself with those negotiations, not all of it flattering," he said. "And the Salviatis won't hesitate to make life difficult for you—in truth, for any of us. Master Fordun is right. It's best if you're hidden away for a while. Safer."

Signora Foscolo nodded. "I agree. There will be ruffled feathers when word gets out about your wedding. We should keep it a discreet affair."

"As you wish." Anica glanced up at Drummond and smiled.

"Will we need to make arrangements at a church for the ceremony?" He groped for the words, dazzled, as usual, by her smile.

"You will marry here," Signor Foscolo said.

"In your home?" Drummond asked in surprise.

"Greeks often celebrate weddings, baptisms, even masses in their own homes," Signora Foscolo informed him. "We don't follow your Latin customs in all our ways."

"Signora, I'm no Latin," he said.

She raised an eyebrow, and the faintest hint of a smile appeared on her face. "Praise all the saints. Some good news at last." She looked at Anica. "We'll have to omit much of the traditional preparation, and if we want to keep this quiet, there will be no chance of a wedding banquet. A morning ceremony will be best, with a modest meal afterward."

"Then you can depart for Archangelos in the afternoon," Signor Foscolo put in.

Anica nodded. "We'll do what we must." Though her voice was steady, the disappointment in her eyes was obvious.

"The ceremony will be just as it should," her mother went on, slipping an arm around her daughter's waist. "We'll use my family's golden crowns. Valossi has them—his marriage was supposed to come next. He can bring them back from Lindos for the wedding."

"Who will be the *koumbaros*, though?" Signor Foscolo asked Drummond.

He shook his head. "The what?"

Signora Foscolo sighed. "He knows nothing of the *koumbaros*, I suppose."

"Groomsman," Anica translated. "He's an important part of the ceremony. Who will you choose?"

"The only man in Rhodes Town I trust with my life," Drummond said. "Sir Peter."

CHAPTER 49

Spring, 1460
Rhodes Town

Anica gazed around the courtyard of her family's home, overcome
with wonder. It had been transformed. Flower garlands were strung in
elaborate patterns above her head. Fragrant beeswax candles infused
with lavender and rosemary oils burned in sconces on the walls. Not a
single cloud marred the sky. As if in concession to the wedding, a
gentle breeze floated down from above, setting the garlands aflutter.

She took her place next to Drummond, facing the priest. With
trembling hands, she smoothed the soft folds of her pale blue silk dress
and adjusted the gauzy headpiece around her shoulders. The priest, a
cousin of her mother's, wore his finest embroidered robes. Before him
stood an altar table covered with a cloth. When her gaze fell to the
golden crowns on the table, Anica's pulse quickened.

The priest's words washed over her, a rich tide of Greek streaming
through the jumble of thoughts in her mind. The scents of beeswax,

herbs, and flowers mingled with the spicy aroma of incense, making her light-headed.

She studied Drummond from the corner of her eye. He wore a shirt of fine linen with a black velvet doublet over it, dark wool breeches, and polished boots. His long curls were tied back with a silken cord. Even his usual growth of stubble had vanished, carefully shaved by Sir Peter as part of his groomsman's duties. His gaze was fixed on the priest, his expression unreadable, his powerful body completely still save for a muscle working in his jaw. The energy coiled within his long limbs felt palpable to her.

Anica's mouth grew dry. She was about to marry a foreign-born privateer. A man who spent his life engaged in combat, a man who looted and raided for a living. A man who was paid to kill.

Santa Maria, who is Drummond, really? Has he been honest with me? Has he concealed things from me?

Her mind jumped to the women she knew whose husbands beat them, abandoned the marriage bed, filled their homes with the children of servants, slaves, and prostitutes.

Fixing her eyes on the priest, she slowed her breath and fought the panicked thoughts.

The time for such worries has passed. You've made your choice. Your path is set.

When the priest slipped the rings on their right hands, he nodded to Sir Peter. The English knight carefully removed the rings from their fingers, exchanged them three times, and replaced them again.

Anica searched Drummond's face once more, seeking reassurance in its defined angles, the wide, expressive mouth, the gray-green eyes that so mesmerized her. She took a tremulous breath.

The priest joined their right hands together. At the warmth of Drummond's touch, the anxiety that had enfolded her like a shroud moments before began to lift.

When the shining crowns were placed on their heads, Drummond's tender expression made Anica's eyes burn with tears. A deep sense of peace settled over her. Drummond *was* a good man. An honorable man. She had seen his true character in Archangelos, on Admiral

Loredan's galley, on the road to Lindos, here in Rhodes Town. He kept his word. He made her feel safe. And he loved her.

Her heart swelled with joy as Sir Peter fulfilled his task of interchanging their crowns three times, then settling them in place again. The solemn nod that Drummond gave his friend spoke of the trust between them. Finally able to give her full attention to the marriage ceremony, Anica savored each word as it rang out.

Our joys will be doubled and our sorrows halved, she recited silently along with the priest. *Because they are shared.*

When the priest led them three times around the altar table, Sir Peter following in their wake, she saw her parents clinging to each other. Heleni sat next to them, resplendent in turquoise-green silk the color of a peacock feather. Her eyes were bright with tears. And just behind Heleni, Aunt Rhea watched the proceedings with an uncharacteristically sober expression on her face.

After the priest removed their crowns and gave his final blessings, the small wedding party gathered at the cypress-wood table for a meal. Folk melodies poured forth from the alcove where Aunt Rhea had installed a group of musicians. Servants offered chicken baked in saffron-infused rice, lamb stewed with onions and garlic, and grilled fish to the guests.

"Is it what you imagined, this wedding?" Anica asked Drummond. "Normally, feasts would go on for a week, and the dancing would go on all night."

"I prefer it this way," he replied. "There are only so many Greek names I can remember over the course of a day." He grinned at her, glancing around the space, and his eyes came to rest on the bronze boy in its niche. "I'd heard some families on Rhodes possess ancient statues of the old gods. I see the rumors are true."

Anica swallowed. Even if Greeks no longer openly prayed to Aphrodite or Demeter, possession of their likenesses was seen as flagrant opposition to the knights' own religious beliefs. Of course, the knights were not above collecting such items for themselves.

"That one is no god. It's simply a boy," she retorted. "The likeness of a servant or a slave, perhaps."

His expression sobered. "Don't worry, my love. I won't tell the knights, nor will Sir Peter."

Across the table, Sir Peter and Aunt Rhea were discussing the merits of Cretan wine versus Burgundian wine.

Anica leaned forward. "When did you taste wine from Burgundy, Auntie?"

"Never," her aunt replied. "But Sir Peter has promised to find me a cask."

"What did you promise him in return, Rhea?" Uncle Valossi asked, unsmiling. He had not been pleased that a foreigner had been chosen as *koumbaros*. Anica was sure that Aunt Rhea shared the same misgiving. And they likely disapproved of her Scottish husband, too.

For a moment, the mood around the table shifted. A current of tension snaked through the air.

Sir Peter put his cup down and turned mild eyes on Uncle Valossi. "An assortment of fine spices to liven up the cooking at the Inn of the English. If our cooks could turn out meals half as tasty as this one, I'd be a happy man."

Uncle Valossi nodded, his expression softening. "A fair trade indeed."

The fraught moment passed.

Anica barely touched her food. Neither did Drummond. Her happiness was tarnished only when Aunt Rhea and her mother helped Heleni up from the table and led her away. Anica watched them disappear, seized by a familiar tug of sorrow. Thanks to the efforts of Signorina Giovanna, the oleander poison had not killed Heleni—but it had stolen her strength.

Drummond leaned close and kissed her cheek, his eyes alight with joy, and she fought off her dark thoughts.

The clink of ceramic cups, the clatter of spoons against plates, the murmur of conversation all fell away.

"My wife," he murmured. His smile was shy, as if he couldn't quite believe the words he'd just uttered.

She fitted the top of her palm over his hand, laced her fingers between his.

Drummond's smile deepened. A pulse of desire thudded in her veins.

Whatever happened, she told herself, one thing was certain.

Somehow, as fantastical as it seemed, she had married a Scotsman.

CHAPTER 50

Spring, 1460
Archangelos

STANDING IN THE ENTRYWAY, Anica bowed her head as Mamá covered her in a cloak made of sea-blue camlet—a blend of silk and wool woven by artisans in Cyprus.

"I've been saving this fabric for you since you were a small girl. Maria sewed the cloak while you were in Lindos. Your dowry chest is full," Mamá told her. "Aunt Rhea and I made sure everything is in place. It will help you feel at home in Archangelos."

Maria entered the room carrying a battered satchel, her eyes swollen from weeping.

Papa had granted Maria her freedom and given her the choice of staying on in his household or working for Anica. She had put her lot in with Anica, but it had not been an easy decision.

"Come, Maria," Anica said to her gently. "Your new life awaits."

In the lane, three cloaked figures waited by the mule cart. She sucked in a sharp breath, then let it out, relieved to see Aunt Rhea and two of her sons.

"I'm coming with you to the harbor," her aunt announced. "And my boys, too."

Anica climbed with her parents, Maria, and her aunt into the covered portion of the cart. As the wheels creaked into motion, her cousins fell into step behind them. In the privacy of the cart, the only sound was that of weeping. Both Mamá and Aunt Rhea swiped at their tears with handkerchiefs, ignoring Papa's admonishments to be cheerful.

"You'll make Anica weep, too," he scolded. "Her husband won't want to see her looking sorrowful on her wedding day."

This prompted a new round of sobs. Papa leaned close to Anica and patted her arm.

"Don't mind them," he whispered. "I, for one, am filled with joy. You are married, you are happy, you are safe."

She smiled at him and nearly burst into tears herself.

They exited the city walls and came to a stop by Drummond's galley in the small military harbor.

Drummond disembarked and greeted them all, then helped the men load the dowry chest and Anica's other belongings aboard.

Anica bade her father and mother farewell, her chest tightening with emotion. Aunt Rhea enfolded her in a long embrace. Then Drummond escorted Anica aboard the galley, Maria following in their footsteps.

As Drummond's ship maneuvered out of the *mandraki,* Anica stood at the gunwale blinking back tears, one hand raised in farewell to her family. The rowers powered the vessel through the mouth of the harbor, past the massive stone towers that stood sentinel over its sheltered waters.

Drummond came to her side. "I've set up your woman in the shade. Are you ready to join her?"

The fine spray of mist that the rowers sent up with each flash of their wooden blades set Anica's skin tingling.

She glanced at Drummond. "I could get used to this."

"Let's hope you never sail in a storm," he replied, his face creasing in a smile.

With the clear sky above him and the deep blue of the sea beyond, the gold flecks in his eyes jumped out at her. She looked more closely, counting them by twos.

He laughed. "What are you doing?"

"Just . . . noticing."

Below them, the head oarsman called to his crew. Their grunts were a rumbling backdrop to the slap of waves against the hull.

Maria sat under the canvas shade next to the dowry chest, shoulders slumped. Her skin had taken on a sallow, greenish undertone.

Drummond frowned. "Your slave doesn't look well."

"She's not my slave," Anica corrected. "My father granted her freedom. She's my maid now."

"I'm glad to hear it because I've no slaves in my household. I can't abide the practice."

She stared at him in astonishment. "But you take captives for the knights. Some of them end up slaves, don't they?"

"It doesn't sit right with me," he admitted quietly.

He squinted at the horizon, watching a trio of gulls glide ahead of the galley, and shook his head a little.

"What is it?" Anica asked.

"I was just thinking back to my first voyage, when I was meant to come here to Rhodes but only made it as far as Genoa. But I knew, deep in my gut, that I would get here eventually."

"How did you know that?"

"Something was waiting for me here."

"What?"

He looked at her. "Can't you guess?"

Warmth ignited deep within Anica, cresting just below her belly. That thrum of longing, of desire—it had begun the day she saw Drummond at the harbor for the first time. Since then, it had grown stronger with their every encounter.

One of his men called out a question, and Drummond left her side. For the rest of the short voyage, Anica could think of nothing else but what was to come tonight, in the marriage bed.

As they neared the half-moon-shaped bay where Archangelos lay, she knelt at Maria's side and put an arm around her shoulders.

"Almost there," she whispered. "You'll feel better when you're back on land."

Maria nodded, unable to muster a response.

The tiny harbor of Archangelos was a far cry from the bustling port of Rhodes. Anica disembarked with Maria clinging to her arm. Her childhood memories of this place had been happy ones. Yes, it was sleepy and rustic, with none of the amenities of a merchant town. But it was still beautiful. And for now, peaceful.

After Drummond dispatched his men to the fort, he led Anica, Maria, and several guards to his home overlooking the bay.

It was surrounded on three sides by a high stone wall. On the fourth side, cliffs fell away to the sea. As Anica followed Drummond along the garden paths to the viewpoint overlooking the calm bay, the faint sound of waves crashing against the rocks below whispered in her ears. She would have to adjust to the constant murmur of the sea. On a calm day like this, it was soothing. But during a storm, it would be frightening, she imagined. She glanced behind them at Maria, who wandered through the garden, her face regaining its normal color.

The whitewashed villa rose up beyond Maria. One by one, servants flung open the shutters on the second floor.

Drummond pointed at the upstairs windows. "Your rooms. One's a bedchamber; the other can be for whatever you wish."

When he led them inside, Anica admired the polished wooden furniture and hand-knotted Moorish rugs. The villa was a stark reminder of how important her new husband was to the knights. After all, it had been a gift to him. It rivaled any merchant's home in Rhodes Town, though it lacked the ostentatious details of silver plate and other shiny trinkets.

The cook and a kitchen servant took Maria into the kitchens while Anica followed Drummond upstairs to the second level. He led her through an open door.

Anica stood in silence, her gaze drawn by the view. She moved to the windows, transfixed by the breeze riffling the garden plants, by the undulating sea beyond.

Drummond chuckled. "Are you dreaming, lass?"

"It's so beautiful. I never had a reason to look outside my windows before," she admitted, turning to examine the space.

There was a broad chest and a wardrobe in the room and a little table with a piece of Venetian glass fitted into a wooden frame on the wall above it. Behind a wooden screen stood a copper tub.

"Have the servants fill that if you want to take a bath tonight," Drummond said.

Anica's eyes fell next on the bed, which was made up with white linen sheets and a stack of cushions. It had tall posts jutting up from each corner, and was situated opposite a window, the wooden frame high enough that she'd be able to see the ocean from it.

She studied the bed for a long moment, biting her lip. Drummond would come to her tonight and consummate the marriage. Excitement flooded her, quickly followed by trepidation. Would it hurt? Would it bring her pleasure? A flush rose on her neck and she glanced at him, then dropped her gaze. She felt awkward in her new husband's presence, overcome by a dizzying combination of shyness and desire.

Drummond seemed to know her thoughts. "We have a lifetime ahead of us, Anica," he said softly. Taking her hand, he pressed a gentle kiss into her palm and led her from the room.

CHAPTER 51

Spring, 1460
Archangelos

AT SUPPER, Anica barely touched the fish and vegetables. She studied the swirling blue designs on the ceramic dishes, watching Drummond from beneath her lashes. He quietly chewed his food, occasionally sipping from his wine goblet.

"I have so many questions," she confessed. "There's so much about you I still don't know."

He leaned back and set down his goblet. "Ask away."

"Why do you speak such beautiful French?"

Drummond smiled. "My mother and grandmother were French. I'd no choice in the matter."

"You're like me, then. Born of two different worlds."

He considered that a moment, then shook his head. "Scotland is in my bones and in my blood. It's where I was born, where I was raised, and God willing, where I'll die. Never thought of myself as a Frenchman."

She picked up her goblet and admired it in the candlelight. It was made of Venetian glass, a luxury few on Rhodes could afford.

"Why do you still risk your life at sea when you live like this?" she asked impulsively. "Surely, you have everything you need by now."

Drummond's expression sobered.

"I only have all of this because of what I do for the knights. Were I to give that up, I'd no longer be welcome on the island, nor could I send money home to my family."

Anica shifted in her seat, her color rising. "Of course. Forgive me."

His eyes never wavered from hers. "There's nothing to forgive."

A servant carried in a plate of fruit and sugared almonds.

When Anica refused the sweets, Drummond stood up. "I've got to check on the horses in the stables," he said. "If you need anything, the servants will help you in whatever way they can."

She watched him leave the room in a few long strides, then instructed a servant to bring hot water and towels upstairs for a bath. Climbing the steps to the second floor, she bowed her head and succumbed to a wave of uncertainty. Her family, everything she'd ever known, seemed a world away. Somehow she had to navigate this new life with grace.

When she entered the bedchamber, her eyes widened. Draped over the bedposts was the *spervani*, the embroidered cloth that traditionally hung over the bridal bed.

Maria paused from her task of lighting candles, turned to her, and beamed.

"You did this?" Anica asked in wonder, approaching the bed. Then she clapped her hands and laughed. "The *krevatia*, too?"

Flower petals and golden coins were scattered across the bed linens.

Maria smiled. "Your family's love is here, even if they can't be."

Anica clasped Maria in her arms. "Thank you. This means more than you can imagine."

"Let's get you ready for your bath," Maria said, her voice rough with emotion.

They unpacked her belongings. She'd not brought much. Just a few skirts and blouses, shifts, cotton headpieces. Cloaks made of sturdy wool. The silk dress she'd worn for the wedding stayed at the bottom of her trunk. There was no reason to bring it out. Where would she wear such a fine garment in Archangelos?

When the servants brought hot water, Maria added a few drops of lavender oil to the bath, set out a bar of sweet-smelling soap, and left her alone. Anica sank into the tub, leaned back, and closed her eyes. The waves were audible under the breeze. The soothing sounds nearly lulled her to sleep.

The water grew cold, and she dried herself, then put on a white cotton shift. The beeswax candles Maria had lit emitted a pleasing scent that hinted at honey.

The sound of footsteps outside in the garden caught her attention. She went to a window and peered down. Drummond was walking along the curving paths lined with rosemary and lavender plants. He wore sandals, not boots, and his feet struck the ground lightly.

He looked up, saw her framed in the window, and raised a hand.

"Come up," she called. "Come to bed."

His hand dropped to his side, and his gaze lingered on her a moment longer. He headed for the house, his pace no more hurried than it had been before.

Anica looked around the bedchamber with wide eyes. What should she do now? She stood frozen, unable to make a decision.

She was still standing by the window when Drummond entered.

He did not speak. He simply came to her and put his arms around her. Without hesitation, Anica lifted her face to his.

When he led her to the bed, she followed him willingly. With trembling fingers, she tugged at her shift and let it slip to the floor.

"You are so lovely, Anica." The quiet words were a caress, and the desire in his eyes made her body ache with longing.

A gust of wind blew in, making the flames dance on the candles.

He stepped closer, running gentle hands along her shoulders and down her arms, tracing the dip of her waist, the swelling curves of her hips and breasts. Her breath came in jagged, uneven bursts as he lowered his mouth to hers.

She reached for his shirt, loosening the laces at his neck, and helped him slip it off. His chest and arms were lean and muscular, as beautiful as she'd imagined. Her gaze was drawn by the golden amulet he wore on a leather thong around his neck. It was burnished with age, worked with delicate, intricate patterns. She laid a hand next to it, on the warm skin over his heart.

"Drummond," she said, so shaky with anticipation and desire that the word came out as a gasp.

"Don't fear me," he said in a hoarse whisper, shedding the rest of his clothes. "I would never hurt you."

Instead of answering, Anica reached for him. She lost herself in the exquisite sensation of his skin on hers, his lips lingering on the cleft at her collarbone, the sensitive skin on her neck, her inner wrists, her thighs. He slid his hands along the curves of her hips and traced feather-light circles on her breasts.

She drew in a shuddering breath, hungrily leaning into his touch, yearning for more. He helped her into the bed, then cast a quizzical eye at the coins and flower petals.

"Will this be a nightly occurrence, my love?"

Anica laughed. All of her worries about what would transpire in this bed disappeared from her mind. "It's a wedding tradition."

He nodded. "A good one, too."

As he trailed kisses over her body, discovering her most sensitive places with his fingers and lips, she moaned aloud. She returned his caresses and kisses, tentative at first, then with a passion that matched his own. His touch intensified, and when he found the very core of her pleasure with his fingertips, she cried out.

"That took me by surprise," she admitted after a moment, running her fingers through his wild hair. Her entire body throbbing with languid warmth, she smiled. "A surprise I'd welcome again."

He nuzzled her breasts and looked up at her with a wicked grin. "And that was just the beginning."

The sky was rose-gold outside when Anica drifted into sleep curled against Drummond's chest, faintly aware that a new day was dawning.

CHAPTER 52

Spring, 1460
Archangelos

ON THE NIGHT before Drummond had to return to Rhodes Town, they slipped out at dusk and went to a small cove near his home, where moonlight gleamed on the water and small waves broke upon the shore. The warm air hinted at summer.

"Can you swim?" Drummond asked as he shed his clothes.

"I've always loved swimming." Anica untied the laces of her shift and slipped it off. "Papa and Mamá used to bring us here to this bay when we were small, and we splashed in the waves together. You should see my cousins, Aunt Rhea's sons. They go out so deep it frightens me. Sometimes they bring back bits of marble, crockery, even coins and jewels. Papa used to dive with them when I was a little girl, and once he found a bronze statue no higher than my knee. The one in our courtyard."

Together, they walked to the water's edge. The waves lapped at their toes.

"The Order may rule this island, but they don't need to know everything that happens on it, do they?" He raised her hand to his lips. "Believe me, I've tucked some things away over the years that I'll never reveal to the knights."

She tilted her head toward the dark face of the cliff rising up to Drummond's villa. "When I was a girl, Papa made up tales about your house," she confided. "He told us Neptune lived there."

Drummond laughed. "They say the villa's been there in one form or another since ancient times."

They waded into the water, watching luminous flecks of foam ripple away from them.

"Papa used to say those glowing points of light in the sea were angel's tears."

"I'll have to remember that the next time my galley is caught in a gale and I'm cursing these waters."

"You once said you'd tell me the story of your arrival in Rhodes." Anica swept her fingertips over the water's surface, making patterns in the sea foam. "Will you tell me now?"

He stayed quiet a moment, eyeing her sideways. The grace of her movements was something he'd never tire of. Gliding away from him, she treaded water and waited.

Drummond swam to her side. "When I was hired by a Scottish knight to be his valet on the voyage to Rhodes, I'd never spent a day in my life at sea."

"What? But you're the best seaman the Order has."

"I don't know if I'd go that far," he said. "I'd spent my entire life on solid ground before that day, and I was happy."

"So you didn't want to leave, but you had to."

"Aye. My family wanted to protect me. I was hiding from a man who wanted vengeance upon me."

"Why?"

He turned over on his back, studying the night sky. Anica did the same, slipping a hand in his. Overhead, the three-quarter moon nestled in its shimmering cloak of stars.

"I'd killed his son in a battle," he said. "His favorite son, as it turned out. The English lord who wished me dead sent men into Scotland searching for me. When they started threatening the family my father worked for, things got desperate."

"What did you do?"

"I took refuge in the Highlands with relations who'd taken me in. A man not far away had died in a brawl. He was a thief and a murderer, without kin, without honor. And his face was so horribly broken by the fight that had taken him to his death that he barely resembled a human being."

She grew very still.

"We decided he would become me, and I would disappear. He was taken back to my family, and a funeral was held. The English lord's spies witnessed it and told their master I was dead. He stopped harassing my family and the nobles we worked for. But I was told I could not return until the English lord himself died, in case word trickled south that I had deceived him."

"So he's still alive, then?" Her eyes glinted in the moonlight, and her dark hair swirled around her shoulders. Dazzled, he couldn't resist the urge to draw her into his arms.

"No. He died not long ago. That's why my family sent word, told me it was safe to return."

He stood on the sandy sea floor and embraced her. The world slipped further and further away. Waves broke and crumbled softly on the sand. The gentlest of sea breezes lifted strands of Anica's hair and floated them around his neck and shoulders, sending shivers of pleasure down his spine.

Thank you, Santa Maria, for giving me happiness in this place, so far from everything I've lost.

He lifted his head, chuckling.

"What is it?" Anica's breath was warm against his cheek.

"I was thinking back to when I left Scotland. I'd kissed a lass once or twice; I barely knew how to swim in those days. And here I am, standing in the Greek sea with my naked wife, looking forward to a night of lovemaking."

She laughed. "Were you just a boy when you left?"

"No longer a boy, but not quite a man either. On that journey, we sailed first to the port of Sluys in Flanders, where we boarded a ship owned by a Flemish merchant whose hold was full of hemp and linen cloth. When we arrived in Genoa, the knight I worked for took ill and died of a sweating sickness."

"So far from home," she said. "What did you do?"

"I notified the Order of their brethren's death and found lodging in a tavern near the shipyards and harbor. I spent my evenings playing dice and cards with all manner of seafaring men."

"Did that include pirates?" she asked wryly.

Drops of seawater on her skin sparkled under the moon. He watched a smile bloom on her face and was struck speechless.

"I'd be lying if I said no," he continued when he found his voice. "When a spice merchant offered me a job on his galley and said he would pay me in pepper if I did the work well and returned alive, I only hesitated a moment."

"Spice brings gold," Anica said. "And danger."

Drummond treaded water again, releasing Anica's hands. She regarded him with an air of anticipation, eager for more.

"I hated Genoa," he went on. "I figured when this spice venture was over, I could get myself to Rhodes, see it for myself—maybe find work with another knight. A week later, we set off along with several other vessels for Alexandria. My eyes nearly popped out of my head when I saw the weaponry on that vessel—crossbows and arrows, lances, swords, shields, daggers."

"That seems excessive." Anica treaded water, too, matching his rhythm.

"I wish it were. No, we deployed just about every method of violence imaginable to survive."

She touched the amulet dangling from his neck. "Do you ever take this off?"

He shook his head. "I don't dare to. It's kept me alive all these years. Along with Santa Maria, of course."

By rights, I should be dead.

His mind went to the worst seafaring experience of his life. As usual when he recalled the incident, shame and regret welled in his chest, choking him. He pushed away the memory. There were some things he wasn't ready to tell Anica yet.

"How did you find it?"

"My Granddad dug up some metal trinkets as a lad, relics of the Celtic kings, and this amulet was among them. I'll need it on my next mission, more than most."

"Where will the knights send you this time?" Her voice betrayed a trace of worry.

"The fortress of Bodrum, in Turkey."

"That's enemy territory, Drummond." Anica's words were slow, halting.

"I have faith in my crew and the speed of my ship." He tried to sound confident. "In my crossbows and swivel gun. The only worry I have about this voyage are the people I'm carrying along with me. High-ranking officials of the Order who couldn't defend themselves against a bumblebee."

"And Émile de Chambonac."

"He's got no battle experience and the wits of a young pup," Drummond admitted.

"He's a scoundrel, Drummond." Her voice regained its strength. "You cannot risk your life for his. Promise me that."

He sighed. "I made a vow to Lord de Milly. I can't break it. I'm bound to protect him, Anica, even if he is a scoundrel."

Anica paddled toward shore, emerged dripping from the water, and snatched her shift off the sand.

Drummond followed her to the beach, stood facing her with his back to the sea.

"Your life is worth a thousand Émile de Chambonacs," she said, dragging the shift over her head and shoulders.

"Not in the view of the Order."

Anica sank down on the sand, knees drawn up, and buried her face in her arms. He kneeled beside her. To his dismay, he realized she was crying.

"Tears won't stop me from leaving, my love," he whispered against her wet hair. "I've no choice."

She raised her eyes to his. "I can't bear thinking of you at sea, shielding him from the iron and fire of enemy weapons, perhaps dying to keep that devil alive."

No words would change the course of his fate or ease her sorrow at this moment. So he kept silent. Under the glowing eye of the moon, he did the only thing he could do: he held his wife in his arms as she wept.

CHAPTER 53

Spring, 1460
Aegean Sea

THE FLEET SET out under cloudless skies. Once they pulled clear of
Rhodes harbor, Drummond stood at the bow deck calculating the
distance in his mind to their destination. They were headed to the
castle of Bodrum on Turkey's mainland, which the Order had built
many years ago from the stones of an ancient, crumbling structure.

Previous delegations had traveled to Edirne, Turkey's capital city, to
negotiate treaties with the sultan. But as far as Drummond understood
it, this was not an official delegation. There was no *legate* in the fleet
representing the pope, for he had expressly forbidden tribute
payments to the Turks. Instead, there were several merchants of
varying backgrounds, as well as some high-ranking Hospitaller officials.
He thanked God and Santa Maria that Guillaume Lopic was not on his
vessel. The man's smug, knowing demeanor made his skin crawl.

Their first stop was the island of Kos, which was controlled by the

Order. They would take a night of rest there, then continue on to Bodrum, where delegates of the sultan's court would meet them.

The dread in Drummond's gut loosened a bit by the time they arrived in a sheltered bay on Kos and dropped anchor. Supping on bread, cheese, and sausages under the canvas cover with his officers and the half-dozen knights who had joined his crew for the voyage, Drummond almost forgot his worries about the mission.

While they were eating, a familiar galley rowed into the bay, drawing up alongside Drummond's craft. It bore the banner of a Genoese privateer who worked for the knights.

Drummond plucked a lamp off a post, then hurried to the gunwale. "What news?"

"The Turkish delegation has arrived in Bodrum. They await the fleet." The captain's face glowed in the light of his own lamp.

"How many are there?" a voice cried out from behind Drummond. "Do they match our numbers?"

Drummond looked over his shoulder at Émile de Chambonac. "I don't recall inviting you to speak," he said tersely. "Sit down."

"Yes, Captain," the young man said with exaggerated deference, sauntering back to the others.

Drummond had half a mind to plant his booted foot in de Chambonac's backside and push him facedown on the deck. Turning to the Genoese captain again, he asked, "Anything I should know about the crossing?"

"Most of the villages near Bodrum are abandoned."

This was no surprise. The knights had taken many of the locals captive, forcing them into service or selling them at the slave market in Rhodes.

"But we saw activity on the peninsula by the bay near the castle," the privateer went on. "A herd of goats and a few shepherds, and smoke —maybe from a cooking fire."

"Will you anchor here with us tonight?" Drummond asked him.

"No. My orders are to continue on to Symi; I've a message to deliver there. And the winds are favorable now—I don't want to tarry here."

"Safe journey to you." Drummond watched the rowers turn the vessel and point it out to sea again.

Émile de Chambonac spoke up. "Goats and shepherds? What kind of enemy threat is that? Will we even see battle on this voyage?"

Drummond did not look at him. He reached for a hunk of cheese. "It's bad luck to wish for violence when you're at sea."

Several of his crewmen grunted their agreement.

One of the other young knights said, "But we need experience if we're to fight in the siege."

"Patience will reward you," Drummond said. "Just wait."

The man looked at him as if he had grown another head. Drummond exchanged an irritated glance with his first mate, whose expression told him they shared the same thoughts. These young men were a burden. Their insubordination and lack of experience could endanger the entire crew.

Anica's distress about Émile de Chambonac came tumbling back. Yes, the young knight was an arrogant little cockerel—but was he also a murderer? Such a calculating plan seemed beyond him. This voyage would reveal more about de Chambonac's character, if nothing else.

He left the group again and stood with his face turned up to the stars, imagining the Genoese privateer navigating his way to Symi using these luminous markers in the sky as his map. For a moment, he was jealous of the fellow, of the ease with which one vessel could travel the seas. No fleet to stay abreast of, no trailing ships to worry about, no chance of being separated in a storm and scattered to the winds. Of course, a single ship was at much more risk than a fleet—not from storms, but from attack.

Drummond slept little that night, his mind flicking back and forth between thoughts of Anica and anticipation of the coming dawn. When he finally dozed off, a light rain had started falling.

The sky was gray and brooding when they pulled up their anchors and set sail for Bodrum. Mist clung to the surface of the sea, and the inviting sapphire-blue waters of yesterday had transformed into a seething cauldron of leaden swells capped with foam.

Soon after they left Kos, patchy mist rolled in, making it hard to see the other vessel. They separated a bit, wary of colliding in the poor visibility.

Turkey was somewhere ahead, a hulking mass rising above islands strung along its coast. As the morning progressed, the wind blew harder from the northwest, pushing them faster toward their destination.

"Light more lanterns," Drummond called out.

As his men hurried to comply, the wind picked up and the galley began to roll in the deepening swells. The sails snapped against their riggings.

The combination of mist and high seas filled Drummond with trepidation. These exact conditions had led to his worst failure at sea. Though it had been his own reckless behavior that lay at the root of it all.

It had been one of his early voyages from Genoa to Alexandria, on a spice merchant's vessel. They had been returning from Africa, nearing Crete. He and one other man had been on watch during the darkest hours of the night. By the light of a single lantern, they'd whiled away the time telling stories and drinking wine. They'd established the routine early in the voyage. Every night had unfurled like the night before, calm and uneventful. Until this one.

Drummond had uncorked a second jug of wine, inciting surprise on his companion's face. But once they began drinking it, the man's hesitation had vanished. They'd swapped stories and guzzled the wine while a thousand stars winked down at them.

Then, lulled by the drink and the gentle action of the waves, they'd both fallen asleep. He vaguely recalled noticing a veil of gauze had been drawn across the stars just before he lost consciousness. And when he woke, he was in the sea.

A gale had descended upon them with savage power, sent them skittering across the water like a toy boat. They'd smashed into rocks, losing the cargo and most of the men, the ship taking on water and sinking with astonishing speed.

He had drifted until dawn, clinging to a wooden cask, alone in the sea.

When he'd sighted land, he'd kicked his way to shore, stumbled onto a strip of beach, and collapsed, sobbing.

Since then, the story had festered within him like a rotting wound. He'd never seen any of his crewmates again, nor the captain. And he'd never told a soul.

"Master Fordun, we've got to rely on your compass to navigate." The first mate stood at his elbow, a worried look in his eyes. "There are no land markers to sight."

"Right." Drummond withdrew the instrument from the pouch at his waist, cursing his memories. While he'd ruminated over the past, the mist had thickened again. "Trim the sails and the yards. We're picking up too much speed."

"Aye, Captain."

Drummond touched his amulet. If the wind kept growing stronger and visibility did not improve, they would have to deploy sails in the water behind each craft as sea anchors, relying on the drag to slow them down as they neared land.

God be praised, de Chambonac and his comrades were in the hold with the rowers. The last thing he needed was a novice knight sliding overboard in these seas.

Shortly, the mist thinned and the wind let up a bit. Drummond caught sight of the other ship and breathed a sigh of relief. They had stayed close despite the conditions.

Thank you, Santa Maria.

Ahead loomed a land mass that he assumed was one of the outer islands bordering the Turkish mainland. Or was it the peninsula jutting out from the mainland, near Bodrum?

A column of smoke rose from the land. He recalled the Genoese captain's words. This must be the peninsula before them, then. He turned a slow circle, trying to get his bearings, confused by the patchy, swirling mist.

"Fetch my portolan," he told his first mate.

The handwritten navigation guide described each feature of land and sea in the area. He only used it when times were truly desperate, for he knew the region so well that he could have written the thing himself.

The man hastened away, apprehension etched on his face.

From the corner of his eye, Drummond saw flashes of bright light.

"What was that, for God's sake?" he muttered. "There's no thunder or rain. It can't be lightning."

It must be the sun, then. Rising over the east. Even as he had the thought, he doubted it.

"Captain, the yard on the mainsail's broken loose on one side," shouted a seaman.

He flinched. "Then lash it! I need two men up there now. And tie on, do you hear? I don't want you flung into the sea."

"Aye, Captain," his men chorused.

Through a gap in the mist, he saw another glimmer of light. This time, his stomach twisted. It was the orange light of a flame, not the sun trying to break through the clouds.

"Hard to port!" he yelled at the crewman handling the rudder. The swells had subsided some, not enough for his liking, but he had no choice. Hurrying aft, he shouted below decks to the master oarsman, "Deploy the oars now, and power up the starboard side."

A muffled explosion sounded off the port side.

"God's teeth," Drummond swore. "To arms!" he roared into the hold. His gunner appeared first. "Ready the swivel gun," he told the man. "And watch yourself getting to the bow deck. These seas are treacherous."

Just behind the gunner appeared Émile de Chambonac. "I'll assist him," he announced, his face alight with excitement.

"Oh no, you won't," Drummond growled. "You've no experience with guns. I know you can wield a sword and a crossbow. If it comes to that, you'll get your chance."

The young man's expression tightened, but he did not protest.

The rain let up a bit, revealing two Turkish *fuste* bearing down on the galley containing Guillaume Lopic and the other officials. The archers on the enemy craft launched a torrent of flame-tipped arrows at the galley. Most of them fell short, but a few hit their marks. Screams rang out, and one of the galley's sails burst into flame. Drummond grasped the amulet around his neck, sucking in a great gulp of air.

"All rowers, full power," he bellowed. "Gunner, prepare to fire."

CHAPTER 54

Spring, 1460
Aegean Sea

THEY BARRELED toward the enemy vessel closest to them. When the *fusta*'s archers caught sight of Drummond's galley, they turned and started shooting arrows in his direction. Luckily, there was still too great a distance between them for the arrows to meet their target.

"Crossbowmen, attack!" Drummond shouted.

With the mounted crossbows on the gunwales and smaller hand-held crossbows, his men returned fire. The snap and clang of the weapons deploying rang out, followed by the whine of arrows slicing through the air at high speed. Cries rose up as the arrows buried themselves in human flesh.

His galley gained speed, the rowers dipping their blades in the sea with unflinching precision.

"Gunner, fire!" Drummond bellowed.

The deck boards shuddered as his gunner fired. Several crewmen on the enemy ship fell. Their screams resonated over the water. Its oarsmen paddling furiously, the *fusta* veered, heading straight for his own vessel.

"Starboard, power up! Port, hold," he shouted to the master oarsman, the acrid scent of gunpowder filling his lungs.

In the stern, the navigator put all his weight against the rudder. The galley groaned as she listed in the water. The oars of both vessels came within a hair's breadth of tangling. With astonishing precision, several of the crewmen on the *fusta* tossed iron hooks aboard Drummond's galley and pulled their craft toward his.

"Prepare for enemy boarding!" Drummond shouted. He scanned the deck for Émile de Chambonac, but there was no sign of the young knight.

Turbaned men began to scramble aboard his ship, their daggers and swords held aloft.

"Lances and shields," Drummond bellowed. "Attack! Attack!"

More of his crew poured out from the hold, rushing the invaders. An enemy seaman leaped in front of him, dagger outstretched, letting loose an ear-piercing scream. Drummond feinted to the left, then brought his sword up and knocked the man's weapon from his hand with one decisive blow. It clattered onto the deck. Drummond plunged his blade into the man's gut and watched him crumple.

He wheeled. One of his crewmen grappled with an attacker near the hold. Drummond rushed at the attacker and ran him through the back with his sword. The man collapsed, unconscious.

Where in the name of Santa Maria is that daft bugger de Chambonac?

A movement across the water caught his eye. With relief, he saw the other war galley bearing down on the second *fusta,* oars flashing. The boom of their swivel gun echoed again over the swells. And they'd cut down the burning sail, praise all the saints.

Ahead of him, a knight garbed in a red battle tunic stabbed his opponent with his steel blade, letting out a roar as he did so. "I strike you down before God," he cried, stabbing the fallen man again and again.

De Chambonac, no doubt.

Reaching his side, Drummond saw it was not de Chambonac after all, but one of the other new recruits.

"Keep your wits about you instead of crowing over your kill," he ordered.

The man turned to find another combatant, his face flushed with excitement.

Drummond spied another red tunic near the gunner in the bow. Of course. The lad was gun-obsessed. He fought his way through the chaos toward the bow deck. Before he reached de Chambonac, though, two attackers sprang over the gunwales and advanced on the young knight. He drew his sword and assumed an anticipatory stance, both hands gripping the hilt.

The gunner stopped reloading and turned to flank de Chambonac, picking up a lance as he did so.

There was a crack and a whoosh overhead as the rope supporting the broken yard on the mainsail gave way. The heavy yard hurtled onto the deck, pinning two of his men underneath it and blocking Drummond's path.

"Help these men!" he roared to anyone within earshot.

He scrambled over the pile of splintered wood and sodden canvas. Ahead of him, the two attackers advanced on the gunner and de Chambonac.

The gunner struck out with his lance just as de Chambonac raised his sword high. The sword clattered against the lance, knocking it out of the gunner's hands. One of the attackers pulled a dagger from a sheath and flung it at the gunner. It impaled him in the throat, and he staggered back and collapsed.

The two assailants rushed De Chambonac as Drummond closed the distance between them. He struck one in the neck with his blade from behind, a deep, lethal cut, then sidestepped the body as it fell.

The other man executed a neat little roll and came up alongside the knight with a dagger in his hand. From a crouch, he struck upwards, aiming for the gut, but de Chambonac shifted slightly and blocked the attacker with his arm. The man's blade flashed out again, slicing into de Chambonac's leg.

The young knight screamed in agony and dropped his sword. He buckled, folding in on himself, and pitched forward.

At that moment, Drummond landed a powerful kick on the

assailant's back. He sprawled on the deck, scrabbling like an upended beetle. Without hesitation, Drummond ran the man through with his sword, then picked him up as easily as a bag of feathers and heaved him overboard.

Breathing hard, Drummond spun on his heel, sword at the ready.

But his men had the upper hand now. Those Turkish vessels had the advantage of speed, but their small size and relative lightness meant they could not carry the numbers of men and quantity of weapons needed for prolonged naval combat, nor could they bear the weight of iron swivel guns and mounted crossbows. And these men weren't armed for serious combat, anyway. They'd no shields, no lances. Their armor was laughable. From the few words he'd heard them utter, they spoke a mixture of Turkish and Arabic.

Frantic men heaved themselves overboard, some landing within their own craft, others splashing into the water and swimming to its side. The *fusta*'s crew cut the ropes attaching their vessel to Drummond's. Their oarsmen paddled away, aided by a favorable wind. Several of the attackers were dead, their bloody bodies slumped on the deck of Drummond's galley. But a pair of them lay groaning on the bow deck, too injured to escape.

"Disengage the hooks and toss them overboard," Drummond ordered his crew. "Take those two prisoner," he added, gesturing at the wounded men. "Bind their injuries."

"I can't move my leg," de Chambonac gasped from behind him. "It hurts too much."

Drummond's chest constricted. "We'll see to your wound." He wrapped one arm around the young knight's waist and helped him into the hold.

"Clean and bind this injury," he ordered the man who served as nurse on his vessel.

"Wait," de Chambonac said as Drummond turned away, reaching out to him. "Don't leave me, please."

Drummond hesitated. "What is it? I've got to see to the others."

"It's my fault, Master Drummond." The soft lamplight made the knight's features look even younger than usual. "The gunner died because of me."

"It was an accident. You wouldn't kill your comrade on purpose, would you?"

De Chambonac's nostrils flared with indignation. "Never. It would be a sin to kill anyone but our sworn enemies."

Drummond bent down and looked him in the eyes. "What about that mistress of yours? She nearly died by poison, they say. Sent by a knight who was her lover."

The young man stared at him, aghast. "It wasn't me who sent the potion. It was Lopic." He lowered his voice. "She was with child. He told me it would end the life in her womb so we could avoid a scandal. He never said it was meant to kill her." De Chambonac's blue eyes filled with tears. "My family owns a house in Rhodes Town. She could have lived there—she wanted to. Other knights keep mistresses in town, you know." His tone grew defensive. "But my desires were ignored."

Drummond rubbed a hand over his face, fighting to maintain his civility. "A first for you, I'm guessing."

The knight turned his face away, closed his eyes. "You'd never understand."

"I understand better than you think I do. No man gets what he wants all the time," Drummond growled. "You're luckier than most, whether you realize it or not."

The crewman began cutting de Chambonac's breeches off his leg, prompting a howl of pain. Drummond grabbed a ceramic jar of wine and pulled out the cork.

"Here." He held the jar to the young knight's lips. "It will ease the pain."

CHAPTER 55

Spring, 1460
Archangelos

As was her habit since Drummond left, Anica woke late and drowsed in bed until Maria came to open the shutters. The rumble of waves battering the cliffs drifted inside. A songbird trilled outside in the garden, then flitted past the open windows.

"Let's walk to the beach before we go to the shrine today," she said to Maria, sitting up. "We can collect shells for sandpaper."

Climbing out of bed, she waved off Maria's attempt to help her change.

"Fetch me a piece of bread and some grapes. I'll work for a bit before we leave."

Maria closed the door softly behind her.

After dressing, Anica looked in the mirror while she unbraided her hair, brushed it, and pinned it up again. She assessed her reflection, turning her head from side to side. Since arriving in Archangelos, she'd made an effort to eat more, and she'd gotten much more rest. Today, the sharp edges of her cheekbones were less pronounced. There were still dark shadows under her eyes, but the color had returned to her skin. It shone like honey in the sunlight.

When Maria returned with the bread, Anica devoured it and asked for more, with cheese this time.

It was good to feel hungry again.

Invigorated, she went to the adjoining chamber. She stood in the doorway, looking around in satisfaction.

Her father had sent panels and easels soon after she'd arrived in Archangelos. This room was her studio now. She surveyed the two easels, the table filled with ceramic jugs of linseed oil and small wooden boxes of pigment, the paintbrushes lined up in rows on squares of tanned leather.

A bird's nest made of grass and twigs sat on the edge of the table, her most recent gift from young Angelos. He often stopped at the villa on his way from the fort to fetch supplies at the village. She and Maria plied him with flatbread, nuts, fruit, and cheese whenever he appeared. In return, he collected small treasures from the beach and the hillsides for them. She smiled a little, cupping her hand over the nest, then turned to her easels.

Both of the easels bore works in progress, icons for a merchant who wanted to send home examples of local art to his wife in Flanders.

She had made them with egg tempera and enjoyed the ease of reverting to the technique her father had taught her when she was just a child. She'd already applied the gold leaf to brighten the backgrounds. Today, she would deepen the red and blue tones, then paint the details of embroidery on the saints' robes. Tying on her leather apron, she got to work. The morning slipped by as she cracked the eggs, mixed her paint, and applied it to the panels with quick, confident brush strokes.

When hunger got the best of her again, she ate the cheese and bread that Maria had left for her on a plate.

Then, standing back, she surveyed her work. Satisfied, she put away her apron, washed her hands and face, and went downstairs.

She and Maria strolled down the sloping path to the beach, a guard following at a short distance. Drummond had made her promise to bring one of his trusted men along every time she left the house, even on quick outings to the village to visit Spiros and his family. Anica carried a canvas bag for shell collecting. Maria would smash the shells and glue them to parchment for sanding sheets later this week.

When they got to the beach, Anica slipped off her sandals, swept up her skirts, and waded into the water.

"Careful, mistress," Maria cautioned her. "Don't go too far."

"I'm no child, Maria."

Shading her eyes with a hand, Anica searched the horizon. Two seabirds hovered just over the waves at the mouth of the bay. A small fishing boat cut through the water from the open sea, its single sail straining in the wind.

The sight of the boat pushed Anica's thoughts inevitably to her husband. When would Drummond be home?

Later, they'd walk to the little shrine she had visited with her father last summer and pray for Drummond's safe return. She always brought fresh candles and removed the ones that had burned to nubs while Maria dusted the altar and the portrait of the Virgin.

Maria hung back on shore, collecting shells. When she had filled the canvas sack, she joined Anica at the water's edge, staring out at the open sea with a preoccupied air.

"You've not been yourself for so long," Anica said softly. "Do you fear this place? Archangelos lacks the walls and towers of Rhodes Town, but we have the fort to retreat to if necessary. And Drummond's guards to protect us."

"I'm not afraid." Maria kept her gaze straight ahead.

"What troubles you, then?" Tiny waves lapped at Anica's ankles. She lifted her skirts a bit higher.

Maria bent down and rinsed the sand from her hands. "Your sister. She's in my thoughts day and night."

"Mine, too," Anica confessed.

Heleni's face loomed endlessly in Anica's mind. As did the stab of guilt that accompanied her memories. If only she had told her father at once about the French knight's proposition to her. Perhaps Heleni would be looking ahead to a future as the wife of a merchant or a prosperous shipmaster. Instead, her sister was a wan, faded version of her former self. The exuberance and high spirits that drove Anica mad with frustration at times had vanished. The spark had gone out of her, and Anica was beginning to doubt it would ever return.

"I could have prevented everything from happening," Maria said miserably, meeting her eyes at last. "It was my fault, all of it. When you left for Archangelos with your father, she told me she would meet with the knight in private. I said I would go to you, I would tell—and she struck me. I told her I didn't care if she beat me with an iron poker, I could not let her ruin her honor." Maria's face twisted, and she fought off a sob. "That made her furious. She said she would hide some of your mother's jewels and claim I stole them. I was afraid your father would not free me, that he would turn me out into the streets or sell me to another master."

"I believe you," Anica said. "Heleni told me she'd been cruel to you. She was possessed by romantic notions about the man. All the sense was driven from her mind."

Maria's shoulders slumped. "I've had far better fortune than most slaves. I thank God for your family every day. And yet I've failed you."

Anica dropped her skirts. She went to Maria's side, oblivious of the sodden fabric dragging through the water, and took her servant's hands in her own.

"I blame myself for Heleni's predicament, Maria," she said. "My father blames himself, too. So does my mother. We all have our reasons for feeling responsible. But none of us are. We must try to forgive ourselves. We must try to live the rest of our days with joy, for there may not be many of them left."

Maria edged forward, leaning her cheek against Anica's chest. Taken aback, Anica folded her former slave into her arms.

After a moment, Maria mopped her tears with a sleeve.

"Your skirts are soaking," she scolded, sniffling. "The salt water will stain the wool if we let that dry."

Anica laughed. "Now that's the Maria I remember. A proper mother hen."

Maria allowed a brief smile, her earnest face lit up by the afternoon sun. They stepped away from the water's edge and she kneeled, wringing out Anica's skirts with both hands.

The fishing boat drew closer. As it approached, the fisherman waved and Maria stood, raising an arm in response.

"You know him?" Anica asked.

"He's the son of a potter who lives in the village. I met him at the market."

A silvery fish broke the water's surface. The seabirds saw it, too. They glided closer, skimming the waves with silent grace. One hurtled through the air, slammed into the water, and came up with the squirming fish in its beak.

"Anica!" A man's voice rose from behind them.

Turning, she saw Cousin Spiros lumbering toward them over the sand. A manservant trailed in his wake, trotting to keep up.

"There you are," he huffed, coming to a stop. "I've been searching everywhere for you."

"What is it?" she asked.

"I've been to the fort. The youngster Angelos has taken ill. He needs comfort and care, and he'll not get it there."

"Have your man go back with a donkey cart and fetch him to the villa. Maria and I will look after him."

Relief softened Spiros's perspiring face. "I was hoping you'd say that." He turned and dispensed orders to his servant. Then his gaze dropped to the basket the two women had brought, with its assortment of candles and cleaning rags. "Were you on your way to the shrine?"

Anica nodded. "We've been going every day since my husband left."

"Would you like me to send someone in your place today? I'll make sure the candles are fresh and the painting is dusted."

She smiled in gratitude. "Thank you, Spiros. Come, Maria. Let's get a bed ready for the boy."

CHAPTER 56

Spring, 1460
Rhodes Town

ANGELOS'S small frame was nearly lost beneath the bedcovers. He lay still, his eyes glassy and his expression listless.

"It's been three days, and his cough hasn't improved." Anica dipped a cloth in cool water, wrung it out, and applied it to his forehead. "He's still feverish."

Maria crossed her arms over her hands, shaking her head. "He needs soup. But he won't eat."

"We'll take him to Rhodes Town," Anica decided. "He needs the care of a skilled doctor, and the herbs we need for a proper tonic aren't available in Archangelos."

Maria looked doubtful. "Are you sure?"

Anica stood. "I can come and go as I wish. And it will be a chance to see my family. Perhaps I can brighten Heleni's spirits a bit."

"No." Angelos pleated the coverlet with his fingers and gave her a beseeching stare. "I won't go back. I hate it there."

"We'll be with you." Anica covered his hand with her own. "You'll be safe with us."

Maria studied him for a moment. "If you eat and drink, you'll get well. Then you won't have to go." She dipped a spoon in the ceramic bowl on the bedside table and offered him a bit of broth.

With reluctance, he opened his mouth and accepted the spoon. His face contorted as he swallowed. A moment later, he leaned over the edge of the bed and vomited into the basin they'd placed on the floor.

"My belly doesn't want anything."

He gave Anica an apologetic look, turned his face to the wall, and closed his eyes.

Anica held Maria's gaze over the bed. She dreaded an encounter with the Salviatis, but her desire to see her family was stronger. Straightening, she mustered her resolve.

"We'll leave in the morning," she said. "At dawn."

As soon as they rolled through the city gates of Rhodes Town the next day, Anica directed the driver to take them straight to Signorina Giovanna.

Grateful for the privacy afforded by the cart's arched canvas cover, Anica fixed her eyes on Angelos's face. The familiar sounds and smells of the city washed over her with every lurch of the wheels. Her muscles had been tense for the entire ride; now they felt practically rigid. And her lungs seemed to have sealed themselves off. She struggled to breathe but could only force in tiny sips of air.

Drummond's guard on the bench beside the driver should have reassured her, but even he with his sword and dagger did little to assuage her anxiety.

Maria slipped a hand into her own. The steady pressure of her touch was calming. As they neared the Tower of Italy and the doctor's residence, Anica closed her eyes and focused on steadying her breath, using the rhythm of the cart's wheels to count to six for each incoming breath, six for the outgoing ones.

Soon you'll see your family again. Think of them, not of your enemies.

By the time the cart drew to a stop, she felt ready. Leaning close to Angelos, she said, "We're here. You'll feel better soon, I promise."

He blinked up at her and attempted a smile.

When Signorina Giovanna came outside to greet them, her face registered astonishment. "Signorina Anica? But I thought you'd left . . ."

Quickly, Anica explained the situation, gesturing to the cart.

"He should go to St. Catherine's," the doctor said after questioning Anica about the boy's symptoms. "I can examine him there and procure what is needed to help him."

Anica shook her head. "He won't go there again, nor will the nuns take him in."

At the doctor's raised eyebrow, she added, "Fate has been cruel to him, but he has a good heart. This island needs the man he'll grow into if he can just survive his childhood."

"Very well," the doctor said. "I have a small chamber upstairs where he can stay. But I'll need to go to the convent myself. Yesterday, I delivered a half-dozen bottles of an elixir of honey, poppy milk, and herbs to them. He needs some of that medicine."

Anica put a hand on the doctor's arm. "Let Maria and I go after we get him settled here."

Drummond's guard carried Angelo upstairs to his quarters and deposited him on the narrow bed. Dr. Giovanna eyed the man's weapons with trepidation, but said nothing.

At the convent, Anica and Maria climbed the broad stone steps and waited for a long moment under the waning light of the sun. When the door creaked open, Anica explained their errand to the nun who greeted them. Frowning, she waved them inside.

"The mother abbess will not be pleased. She paid good coin for those bottles. And we've several sick children who need the medicine."

Anica dug in her purse and came up with thirty silver aspers. "This should cover the cost of one bottle."

Her frown fading a bit, the nun took the coins and disappeared.

When she returned a few moments later with the bottle, Anica asked after the young woman she had seen cleaning the floor during her last visit.

The nun shook her head. "She's gone."

Anica stiffened. "Gone? Is she dead?"

"Oh, blessed mother, far from it. She came into some money." The nun's eyes gleamed as she imparted the gossip.

"But she was a servant, I thought. With no family, no place to go."

"Yes, she was a servant. Her master was cruel to her. He beat her, sliced off an ear. But when he died, he left her some money. All the servants he'd abused got money, or so the story goes. It was his way of trying to absolve himself of his sins. Only God can decide if he's worthy of absolution, of course."

"Who told you this?" Anica asked, skeptical.

"I swear it's true, on all that is holy." The nun crossed herself and cast her gaze to the heavens. "A notary came here not long ago and asked to see the mother abbess. He told her what I've told you. Said his employer, a Genoese merchant, died at sea in a gale. The merchant left the woman a sum of ducats in his will."

Maria let out a gasp. Dread rippled down Anica's spine.

"Was the merchant's name Marino Lomellini?" she asked, her voice dropping low.

"How should I know?" the nun said, pursing her lips.

"Surely, the mother abbess knows." Anica thrust out another silver coin. "Please ask her."

When the nun bustled back through the doorway, she bore an astonished expression. "Yes! His name was Marino Lomellini. But how did you—"

Anica wheeled and pulled Maria toward the door. "Thank you, Sister," she tossed over her shoulder.

She barely recognized her own strangled voice.

CHAPTER 57

Spring, 1460
Symi Island

ON DRUMMOND'S ORDERS, the galleys headed for Symi. The other vessel had sustained so much damage to its sails that it had to be powered by oars, and the seas were so choppy that progress was slow. Things weren't much better on his own galley, which was gravely hobbled by the loss of the mainsail yard.

When he sighted Symi, relief washed over him. Along with several other islands, Symi had been attacked by the Turks a few years ago; repairs on its ancient hillside fortress ordered by Lord de Milly were almost finished. They would bring their wounded to the fort and light the signal fires. With a little luck, reinforcements would soon arrive from Rhodes Town.

His neck and shoulders screamed with tension all the way to the sheltered bay where they dropped anchor late that afternoon. The clouds lifted as they disembarked. It was slow work transferring the wounded to skiffs and rowing them to shore, but finally it was done.

A group of local men appeared at the base of the hill. He recognized one as a sea-sponge diver who'd once gifted Drummond a half-dozen sponges in return for his help with a boat that had sprung a leak at sea.

"Kalimera," Drummond greeted him.

The man returned the greeting and approached with his companions. After hearing about the incident, the men said they would bring several pails of shrimp and fish up to the fortress to feed the crew.

"I'm grateful," Drummond said. "We'll look forward to it. Tell the villagers the signal fires will be lit tonight. We weren't followed and don't expect an attack on Symi, but if the people wish to shelter in the fort, they're welcome to. We have several wounded men among us. Can we borrow a few donkeys and carts to transport them up the hill? And if your apothecary has poppy milk or any other remedies for pain, can you send some along?"

The men agreed and went to fetch the carts.

As they prepared for the steep climb to the fortress, Drummond settled Émile de Chambonac in a donkey cart. The young man's skin was waxy, and his eyes were closed. Occasionally, he emitted a long, low groan. Next to him, Drummond had his men place the wooden cask containing the tribute payment meant for the sultan's negotiators.

"You'll receive good care in the fort," Drummond assured him.

If only he could believe his own words. This fort was sparsely manned and had few comforts. But they could not sail all the way back to Rhodes without carrying out the necessary repairs to their crafts, so it would have to do.

Drummond did not look forward to the climb, but he did eagerly anticipate a bowl of hot, garlicky shrimp for supper.

A haughty voice rang out behind him. "There are only three carts, and they're all full," Guillaume Lopic said. "What about me and the other officials of high rank? We cannot be expected to climb this hill on foot."

Drummond turned on his heel and eyed the man. His face was set in a petulant scowl. A breeze careened off the sea, lifting the hem of his silk tunic and revealing soft leather boots soaked through with salt water.

"Anyone who can walk on his own two feet is required to do so," Drummond growled.

"There should have been provisions made for our transport," the Frenchman protested.

Drummond ignored him and instructed the drivers of the carts to make haste for the fort.

Behind the carts, the disheartened men shuffled in near-silence, sobered and exhausted by their ordeal at sea.

Drummond's lungs burned with exertion. The sun slid down in the west, streaking the sky with copper. The fort loomed above them, its thick walls and towers a welcome sight. Never had he yearned for the dark of night with as much fervor. The moment the sun vanished below the horizon, he would order those signal fires lit.

As soon as they arrived in the fortress, Guillaume Lopic and the other agents of the Order clustered around the hearth in the drafty great hall. Soot crusted the walls and ceiling, and the space stank of tallow from the candles burning in iron candelabras around the chamber.

Drummond accompanied de Chambonac and the other wounded men to the small infirmary. It had its own hearth and seemed more airtight than the great hall. A few faded tapestries hung from the walls, creating an illusion of warmth.

When the villagers arrived with food and a modest assortment of medical supplies, Drummond cleaned and bandaged de Chambonac's wound again. It was a deep gash on the outside of the thigh, stretching around to the back of the knee. Every time he came near it, de Chambonac yelped with pain.

As the knight drifted into an uneasy slumber, Drummond raced to the signal tower. He supervised the lighting of the fire just as the last glow of sunlight shimmered on the edge of the sea. The dry branches and logs crackled and hissed as the fire took hold. He ordered two guards to replenish the wood all night, then trudged back down the stairs to the great hall.

Servants laid bowls and cups on the long table and dragged benches alongside it. The cook brought out platters of fish, shrimp, fried onions and greens, and flatbread. When the men took their seats, they fell upon the food as if they hadn't eaten in days. Lopic sent servants back to the kitchen repeatedly for more wine.

Drummond ate his fill, drank sparingly, and excused himself twice. Once to check on the kitchen, making sure the oarsmen and sailors were fed. And the second time, to ensure the signal fire burned at full strength.

Satisfied on both counts, he headed back to the great hall, suddenly conscious of a searing exhaustion in his muscles—in his very bones. The pressure of his responsibilities squeezed his lungs like a vise, sucking the breath out of him. He paused, leaned against a wall in the shadows, and fought for air.

Closing his eyes, he conjured up Anica's face. Her large brown eyes, their veil of black lashes, the pleasing angles of her arched eyebrows, all swam before him. He longed to put his hands on her, feel the gentle sweep of her cheekbones, brush his fingertips over her full rose-colored lips, watch them part in a smile. Just the thought of her calmed his racing heart. He willed away his fear, his dread, and imagined himself in her arms, drinking in her sweet scent, listening to the soft thud of her heartbeat as she slept entwined with him.

"Master Fordun!"

He opened his eyes and reluctantly came back to the moment he had been trying to escape.

"What is it?" He stepped out of the shadows.

"The men demand your presence," the guard said.

Drummond stalked across the courtyard by the light of flickering torches. Inside the great hall, he joined the group at the table, sitting as far from Guillaume Lopic as possible.

"We'll have to prepare for war," Lopic was saying. "The sultan betrayed our trust. We can never attempt a negotiation again."

One of the other men objected. "Were those even the sultan's men who attacked us? I did not see his banners on those *fuste*. The boats were unmarked. They were pirates, I wager."

Several men turned to Drummond, awaiting his opinion.

He wanted to seize the nearest pitcher of wine and gulp it down.

Instead, he placed his hands on the table, curled into fists, and stared at Lopic.

"I agree that there was no evidence the sultan sent those boats. Some of the attackers spoke Arabic, some Turkish. Surely, you heard their words as well?"

A few men nodded their agreement.

"They could be pirates or perhaps mercenaries sent by the Mamluks to create mistrust between the Order and Sultan Mehmed," Drummond continued. "It's happened before."

His mind went to the prisoners they'd seized during the melee. Drummond always did his best to treat such captives well because they were potentially valuable for ransom exchanges. He'd ensured their wounds were cleaned and bound, and had scavenged some salted fish and twice-baked bread for them to eat.

"It's easy enough to learn the truth," Lopic said. "Let's interrogate the captives." He looked at Drummond. "You can take charge of the matter. I'm sure with the proper persuasion they'll reveal their employer's name."

Drummond stiffened. "I'm a privateer. A sea captain. Not a torturer of prisoners in fortresses."

"You work for the Order. You'll do as required for the knights."

"I don't work for you, Monsieur Lopic. I work for Lord de Milly. And I'll await his word on the matter. We should be back in Rhodes within a few days."

"In his absence, you answer to me." Lopic rose. "Guards!" He signaled to a pair of men standing at either side of the doorway. "Accompany Master Fordun to the dungeons. He'll be interrogating our guests tonight."

CHAPTER 58

Spring, 1460
Rhodes Town

AFTER DELIVERING the elixir to Dr. Giovanna, Anica and Maria hurried through the streets toward home. The warm glow of the setting sun traced gold across the limestone and marble façades of the buildings around them. A fragrant burst of jasmine drifted out from a garden behind a decorative iron gate, filling her lungs with sweetness. She savored the scent, trying to put aside thoughts of Marino Lomellini.

They turned up a narrow lane. Children's laughter rang out from an open window. For a fleeting instant, memories of Benedetto flooded Anica's mind. Her breath faltered. She bowed her head, forcing down an unexpected sob.

Rounding the final curve, they came face-to-face with her father and Aunt Rhea.

"Anica!" Papa cried in astonishment.

The sorrow that had knifed through Anica a moment ago ebbed as she embraced her father and aunt, explaining what had brought them to Rhodes Town.

Papa glanced over her shoulder at the guard, raising an eyebrow. "He looks fierce."

"Drummond assigned him to watch me. He's always a few steps behind, wherever I go. I trust him."

Her father nodded in resignation. "It's probably best." He turned to Maria. "How does Archangelos suit you?"

She smiled, her expression open and unguarded. "Very well, signor. Better than I thought."

"Let's go inside." Papa took one of Anica's arms and Aunt Rhea the other. "Your mother will be overjoyed."

They ascended the steps to the house. "And Heleni? How is she?" Anica asked.

Papa hesitated.

"Better all the time," Aunt Rhea put in, a bit too jovially. "She's embroidering veils with gold thread for you to wear to Valossi's wedding."

They entered the house.

"Mamá!" Anica could not help calling. "I'm home!"

Her mother appeared through the door to the prayer room. With a cry of delight, she drew Anica into a long embrace.

A movement beyond Mamá made Anica step back, startled. "Heleni?"

Her sister walked with slow, uncertain steps into the entry hall. Her eyes widened at the sight of Anica.

"I've missed you," Heleni said in a halting voice.

Anica wrapped her arms around her sister, her throat tightening with emotion. "As I've missed you."

Heleni clung to her for a moment, then turned to Maria and held out her arms. "Maria."

With an expression of complete shock, Maria accepted Heleni's embrace.

"Into the courtyard, everyone," Mamá ordered. "We'll have lemon tonic and sugared almonds." She met Maria's gaze. "Will you fetch the refreshments, Maria?"

Nodding, Maria scurried off to the kitchen.

The rest of them entered the courtyard. It was even more lushly planted than Anica remembered, with new terra-cotta pots filled with roses, lavender, and pomegranate trees.

"It looks lovely in here," she said, gazing around in admiration. As they took their seats on cushioned benches, she knew something else had changed in the space, but she could not put her finger on it. "I've been longing to see you all. What have I missed?" She turned to Papa. "Is there word from the apprentice?"

He nodded. "The young man's called Francesco, and he wrote me not long ago to say he'd be sailing from Venice soon."

"Praise the saints. And your eyes?"

"Better and better," her father assured her.

Maria appeared with the lemon tonic and sugared almonds on a tray. She set it down on the cypress-wood table and poured for them, then retreated into the shadows and began lighting torches around the perimeter of the courtyard.

Anica studied her sister's face. An unsettling blankness had veiled her eyes, and she was still too thin. But on balance, she looked better than she had when Anica left Rhodes Town.

"How are preparations for Valossi's wedding coming, Aunt Rhea?" she asked, turning to her aunt.

"I believe it will be the most extravagant wedding in Lindos in some time," her aunt replied. "Valossi does not want to spare any expense for his lovely little bride, and why not? He deserves every happiness."

Following Maria's movements, Anica's gaze fell on the niche where the bronze boy customarily stood. "He's gone," she said in surprise.

"Yes." Her father sipped from his cup.

"Where did he go?"

"Across the sea to Italy," Aunt Rhea answered. "To a collector in Verona with a deep purse."

"What?" Anica asked, stunned. "You sold him?" She shot a perplexed look at her father. "Why on earth would you do that?"

"I had no choice, Anica. The Salviatis did not take the news of your marriage well. Their pride suffered, and for that, they wanted us to suffer, too."

"How do you mean?"

Her father sighed. "They threatened to take me to court for defaulting on my loan."

"But you didn't default—"

"I know. But it was Signor Salviati's word against mine. He's a wealthy Florentine banker with ties to the Medicis, I'm a Venetian artist. Venetians aren't held in the highest regard by the Order just now."

"No," she admitted, watching him with apprehension. "So you got the money to pay off the loan by selling the boy?"

"I did. Rhea helped find the buyer, and the sale went smoothly. I paid off every ducat I owed the Florentines, down to the last asper. But Signor Salviati set out to destroy my reputation with other moneylenders nonetheless, claiming I tried to cheat him."

A wave of anger struck Anica in the gut. "That devil," she muttered.

"Anica!" Mamá looked shocked.

"It's no lie to call him that." Aunt Rhea slurped from her cup, then tossed a few sugared almonds into her mouth. "Your father's reputation is intact, though. And we have Troilo to thank for it."

"How can that be?" Anica asked. "He wouldn't lift a finger to help any of us."

Aunt Rhea snorted. "I can't decide if he's an idiot or if he's some kind of madman."

Anica cast a questioning look at her father.

"Troilo had his hand in the till at the Order's treasury," he said. "He dispensed salaries for the falconers, stablemen, and other servants of the Order. Apparently, he developed a trick of holding back a coin or two here and there, perhaps assuming that the men weren't capable of counting their money. Cédric de Montavon collected evidence from those affected over a period of a few months, then took it to the grand master."

"What happened?"

"Troilo is in the Kastellania. In a cell that will be his home for—how long is it, Rhea?" Papa asked.

"God willing, a year at least. Perhaps two. He was lucky to avoid a public flogging. I'm sure his father paid dearly to ensure he got off with a mere incarceration."

Anica glanced from her father to her aunt, her mind reeling with the news. Then her gaze slipped to the empty niche in the wall again.

"I'm sorry, Papa."

"Why, my dear? I plucked the bronze boy out of the sea, but he was never ours. He was crafted by the ancients hundreds, maybe thousands of years ago. He was in our home for a time, yes, but the boy was simply passing through our lives on the way to—"

A deep chorus of blaring horns rumbled through the streets, silencing her father. They all froze in place, dumbstruck. The sound came again, reverberating in Anica's chest with ominous force.

"Dear God. The knights have sighted signal fires." Papa's words were slow and halting.

Trumpeters at the palace signaled the call to the knights to assemble in the Mandraki.

"They'll dispatch war galleys from the harbor," Aunt Rhea said as the sound faded. "It must be serious if they're launching a fleet at twilight."

Heleni dissolved in tears.

"God help us," Mamá murmured, drawing Heleni into her arms. "God help us all."

Rhea stood, her ceramic cup smashing on the stone floor. "I'm needed at home."

Anica felt pinned to her seat by terror. She barely heard the murmured voices of her family. All she could think of was Drummond.

A chill struck her, driving deeper into her flesh with each plaintive blare of the horns.

She struggled from her seat. But before she could take a step, her knees buckled. She sank to the floor, her skirts pooling around her.

Santa Maria, I beg you, bring my husband back to me.

CHAPTER 59

Spring, 1460
Symi Island

DRUMMOND PASSED a hand over his face, studying the two men at his feet in the weak light of a single torch. One of them was worse off than the other. His eyes closed, he bled from the head and the gut, and would likely not last the night. The other was a gaunt man of middle age with silvering hair revealed by his missing turban. His wounds were not so grave. He bore a resigned expression, and had no apparent regard for his comrade, making no attempt to comfort the man.

Drummond repeated his question to the bare-headed man, this time in Arabic. "Who pays you?"

Turkish had prompted no response.

The man's eyelids drooped. But Drummond thought he saw a slight shift in his expression, so he said the words again, pronouncing each syllable with care.

"Who pays you? If you tell me, we'll see that you're ransomed and returned to your home. If you don't, God help you."

"I have no home to return to," the man said dully, breaking his silence. "The Christians came to my village and took my wife and children captive two years ago. I was in the next valley when it happened. I could do nothing to stop it."

"Where is your village?" Drummond asked, his tone softening.

"South of here. In Syria."

"So where did you launch from?"

The man stared at him stone faced. "South of here."

"In Syria?"

No reply. The man turned his face away, setting his jaw.

One of the guards at Drummond's side slid his dagger out of its scabbard.

"He needs some prompting," said the man in French. "The sharp end of a blade will jog his memory."

"I'm conducting this interrogation," Drummond ground out. "If I want you to raise arms against this man, you'll know."

Reluctantly, the guard stilled his hand.

Continuing in Arabic, Drummond said to the prisoner, "I've been ordered to torture you if you don't tell me who hired you."

The man gave him a bleak look. "I'm paid by the captain. He sails from village to village collecting men who've been wronged by the Christians. Then he attacks Christian ships. They say his brother captains the other *fusta*. They always travel together, that's certain."

"So he's a pirate, then?"

"I don't know. He's a man with anger in his heart."

"Is he Turkish? Syrian?"

Next to him, the seriously injured man moaned, blood leaking from his bandaged abdomen to the cold stone floor.

The other captive gave his agonized companion a cursory glance, then returned his gaze to Drummond.

"He speaks Turkish and Arabic equally well. I don't know where he comes from."

"Your vessels bore no banners."

"That's because the captain has no allegiance to anyone but himself." The man's voice was hoarse. He coughed, a loose, rheumy sound that rattled ominously in his lungs.

"So he *is* a pirate."

"He pays well, and that's all I care about. I was a fishing net weaver before the Christians destroyed my village and stole my family. Now I've no other way to earn money but this." He coughed again. "It's the truth, what I've said. I don't know any more."

Drummond nodded. "You've said enough."

He turned to the guards. "This man must live. He's a valuable captive. I'll be back to check on him at dawn, and I expect him to be in the same condition he's in now."

Before returning to the great hall from the dungeons, he climbed the stairs of the signal tower to check on the fire. It was crackling fiercely in the cool night air, the guards feeding it fresh logs at frequent intervals. Taking a long, slow breath, he tilted his head back, quieting his mind as best he could.

Stars glimmered overhead. Not a wisp of cloud marred the sky. Drummond was tempted to stay up there until dawn broke. But he had to descend the stairs, had to honor his vow to Lord de Milly. Emile de Chambonac needed his attention. Guillaume Lopic, on the other hand, could rot in Hell for all he cared. Drummond would not step foot in the great hall until daybreak, consequences be damned.

CHAPTER 60

Spring, 1460
Rhodes Town

DRUMMOND CLENCHED his amulet with stiff fingers as the galley glided into the Mandraki. He raised an arm in greeting to the guards atop the walls. Trumpets blared to signal their arrival, the sound rippling up toward the palace.

"Cast on the ropes!" His voice was raspy with fatigue. He'd barely slept since their ill-fated attempt to reach Bodrum. And for the life of him, he could not recall how many days had passed since then.

He supervised the landing with bleary eyes, his entire body aching, his brain throbbing.

It was quiet in the harbor this evening, as Sundays usually were. But as they tied up the vessel, dozens of church bells heralding the hour of Vespers shattered the calm. Though the nearby bell tower of Santa Maria was concealed behind the city walls, its chimes washed over him with the familiar pattern he'd heard daily in his rented chambers near the church.

Thank you, Santa Maria. I don't know what I've done to deserve your protection all these years, but I'm grateful all the same.

As the crew prepared to disembark, he handed out an extra portion of coin to each man. They had performed well, both during the attack and in the tumultuous days afterward.

Drummond performed a last inspection of his craft with slow, fumbling movements. Tomorrow, he would return to the harbor and look at his galley with fresh eyes. It had made the journey back from Symi without mishap, but there might be some damage he'd over-looked, some crack in the hull he'd missed.

Finally satisfied, he disembarked. It felt good to stand on solid ground in a familiar place. What he wouldn't give for a bath, a pitcher of wine, and—most of all—a leisurely night of lovemaking with his wife.

Squaring his shoulders and heaving his sack of nautical instruments and possessions over his shoulder, he strode toward the city walls. His leisure time would have to wait. First, he'd have to muster the energy to face questioning by the grand master this evening. His mind flicked to Émile de Chambonac. The same day a rescue fleet had arrived in Symi harbor, de Chambonac and all the other injured men—including the lone surviving captive—had been ferried back to Rhodes. Lopic and the rest of the contingent of negotiators had accompanied them.

In the intervening days, while he'd supervised the repairs to his galley, his thoughts had alternated between images of a dying Émile de Chambonac and worries about Anica. Had word of the attack trickled south to Archangelos? News spread rapidly on the island. She probably had learned the signal fires of Symi and Kos had been lit, had discovered a fleet was dispatched in response. And now she likely harbored fears that he was taken captive, wounded, or, worst of all, dead.

As soon as he made his report to Lord de Milly, he would go to the Foscolo home and arrange to send word to his wife that he was safe and well.

After exchanging a quick greeting with the guards at the city gate, he made straight for his residence. He could at least put away his things and wash up a bit. But before he got to the doorstep, a voice cried his name. He pivoted on his heel to confront a cloaked form hurtling at him. He dropped his sack, threw his arms wide, and Anica rushed into his embrace.

"You're alive!" She sobbed the words, her voice muffled against his neck. "I heard the trumpets and I hoped—prayed—you'd returned to me."

Drummond felt like weeping, too. "By the grace of God and Santa Maria, I'm still breathing."

She pulled away a little, examining him with concern. "And you're unhurt?"

He nodded. A pair of monks exited the hospital and glanced their way, eyes full of curiosity. Drummond scooped up his things again and led her to his doorstep. "What are you doing in Rhodes Town, my love?"

"Angelos fell ill. He needed more care than he could get in Archangelos. Maria and I brought him here."

Drummond's worry spiked again. "How is the lad now?"

"Better," she reassured him. "He's staying with Dr. Giovanna. His cough is much improved, and he's eating again."

"I'm glad to hear it." He fumbled the key into the ornate iron lock. "Come upstairs?"

Anica smiled at him, dipping her head in a slow nod.

The veneer of hard indifference he'd worn since the moment he sailed away from Rhodes Town cracked.

"I wish we could spend the evening together, but I don't have much time," he said with regret. "I'll need to clean up before I head to the palace."

She put a hand on his cheek, caressing it with astonishing tenderness. His heart swelled again. At her touch, the iron vise of tension and anxiety gripping his heart vanished under a tide of warm, rich desire.

"I can help you with that," she said, her voice silky and low.

He grinned.

Their hands entwined, he led her through the door.

Drummond waited outside the great hall, trying unsuccessfully to banish thoughts of his wife's loving ministrations to him not an hour ago. His skin still pulsed with pleasure where she had bathed him with gentle hands, kissed him in his most tender, sensitive places. His loins stirred with longing as he recalled the sight of Anica shedding her cloak, skirts, and blouse by the light of a single guttering candle. She'd unbraided her long black hair and let it tumble around her shoulders, lips parted, eyes shining with desire—

"Master Fordun, you may enter now."

The guard's voice brought him back to the present with harsh finality.

Inside the vast chamber, he saw Guillaume Lopic at Lord de Milly's side on the dais. A group of other officials stood near the doors, heads bent together in quiet conversation. They fell silent as Drummond stalked across the floor.

"My lord." He bowed to the grand master, ignoring Lopic.

"I'm glad you've returned safely," his employer said in a sober voice.

"How is young de Chambonac faring?" Drummond asked.

"He is improving. That leg injury will be difficult to mend, but it's not festering."

"Thank God and all the saints."

Drummond was sincere. He did not want the lad to die despite his abominable behavior toward the Foscolo family.

"It is unfortunate that the sultan saw fit to betray our agreement," the grand master went on. "I'd never held out much hope that the negotiations would foster a real truce, but attacking the contingent before they even arrived at Bodrum . . ." he trailed off, shaking his head.

Drummond's jaw tensed. He shot a glance at Lopic, who was watching him with shrewd eyes.

"We don't know if the sultan was behind the attack, my lord—" he began.

"You haven't heard the news, it seems." Lopic folded his hands together and pressed them against his belly, just above the bulge of his purse. "That captive we took? He confessed that the sultan hired the captains of those *fuste.*"

Drummond looked at him in astonishment. "That's not what he told me."

Lopic frowned. "I interrogated him myself in the Kastellania last night. Your questioning of him was insufficient, according to the guards who witnessed it. So I took it upon myself to do the job. My methods extracted the truth. The sultan ordered the attack, I promise you."

"If the sultan was responsible, why would he send half-starving old men who were shite fighters? You're truly telling me that the man who captured Constantinople with an army of one hundred thousand men would hire a ragged crew of desperate souls to interfere with a truce agreement? It makes no sense at all."

The grand master leaned forward in his high-backed oak chair, training a hard gaze at Drummond. "What are you getting at?"

"The crew of those *fuste* were poorly armed. Some of them wielded daggers with skill, but they were not trained soldiers, my lord. They were easily overpowered."

"You're wrong." Lopic's voice rang out shrilly, piercing the air. "I got the truth out of that captive. My interrogation was so thorough he died after making his confession."

"A waste," Drummond retorted. "We could have used him for a ransom swap. I don't hold with killing captives for no reason."

"He was an infidel! His death means nothing."

Drummond fought to keep his hands from curling into fists. How he longed to strike that smug little bastard in the face.

"Every life has value, Monsieur Lopic." The grand master laid his hands on the carved armrests of the chair and leaned back, eyeing the Frenchman speculatively. "Lately, though, I've learned that you do not share this view."

"Every *Christian* life has value, my lord." Lopic's tone was conciliatory.

"Yet you ordered the murder of a Christian woman not long ago, didn't you?" Lord de Milly dropped his voice to a predatory growl.

"I'm not sure I know what you refer to, my lord."

"Heleni Foscolo," Drummond said, meeting Lopic's gaze. "My

wife's sister. She believed herself poisoned by Émile de Chambonac. But it was you who sent the poison. Émile himself told me so."

"What is this nonsense?" Lopic spluttered. "You insult me."

The grand master shook his head. "Master Fordun is correct. I've looked into the matter. You ordered the potion from our apothecary. You copied Émile's hand, inked a note telling her the stuff would end the life in her womb and no one would be the wiser."

Lopic's expression of wounded indignation crumbled. His gaze slid from Lord de Milly to Drummond. A hint of fear glinted in his eyes.

"I was protecting the boy's honor. The reputation of the Order. There is no shame in that."

"You usurped my authority. You proved yourself untrustworthy. If the girl had died, our most valued Greek allies—men of the first families, the ones who've supported the Order since our early days in Rhodes—would have risen up in protest. For that, I will not suffer you as my counsel any longer."

"My lord!" A look of utter shock came over Lopic's face.

"You'll leave on the first ship back to Narbonne. I'm assigning you as under-administrator of the preceptory in Auvergne. My trusted sergeant will be your superior. He'll be reporting back to me on your activities."

"What? Auvergne? Tucked away in the mountains? No, I cannot—"

The grand master rose. "You can and you will. It is better than you deserve. Now get out of my sight."

He remained standing until Lopic's footsteps faded, then sank into his chair again.

"Master Fordun." Lord de Milly turned his eyes to Drummond, his weariness evident. "I am ready to put this matter behind me. But first, I must express regret for my treatment of your wife. She told me the truth, and I did not believe her. She's entirely too bold, but she also possesses admirable courage. Before you leave the palace, I'll have a secretary write a letter to her father."

Drummond took that in. "To what effect, my lord?"

The grand master's lips curved in a half-smile. "I find I'm in need of a few more portraits in oil, so I require the services of the finest artists on the island once again."

"Artists?" Drummond repeated, sure he had misheard.

"Indeed." Raising his voice so it echoed all the way to the doors, he added, "The Foscolo family studio turns out highly skilled work. I've never seen its equal."

The chatter amongst the other men in the room died away.

Drummond couldn't help himself. He grinned.

Lord de Milly raked his gaze over the officials clustered beyond Drummond. He pitched his tone low again. "And where I lead, these men will follow."

Relief loosened the tension in Drummond's chest. It took a moment to find his voice. "Thank you, Lord de Milly. My wife and her father will be pleased."

CHAPTER 61

Summer, 1460
Lindos

ANICA STAMPED AND SWAYED, clapping to the beat of the drums. Drummond clasped her hands and spun her around, his eyes glowing with merriment. Planting a kiss on her mouth, he wheeled her in a neat circle, then executed a courtly bow, one eyebrow tilted at a suggestive angle. Anica burst out laughing. She whirled, ducked, and sidestepped, avoiding a crash with two cousins who had imbibed a bit too much wine.

"I have to catch my breath," she told Drummond between gasps for air.

His eyes dropped to her swollen belly, his smile vanishing.

"I'm fine," she reassured him. "Never better."

He nodded, relieved.

They stood a little apart from the dancers, watching them assemble amidst much laughter and good-natured argument about which song the musicians would choose next. At a signal from her aunt, the musicians launched into a rousing folk tune, and a circle of dancers materialized at the center of the courtyard. Uncle Valossi and his new wife took their places at the heart of the group and raised their joined hands in the air, prompting an eruption of joyful cries.

All around them, people wove complex patterns in the dance, first merging, then splitting apart again. The flower garlands on the walls and rafters trembled and bounced. Through the open windows beyond the dancers, the inky sea spread out to the western horizon.

Anica swept her gaze around the space, cherishing the sight of so many beloved, familiar faces. Her parents, Heleni, Aunt Rhea, Uncle Vallosi, dozens of cousins and friends, all of them wreathed in smiles. Spiros danced through the crowd, flinging his arms wide to embrace everyone in his path.

Mamá came to her side.

"Let me look at you," Mamá ordered, cupping her hands over Anica's belly. She gave Drummond an approving nod. "You're taking excellent care of her, I see."

"I take my duties as husband seriously," he replied with a gleam in his eyes.

"As you should, Scotsman," she said. "As you should."

Aunt Rhea bustled up and took Anica in her arms, planting kisses on both cheeks. "You've plumped up nicely." She shot an appraising stare at Drummond. "Now, if you could just get your husband to stop his seafaring ways."

He dipped his head at her. "I only wish I could."

"We'll talk later," she told him. "You might be surprised how a man can make a fortune on this island."

He chuckled. "That should be an interesting conversation."

"I don't know how it's possible, but I'm hungry," Anica announced.

"I do," Mamá said tartly, gesturing at her belly.

Exchanging an amused glance with Drummond, Anica allowed her mother to lead her to a table. She sank down on a bench, grateful to be off her feet. Before her lay the remains of the wedding feast: fish stew, grilled octopus, grape leaves stuffed with rice and raisins, lamb laced with garlic and rosemary, fragrant flatbreads. Aunt Rhea had provided the wine, naturally, from her best Cypriot casks.

Though she'd already eaten plenty of food today, Anica fell upon the dishes ravenously, her appetite whetted by all the dancing.

"Aren't those musicians from Rhodes Town?" she asked her mother. "I recognize them."

"Yes," Mamá replied. "They rode here with your cousins in a mule cart. You know your aunt. Rhea wouldn't dream of relying on provincial Lindos for entertainment."

Anica looked at her father, who was standing near the windows immersed in conversation with a lean, fair-haired young man.

"Papa's finally found an apprentice he not only tolerates but respects," she observed.

Though a small part of her was envious of the role Francesco now played in her father's workshop, Anica was relieved Papa finally had a reliable assistant. Even more reassuring, Papa's eyes had completely healed. He had regained both his vision and his confidence before the easel.

"Your father says Francesco is far more talented than any of the previous ones," her mother said. "He's got an agreeable temperament, too."

"Look!" Anica put a hand on her mother's arm as Heleni, dressed in a gown of pink silk, approached Papa and the apprentice. "She walks with assurance now, doesn't she? And she's got her color back."

Francesco bowed to Heleni as Papa engaged her in their conversation.

Mamá nodded. "Once, she was the first to join any circle of dancers. She hasn't danced all night. I fear she still longs for that French knight."

"He'll never hurt Heleni or any other Rhodian woman again, Mamá. For that, at least, we can be grateful."

Émile de Chambonac had sailed back to France a month ago, his lame leg condemning him to a sedentary life. Drummond had told her the knight refused an administrative position in the palace, preferring to return to Auvergne rather than give up his sword.

Good riddance, Anica thought.

Then Anica and her mother both gasped. They watched, mesmerized, as Heleni followed Francesco to the circle of dancers. Anica's father caught her eye. Beaming, he raised an eyebrow, tilting his head at Heleni's retreating back.

She returned his smile and stood. Looking down, she saw Mamá's eyes glistening.

"Tears of joy?" she asked softly, extending a hand.

Her mother nodded. "Let's dance."

They wove through the celebrants to Papa, who was resplendent in a silk tunic embroidered with gold thread.

Anica couldn't help herself. She flung her arms around him. "You look happy."

"You make me happy, dear girl," he returned. "You gave me my sight back. You fought for your sister's honor—for her very life. You married a good man. And you'll soon make me a grandfather. What more could I want?"

He looked at Mamá as if he'd forgotten something.

"Commissions from the grand master?" Mamá prompted him.

"Ah, yes. I delivered the paintings to Lord de Milly. We've been so busy celebrating that I haven't had a chance to tell you."

Anica's heart leaped. "Was he satisfied?"

Papa had made one painting; she'd been responsible for the other. In the end, no one would ever be able to tell two different artists had produced them.

Her father nodded, his eyes twinkling. "He asked me to give you his thanks."

A warm glow spread through Anica's body. She took her parents' hands, and they joined the revelers whose pounding steps shook the rafters. Heleni danced nearby, her wide smile matching their own.

I choose joy, she told herself. *I choose hope.*

Despite the sorrows of the past year, despite the injustice her family had endured, despite the pain that all Rhodians had suffered with every pirate attack, every assault by the Mamluks and Ottoman Turks, every diminishment of their independence under the rule of the Order, they were still here. They still had love in their hearts.

Tears pricked at Anica's eyes. She blinked them away defiantly.

I choose joy. I choose hope.

Across the room, she glimpsed Drummond with her aunt. His head was bent toward Aunt Rhea's, his face composed in a polite smile. Feeling the pull of Anica's gaze, he glanced up. When she smiled at him, he straightened, his face splitting into a grin. Excusing himself, he strode to her side.

A shiver of happiness struck her.

Gripping Drummond's hands in her own, Anica let out a cry of delight. He threw back his head, smiling, and a shout of exultation tore from his throat. One by one, the other dancers joined in, bellowing their joy. Whoops of wild energy rose up and exploded into the night, hurtling toward the stars. Anica's voice mingled with a hundred others, sailing over the torchlit streets of Lindos to the dark and restless sea.

A siege would come. It menaced the islanders from the whispering waters even now, gathering strength in the East. One day soon it would roll in with the relentless tides, propelled by wind and waves. And everything would change forever.

But the horrors of the future could not harm them now.

All that mattered, Anica knew with certainty, was this moment.

And in this moment, life was exquisitely, unspeakably beautiful.

HISTORICAL NOTES

Sea of Shadows is book 2 in the *Sea and Stone Chronicles*, a series of stand-alone romantic suspense novels set in 15th-century Rhodes and Cyprus.

Readers are always interested in what is real and what is imagined. The following will give you an idea of what I found in the historical record and what I created.

I visited Rhodes, Greece, with my family ten years ago and fell in love with the island, its culture, and its history as a crossroads of maritime trade and as the seat of power for the Knights Hospitaller in the medieval era.

After their occupation of Jerusalem was ended by Muslim forces, the Knights of the Order of St. John, otherwise known as the Hospitallers, moved their operations to Rhodes in the early 1300s. The organization also possessed a stronghold called Bodrum in Turkey and was a dominant presence on the island of Cyprus.

The Order would rule Rhodes and surrounding islands for roughly two centuries, until a siege by the Ottoman Turks in 1522 forced the knights to withdraw to Malta.

The *Sea and Stone Chronicles* takes place midway through the Order's occupation of Rhodes. After Sultan Mehmed II of the Ottoman Turks sacked Constantinople in 1453, the knights shored up defenses on Rhodes, preparing for an inevitable siege by the Muslim people they called "infidels" from the East.

Most of the Order's time was spent engaging in naval warfare with the Turks and the Mamluks of Egypt, taking goods and captives at sea or raiding coastal villages. Captives were either kept as slaves, sold at auction, or ransomed in return for Christian captives. The Order hired privateers to supplement its naval force, both for business operations and military missions.

Rhodes Town has a long, rich history as a thriving port community. By the time the knights took over, Rhodes Town was home to a mixture of Greeks, Italians, French, Catalans, Turks, Armenians, Jews, and others.

Of the approximately eight thousand people in Rhodes during the era of *Sea of Shadows*, about two thousand were connected in some way to the knights, and about three hundred were noble-born knights. The knights hailed from various Western European kingdoms and were divided up into "langues" (tongues) according to their nationalities.

French and Italian were the dominant languages among the so-called "Latin" citizens of the island, and by necessity many Rhodians became multi-lingual. Intermarriage between Greeks and Latins was common. Citizens of Rhodes Town were traders, notaries, mercenaries, artisans, shipbuilders, sea captains, moneylenders, lawyers, and more. Rhodes was known throughout the Mediterranean for its large slave market and thriving brothel industry.

Grand Master Jacques de Milly was the elected leader of the Knights Hospitaller during the era of the *Sea and Stone Chronicles* series. His permission was required for marriages and other civic matters, including the freeing of slaves. Some Greeks rose to great heights as "burgesses" who served as political representatives helping the grand master govern Rhodes.

The city-state of Genoa was a longstanding ally of the Order. Genoa and Venice were enemies, so relations between the knights and Venice were rocky as well. (Venetian citizens were forbidden from joining the Order.) There were several incidents over the period of Hospitaller rule involving bloody conflict between the knights and

Venetian fleets. Two Venetian ships did take refuge in Rhodes Town during a storm and had their goods and passengers confiscated. Jacques de Milly is credited with preventing a major schism within the Order over the incident.

The Loredans were a powerful Venetian family. There were several generations of Loredan men who served as military leaders for the Venetian navy. A Loredan did own the island of Antiparos in the 15th century and built a home there.

Venice was the mightiest naval power of the Mediterranean at that time. Its galleys brought the goods of the world—spices, silks, timber, fur, wool—to Venice, where they were taxed and shipped on to other ports. On a smaller scale, Rhodes Town enjoyed similar status. Galleys from the Middle East, Asia, Africa, and Eastern Europe brought valuable goods to its thriving marketplace, where traders and merchants purchased them for resale elsewhere. Because of this, wealthy merchants from all over Western Europe established residence in Rhodes, many of them splitting their time between the island and their home countries. This was the inspiration for Marino Lomellini.

Artists trained in Italian traditions worked in Rhodes, and there are still examples in Rhodian churches of artworks in a transitional style that combines Byzantine and Sienese or Tuscan techniques, probably commissioned by knights or feudal lords connected to the Order. Knights commissioned icons painted in the Greek style as well. Anica Foscolo was inspired by examples of women in the medieval and Renaissance eras working alongside their husbands, brothers, or fathers to produce art for patrons. Most of these women remained anonymous or their work was attributed to male colleagues.

The mid-fifteenth century saw the rise of oil painting, which heralded the decline of tempera painting. Tempera paint was made from egg and pigment; oil painting relied on linseed oil instead of egg. The style took off first in Flanders and other northern European locales and then dispersed to other countries.

In Rhodes, there were knights from England and Scotland. Drummond Fordun was inspired by a man called Digeurus le Scot who was not a knight (probably because he was not of noble birth). He traveled to Rhodes in the mid-1400s and worked for the Order for a number of years before returning with a generous pension to live out his days in Scotland.

Women owned property and businesses at the time. I found evidence of women purchasing large quantities of wine for their taverns in Cyprus, and women bequeathing property and vineyards to female descendants in Rhodes. This inspired the character of Aunt Rhea.

A school for physicians in Salerno, Italy, accepted female students during the medieval era. This inspired the character of Signorina Giovanna.

Rhodes was a favorite stopping-off point for Western pilgrims sailing to Jerusalem. There are many accounts of these early travelers marveling at the beauty of the island and the lush gardens and villas, mostly owned by knights, located just outside the walls of Rhodes Town.

In the fifteenth century, Italians began to seek out ancient statuary for home décor. Rhodes was full of such relics. For the right price, Rhodians sold these statues to collectors in Florence, Siena, and other Italian cities. Officially, these antiquities were the property of the Order, so such transactions were kept under wraps.

In 1452, the Medici bank in Florence set up a satellite operation on Rhodes. A man named Bernardo Salviati was in charge of the operation; he inspired Signor Salviati in *Sea of Shadows*. The Medici bank went on to become a major partner for the Order, helping it funnel rents and donations from Western kingdoms to Rhodes.

Rhodes was known for its soap, which was made from olive oil and the ashes of a beach plant. It was often enhanced with flowers or herbs to become fragrant, making it a far superior product to the stinky animal-fat-based northern European soaps.

The *fusta* (plural: *fuste*) was a small, light, extremely fast boat favored by the Turks. The attack in *Sea of Shadows* by two *fuste* was based on a true account of two Hospitaller galleys that were attacked near Symi by two Turkish *fuste*. A nephew of the grand master, aged 22, died in the battle; he had recently arrived from the West.

The knights generally used heavier war galleys that could support the weight of mounted swivel guns, crossbows, and ammunition. Most merchant galleys at the time deployed such weapons as well; piracy was a constant threat.

In Rhodes, the knights allowed Greeks to continue worshipping in Greek Orthodox churches. There is evidence of Latins attending Greek churches and vice versa. There is also evidence that Greeks sometimes held religious ceremonies—baptisms, weddings, masses—in their own homes during Hospitaller rule. This is why the wedding scene in *Sea of Shadows* is set in a private home. Because I found no evidence of how exactly marriage ceremonies were performed in fifteenth-century Rhodes, I based that scene on traditional Greek Orthodox wedding rituals.

No matter their religious tradition, everyone in Rhodes and the surrounding islands flocked to certain pilgrim destinations such as shrines to Santa Maria (the Virgin Mary), the patron saint of sailors.

In the late 14th century, the Pope prohibited Greek wailing women at funerals.

The character of Dr. Syriano, the Syrian physician to the Grand Master, was based on a real person called George Syriano. In the early 1450s, Syriano was hired by the Order to move his practice from Egypt to Rhodes and was given safe passage for sea voyages, along with "burgess" status in Rhodes Town.

Arabian medicine during the medieval era was vastly superior to that in the West. Successful cataract surgeries using a suction method were invented in Iraq in the 10th century, but this method didn't reach the West until the 18th century. I found evidence of an Italian doctor living in Cyprus who traveled to Damascus in 1448 for treatment of his failing vision. He returned a few months later with his vision restored.

Oleander is a shrub with vivid, colorful flowers that is native to the Mediterranean. It is highly toxic. Activated charcoal has been used since ancient times to treat ailments and absorb toxins. It counteracts oleander poison by binding to the toxins in the victim's stomach and intestines—as long as it's administered within a few hours after the poison is ingested.

For more details about my research, please visit my blog at www.amymaroney.com

ACKNOWLEDGMENTS

As with *Island of Gold*, I am deeply grateful for my writing critique partners, Elizabeth St.John and Cryssa Bazos. Thank you both for your friendship and for helping me go farther with these stories than I ever could on my own.

Another huge thank you goes to Patricia Riak, Ph.D., whose research about Rhodes has been invaluable during this project. I also found treasured books and papers by playing "chase the footnotes" in her doctoral dissertation.

Jenny Quinlan, thank you for your excellent guidance both at the developmental and copyediting stages. Big thanks to Patrick Knowles for the beautiful cover and to Tracey Porter for the fabulous map. Thank you to all the members of the Coffee Pot Tweet Group for encouragement and inspiration, and particularly to Vivienne Brereton for connecting me with so many helpful books about medieval Europe.

I am indebted to the academic researchers whose work is available on Academia.edu, and I've been lucky enough to locate critical documents through Interlibrary Loan and through communication with individuals. I am particularly grateful for the work of Diana Gilliland Wright, Anthony Luttrell, Nicholas Coureas, David Jacoby, Helen Nicholson, Ruthy Gertwagen, and Alan Macquarrie. This book also benefited from the entertaining and informative *The Taste of Conquest: The Rise and Fall of the Three Great Cities of Spice* by Michael Krondl.

As ever, thank you to all my family and friends for supporting me and cheering me on, with a special shout-out of gratitude to Julie Cassin.

To my daughters Dahlia and Nora, thank you for inspiring me to write about strong women of the past.

Finally, the *Sea and Stone Chronicles* would not exist without my husband Jon's encouragement and love.

MEET AMY MARONEY

Amy Maroney studied English Literature at Boston University and worked for many years as a writer and editor of nonfiction. She lives in Oregon, U.S.A., with her family. When she's not diving down research rabbit holes, she enjoys hiking, dancing, traveling, and reading. Amy is the author of *The Miramonde Series*, an award-winning historical fiction trilogy about a Renaissance-era female artist and the modern-day scholar on her trail. Her new romantic suspense series, *Sea and Stone Chronicles*, is set in 15th-century Rhodes and Cyprus.

Join Amy's community of readers and get monthly updates about her research and next books (plus great deals on historical fiction) at www.amymaroney.com.

If you enjoyed this book, please take a moment to leave a review online or spread the word to family and friends.